T0367237

HELL
IS THE
NIGHT

HELL
Is the
Night

The Second Gomer Wars

Michael S. Pauley

authorHOUSE®

AuthorHouse™
1663 Liberty Drive
Bloomington, IN 47403
www.authorhouse.com
Phone: 1-800-839-8640

Published by AuthorHouse 10/24/2014

ISBN: 978-1-4969-4872-4 (sc)
ISBN: 978-1-4969-4873-1 (hc)
ISBN: 978-1-4969-4871-7 (e)

Library of Congress Control Number: 2014919008

Contents

AUTHOR'S FOREWORD

After countless hours and some serious soul searching, I've finally decided to cut this book loose into the wild and wonderful world. In the humble opinion of my lovely bride, this one is "awesome." I will freely admit that she is probably right, but then that is my bias showing, too. I'll leave it to you as the reader to decide if it is worth it or not. Still, before you dive in with both feet, let me offer a few thoughts.

Unlike the first book in this series, I've consciously decided that a little explanation might be in order. So, let's talk Gomers! What is a Gomer? First, I'd caution that you will need to read the books as a series. We have some pretty good descriptions for you, and in this the second book, these descriptions are even more complete than in the first. Still, what generally is a Gomer? A Gomer is a term that soldiers often use to describe a nondescript enemy. If you don't have a clue what else to call them, then he/she/it is a Gomer. Similar to the Air Force calling an unidentified target on the radar "a bogie," the Gomer is something out there that goes "bump in the night." You will find in the second book that the Gomers actually come from somewhere, but when a name sticks, it sticks. So, despite the Gomers having a place from which they originated, in the hearts, minds, and even psyche of the characters, they will always be known as Gomers.

Aside from the description of the Gomer, there will be some slightly more graphic details about their Ships. In the first book, there was a vague description about the size, type, and purpose of each Gomer Ship encountered. I did this for two reasons. The first is to replicate situations on a battlefield, where oftentimes this is about all you have to go on. During World War II, it took us quite a while to get a handle on several new aircraft put forward by the Japanese. I would just ask the reader to remember there is at least one more book in this series, and there will be more answers as each book unfolds. I will crassly admit that the method here is to tease you. Besides, what you can conjure in your mind just might be far scarier than anything I could create for you.

Similarly, I like to let people use their imaginations to "see" the threat. Call me old school, but of the two versions of the movie *Psycho*, the first one is far more frightening to me. Sometimes it is the horror you don't see that will trigger your own imagination as the reader. I assume that the average science fiction reader already has a vivid imagination, and as someone who can dream within the realm of science, you can create something far more frightening to you than I ever could in a million years.

In the first book, you were introduced to our alien attackers. As someone on the ground, I doubt seriously you will have a Back Story for anyone who is trying to exterminate you, especially when they first show up and aren't exactly talking to you. The Back Story, as it were, will take time to develop. In this case, there is at least one more book coming, and I can assure you, that this, the second one, will definitely open eyes on a large number of these questions. I can also assure you that in the third book, you will actually find out far more detail, and precisely what that Back Story really means for us as a civilization.

While a lot of time isn't spent solely on the subject, make no mistake, the civilian population is important. Extremely important, which is why the character John, General Patrick's son-in-law, allowed us some insight into the initial phases of the invasion in the first book. He was forced to seek refuge along with other civilians, and it was his journey that provided that background color to what was just a part of an overarching story. Through his eyes, you saw how the military was forced to deal with refugee issues which, from a soldiers' point of view, is by necessity part of the job. Face it, if not for the civilians, there would be no need for protection of anything.

When it comes to refugees, and the evacuation of a civilian population, history is always a good teacher, and in this series of books, this concept is no exception. When France was invaded by the Nazis in 1940, part of the Nazi strategy was to flood the roads with refugees, and then literally clog the system so that troops could not move into, or out of, any particular position. Since France fell quickly, and the British had to leave via Dunkirk, this strategy appears to have partially worked. This is covered in some detail in the first book, along with an extensive discussion about setting up schools, trying to feed the population, etc. Now in this, the second in the series, the story is told from the perspective of those trying to fight an enemy, as opposed to dealing with the civilian population. In other words, there isn't a lot of discussion about civilians. Besides, this is not a civilian story, instead it is the story of the "Old Guy" General who is thrust in the middle of something he didn't want. We are at war with an alien race, and therefore, there also won't be time for the romantic interludes in a hay loft. If that is the kind of story you want, then move along, because there is nothing to see here!

I probably also need to point out one other pretty major point in these stories. In the first book, there was a greater emphasis on the American side of the story. General Patrick is an American, and therefore, the story begins here in America. It also takes our lead character on a journey from an Army Reservist to the leader of a combined international force. This is a huge change of perspective, and as a result, this is a journey or a process for him as a leader. His journey begins in *They Own The Night, the First Gomer Wars*, and will now continue here. I will admit that during my own military career, I have worked with a number of nations, and their military personnel, all at a number of different levels. Right now, just from a "geo-logistical" standpoint, we have some of the finest equipment in the world for doing what is described in the book, as do many of our allies that have acquired much of their equipment from us. Still everyone contributes as the story expands.

While we're on this subject, I do not give short shrift to the Navy or the Air Force either. We fight together, train together, and have endured hardships around the world, all together! This is why the Navy and the Air Force are key players throughout these books. Granted, in the first book, the initial focus is more local, and therefore the Army is in a lead role, but I can assure you, as the series continues, there is, by necessity for General Patrick, a more expanded difference in perspective that will be even more inclusive of all involved. You don't fight a global war without forces from around the globe, to include all of the Armies, Navies, and Air Forces from various nations.

In the first book, there is a paradigm shift, from the local (in America) and more tactical perspective, to a later global and more strategic campaign. The more global campaign by necessity includes other nations, and as you will discover now in the second book, this expansion is exponential. This is a natural progression, but it must also take into account what is left, and where it is left, to allow for the unification of these global forces. You could write a book just on this type of relationship, and what it takes to forge such a thing, but that was not my intent with these books. In the first book, you begin to see these relationships build on a smaller level until they lay the ground work for what is coming now in this the second book. In the first book, I tried to flavor it some by referring to the initial resistance by the Argentine Government from ever allowing their military forces to fall under the command of a General from the UK. (For those of you who remember the Falklands, this might have some meaning.)

As this book unfolds, you will also be introduced to a number of staff officers and commanders from a number of different nations. This is not just an American Show, but if you've ever read a history of World War II, you will quickly realize that if the book is written by a General from England, then it will have an English bent, just as Patton's memoirs are from a decidedly American bent. In the first book, General Patrick develops a closeness to General Fuller, who is an officer from the UK. Now in the second book, you find that there are a number of other Officers from a number of other countries that will forge equally solid bonds. So, is it an American show? Not at all. Still, it is told from the American perspective, but no more than a standard World War II history written by any other American officer. Rest assured, this is not an American show, or an English show, or a Russian show, but instead, it is hopefully a global show.

Now for the more mundane. Just like the first book, there are a lot of logistical considerations. Aside from food, fuel, ammunition, etc., there is also an Order of Battle, along with a number of other military details to support that Order of Battle. I won't apologize for this, because if you were to read a true history of any warfare, you will find these things as part and parcel to any war. (For example, Samuel Eliot Morrison's History of the United States Navy in World War II, is jam packed with this type of information.) It is my absolute intention to include realistic concepts, hard science, logistical considerations, and a description of how all these things must come together in any conflict. "No Beans and no bullets, means no victory." I, for one, hate those old movies where the hero fires a six shooter with 3000 bullets in it. At some point, you need to realize that nothing comes without a logistical trail, even if it is a trip with your family out of town. As a result, I've strived to write as authentic a story as possible.

Finally, I've had a great deal of help in the scientific research from my absolute favorite "Nerd." As you can guess, this would be my lovely Bride, who should get all the credit for discussing a number of scientific concepts with me. Her research, and attempts to convey that knowledge to me, only showed that I'm way out of my league when it comes to the physics involved here. Having said this, I will accept full responsibility for any errors, since after all, my wife was trying to teach a pig to sing and dance.

I sincerely hope you enjoy the story half as much as I did writing it.

September 2014

~ Michael S. Pauley

SECTION 1

THE GOMERS RETURN:
SECOND CONTACT

CHAPTER I

North of the Main Channel of the Savannah River near Hilton Head Island:

Captain Brian Harris was a third generation Shrimper. A hard drinking old man of 59 years of age, Brian was rather squat in frame, and even shorter in temperament. He and his boat, the *Anna Marvel*, were still plying the same waters as his Father and Grandfather before him. Despite the Gomer invasion almost three years ago, he refused to find somewhere else to go, even though there was now only marginal fishing. Up early in the morning and fishing until very late in the evening, the numbers for his daily catch were now much harder to maintain. To add insult to his injury, the wreckage from the earlier Gomer battles around the mouth of the Savannah River made navigation even more treacherous than ever. His nets were almost constantly being caught on something, and occasionally something nasty would get caught up in the nets that, when hauled to the surface, would scare the hell out of both him and his crewmen. Still, his frustration was tempered by the thought that at least he had survived, which is more than he could say from many of the people he knew from before the war. It was his connection with these waters that drew him back and held him now as he tried to earn a modest living. These days, he was just lucky to make enough money to keep the crew paid and the old boat running.

The thought of the "before" would always haunt him. He still had a hard time shaking the fact that he had been out fishing when the

Gomers first hit, and was so drunk the first few nights that he missed the initial invasion as it had passed over his head. When he finally sailed back into his home port at Lazaretto Creek, it was only to find a deserted marina completely devoid of all humanity. His family and almost everyone he ever knew were simply gone. He and his crew of two other men were all that was left, and they hid and stayed drunk until a bunch of Marines showed up to move into Fort Pulaski. It was from them that he finally learned what was going on, and it was from them that he learned to stay hidden during the night and to keep his power and radio off. It was after the first night of the battle near the River that he decided that they should probably go back to sea and head somewhere to just hide out. After making that monumental decision, both he and his crew remained gone until they finally got word that the war had ended. Even that was pure luck, since he heard about it from a Coast Guard Cutter that had intercepted them while they were trying to find fuel near St. Simon Island.

Now here he was, almost three years later, still trying to make a living by catching shrimp. It wasn't easy, because now he was going further out from the shore, burning more fuel, and hoping not to get his nets ruined from dragging over the Gomers' wreckage stuck in the muddy bottom. They had left the dock around 2:30 a.m. and were making their way out to sea, when he noticed something that just didn't look right with the horizon. Usually at this hour, as they were clearing the river's entrance and turning north to run up the coast of Hilton Head Island, the view of the stars was magnificent. As he peered into the darkness, he could see nothing. There were stars overhead, but absolutely nothing out to the southeast of his position except total blackness. He was puzzled, since the weather report had been for "severe clear." No clouds, no bad weather, yet here he was looking to the east and southeast into an abyss of nothingness.

Confused by it all, he called down to the Mate, and asked him to look out ahead to see if there was something that might be ahead of the boat. "Hey, Crank, do you see anything at all?"

"Nope, nothing, skipper."

"Something just don't seem right. Does it seem like fog or something blocking the stars?"

"No. It looks clear, but like a line of dark down lower."

"Wonder what the hell......"

As he and the Mate looked south and north, there were no obstructions to their vision and up higher, the stars shimmered against the night sky. Then the Captain noticed that he was seeing more beach than usual, and he again turned back to the Mate to get him to confirm that the water line was receding. It was then they noticed that the total blackness was now extending much further upwards into the night sky. To the southeast and off towards the east, there were more missing stars, and when they looked back towards the beach, the water level was dropping dramatically against the shoreline. Then suddenly the *Anna Marvel* was scraping the bottom near the main channel along the coast and, as it finally dawned on the Captain what was happening, there was nothing he could do but watch. He asked himself, "what in the hell could cause a wave like this here?" Within seconds of his asking the question, the giant wave that extended at least 350 feet into the air came crashing down on him, destroying the *Anna Marvel* and her entire crew.

After crushing the *Anna Marvel*, the huge wave continued into the Lowcountry of South Carolina until it finally dissipated almost 20 miles inland from the coastline. In the wake of the mammoth wave, the destruction was complete and total. The apex of the tidal wave was centered along Hilton Head Island and into the Port Royal Sound, with the flooding and destruction extending inland over Parris Island and Beaufort, South Carolina. In some places, the flood waters extended almost to Interstate 95, along the Coosawatchie River. How Savannah and the coast of Georgia were spared was a mystery to those who witnessed the event and were lucky enough to survive to talk about it later. What was clear was that the death toll was only mitigated by the fact that the area had not been heavily resettled after the Gomer invasion. The other good news was that the Marine Bases at Parris Island and the Beaufort Marine Corps Air Station were no longer being occupied. Thanks to the war, those units, missions, and personnel were now all relocated to other parts of the world.

South of the Puerto Rico Trench:

Just 6 hours earlier, the USS Thadaeus Morton, DDG 1001, was engaging in her first patrol after her initial shakedown cruise. A brand new, highly modified, Zumwalt class Destroyer, she was completed after the Gomer war, and named for Admiral Thadaeus Morton, the Former Chief of Naval Operations and Chairman of the Joint Chiefs of Staff. The Admiral had died fighting as the Chief of Allied Naval Operations onboard the USS Iowa, during the Gomer war, and this brand new ship was his legacy. The USS Morton, aside from being almost brand new, displaced roughly 15,000 tons full loaded, with a hull of 610 feet. Her 2 Rolls Royce gas turbines, plus 2 Rolls Royce gas turbine generator sets, could turn about 30+ knots, and her sonar and radar equipment, along with her Kingfisher mine detection system were as advanced as possible. What separated her from the earlier ships of the class, and was even argued by some to justify calling this the new "Morton" class destroyer, was that she was fitted out with a greatly different armament system. She was sporting three 6" or 155mm main guns with a range of over 100 miles, along with two 20mm Phalanx mounts, and a number of other Gomer killing weapon systems, to include a highly classified and somewhat experimental weapon that was forged from the lessons learned from the Gomers themselves. Each of these systems was designed to kill as many Gomer-type smaller objects as possible and maybe even make a dent in the big ones, should they show up again.

The military always learns from the last war and, more often than not, it is doomed to fight the last one instead of the next one. Still, in this instance, it seemed quite prudent to create a new class of Gomer-ready combat ships, in the hope that it just might be a counter to any threat, even the extra-terrestrial ones. This philosophy even carried over into the latest in Battleship design, and the modified Montana Class was well underway, with the first such ship of the class expected to be operational within the next few months. Scrapped at the end of World War II, this particular class of Battleship would carry an extra main battery aft, and was about a third larger than the Iowa Class Battleships used to fight the Gomers. These huge battleships were going to be the eventual replacements for the sunken USS Iowa, as well as for the USS North Carolina, USS Massachusetts, and USS Alabama, which had all been pulled out of their museum status to be returned to active service. The second of the class, the new USS Iowa, was to be commissioned in about 6 months, with the follow-on ships to be commissioned at a rate of one a year for the next four years thereafter. As with the USS Morton, they were incorporating the lessons learned from the Gomer Wars and were the brain child of Admirals Steadman and Lynch, with tweaks from the great Drs. Abramson and Clarkson, all heroes in their respective fields from that earlier war.

The USS Morton was just making a high speed turn back towards Puerto Rico as part of her patrol pattern, when her Captain, Commander Joshua Bennett, USN, received an URGENT FLASH message via the ELF (extremely low frequency) system.

FLASH IMMEDIATE

TO:　　　*Commander, USS Morton*
FROM:　　*Commander, Supreme Allied Headquarters*

1. *Large object from direction of the Moon, with anticipated track taking it to position at or near the Puerto Rico Trench;*

2. *Object appears to be Gomer Mountain Ship; however, travel signature appears different, behavior pattern is altered, and general tracking information is also confusing;*

3. *Object struck an outer mine, but is still slowing as it approaches Earth, and may enter low Earth orbit,*

or may continue descent to impact at or near your position;

4. *All allied forces on alert for defense as required;*

5. *Suggested you utilize passive surveillance systems only, but you are authorized to take whatever action you deem necessary to maintain contact and to protect your ship from attack;*

6. *Report via ELF all movements of the object directly to this headquarters;*

7. *Priority is for you to maintain contact with the object until relieved, and NOT, say again NOT, take any offensive action;*

8. *USS Virginia en route to your position and will relieve you of surveillance mission, anticipated arrival within 23 hours of this message.*

Signed: s// Patrick,
   General of the Army,
   Supreme Allied Commander

Captain Bennett finished reading the message, and immediately remembered his experience as the gunnery officer onboard the USS New Jersey during the Gomer battles near South America. He was forced to sit in an ancient Gun Director position as the big Gomer Ship passed overhead and reading this message, just like that night three years earlier, made him feel as though his blood was running about 10 degrees cooler. Nodding to his Executive Officer, or XO, he waved him over next to his chair on the bridge. "Okay, Doug, we've got a little problem." Passing the message to the senior Lieutenant Commander, the XO read it and immediately looked up and aft of the bridge. "Sir, how can they be sure that it is coming this way?"

"Commander, I have no idea, but if memory serves me, they did a pretty righteous job of tracking them the last time. Sound General Quarters, and make it 'no drill.' If we have the Gomers coming back, then we had damn well better be on our highest alert!"

"Aye, Aye, Sir!"

"Oh, and Commander, you might want to make sure we're completely in the passive mode. I think the expression is to make us into a hole in the water! I have seen what happens when they know we are here, and I have no intentions of letting them know shit! Got it?"

"Aye, Aye, Sir!" The XO stepped away and told the officer of the deck to sound General Quarters, and to advise the CIC or Combat Information Center to go to passive systems only. With that command, the USS Morton entered a state of quiet readiness.

Supreme Allied Headquarters, (SAHQ):

I was within a few days of telling the whole bunch to kiss my ever-expanding ass! The folks in Congress were convinced that there were no more threats around the world, except the Gomers, and thanks to me, there were no more Gomers. A winning scenario if ever there was one, at least to most of the members of Congress that weren't from States that had been heavily impacted by the invasion. The States devastated by the invasion, on the other hand, were a little friendlier and far more supportive of the concept that the bad guys could return. They knew that the situation could be repeated, that they were vulnerable, and that the military re-building could be vital in rebuilding their States. After all, a Montana Class Battleship would put people back to work in the ship yards, which was a boon to the economy, and would get people back to work near the coast, which in turn would repopulate the most devastated areas.

President Blanchard was having to fight for even the simple things, and I was doing my best to make things work on a ludicrous budget. The Army was still in Khaki, not as a fashion statement, but because the government was refusing to expend any additional funding for silly things like uniforms. (We were keeping places like Wrangler and Dickies in business by buying in bulk from existing stocks). I knew it was a matter of priorities, and the expansion of various key weapon systems to include the recruitment of talented personnel to operate them were far more important to the overall mission than the appearance of the average trooper. Still, keeping people convinced that a larger, better trained military was important was tough since it was clear that the Russians and the Chinese were no longer really global threats. Even the classic terrorist had bigger things to be concerned about these days, so the threat was more about starvation and keeping people employed than it was to project a force with any sort of global capability. I understood it and was learning to live with it, at least to a point. Still, I was getting sick and tired of being sick and tired.

President Blanchard knew all of this, and so did I, but the President was better at doing the balancing act. From my perspective, the Gomers weren't really gone, they were probably just on break, and the longer it took to get ready for their return, the harder it was going to be to get rid of them the next time. I still remembered how lucky we were the first time, and I was very concerned about whatever it was on the back side of the moon. Did they still have a base and personnel that close to us? Was it a refueling point? Was it a staging point for later operations? I was having daily battles with Congressmen, trying to justify why we needed to keep the passages around the Moon mined, and why we needed to maintain stockpiles of various munitions. My frustration was carrying over even to my eggheads. Dr. Clarkson was highly upset, often for the same reasons, because he watched the last Gomer Mountain ship pull out. Like me, there was no doubt in his mind that they would return and that, when they did, they would probably be a whole lot smarter about it.

I was just discussing my decision to retire, for the second time in my career, with my bride, Leah, when the red alert phone went off in my quarters. I have to admit that it caused me to jump about halfway out of my skin, since the damn thing hadn't rung since the last test of the system almost three weeks before. I caught it on the third ring, and it was the Operations Duty Officer of the Day, Colonel Feldman. "Sir, we have three extremely large bogies headed towards Earth, passing Jupiter on a course that we believe is inbound."

"Colonel, what do they have for a possible ETA?"

"Sir, in about 36 hours, they should be in orbit. It appears that they are slowing down, and are coming from a course direction that is not entirely consistent with the prior tracks of the Gomers."

"Okay, Colonel, assemble the staff, and you can update us in about 25 minutes in the War Room. In the meantime, get the information to the White House, and set up a conference call with the President. I should be at your location in 10 minutes."

"Yessir."

"Oh, and Colonel, activate the initial alert system, and get messages out to the major commands and all senior commanders that we might be getting company, and to act in accordance with the Alert Plan Yellow."

"Yessir." With that, I hung up the line and immediately started out the door towards the War Room which, given our Allied Headquarters set up, was only about 8 minutes walking distance from the front door of my quarters. As I was leaving, my wife stopped me, "Mike, is that what I think?"

"I'm afraid so...."

"Crap, should I call your mother, Christine, and Holly to get them over here?"

"It shouldn't be anything that eminent, but yeah, you might want to circle the wagons and we'll see what we need to do over the next few hours. If nothing else, you can get them in the mind set to move in a hurry, just in case it becomes necessary."

"Okay. . . . . . Honey?"

"Yeah?"

"Please be careful, remember the last time you wandered off to Hawaii? It took you months to get all the chunks of metal and concrete out of your hide."

"Very, very, funny! Now can I go and see what the hell is going on?"

"Yeah, sorry. I love you!"

"I love you, too, sweetie!" I planted a kiss on her cheek and then turned on my heel. "Honey, you know I'll be home later, don't you?" She responded by smiling and flipping me the bird. I couldn't help but chuckle as I headed out the door to the unknown of what could be another huge problem for all of us. This time we were at least semi-prepared, but that was little comfort, since facing the unknown is seldom something you can plan with any effectiveness.

Supreme Allied Headquarters - War Room:

I stepped into the heart and soul of our Allied Operations, an extremely high-tech command center that had a lot of low-tech touches. We'd seen our "gee whiz" fail before, so for every high-tech 'gizmo,' there was at least one low-tech back-up system. We no longer used the HF, UHF, VHF, or FM radios for communications. Now it was all LF (low frequency), VLF (very low frequency), and ELF systems. Even the Commercial Radio stations were transmitting on AM again, with FM radio almost a complete thing of the past. Even those who weren't "worried" about the Gomer threat anymore were still very reluctant to send a signal on an FM or higher frequency radio. Internet radios and television were the thing now, assuming the internet was working properly, and so there was a resurgence of live entertainment in the post war world. My being old school, I personally preferred the telephone for the more serious conversations, and so did our President.

"General?"

"Yessir, Mr. President?"

"What is your recommendation as to the threat level?"

"Sir, I would have to assess it as high, and I've alerted all major commands and senior commanders to be on alert accordingly at Alert Level Yellow."

"Do you have a recommendation about evacuation of the cities?"

"I don't have enough information to answer that yet, sir, but given our history, I would seriously consider maybe moving key personnel to more hardened facilities, while putting the public on some sort of alert."

"I just hate to cause a panic for no reason."

"I agree, Mr. President. Just as an idea, maybe you could treat it like a weather type event. Maybe make evacuation non-mandatory, like with an oncoming hurricane, at least for the next 12 to 24 hours. Then as the objects move closer, make it mandatory for the final 12 hours. It might move the bulk of the population out to safer ground, while the infrastructure can manage it. If you wait until the last minute, then the roads will be jammed, and panic will really set in."

"Okay, it is an idea. I'll talk it over with the cabinet. Can I quote you as making that recommendation?"

"Sure! Marty, you can quote me whenever you want, but if you do, make sure it starts with 'hey you assholes, listen up.'"

"Funny! I knew giving you the 5th Star would make you the consummate smartass!"

"Sorry, Mr. President, but you know most of those guys don't want to hear from me. I've been accused of being 'Chicken Little' one too many times."

"Yeah, I know, but if you will recall, I was the 'Chicken Little' last time around."

"Yessir, and you saved more than a few lives, to include mine, for those of us who listened."

"Bingo! My point exactly. Now get to work, get the latest intelligence, and then be prepared to brief when I get there."

"Yessir, and I can assume you'll be bringing the key players with you, so we will open up your new facilities and have security teams prepared to receive you."

"Roger that, and we should have everyone out and on the way to you within the next 6 hours."

"Can do, sir! Your new home will be ready, and don't forget to bring the grandkids." With that, the President chuckled and broke the connection. I turned to get the staff fired up, briefed, and moving in the right direction. Within minutes, our first war briefing in three years began in earnest. As Colonel Feldman briefed the course, speed, and anticipated progress of the new ships, Dr. Abramson and Dr. Clarkson entered the room. Dr. Clarkson sat in rapt attention studying the track of the objects, their movement patterns, and course projections. As one of the few people on Earth who had experienced first-hand the Gomer ship and technology, his opinions would be vital to our understanding, and to identifying the proper tasks we would need to accomplish over the next few hours.

Dr. Abramson and Dr. Clarkson were in the middle of their equations when General Whitney arrived with more news. The three large objects were now turning more towards the Moon, almost like that was their initial target, and were on a course to enter the Moon's orbit. Once he said this, both Dr. Abramson and Dr. Clarkson said, almost in perfect unison, "Orbit?" Again conferring and checking the numbers, they confirmed General Whitney's information. Sure enough, these objects were moving on a course to enter an orbit of the Moon, as opposed to holding a course to remain behind the Moon. This was something new and for many of us in the room, something far more sinister. Did this mean that these Gomers don't have a problem with sunlight? If not, then are they even Gomers?

Several more minutes passed, and finally our resident "eggheads" stepped up to the plate. Dr. Abramson began by saying, "General, it would appear that these objects did not originate on a track that would be the normal heading we would associate with the Gomer home world. It is close, in fact painfully close, but not quite an exact track. They also do not appear to be tracking a course using quite the same pattern as the Gomer craft we have encountered, and by that we're referring to flight patterns. Finally, we are not seeing a 'signature' that is completely consistent with the Gomer technology we have previously encountered. In short, General, we cannot confirm that these are the same Gomers that were here three years ago."

"Doctor, you are telling me that these might not be Gomers at all, is that right?"

"General, I am telling you that I can't confirm they are Gomers, but I can't rule it out either."

"Can't rule it out?"

"Sure, they may be Gomers with later technology available to them. Similar to our having made advancements of our own over the last three years. OR, it could be that they have modified their patterns, based on the prior experiences with us."

"Okay, fair enough. It could be Gomers with advances in their technology, but either way, it might mean that our normal defenses have been compromised. If they are Gomers, then perhaps they have ways to counter what we have developed to fight them. Similarly, if they aren't Gomers, then whoever they are might not be impacted by any of our anti-Gomer weapon systems. Hell, they might not even have the same weaknesses."

"I think that is a fair assessment, General."

"Okay, anybody, can we read intent from their movements? Is there anything here that would indicate that they are friendly?"

After several moments of silence, Dr. Clarkson finally weighed in, "General, they are going to the Moon first, and this may be something that isn't a threat as we know it, especially since it might give us a chance to get a visual image or two. I don't think we can assume that their intentions are hostile, but at the same time, I would NOT want to be the one who just assumed they weren't hostile and then have something bad happen. That is what got us in trouble the last time."

"Thanks, Doctor. That is precisely what I was thinking." With that I turned to General Whitney and asked, "Well? What are your thoughts about what we tell the President, evacuate the population or not?

General Whitney paused, and then began, "Sir, I know this is probably not a basis for making sound policy judgments, but my gut says evacuate. At least until we know more about these...... Okay, if they're not Gomers, then what DO we call them?"

"I'm sticking to Gomers for the moment, but you're right, if they're not what we know as Gomers, we'll have to come up with something else to call them, since I don't want to get the tactics confused later on down the road."

"Sir, if I may?"

"Sure, Doctor Clarkson."

"Sir, I would stick to Bogies right now. Once we get more visual intelligence based on our photographic information, we can find something to call them. Assuming they actually orbit the Moon, we should have some great panoramic views of them within the next several hours."

"Okay, General Whitney, advise the President, and tell him our recommendation is to move forward and order the evacuation of the cities. We can't afford to repeat our mistakes, and this could be just such an instance. In the meantime, move our forces to Threat Level Red, and keep them in the passive mode on all radars and radios."

"General, if they decide to evacuate based on your recommendation, you do know that if this turns out to be nothing, it will be your ass on the block."

"Whit, right now I don't give a flea turd on a rat's ass. I can promise you that if we don't tell them to evacuate, and this IS something to worry about, then not only would they have my ass, but I would want them to have it. I'd rather be wrong and unemployed, than wrong and not be able to live with myself."

"I know, sir, but I wouldn't be a good staff member if I didn't at least point out the down side."

"Geez, Whit, in all the time I've known you, you have excelled at being my conscience, which is Latin for one huge defacto pain in the butt. Now, tell the boss to get everyone away from the cities and the coast, and I'll be happy to take the heat if it becomes necessary."

"Yessir!" With his response, the entire War Room took on a whole new purpose. We activated all recall procedures, initiated the evacuation plans, and took every step we could think of taking to get the ball rolling.

Chapter II

Supreme Allied Headquarters:

The next few hours passed quite quickly and, as predicted, the three objects did enter an orbit pattern around the Moon. The President was relocated, along with his cabinet and most of the members of Congress. There were absences and individual instances where several Congressmen were at home when the alert went out, but as they were rounded up, they were being brought to the mountains to their temporary home at "New Washington." This "New Washington" was different from the one used during the first Gomer War. Deeper into the mountains and far further underground, the new seat of our government was located much nearer to our Allied Headquarters (at the old new Washington), and to the New Pentagon, which never moved after the war's end. As for the public, they were now making their way into the various mountains and hiding places that were closest to their homes. Most were being housed in 'displaced persons shelters' that had been built both during and after the last Gomer War, and a few were attempting to shelter in place.

All of these steps were a far cry from a perfect solution, but it was at least a step up from how we started the last war. The good news was that the entire process moved a lot smoother than anyone could have predicted. When the President spoke to the nation, he made it clear that we had no idea of the actual threat and, therefore, he would not make evacuation mandatory; however, unlike hurricane warnings of recent years, this time very few people decided to hang around where they were along the coastal regions. People were also heeding the advice to travel light and travel far. I think unlike a hurricane, many of these people who survived the first Gomer war realized that the Gomers didn't mess with their homes or take things. It was the looters that would do that, but with the new "normal", looters weren't likely to hang around and risk being Gomer bait over a cheap TV.

As the Bogies orbited the Moon, our eggheads were engaging in a massive evaluation of the questions, "Just who the hell are these guys, and what do they want?" The pictures were of little help, not because their resolution was poor, because they were almost perfect in resolution. No, the problem here was that the designs of the ships appeared to be VERY Gomer. The eggheads were split about some of the individual features on the craft, but what they were describing was a force of three Gomer Moon Ships. We had faced one, and the results were pretty devastating to us. Now there were three, and this was definitely not a good thing. Armed with this information, we began to deploy various naval forces around the planet to maintain observation, just in case they decided to come down to play. The most confusing and disturbing aspect was that these Gomer Moon Ships did not feel compelled to hide behind the Moon.

Maintaining constant observation on all three of the Moon Ships, the scientific observers were very quick to notice what appeared to be just one Mountain Class Gomer as it was launched from one of the Moon Ships. It circled the Moon for one orbit, and then began to travel towards Earth. Within minutes, the scientific team and our naval observers all came to the same conclusion; it was headed towards the Southeastern part of the United States. Right back to the

SRS area. The observers also detected some differences in the overall configuration of this Mountain Class ship but they were minimal, and everyone on the staff was convinced that this was a Gomer returning to SRS. It passed the initial line of our 'space mines,' but as it approached the second line, there was a massive explosion along the port side of the huge Gomer ship. With that explosion, there was a significant change in the Gomer ship's course, and our resident eggheads were working feverishly to determine the probable points of impact. The result of their computations was to now put the ship as striking the Earth somewhere adjacent to or on top of the Puerto Rico Trench in the Caribbean. With that revelation, I called for the Chief of Allied Naval Operations, Admiral Carl Lynch.

"Admiral Lynch?"

"Yes, General?"

"What do we have that might be near that location?"

"Sir, I think we have a submarine . . . yeah, the USS Virginia is returning from patrol in the South Atlantic, and let's see........... AH, yeah, the USS Morton, that new destroyer, is on patrol near Cuba and right in that area."

"Okay, let's get her a FLASH message to keep an eye on this thing, and tell the USS Virginia to move their asses towards the USS Morton's position. Doctor Clarkson? Is this thing about to crash, or is it more controlled in its descent?"

"General, the descent is more like a controlled crash and, while the course is greatly altered, the rate of descent is probably going to make it several hours before it actually impacts the ocean. Our best guess is about 6 hours or so....."

"Doctor? Is this thing going to hit land or water?"

"Could go either way, since there are a bunch of islands in that area, and frankly, our computations could be off as much as an hour or by several hundred miles."

"CRAP! Okay. Admiral Lynch?"

"Yessir?"

"Send this FLASH message to Commander, USS Morton, over my signature. . . . ."

As the message was being sent, Dr. Clarkson approached me and asked a question that I had simply not considered. "General, what if that thing hits the water? We could be looking at a HUGE wave that would devastate the coastline."

"Geez, Doc, how friggin' wonderful is that? Okay, General Whitney, please put that out to the Civilian Authorities along the Eastern Seaboard. I guess that would be a Tsunami Alert?"

"Yessir, but where should we put it out for?"

"All along the eastern coast of the United States, and the Islands in the Caribbean."

"Yessir, but with the AM radio limitations this could be a problem in letting people know."

"Dammit, Whit, tell the Coast Guard or NOAA to let it go in the clear, and to send it via all available means, to include the higher frequencies."

"Yessir. I don't think Admiral Kleener will appreciate making his boys targets, but he will understand."

"Tell Kleener I'm sorry, but it is probably worth a try and the risk. My only question is who listens to FM, VHF, or UHF anymore? At least, besides the Gomers?"

As the time passed, so did the erratic descent of the Gomer Mountain Class ship. Entry into the atmosphere altered the course a little, but largely it maintained a heading that was going to put it at or into the Puerto Rico Trench, just north of Puerto Rico. We waited, and the USS Morton watched.

USS Morton, 25 miles northeast of Puerto Rico:

Captain Bennett was standing on the bridge when his CIC contacted him of the imminent approach of the Mountain Ship. Running out to the bridge wing, the Captain trained his night glasses in the direction of the large object that was passing abeam of his position. The altitude was about 3500 feet, but it was clear that the object was coming down. As he watched, the XO stepped close beside him and whispered, "Sir, did that damn thing just flare like it was coming in for a landing?"

"Sure looks like it, doesn't it, XO. . . . . Wait, now it is pointing the nose almost straight down. SHEEE-IT! Look at that, it is nosing in like it's in a dive!"

"Sir, that damn thing looks like it is diving into the water deliberately!"

"XO, quick, tell the helm to standby, and on my command I'm going to want everything this bitch has in the way of speed!"

"Aye, Aye, Sir!" The XO stuck his head back into the bridge, and gave the Captain's intentions to the Bridge Crew, and then stood by to relay the Captain's orders. They were very precise and quick. The second the object struck the water, several things happened at once. The first was that a giant wave was generated as the nose of the Mountain Ship struck the water at a high angle and rate of speed. The second was that the Captain yelled, "Turn towards the splash, and all ahead flank directly towards the wave!"

With that command, the Captain literally leaped back into the bridge and dogged the hatch behind him. As they plowed through the resulting wave, the Captain could only thank GOD that they were at General Quarters with the ship closed up. As the wave passed them, it would be a few minutes before things even remotely returned to normal on the bridge. Despite the turmoil and noise of the engines winding up, the Captain maintained his wits and yelled over the din, "XO!"

"Yessir"

"We got lucky to be on the down side of that impact, I would hate to see where that wall of water is headed, and I'm damn glad we got the short side!"

"Short side, Sir?"

"Yeah, this side was only about 50 to 75 feet, I can tell you that from the angle that damn Gomer smacked into the water, that the front side of this thing is probably about 3 or 4 times that height."

"SHEEE - IT! Sorry, sir."

"XO, get this off now in a flash via ELF, and......"

"Bridge. Sonar."

"Go ahead, Sonar."

"Sir, contact moving away and into the trench. Speed about 55 knots, direction 265 degrees relative, and depth appears to be level..... no . . . .450 feet and descending."

"Okay, XO, get out our position, and what the Gomer is doing, and ask for instructions. OH, and tell them the bastard executed a water landing that turned into a submarine crash dive type maneuver. It was controlled, I say again, CONTROLLED!"

"Aye, Aye, Sir!" Within minutes, the ELF communications had reached the Allied Headquarters war room. Unfortunately, it would be far too late to assist the Captain of the *Anna Marvel*, who wasn't monitoring any radios, much less the AM bands where a tsunami warning was being broadcast. Within 30 minutes of the Gomers' impact, the large wave crashed into his old fishing boat, and then into the South Carolina coastline. Little did Captain Brian Harris know, but at that moment, he and his small crew would be the first casualties in the next phase of the Gomer Conflict, or as some would later call it, Gomer War Two.

The second group of casualties would be those people who decided to shelter in place along the areas around Hilton Head Island and on up into the Lowcountry of South Carolina, above Beaufort. In this area, the death toll was complete and absolute, but as with the vagaries of a storm, the wave was not as devastating to the areas around it to either side. In those areas, while there was high water and some other more minimal damages, the shipyards in both Charleston and Savannah were quite intact and operational. This was extremely good news to the folks that were now working around the clock to get the new USS Iowa and the USS Montana completed. The sighting of the Gomers put the scores of workmen into a higher pace and, for the first time since construction began, every soul affiliated with the work felt a real urgency. They had been warned of a giant wave, but they made a conscious decision to ignore the warnings to keep the work going. Fortunately, the monstrous wave that was generated only gave them minor headaches.

Supreme Allied Headquarters, (SAHQ):

The line to the President was lighting up within seconds of the impact. Clearly, the President wasn't on the sidelines for this one, and he was on the line asking for me. Picking up the line, "GENERAL, what the hell just happened?"

"Mr. President, I don't know yet. We got the initial Report from the USS Morton, and it would seem that the Gomer, if that is who they are, is settling into the depths of the Puerto Rico Trench. No other ships have moved, and nothing else was launched."

"WELL, just what in the hell is the Gomer doing in Puerto Rico?"

"Sir, she has descended into the trench, and according to the Captain of the USS Morton, she is moving slowly as she settles into the trench itself. Mr. President, I have been informed that the trench is about 497 miles long with a maximum depth of 28,373 ft, which means that this thing can hide in about the deepest point of the Atlantic Ocean."

"Well, can we flush him out?"

"I'm not sure and, more to the point, we don't know that it is still alive. We think it might be, but the damage it suffered may have compromised hull integrity, which means it could be sunk with a boat load of dead Gomers on board. Assuming that they even are Gomers."

"What the hell do you mean IF they are Gomers?"

"Sir, Dr. Abramson and Dr. Clarkson still have not confirmed that these are the same Gomers. They did not see the mines which means they have the same limitations with Lead, and maybe even Sulphur, but sunlight isn't bothering them in their orbit of the Moon. This is enough of a variance that my resident eggheads are having a hard time telling me for sure that they are Gomers."

"So, what if they aren't Gomers?"

"I agree that probably doesn't matter, sir, but only to a point. I mean, it doesn't matter who they are if they are attacking us. Right now, though, that hasn't been the case. More to the point, we've drawn the first blood, so I would prefer to let them reveal who they are before I commit forces to a particular action. I don't want us to be over-committed and worse yet, what if we're bringing a knife to a gun fight?"

"What are you saying?"

"Well, if they're not Gomers, then we could be standing out there waiting on them to make a Gomer mistake, and when they don't, then we'll be in the wrong place, or worse, when we hit them with a Sulphur shell, what if it doesn't work? Then we could be screwed since we fired our best bolt."

"What happened to your being aggressive in the face of the enemy?"

"I guess my having to do this with very few assets just makes me not want to waste a single thing in the fight."

"Okay, you passed!"

"What?"

"You said everything I was thinking, and I wanted to make sure that we were on the same page. I agree with you, and want you to wait and see what the bastards are doing before you commit any forces to offensive operations. I don't know why, but something just seems a little off here."

"I thought it was just me and Whit."

"No. General, I think there are several of us that think things are just not right, and that there is something going on here we just don't grasp yet. Maybe a trap, maybe not, but right now, I agree that we don't need to take any course of action, until this develops."

"Yessir!" With my words, the line went dead. No sooner than we broke the connection, we were getting reports about the latest movements of the three remaining Moon Ships. While two were remaining in orbit around the Moon, the third was going to the opposite side of the Moon and assuming the same type of positioning that the original Moon ship had taken during our first encounter with the Gomers. While not comforting to know it was there, it was a return to a tactic that made us feel a little more at ease about what we were facing. Now we would observe to see if there were any other ships, regardless of size, that might be headed our way.

Lost in my thoughts, I didn't really notice that Dr. Clarkson had walked up next to my seat. When he spoke, I think I must have reacted with some surprise, "General, the launching of the large ship first may well be consistent with the tactics employed by the earlier Gomers."

"Go ahead, Doctor, you've got my attention."

"Well, the last time they must have sent the large Mountain size ships in first, because we were unaware that they were on our planet until later when we got into the Southern Hemisphere. The same goes with the tactic of getting behind the Moon to launch the other size ships. We don't really have all that information because the first time around, nobody was really looking like we are now, or if they were, their data didn't survive any better than they did."

"So, Doctor, are you thinking that we are closer to confirming that these are Gomers?"

"Well, actually, yessir, I am. I think Doctor Abramson agrees, but we're not comfortable in the conclusion just yet. If they aren't Gomers, then they are certainly mighty close to being Gomers."

"So, any clue about what is coming next?"

"Well, sir, if they are Gomers, we can expect them to start launching their fleet of other ships from behind the Moon at any time. Assuming they do, then we can assume that they are engaging in another attempted invasion."

"Doctor, I love how you say 'attempted,' especially since I thought they did a pretty damn good job the first time."

"That's true, sir, but they didn't get to stay around, so ....."

"No harm, Doctor, but right now, we need to figure out their patterns again, and start from scratch on killing the littlest ones. If they do launch and form a fleet, we can at least try to take out the Gomer Moon Ships we can see, and whether they are actual Gomers or not, we can assume that a fleet means business. Fortunately, we should have a thing or two at Vandenberg that will take care of at least some of them."

"True, sir, very true! We've even made some modifications, just in case the Gomers did come back, so this time there might even be some enhancements to the Sulphur Isotope missiles that they will fire."

"I know, Doc, I read your paper."

"You're kidding, I never thought...."

"That old guys could read such complex things? Doctor, remember that your assistant is my own youngest daughter. Her Mom isn't the only one in the family with a science geek hidden somewhere inside. You might even appreciate that Vandenberg isn't my only ace in the hole."

"Oh, what is the other one?"

"Now, Doctor, that would be telling."

"Yeah, I guess it would be."

"Okay, thanks, Doctor, and keep me advised of what the Gomers are doing at the Moon. Right now, I need to find out what the Navy knows."

Fort (formerly Camp) Dawson, West Virginia, HQ, 11th Airborne Division:

The young first Lieutenant was reporting to the Division Headquarters building, and as he ran up the steps, he literally ran over the Division Sergeant Major.

"GEEZUS H. TAP DANCING CHRIST! L-T, what is your damn hurry?"

"Sorry, Sergeant Major, I was ordered to report to the Commanding General."

"Oh, fuck me running. You must be the Mouse's boy."

"Huh?"

"L-T, is your name Robert Patrick?"

"Yes, it is." Growing a little annoyed at the quizzing from this old guy, Robbie was about to make a typical lieutenant error. He was about to believe for that one magical nanosecond that he 'out-ranked' this Sergeant Major. "Look, Sergeant Major, as much as I would enjoy a little chat, I was told to report to the General and, well, you're dismissed." With that wonderful remark, the Sergeant Major not only didn't move, but a rather twisted grin shot across his face. "L-T, you have a thing or two to learn, even if you did start off enlisted. So here is lesson number one, and please pay very close attention. SON, I happen to be the Division Command Sergeant Major and, with all due respect, I have shit turds way bigger than you. It is only out of respect for your Dad, who I've known since he was a fucking puppy, that I don't drop kick your ass all over this parade ground."

The look of horror hit my son immediately, since he had discovered the one thing on the entire planet meaner than a boat load of Gomers. This wasn't just the Division Command Sergeant Major, this was the famous, or was that infamous, CSM Clagmore. Knowing when he had his hand in a bucket of rattlesnakes, Robbie at least had the good sense to apologize and ask where he could find the General. "General is in there, but don't worry, I've got you covered. All his stuff is ready to go, and he will be out in a minute. He picked you to be his new Aide, probably because he knows your Dad from years ago too. Please, Please, do NOT disgrace your Dad. He is about the only officer I ever met that I halfway like, and that list includes you and the General who is about to walk out that fucking door."

"Thanks, Sergeant Major, and again, I apologize if I was too brusque."

"L-T, I have no idea what brusque means, but if you mean being an obstinate pain in my fourth point of contact, then apology accepted. Now then, make sure your shit is in one sock, because all the panic around here is that we're on alert, and from what we hear, the Goddamn Gomers are back."

"Roger that, Sergeant Major, and I'm ready!"

"Bullshit, L-T, ain't nobody ready for a fucking Gomer." With that, CSM Clagmore bounded on down the steps and leaped into the HUMVEE. He was going to shake a few people up and do all he could to get the Division on the move. When the General walked out, he looked at the lieutenant and could only shake his head. He could tell with one look what had happened, and as he chuckled to himself, all he said to the lieutenant was, "Welcome aboard, Lieutenant Patrick, I see you've met our beloved Sergeant Major." Motioning Robbie to follow him, the Division Commander hauled himself into his HUMVEE, and told the driver to get them to the airfield.

Movement was ongoing all over the Army. Each unit, from the rifle squad all the way up to the individual Field Army Headquarters, was making preparations for what they all knew was inevitable. At least this time, they weren't caught with their faces hanging out and the leadership cut off before they even had a chance to process what was happening. Now they were getting moved to their defensive positions to keep the leadership from being culled from the herd, and to make sure that the force would survive intact so they could strike back. Within hours, the entire Division, along with the 13th Airborne Division, was relocated to provide for the defense of the New Washington perimeter. Similarly, the 82nd and 17th Airborne Divisions were providing security for the new Pentagon system, and the 101st Airborne Division along with the 1st Marine Division were set up around the Supreme Allied Headquarters mountain complex. The individual taskings were more complex, with each Corps and Army Headquarters taking positions in and around various strategic positions around the country.

The question now would be what would they do next? As CSM Clagmore had explained to the young Lieutenant Patrick, "ain't nobody ready for a fucking Gomer." We could only hope that this time, we were as ready as we could be under the circumstances. Aircraft were placed in hardened revetments, shielded from energy drain and EMP. Ships were becoming holes in the water, and the newer task groupings built around both Battleships and Aircraft Carriers were rapidly becoming better at the game of being silent. Our submarine fleet was also getting scarce and quiet and, as of midnight the first full day after the Gomer Ship entered the Puerto Rico Trench, the only military assets that were still openly moving with a purpose were the USS Virginia and the USS Morton.

CHAPTER III

Supreme Allied Headquarters, (SAHQ):

Checking the main board I felt fairly confident that we had our leadership protected, dispersed, and our forces were as alert as possible under the circumstances. Similarly, I was able to follow the steps being taken by our allied forces. Field Marshall Sir William Fuller, OBE, was on top of his forces and, like us, they were finding places to go to disperse and protect themselves. Our Chinese allies, under the guidance of Admiral Li Dejiang, my former Chinese Liaison Officer, were also as ready as they could be, given the limited rebuilding of their military forces. As usual, the Russians were either unable or unwilling to provide meaningful assistance, preferring instead to remain aloof and disconnected from any global coordination. Other countries were stepping up, with either rebuilt forces or forces that were at least in the process of rebuilding. The German Navy and Army were functional, and a new liaison appeared at my headquarters within hours of the arrival of the Moon Ships. Sadly, their Air Force was still a shadow of its former self, but it was there and operational. Canada, France, Spain, Denmark, Sweden, and Norway were all providing forces this time, and their units were on standby for any movement as necessary. The Central and South American forces were largely on board, with the exception of the "usual suspects" in Cuba and Venezuela. All in all, there were reports coming into my headquarters from around the world as to the readiness status of the individual units and forces.

With some satisfaction, I was thankful that I had insisted on taking the last two years to get many of our allies trained and equipped to assist with any future Gomer incursions. We also took the time, whenever possible, to facilitate joint training among the allies. The only thing we did not do was allow for the proliferation of Gomer weaponry. Some allies did have access to portions of the alien technology, but such access was based on their earlier participation levels, and desire to cooperate in the building of a force that would be able to address the global threat. Non-allies or forces that were refusing to cooperate were denied both the technology and most of the information we had built up as to alien tactics and weaknesses. One thing we did share with anyone who would listen, stay the hell off the HF/UHF/VHF/FM radio bands. Making that long story short, only the forces from United States, Germany, and the United Kingdom came anywhere close to having the ability to fully meet the Gomers with their own technology.

My only real issue at this point was whether we were actually facing Gomers, or some other alien threat. We had issued all we could in "anti-Gomer" munitions to just about anyone that could or would use it. Now it was a matter of standing by to counter any threatening moves that might come from the unidentified force that was gathered around our Moon. It didn't come immediately this time, but instead, we waited for almost three days before the alien force began its next move.

I was now sleeping on a cot inside my office, because it put me within about 50 feet of the War Room. When Chris, my daughter and beloved "gate keeper," shook me awake, I could tell immediately from the look on her face that something was going on. Her words just confirmed it. "They're moving!" That phrase ran through me with a bigger jolt than a gallon of coffee. In an instant, I was up and moving towards the War Room at almost a dead run. When I entered the room, I could feel the tension. The silence and watching were more unnerving than the normal din of activity, and I was standing there for almost a minute before one of the duty officers noticed I had entered the room. Colonel Feldman sidled over to me and said, "Sir, one Moon ship has moved into position behind our Moon, and the other two have shifted out of the Moon's orbit and appear to be heading towards Mars."

"Mars? What the hell is on Mars?"

"Sir, I haven't a clue, but the one ship appears to be taking a page from that Gomer playbook you're always talking about."

"Seems they have. Anything moving this way?"

"No, sir. So far it is quiet."

"What's the latest from the USS Morton?"

"Nothing, they report that the Gomer in the trench is being as quiet as a tomb, and that was as of 5 minutes ago, in response to our inquiry."

"What about the USS Virginia?"

"Nothing either. They confirm that it is quiet, BUT, the Captain said he was descending closer to hopefully get something without having to go 'active' with his sonar."

"Okay, make damn sure that the Virginia does NOT go active. I say again, DO NOT go active on any systems. He is to wait, watch, and report only. Is that clear?"

"Yessir."

"Good. Get that out, and while you're at it, make damn sure that the USS Morton is copied on everything we're sending and getting from the Virginia."

Looking over towards the naval section, I said, "Admiral Lynch?"

Admiral Lynch turned immediately and came over to my station in front of the big board. When he got within earshot, I asked him quietly, "Admiral, which Battle group is closest in position to the Morton and Virginia?"

"General, the USS North Carolina battlegroup and the USS Roosevelt battlegroup are both within about 5 hours steaming time to the trench. The Roosevelt's airgroups are on standby for an Alpha Strike, and she is already within aircraft range of the target box."

"Excellent. Thanks, Admiral. I hope to hell we don't need them, but you never know. Now what battlegroup is that next to the South Pole?"

"Sir, that is the British flotilla. They don't have any big gun support, but they do have their version of a heavy guided missile cruiser."

"Okay, where is our nearest big gun support to either pole?"

"Sir, we've been moving the USS Alabama Group and the USS Massachusetts Group in the direction of both poles. The Alabama is headed north, while the Massachusetts is headed south. Each should be on station within the next 24 to 48 hours at the latest."

"Great, at least that puts us in the ball park if they try that crap again. Now where are the other big guys?"

"Sir, we have the USS Missouri and the USS New Jersey battlegroups in the Pacific with both groups covering the passages off the West Coast. The USS Wisconsin and the USS North Carolina battlegroups are essentially doing the same thing on the Atlantic side. We've just moved the North Carolina a little further south from her original station near Florida, and the Whisky is set up nearer the New Jersey area."

"Well, looks like coverage to me, and now we wait again." I was finishing my discussion with Admiral Lynch when General Whitney joined us. "Whit, I guess I don't have to tell you and your folks to keep a close eye on the Moon. If ANYTHING comes around the corner, let me know."

"Yessir. So you'll know, the Moon ships are definitely headed in the direction of Mars, and it would appear, at least according to Dr.

Clarkson, that they will likely enter an orbit pattern there within the next few hours."

"They must be hauling ass to get there within 10 hours!"

"Yessir, Dr. Clarkson doesn't have a full estimate of speed, but yeah, 'hauling ass' essentially covers it."

"Make sure we clock the time it takes them, since it might come in handy later if they break that orbit and start heading our way. We may need to know exactly how long we have if they decide to join the party."

"We are already doing that, and we can give you start times at varying stages, since we have one that runs from when we first detected movement of any kind, one for when the beast actually began to move forward, and finally, one from when it broke orbit around the moon."

"Whit? You're getting this from the new Hubble2?"

"Actually, no sir, if you will recall we had the 'Red Light' telescope put up to keep track of that part of space where the Gomers live, and we ...."

"Wait a minute. If Red Light is looking at Mars, just what the hell is still looking towards Gomerville?"

"Well, uh....."

"Son of a bitch, you mean there is nothing looking at that part of space?"

"Well, ground stations are looking, but NASA hasn't shifted Hubble2 around to that part of the sky yet."

"Dammit. You mean a battle fleet or a half dozen of these Moon critters could be flying up my ass, and I wouldn't know it until they were here?"

"Well, sir, it was a calculated risk......"

"Okay. Dr. Clarkson? How long to get Red Light back where she belongs, and get Hubble2 set on those SOBs headed to Mars?"

"About 14 hours, Sir."

"Dammit! Okay, Doctor, how long to get me something, like Hubble2, looking towards Gomerville?"

"We can send Hubble2 in that direction and have the passage covered in about 5 hours."

"Okay, make it happen, Doctor, and sooner than 5 hours will make me very happy. Right now we're blind, and I do NOT like being blind!"

"Yessir."

I sincerely hoped beyond hope that this was NOT the same kind of conversation had by Admiral Kimmel prior to the attack on Pearl Harbor. Poor bastard was quoted a few days before the attack saying, "You mean the whole Japanese Fleet could be steaming around Diamond Head right now, and I wouldn't know it?" This was that kind of moment, and I only prayed that we had at least somebody on the ground with a really good telescope and a great set of eyes. I could just see how history would excoriate me if we let something sneak up on us that we couldn't handle. So, for the second time in so many days, I issued yet another warning order to all units within my command. This time it was invasion possible from ANY direction, be on alert accordingly. "Threat level RED ALPHA is in play, all units to continue dispersion and maintain your conditions in accordance with War Order number 1."

I felt a little guilty after issuing the Order, but again, better safe than sorry. The idea that we might not have a full view of the sky made me damn nervous, especially since we already knew that somebody was on the front door step with a shotgun. It was now the back door that had me nervous.

USS Morton near the Puerto Rico Trench:

"Captain, here is another alert that has gone out to all Allied Units. I'm not sure what they're concerned about, but something has them kind of spooked."

"XO, I'm spooked too, and frankly, that alert only confirms my really bad gut feeling about all of this."

"Sir, what can we do that we're not already doing?"

"XO, I suggest prayer, and a sharper eye on the Sonar and in the sky. Double the lookouts for the old fashioned visual checks. Only this time, get somebody looking WAY the hell up."

"Way the hell up?"

"Yeah, as in up in the sky, only way the hell beyond where they normally look. I mean all the way up and overhead into space. If it looks weird, report it to the bridge."

"Aye, Aye, Sir." The Captain had been truly concerned about several things here lately. The first was that with their onboard optical equipment, they could visually confirm the Moon ships in orbit around the Moon. They were able to confirm that the Moon ships were moving away from the Moon, and the thing below them was now making like a 'hole in the water'. The Captain was having visions of them about to stuff one up his ass like the Gomer had that night on the USS New Jersey. Not a happy place at all, and he sure wasn't comfortable with any of it. Nope, his "Spidey" senses were going absolutely berserk, and something told him that he wasn't the only one feeling it. He was thinking so hard, he said out loud, "I'll bet General Patrick is probably shitting bricks, along with the rest of his staff. That's why they sent that message." The XO, not knowing that his boss was just thinking out loud, simply stared and felt a cold shiver pass through him. He wanted to say something, but frankly, he was just too damned scared to even open his mouth. When the 1MC went off, the XO almost fainted.

"Bridge! Sonar! Contact moving!"

"Captain here, which way is it moving, Sonar?"

"Sir, it is moving deeper into the trench, 270 degrees relative, and at a speed of about 30 knots."

"Crap, okay, keep course and speed information coming. Helm, make your heading 270 degrees and increase speed to 30 knots. Let's try to keep up."

"Aye, Aye, Sir."

The little destroyer almost heeled over as she made the turn and increased her speed to parallel the contact's movement in the trench. Once out of the turn, she shot forward, and the USS Morton was now in pursuit of the contact. "Bridge, contact increasing speed to 45 knots, increasing depth to 10,000 feet."

The Captain whirled around and said to the bridge crew, "All stop! Power down!"

The XO looked at him like he had something growing out of his head, but the Captain knew that he wouldn't be able to keep up. "XO, notify the Virginia via ELF. We've broken contact, and pursuit. Give our position, and remain passive. There is no way we can keep up, and even if we could, I'm thinking we might be catching the garbage truck or worse yet, sailing into a trap."

"Aye, Aye, Sir." The XO ducked into the CIC to get the message out, and the Captain sat down in his chair to contemplate the next move. It would be dark soon, and then GOD only knew what might come out of that thing. It was this thought that bothered him the most, since he knew that these Mountain Class Gomers could launch Fighters, and if he was too close or making noise, then it would be a bucket of something very nasty! He then turned to the helmsman and Ordered, "Make turns for 15 knots, on a heading of 360 degrees, and get us from this position. We have only an hour before sundown, and I want to be as far as we can be from here by then." He thought to himself, "yep, they're up to something, and sundown will be the trigger." The Captain then told the crew to stand easy and for the galley to start handing out chow and hot coffee. Somehow he knew it was going to be a damn long night.

Onboard the USS Virginia, near the Puerto Rico Trench:

The submarine was at its classified maximum depth and holding position at the Dominican Republic end of the trench. She was passively listening back towards the USS Morton, which was at the far end of the trench nearer the Virgin Islands. She had heard the run of the Gomer Ship from where the USS Morton was located, mainly because there was something loose on board the Gomer. The Captain assumed it was battle damage, but with these guys, you could never be sure. He'd read the intelligence reports about the Gomers' visual acuity, and their problems seeing things through or under seawater. He was more than perplexed at the idea that something the size of the Gomer ship could navigate submerged, in confined space, at a speed nearing 45 knots. He turned to his XO, and said, "Okay, just how in the world can they do that kind of speed, in that kind of space, with that size of a ship?" His XO merely looked at him and shrugged. At a complete loss, the Captain continued, "Well, regardless, the bastard is here, and he is doing it. XO, whatever you do, do NOT power up anything. Let's listen, and unless he is on a collision course, we are not going to move. I have a feeling Admiral Lynch is going to want to know what this guy is doing, and how he is doing it. Maintain a silent boat."

Supreme Allied Headquarters:

Monitoring all the message traffic from and between the USS Morton and USS Virginia, Admiral Lynch was truly puzzled. "General, I'm at a complete loss at how these Gomers are able to do this maneuver! Most of my skippers take years before they can run an undersea canyon, much less doing it that speed and blind, or at least we're assuming they're blind. I thought water kept them from being able to detect us?"

Dr. Clarkson spoke up, "Well, Admiral, looking down through it is one thing, but being in the water itself might be another. This is just a guess, but maybe it is similar to when you try to look through a window into a room during the day. Glare keeps you from seeing anything from outside, but if you're in the room already, you can see. So, maybe, there isn't the same restriction to vision once they're in the water? They're also pretty deep, so maybe the darkness is helping them? I also have another theory, but right now I need more data to know if the theory is completely plausible."

While we pondered the ramifications of those notions, it struck me that this discovery could be a game changer for all of us. If they don't have to wait for night time, they can just dive in the water and wait in place or move where they want without our being able to track them adequately. Then what, or does that even matter? If they're under water, then what does that do to their offensive capability? For that matter, what does that mean for our naval units? They can't be holes in the water, or can they? Will the lead-based paint still protect our guys if they're being seen from below? Dammit, the questions were far more pervasive than the answers. Besides, are these even the Gomers we know, or by doing these things, are they something different? Pondering all of this, I could only say, "Crap, well okay, when in doubt, we're going to have to defend ourselves. Advise all units in play that any offensive move by that Gomer in the trench is to be met with instantaneous and overwhelming firepower." Within a few seconds of my giving that Order, the USS Virginia was on the ELF to report her status.

Onboard the USS Virginia, near the Puerto Rico Trench:

The crew was being extremely quiet and more vigilant than most would ever believe possible while inside a monstrous machine. Sonar plot was showing that the Gomer was headed right at them, but about 8,000 feet deeper in the trench. The Captain whispered to no one in particular, "Shit, that thing is going to pass well below us." As it passed, things were so quiet in the submarine that when the Gomer rushed below them, they could actually hear it moving the water before it. Looking at the Sonar operator, and then at the plot numbers, the Captain was honestly shocked. Turning to the XO, he again whispered, "Geezus, that bastard went by at 79 knots, and was picking up speed. I don't think anyone will be able to maintain a viable sonar contact on it."

The XO looked at him in amazement, and could only chuckle and shake his head at the next command. "XO, get the course, depth, and speed off to SAHQ, Admiral Lynch is going to wind up giving birth to a litter of kittens over these damn numbers. Also advise them that we'll try to maintain passive contact, but target is rapidly moving out of range."

"Sir, I just hope that damn thing doesn't turn around and bite at us."

"Me, too! Now send the message." Just as the XO turned, the Communications Officer handed the Captain the message from SAHQ. The Captain chuckled and said, "Good thing we didn't get this a few minutes ago. I would have shot the bastard as it was coming at us, if for no other reason than it was coming right at us."

"Hah, that would have been fun trying to ex...................." The XO's words were cut off as the sound of a massive explosion rocked throughout the boat. In fact, the force was so strong that it moved the USS Virginia almost to the surface. The violence of the explosion threw everyone off their feet, and the currents were so strong that the submarine almost collided with the walls of the trench on her way towards the shallower depth. When the submarine was under control and there was a second to catch their breath, the Captain said, "XO, get that off to the SAHQ immediately, tell them I believe that either the Cuban's did something damn stupid, or that bastard hit the far end of the trench going close to 80 knots."

USS Morton near the Puerto Rico Trench:

Almost 230 miles away, at the other end of the Trench, the Captain of the USS Morton could not only feel it, but he could hear a sharp, cracking sound. When the ELF lit up with the message from the USS Virginia, it only confirmed what he suspected might have happened. Oddly enough, he didn't find any comfort from it. Instead, he knew what was coming. "Chief, get everyone buttoned up, and tell them to hold on. XO, get a message to the beach and let them know that a Tsunami will be coming their way. I have no idea what magnitude that impact might have generated, but if it doesn't kick up a good one, I'll kiss your ass. Helm, make course 270 degrees, and speed all ahead full." Thinking to himself, *dark or no dark, we've got to get our asses over there, just in case the Virginia needs help, or something good floats up from the impact.*

Supreme Allied Headquarters, (SAHQ):

The news shot through headquarters like a dose of salts. If that damn thing hit the end of the trench, then that meant they really couldn't see all that well and got caught with their faces hanging out. If someone like the Cubans did it, then that might mean something else entirely. Either way, we needed eyes on this as quickly as possible. Turning to General Whitney, I asked the $3.00 question, "Whit, what do we have that we can get there quickly, and what are we doing about the USS Morton's warning about the tsunami threat?"

"General, the wave is a problem, but not that huge for the military. Looks as though it will play hell with the Dominican Republic, Haiti, Cuba, Southern Florida, and along the Gulf Coast, but our assets in all those locations are limited and/or well protected. The good news is that it won't impact our shipyards directly. Like the last one, it is more focused. As for assets, the USS Morton is headed that way, and we could put aircraft in the air, but with darkness falling, we might want to wait."

"Gotcha. What about the Virginia? Is she alright?" Admiral Lynch stepped up and said, "Yessir, they're okay. They do have some minor damage, but she is underway, and reports that weapons are green across the board." At least that was some good news, and a check of the Moon ships didn't reveal anything happening. There were no signs, at least so far, of any movement coming around the Moon that would show the approach of a fleet, so things were still oddly quiet. TOO damn quiet. Almost as an afterthought, I asked the status of the Hubble2 repositioning, and was advised that it was now in place, and the skies were clear.

The feeling in my gut was that we were on the verge of a serious knock down fight, but right now I just couldn't get a handle on where the punch was going to come from. The deeper I thought about it, the more disconcerted I was becoming. Pondering all of this, Dr. Clarkson's sudden outburst was almost enough to cause me a heart attack. Looking over towards him, he was looking and acting more like a kid on Christmas morning than the stodgy elder scientist. Turning towards everyone in the room and giving us all his best 'Eureka' kind of face, he announced, "We have finally located the part of the electromagnetic spectrum where these guys are communicating! I KNEW it, I had hoped from my dissection of their equipment that we would find it, and Yee Haw! We finally found it. HOT DAMN DINKY!!" As he peered at us, with his glasses fogged up from his excitement, and just a touch of spittle dangling from his lip, he realized that his outburst, in this setting, was probably just a tad bit over the top. Looking completely crestfallen, he apologized and started staring at his feet, while the rest of us were thunderstruck at what he had just said.

Breaking the silence, I said as softly as I could, "Doctor, you may have just won the war before it ever got completely started." With that, he looked around at all of us and positively beamed.

"Doctor, lay it out for me, and this time without the touchdown dance."

"Sorry, General, but listen, we were watching for any variance in these areas of the spectrum that might indicate a transmission or discussion with their commanders on the Moon Ships. Well, look at this. . . . " With that, he pulled out a long strip of paper that looked more like an EKG strip than anything else, but the long story short was that the spikes were in areas and in a pattern that indicated that there were some kind of transmissions. Seems that the spikes ended from the Trench, at the exact moment as the explosion of their ship hitting the end of the trench. Other spikes coincided with transmissions from the other ships to the one on Earth, and the other ones in space around Mars. At the end of his presentation, we were convinced that he was right. I told Whit to get this information off to the rest of the eggheads and the President. If we could break into their transmissions, then we might be able to either communicate with them, which put diplomacy on the table, or we might be able to listen in and find something useful to use in simply busting their asses. Either way, we had another game changer on our hands, and this one was huge.

Some days are better than others, and this one was starting to shape up that way. No sooner than we were reveling in Dr. Clarkson's new discovery, we got a message from the USS Virginia. Seems that they had just fished a few of the Gomers from the crash site. We didn't have anything solid about them, since nobody on the USS Virginia had ever seen all three types of Gomers. One thing we felt sure about was that what they found wouldn't be a 'dusty' Gomer. Instead, from their description over the ELF, we definitely couldn't rule out the "meaty" Gomer nor could we even confirm that it was a Gomer. We made arrangements to get whatever they found back to Dr. Abramson and his folks first thing after sunrise, and we made sure that the USS Morton was also en route to begin whatever recovery she could in that area. In either case, our answers would be hours away.

Now all we had to do was hope that the Gomers didn't try anything the rest of the night. I was used to such hopes being completely empty, but as the night progressed, it was clear that the two Moon Ships were still orbiting Mars. The other one was still hiding behind our Moon, and there was nothing moving around the Moon. Now that the Hubble2 was in place, we confirmed that there was no movement off in the direction of Gomerville either. This lack of movement, especially given the events earlier with the Mountain Ship in the trench, was unsettling. Fortunately, thanks to Dr. Clarkson's discovery, we did know they were all talking to one another. In fact, they were talking so much that Dr. Clarkson was getting worried that he had over-read something, and that maybe these weren't communications spikes in the spectrum after all. Finally, as dawn approached, the spiking returned to normal, with their transmissions coming at lesser intervals. Dr. Clarkson felt relieved, since it restored his faith in his earlier 'discovery' and confirmed his theories. Unlike Dr. Clarkson, the return to normal transmissions got me concerned that it was not a good thing. In fact, I got damned worried, since the cessation of talking usually always is followed by somebody doing something. In my business, it is the "doing" that usually generates all of the real problems.

CHAPTER IV

Supreme Allied Headquarters, (SAHQ):

The schedule in the War Room was simple. We were on a war time footing, which meant that either General Whitney or myself was physically in the War Room on a 24/7 basis. Most of our staff were operating on the same breakdown, usually working off a 12 hour roster, as opposed to Whit and I juggling what seemed to be 18 to 20 hours shifts. With most of our Staff, either the Chief or his Deputy would be present at all times. Exceptions were made, of course, but those were for staff personnel in other more independent areas, such as the Chief of Allied Special Operations, or ASOC. With the arrival of the three ships, ASOC moved to their wartime positions at Vandenberg, and to their secret location in the Rockies. A representative from the command was send to our War Room but, unlike everyone else, he was often forced to work a lot more hours than just a 12 hour shift. Brigadier General Nathan "Deacon" Jones didn't seem to mind at all and, along with his new Aide, he did his best to keep up. His boss, now Lieutenant General, Daniel Greene, Jr., was running things from the Rockies ASOC Headquarters. As with the first Gomer incursion, Daniel was giving it more than his best in gathering information about these latest visitors. In fact, there was a rumor that he was keeping Dr. Abramson's working team chained to their desks until they came up with some answers.

Similarly, Dr. Clarkson was working overtime on lots of questions with very few answers. The first of such questions was partially answered with the arrival of the first alien that the USS Virginia had picked up from near the Puerto Rico Trench. Since the initial burst of transmissions after the Mountain Class Gomer ship collided with the end of the trench, our 'visitors' maintained what could best be described as routine transmissions. There was also little movement or activity observed emanating from the ships still in position around Mars and behind the Moon. As the day wore on, Dr. Clarkson finally arrived with the initial information derived from Dr. Abramson's autopsies conducted at ASOC.

"General?"

"Yes, Doctor."

"Sir, we have the Dr. Abramson's initial findings from the autopsies of several of the bodies they flew in."

"Sure, hang on. General Whitney? General Jones? Please step over here." With their arrival, Dr. Clarkson continued.

"Sir, these things appear generally to be what we used to call 'meaty' Gomers. I say generally, because there is only about a 97 percent concurrence in physiology. There are some differences, and in some respects, those differences are rather dramatic."

"Okay, go on, you damn sure have my attention."

"Well, sir. In layman's terms, they appear to have the same differences as say, you or I would from a Neanderthal man."

"Huh? You mean these things are the caveman version of the meaty Gomer?"

"No, sir. The opposite. The 'meaty' Gomers we fought before were the caveman version of this Gomer. From what I'm told by Dr. Abramson, and these are only preliminary findings, the Gomers on his table right now are more advanced."

"Crap! How are they more advanced?"

"Well, they appear to have greater brain development, by almost 68%, and they are more capable of manual dexterity. Seems they also evolved an extra finger on each hand, and an extra toe on each foot. In some respects, they are far more humanoid than their 'meaty' Gomer cousins."

"So are they Gomers or not?"

"Well, sir, at this point, we'd have to classify them as Gomer, since they have the same chemical and DNA makeup as the 'meaty' variety. So far, we haven't found any of the 'crab' looking Gomers, and everything that has come up so far is of this latest variety."

"Well, Doctor, any ideas for a name we can call this new class of Gomer?"

"Smart Gomers?"

"As opposed to just plain Gomers, or 'meaty' or 'dusty' Gomers?"

"Yessir. Just smart. Apparently the brain capacity, at least as we know it, is greater with these Gomers than even with what we were calling the Gomer or Crab Gomers."

"Doctor, for some reason that doesn't give me any comfort at all, since what you're really telling me is that the bastards still in space could be our toughest opposition to date. If they're smarter, and clearly they are since they wound up crossing space to get on our doorstep, then we could have a very serious problem on our hands."

"I hate to say it, but yessir, that would be my assessment."

"Okay, great. Doctor, thanks for making my day go from crap to pure shit. Alright, gentlemen, what do you think?"

"Sir, one more thing."

"Okay, go ahead Doc."

"Sir, I have been working on the transmission theory, and I think I know why they can't see our submarines, and then wound up killing themselves while underwater."

"And........"

"Well, I've been comparing our data from our discoveries on the Ship at the South Pole, their weapons, and checking all the other materials involved in the composition of their technology, and I believe that they have figured out some answer to solve some of the issues we've been having in the field of physics. It is a relatively new field, and while we were able to replicate much of it in rebuilding their weapons for our use, some of it has remained kind of elusive. Their transmissions we should have caught sooner, since we've had a form of this technology ourselves. Now, in sub-millimeter studies, of wave pass......."

"Doctor, I hate to seem rude, but this sounds like you're about to take us down a road where you will lose us in the next two seconds. Can you make it simple for this old hillbilly?"

"Sorry, Sir. Okay, I am talking about the area of Terahertz Radiation, or T-rays."

"You mean like what the TSA was playing with to see through our clothes at airports?"

"Exactly. One of the reasons the TSA backed off was that, while originally believed to be harmless, if it were used wrong, there were studies that suggested that it could impact our DNA. Sort of changing or unzipping it, if you will. See, the Terahertz Radiation wave length is on the electromagnetic spectrum between microwaves and infrared light waves. It begins at a wavelength of one millimeter and proceeds into shorter wavelengths, which is why we call it the sub-millimeter band or waves. Being between microwaves and infrared light waves, it can have the characteristics of both, which is why it can pass through clothing, paper, and lighter materials, but it totally dissipates in water. It can't see through water either, assuming that is your primary source for what we would call vision. Our atmosphere is another impediment to that sight, which is why they may not be seeing what we're doing, unless we're leaving some sort of radio signature that they can detect using their other senses."

"Okay, Doctor, you have our complete attention."

"Sir, the impact of this type of Electro Magnetic Radiation on humans would depend on the frequency or the power behind the usage. So, the higher the frequency, the more likely it will do damage at the chemical or molecular level on living cells. So, when they were scanning us, they were literally vaporizing people from their cars and houses. It would take out the living cells, while the metal surfaces or non-living materials would offer some protection, it would not necessarily be sufficient to stop their scans. Meanwhile, using a different frequency, or adding power, would make this same process a weapon. This is what we found as we reverse engineered some of their weapons for our artillery and naval assets. Now, here is the kicker for communications. Pushing the frequency again, you can create, just as we have done with more efficient Wi-Fi Technology, a pretty impressive communications system that would work well within space. In fact, sub-millimeter astronomy uses this same technological thinking for our various observatories. We even had these facilities before the Gomers showed up the first time. There was one in Hawaii and another one at the South Pole."

"Holy Hell! You mean to tell me that the Gomers may have been drawn here to Hawaii and the South Pole because of this Terahertz stuff we were doing?"

"Exactly, sir. Hence my theory about it all, and why I even went so far as to consult with Dr. Marvin who was doing a lot of the development of the Terahertz Radiation in physics. He is an expert in 'string theory' and has ...."

"Doctor, did you really just say, Doctor Marvin?"

"Yessir. He is or was a physicist specializing in string theory from Stanford. He survived the earlier California attack because he was visiting his mother in Denver when it happened."

"Doc, are you familiar with an old 1950s movie called 'Earth vs. The Flying Saucers'?"

"No, sir, a little before my time."

"You are kidding me, okay, well you need to watch it, and then get back to me."

"Yessir."

"Okay, Doctor, if you need to bring him in, get Doctor Marvin onboard, and see if you can develop something that would allow us to either monitor or disrupt their transmissions."

"Yessir, that was what I was hoping you'd say."

"Go for it, with my blessings. Whit, make sure they get whatever they need to get more answers. I see where this could go, and it is well worth the time to explore it." Dr. Clarkson headed off, and I turned to Generals Whitney and Jones. "Gentlemen, that explains just about everything for now. Problems in seeing in the water, and the basis for their weapons. All very helpful. Still, my real problem now is their findings that we may be dealing with a new 'smart' Gomer. Any thoughts?"

General Whitney spoke up first, and said, "Well, sir, whether they're smarter or not, we know at least some of their weaknesses, and given the fact that they smacked a lead painted mine on their way into Earth means that at least some of them are still in effect."

"Maybe. Then again, we don't know if that was as much the same weakness or whether it was just hubris at ignoring something that relatively small to their size. I'm just a little worried that they may either have intelligence about our 'hole in the water' naval tactics, or that the lead isn't a good basis for hiding from them anymore. Lots of lives at stake here, and I guess what has me more worried than anything else is that they may well be ahead of the curve on us."

Whit then turned and asked, "General Jones, you're being quiet, is there a reason? You've seen them up close, at least the previous Gomers, what do you think?"

"Well, there weren't any 'smart' Gomers directing the forces where we were on the battlefield, but that doesn't mean they weren't here in some capacity. I wonder if they might have been working on the last Moon ship, which means we wouldn't have found any. Either way, they are here, they are on our doorstep, and we are going to have to kill them."

"My thoughts exactly, gentlemen. Whit, see if you can sum up what Dr. Clarkson told us, and get a FLASH out to the Senior Commanders and copy the President. I guess we will still have to wait for them to make the next move. Oh, and make sure you bring Vandenberg up to speed, too. Maybe they can come up with some ideas."

"Yessir." With that reply, both General Whitney and General Jones returned to their duties, while I returned to my thoughts. The hours drug on, and still nothing was moving in space. The waiting was unnerving to many of the staff, and the longer we waited, the worse it got. Unlike the last time, these Gomers were taking their time, talking, thinking, and plotting their opening move. I guess what they had originally planned just wasn't working out the way they had hoped. Then again, the silence was deafening.

11th Airborne Division Headquarters, New Washington:

Security duty around the underground Capital was quiet and more than a little boring. As the days wore on, the only traffic into or out of the Mountain were diplomats from the various nations. CSM Clagmore was using his time to make sure that the individual Regiments within the Division were maintaining their training levels. Making the rounds, he was determined to keep the men focused by reminding them just how serious Gomer killing could be, especially when they decided to tear up the landscape like they had in Virginia three years earlier. After tearing into a Regimental Sergeant Major, he was summoned to the Division Commander for what best could be described as a minor ass chewing.

"CSM Clagmore, you can't keep kicking everyone in the ass all the time, especially in front of the troops."

"General, with all due respect, if the Gomers ever decide to come at us again on the ground, we've got to be ready. Half this Division hasn't ever seen a damn Gomer, much less tried to kill one. Hell, that bastard I chewed out was hiding somewhere in the Mountains of Italy when the shit went down last time. The closest he got to a damn Gomer was when he took a dump."

"I know, Sergeant Major, but you can't say that out loud in front of God and everybody. Hell, the President is only a rock toss from here, and if he heard you, it would not be good."

"Again, with all due respect, Sir. Bullshit! First of all, the President knows Gomers like we do, AND he was Army. And while we're at it, he was my first shavetail to break in back in the 101st Airborne. Somehow I think he'd agree with me."

"Just don't do it again in front of the troops, got it?"

"Yessir. Next time I'll politely tell him that his head is so far up his fourth point of contact that he needs a sight glass in his fucking belly button to see where he is going."

"See, Sergeant Major, I knew you could be nicer."

"Gotcha, Sir!"

As Clagmore left the General's CP, Lieutenant Patrick could only smile and shake his head as he looked back at the General. The General looked back at him and smiled. "You know the old bastard is right. The President is terrified of him, for the same reason the rest of us are, he not only knows where all the bodies are buried, but he was usually the one operating the shovel. One of the best NCOs the Army ever produced, too. Nobody has the heart to retire him either, since he knows more about killing than the next three guys put together, with one notable exception, who is probably better at it than even Clagmore."

"Who's that, General?"

"Never mind, so how is your Dad these days?"

"Beats me, sir, nobody in the family has seen him since those damn things showed up. Mom says he is living at or in the War Room, and that he only shows up long enough to shower, shave, and change uniforms. My sister sees him daily, but she is worse than he is about sharing information. I'm not even real sure she isn't the meanest one in the family!"

"Well, oddly enough, I find that pretty damn comforting. Now then, Clagmore is dead right about one thing. We need to start kicking these Regimental Commanders in the ass, too. Sitting around is bad news, and we need to keep these troopers motivated. Grab your hat, and let's see what trees we can shake! Oh, and if your sister is the meanest one in the family, then maybe we should be recruiting her to take on Clagmore......"

"Yessir. She might be his one and only kryptonite."

CINCLANT, Norfolk, Virginia:

Admiral Steadman, as the Chief of Naval Operations, was overseeing the "Montana" project. A lover of all things naval, he was excited to see something that was truly historic in its proportions, and even more beautiful in its aesthetics. The Montana Class was a dream of the battleship sailor from well before World War II and now, almost 75 years later, it was becoming a reality, thanks to a new world threat. He had the new USS Iowa on the ways in the Charleston Naval Ship Yard, and she was about 80% complete.

Here in Norfolk sat the USS Montana, the leader in her class and more advanced than anything ever dreamed of by the naval planners for her originally-1942 scrapped construction. A thing of beauty, she was now being outfitted with the newest weaponry, which would augment the classic guns she would also be carrying. An extra turret aft gave her over twelve 18" gun tubes, along with four batteries of the newer Gomer based weapons. She was also outfitted with a huge array of stealth technology to include a device that would mislead anyone terrestrial, and lots of lead coverings to throw off the Gomer sensors. The real problem was for the shipyard workers and sailors who would have to be protected from her lead outer coating. Thanks to some work from the scientists and chemists, there was some headway in the area, but most of that would not be here in time for her launching. Instead, that would be a retrofit, since time was of the essence. Thankfully, her hull had been launched last year, and the outfitting and final touches were coming together. Sadly, there wouldn't be much of a shakedown cruise for her, since it looked as though it was now a real race to get her ready before the bad guys arrived.

Picking up the phone, Admiral Steadman contacted his counterpart on the Allied Staff, Admiral Lynch, "Carl?"

"Hey, Admiral Steadman, how are you doing this fine afternoon?"

"Look, Carl, I'm fine, but the Montana could use some help."

"Crap, okay, what do you need?"

"Carl, we need someone to kick the production folks into high gear on the 18" Sulphur Rounds. We've only got about half of what we need on hand, and the rest are still stuck somewhere in the rail system. Can you find the log jam and break it loose?"

"I'll check with General Clark, and see about the hold up. How soon before the old girl will be ready?"

"Old girl, my ass. She is a thing of absolute beauty! Get me the shells and we can start an abbreviated shake down in about a week. Just enough time to get in some gunnery practice with the real thing. Computer simulations are fine, but we need some real bang time on these new caliber guns."

"Got it, and I'll get on Clark to see what is the problem. In the meantime, did you get the old man's summary about that Terahertz stuff?"

"Sure did, and I got my Information Dominance and crypto guys on it. I've also given some thought to how to maybe counteract their weapon, at least at the local level. I've even told the BB crews to move forward with it."

"Okay, I'll bite, what do you have in mind?"

"Something simple, fairly low tech for Gomer stuff, and we'll see how effective it works when the fecal material really hits the fan."

"You're not going to tell me, are you!"

"Nope, but General Patrick blessed off on it, and I told him to keep it as a surprise for you. Seems it was an idea hatched by that sicko, Greene, over at ASOC."

"Dammit, I hate it when the Army knows more than we do about stuff."

"Hey, get used to it. The old man is half Navy, you know."

"Yeah, I know, and HIS old man would be rolling in his grave if he knew what was going on these days." With that, they broke the connection and Admiral Lynch went to find General Clark to get the shells moving.

Supreme Allied Headquarters (SAHQ):

Admiral Lynch turned from his conversation with General Clark and was headed to brief General Patrick, when General Whitney intercepted him. Their conversation was short, and it was clear that something was up that made Whit want to keep him out of ear shot.

When they finally approached General Patrick, he was locked into another conversation with General Jones, the ASOC representative. As they got closer, they could hear what was being said. "Okay, Deacon. Tell Daniel that he is cleared to move it forward, but I want the Vandenberg assets and Project Dragon to sit it out, at least until the big ones try to come this way. I just don't want to tip my hold cards until we absolutely have to show them."

As General Jones walked away, Admiral Lynch stepped up and said, "General, what is Project Dragon?"

"Never mind. The fewer that know the better, especially if it doesn't work. That way during the Court Martial, you can honestly say you didn't know a damn thing about it."

"Geez, well, I have a problem a little closer to home, and thought you should know about. The thing that appears to be holding the USS Montana from getting to sea is a shortage of 18" Sulphur shells. She is loaded with her HE rounds but not a full load of the Sulphur ones. General Clark says the hold-up is the usage of the rail system taking some stuff to Vandenberg. Can we break that log jam?"

"I'm sure we can, but right now, I've got to give Vandenberg the nod. Once that is done, which should be within hours, we'll start getting your loads headed towards Norfolk."

"Aye, Aye, sir. Still, I got another secret to ask you about."

"Okay, ask away. Doesn't mean I'll answer, but you can ask."

"Sir, Admiral Steadman said he had an idea that he was going to try onboard ship when the Gomers come back. Can I ask what he has in mind?"

"Carl, you can ask, but unfortunately, Steadman swore me to secrecy. You'll love it though, I promise. Especially if it works."

"Dammit sir, I'm your Allied Chief of Naval Operations, and I'm out of the loop?"

"Actually, you're not out of the loop. It was your idea apparently, and that is all I'm going to say about it."

"Crap!"

"Now Admiral, stay up Clark's ass, and once they get that rolling stock offloaded, they will come to you for the delivery of the 18" shells. Which I'm assured will be on location, assuming the war doesn't go hot, no later than two days from today. Now if the war really gets going, then they'll just have to sail and we'll have to figure out how to resupply either at sea or with a quick trip back into Norfolk. We'll figure something out, but right now, Vandenberg has priority."

"Yes, sir. I don't suppose it has anything to do with Operation....."

"Yes, it does, and don't mention that name again. Read me?"

"Aye, Aye, sir."

As the day wore on, General Clark was faced with more problems. A derailment near the rail hub outside Denver, for example, was just one more of many headaches. Still, the logistical machine was moving forward and as the day progressed, things were beginning to improve. The one upside to the Gomers' reticence to make a move was that it gave us time to get better prepared. Sadly, no matter how much things improve, you never feel as though you've done enough. Finally, on the evening of the ninth day, there was movement from the Gomers. It wasn't much, but it was definitely a move that telegraphed their intent.

I was awakened by Chris, who said I was wanted in the War Room, and without even realizing it, I was coming through the door as I was waking up. With a cup of coffee thrust in my hand, the briefing began. "Sir! A small fleet of Carrier Class ships is moving from behind the Moon and headed through the mine field."

"Whit, what is your best guess? Are they passing through because they can see them, or is it that they're too far apart to take out a smaller ship?"

"We think it is the latter, and so does Vandenberg. The observers noted that the Mountain class will hit them, the Gomer's Battleship might hit them, and Carrier Classes will almost surely get through."

"Okay, crap. First, ask whether we can increase the mines to keep out the Carrier Class, and second, where are the Gomers headed?"

"I don't know about the first part, but as for the second, they are moving straight for the twilight line, which is right now passing over Europe."

"I assume you've told the Germans and General Fuller's people?"

"Yessir. They are all on standby, per your Orders, and the big guns and our carrier battlegroups are all sortied to their assigned positions."

"What about the USS Montana?"

"Sir, she is headed out, but she is still short some of her shells. They got there, but were in the process of being loaded when they got the signal."

"Okay, tell her to just go out to their alternate position, and hold till morning. She is to remain silent, inactive, and she is NOT to tip her hand just yet."

With that last command, Admiral Lynch responded with a quick, "Aye, Aye, Sir. I take it you're holding her back, too?"

"Correct. Let's see what else they have for us this time, and then we can figure out how best to use her. Right now, I want her out of harbor where she can maneuver, but not in the thick of it just yet."

"For whatever it is worth, I concur, sir, and thanks!"

As we watched, the Gomer fleet began its arrival, and we prepared to monitor the pattern. The Civilian population was now all under cover, and our military was on high alert. We had also done all we could to make sure that when the twilight line went by us, the Gomers would have little in the way of things from which to draw much energy. Well, most things. We still had a surprise or two for their favorite watering holes, but otherwise, things were in a complete shutdown. As we braced ourselves, we started listening for the reports from our submarines and from the forces in Europe. Seems that instead of the Eighth Army in the Pacific being hit, like last time, these Gomers had their eye on the Seventh Army in Brussels. Hopefully this time their search for the leadership would yield far fewer results.

SECTION 2

GREENLAND ATTACK AND
THE WAR OF ATTRITION

Chapter V

Supreme Allied Headquarters, (SAHQ):

As we monitored from our observation posts both in space and around the world, the Gomers were deploying in a manner very similar to their previously used tactics. It was eerie to see it play out from this position since the last time they did it, I was running with my wife into a culvert. This time we were ready, and this time, they were bumping up against a dearth of targets. Using their prior information, they did hit several of our former bases and strong points. For example, over the former NATO Headquarters, the Gomer Small ships made their run, and came up with absolutely nothing for their troubles. They had a similar problem as they worked their way into the United Kingdom. Whitehall, Parliament, and even Buckingham Palace were hit again, but there was simply nobody home. Instead, the UK wasted no time after the Three Gomers ships had shown up at the Moon to move everything and everyone into the Scottish Highlands. Then it was our turn. As the Gomers progressed over the Atlantic Ocean, they were being watched closely by our submarines and several of our surface task groups. This time, there were no electronic emissions of any kind, except for the coded short burst ELF transmissions into our Headquarters.

The path of this fleet did approach our coast a little differently than the last time we were invaded. Instead of coming in around New Jersey, they headed straight towards Washington, D.C., where they took the exact same actions as in London. Hitting the Capitol, White House, and the Pentagon almost simultaneously, they then turned south, directly towards the SRS. As before, the radiation levels from our past battles there were reduced to near nothing as the fleet settled in over the SRS location. This time, we gave them a pass, opting instead to see their patterns develop, before taking them out. As a pleasant side effect, they did clean up the SRS from the last time we'd killed their Northern Fleet. Again, they turned to the south of the Appalachian Mountains and swept up towards the Great Lakes before turning back to bypass the Rockies to the south. They then headed to Asia, where they repeated the pattern, stopping in Japan long enough to clean up those radioactive sites, before turning southward to pass along the identical Southern Routes as those used by the Gomers in the last war.

At each place they stopped, we made a note to make sure that we had forces there to handle the issues in the future. Oddly enough, at least for the moment, they were staying completely away from either of our polar regions. We speculated that this move was because they associated these regions with their earlier defeats. We also noted that so far, none of the Battleship Class Gomer ships had made an appearance. Whether this was significant, given what happened to their Mountain Ship, or it was just the fact that they were using scouts now, as opposed to a great assault later, was yet to be seen. For the moment, we were just holding on to watch things develop. At the same time, Dr. Marvin and Dr. Clarkson were busy keeping track of their communications patterns and their scanning techniques. I felt fairly sure that the Gomers had to be a little disappointed at their lack of success in killing off the leadership, but then again, maybe they didn't know the difference. Either way, we were going to give them one more pass to the South, then we were going to make them pay dearly for that mistake.

The day pressed on as the Gomers did their night time sweep throughout the Southern Hemisphere, and as the twilight neared Europe they swept up from the African regions to return to the more northerly route. This time, things were different. As they began to pass into the more northern parts of Europe, the German Army unleashed a swarm of sulphur and lead coated missiles as the fleet passed by them. This continued throughout the rest of Europe and over the United Kingdom. Bypassing Iceland, their fleet, or what was left of it, turned to their southerly pattern, and crossed our shores near Norfolk. This time the USS Wisconsin Task Group was waiting off shore, depleting even more of their fleet using the conventional 16" guns. As the few remaining ships settled over the SRS, a series of ERW(s) (enhanced radiation weapons), were detonated, thereby ending the careers of these particular Gomer Ship Captains.

As we destroyed the Carrier Class and Fighter ships, the Moon sized ships increased their chatter, but they still took no action. In fact, they didn't make any movements at all. What we found even more interesting was that the chatter between them was high, but at no point was there any chatter directed to the Earth bound fleet. There were transmissions as the fleet passed around the globe, but those were all being transmitted from the Earth to the Moon Class ships, as opposed to the other way around. This was an odd development but as Dr. Clarkson explained, our atmosphere might make it easier to send messages out than in. The atmosphere may also work to shield us from their observation, especially from the positions they were holding near the Moon and around Mars. I just hoped he was right.

Several days would pass before the Gomers attempted another sortie onto our planet. Again, this was a mistake, since we repositioned our assets, cleared the areas that were used for our initial defensive positions, and got the USS Montana out to sea. Now she was loaded and ready, at least on paper. Opting to give her crew a chance to get familiar with her, we still kept her out of the main fray, and tried to give her at least a few days to get trained up and ready. It was a race to see which came first, the main assault or her being ready. Having said this, the USS Montana wasn't the only race being run. Dr. Clarkson and Dr. Marvin were also working to see what, if anything, they could do to counter the Gomers' activities. While we might win one of these races, it looked as though the other one might still be a little out of our reach.

This time we didn't wait for their fleet to make it all the way around. Instead, we began to assault them the second they entered the mine field. The first ships were of the Battleship Class and this time, instead of being passive about it, we actually flew the mines into the sides of their largest ships. As a result, the fleet that made it to Earth was already reduced by 20%, with their largest Battleship Class ships not making it at all. The rest of the fleet was attacked the moment they arrived in our atmosphere, with our Air Forces staging a strike from the daylight side of the line. As several of the Carrier ships began to deploy their Fighters behind the twilight line, we began pounding away at them. The USS Morton even got in a lick or two, and the results were very effective as she tested some of her newer Sulphur based rapid fire weapons on the multiple fighters that had approached her as she ran an outer screen for the USS North Carolina. After these several weeks, and at least two combat encounters, the Gomer casualties were high, while ours were fairly non-existent. Unfortunately, this was about to change, and it would be very dramatic when it happened.

After waiting almost another week, the Gomers made their third assault, and this time it was going to be monumental. The fleet that descended was perhaps twice as large as the earlier sorties, and as they rounded the moon, General Whitney made it quite clear that the size of this fleet was something we'd never experienced, not even the first time around. Moreover, they were seeing another class of ship that we'd never seen before. Longer, cylindrical, and with features that included the wings similar to their smaller Fighter Class, this new class of ship was almost as large as their Carrier Class ship. We weren't sure of its purpose, but it wouldn't take us long to find out. The twilight line was now almost off our coast when they arrived in our atmosphere, and despite our best efforts using the mine field to clear them out, their fleet arrived mostly intact and not that far from our major eastern cities. Now we understood. These new ships were Transports or Troop Carriers. There was no question, this time we were being invaded by ground Gomers, and they were a large force that had its own air support.

New Washington:

President Blanchard was highly concerned. Not since the War of 1812 had a force invaded our country, and damned if he wasn't taking it personally. There was no question that the old General was coming out in him, and he made it quite clear to both of the Division Commanders providing New Washington's security that they were to make it count. Naturally, his displeasure didn't take long before reaching the ears of General Patrick.

"God dammit, Mike! Just what is your plan for defense?"

"Sir, you know the plan, and we've got everyone in place. Besides the strategic reserves that we have sitting in your lap, we have the entire First Army arrayed between you and the Gomers. We also have two mountain ranges, with a veritable ton of air defense capabilities, both Sulphur and Gomer based, all located between you and them."

"Mike, that doesn't mean a damn thing. They have ground forces, and their Fighters are providing them cover!"

"I know, sir, but that is no different than what they tried to do last time around at Tierra del Fuego. This time they were able to piece it together, based on their bypassing the oceans, that our Navy is a threat to them. Having said that, we're as ready as we can be, I promise, and we're ready with much of the same capability on the ground as we have at sea."

"Mike, I want you to pull the trigger on Red Dragon."

"Sir, it isn't time yet, since they still have at least two more ships near Mars, which is right at the outer edge of the Red Dragon's range. If we pop that cork now, we won't have it later, and we will be up to our asses in bad guys."

"Shit! I hate it when you make sense."

"Sir, please. I didn't say it would be easy, but we've got a strategy and we've got people working to refine even more dirty tricks."

"I know, but you have to protect....."

"Sir, with all due respect, a General we both know used to love saying 'we can't both fuck this goat. Somebody has to be holding the damn head.'"

"Damn you, Mouse, I can't believe you would quote me to me!"

"Mr. President, you were always my mentor, so please let me take the goat, while you hold the head."

"Dammit, Mouse, you've got it. Still, I want to know exactly what is going on to my front."

"Sir, I'll make sure that the First Army Commander copies you with every move he makes, and I'll be happy to copy you from here, just like I have been doing."

"Oh, hell. Never mind, just let me know when I should move to the back up, and we'll do it. Dammit, I hate it when you're right. You can't copy me on everything, and well, sorry I called raising hell. I'm sure you've got your hands full right now."

"Sir, you are the Commander and Chief, and I'll do what you tell me, when you tell me, but right now, it isn't as bad as it seems. They are bunching up around Washington, DC, and Richmond, Virginia, and it seems that they are pretty concerned about the old James River line, where we have absolutely nothing. I have a feeling they're in for a surprise right before the sun comes up, since we do have something for that occurrence."

"I know, and you're fully authorized, especially since the residual effects from it disappear quickly. What is the half-life again?"

"Sir, this version should be clear in about three hours."

"Yep! Go for it."

"Yessir, it is in place, and ready to rip." When the connection was broken, it was clear that Marty was chaffing at the bit to be a soldier again. So much so that he didn't hesitate after hanging up. He wandered out to the 11th Airborne Division's Command Post, which not only scared the crap out of the Secret Service, it set everyone but CSM Clagmore on their ears. The Division Commander was tracking the events closely, and making sure that everyone in the Division was on their toes and defending their assigned sectors. Sitting down for the first time in about 6 hours, he was more than a little pissed that someone would call the command of attention, when it was his own Headquarters. Turning around he came face to face with the President. "Sir? Mr. President. What brings you to my humble headquarters?"

"General I was just wanting to look around, and se....."

"Bullshit! Mr. President, you were just fucking snooping and wishin' you was back in the US of Army!" It was now the President's turn to be shocked. Without turning around, he looked directly at the Division Commander and said, "General, please tell me that isn't Command Sergeant Major Clagmore standing behind me."

"Sorry, Sir. I can't tell you that, since it is the Sergeant Major."

"Sergeant Major, as your Commander and Chief, I should probably have your ass for such disrespect."

"Mr. President, I've got the Medal of Honor, and 37 years service. So, if you want to call it disrespect, go right ahead. I just prefer to think of it as keeping my former lieutenant from stepping on his crank."

"Dammit, Clagmore! How are you keeping me from stepping on my crank?"

"By telling you to go back to Commander-in-Chief'n, and leavin' the poor soldier boys alone. We got enough to keep these boys in line. Hell, we got the damn Gomers outside the wire, and now we got to worry about keeping a watch out for the boss of bosses."

"Clagmore, somehow, despite your winning personality, I can still find your advice beneficial. Okay, I am busted. I pestered Patrick and when he told me to find something else to do, I came here."

"Then you should know better, sir! Hell, we both know that you don't screw with Patrick. Hell I once saw him take out......."

The Division Commander cut him off with a rather stern, "SERGEANT MAJOR, kindly shut the hell up! His son is my Aide and he is right outside the damn door." With that, the discussion ended with the President returning to his Situation Room. Outside the Division Commander's office, Lieutenant Robbie Patrick made a mental note to find out whatever it was about his Dad that had somebody like Clagmore intimidated. Hell, even the President was intimidated. Just exactly who or what is it about his Dad? He was stern, but not near as stern as somebody like Clagmore. With those thoughts wandering around in his head, Robbie hardly noticed when the President came by and patted him on the shoulder on the way out.

Washington, DC, and along the James River:

The Gomers were consolidating their positions, and were doing their best to start digging into the terrain for cover before dawn arrived. As they landed, the Fighter ships fanned out and were blasting away at the countryside, much as they did during the day after the Battle along the James River during the first conflict. This time though, there were no observers to kill as they blasted away at suspected targets. Instead, there was one lone Cruise missile, fired by a submarine off the coast, that traveled upwards above their positions. It went just high enough to include both Richmond and Washington, DC, inside the air burst radius, and then it was detonated. As the Sulphur Isotope 38 was released, it promised to do the maximum damage to the Gomers, but this time with a half life of about 170 minutes. As advertised by Dr. Abramson and Dr. Clarkson, that is exactly what it accomplished. The disruption to the Gomer ground forces and their supporting Fighter Class ships was immediate and devastating. There were survivors, but not many, and most of those Gomers would not live past dawn, as the impact of the solar rays removed the rest of their ability to function entirely. The ones that did manage to pull through the night and morning light became permanent guests of Dr. Abramson's biological examination teams, who were now in the "prisoner of war" business.

USS Springfield, SSN 761, Near the coast of Greenland:

After several attempts to contact anyone on the ELF/VLF systems, the USS Springfield made her ascent to a depth nearer the surface. Unable to get a message in or out, she had a piece of the puzzle which was vital to get to SAHQ. Taking the chance, she transmitted on the unsecured VHF channels. It was a burst message, which would take the recipients a little time to decipher and pass on. Not perhaps their best option, but at the moment it was all the Captain could think to do in a pinch. Nearing the surface, the crew sighed in relief to realize that it was just past dawn, but knowing that what they were doing was still a high risk, they did anything but rest easy about it.

"Captain, THE message is sent!"

"Good, XO, get us back down nice and deep, and get your people back onto those frickin' radios."

"Aye, Aye, Sir. We still have no idea what went out, or why it went out."

"Tell me, XO, were we being jammed, or is it a mechanical fault?"

"Sir, we got nothing yet. Not sure why the thing tanked, but for some reason, we are not getting anything out of here. The VHF went, and we got a receipt for it, but that is all we got."

"Okay, well, keep me posted. Now let's head back on station, and keep watching."

"Aye, Sir."

Supreme Allied Headquarters, (SAHQ):

The message clattered into the Communications center and because it was on a VHF channel, the communications personnel gave it an extremely high priority. Anyone with balls enough to transmit on those frequencies HAD to be in a hurry, crazy, or stupid. Either way, the information was also probably damned important, otherwise nobody would run that risk. The effect of the message, once they unscrambled it, was immediate. Moving towards the War Room at a dead run, the messenger almost bowled over General Whitney as he burst into the room. Taking the message, General Whitney read it and blanched. Turning to the room in general and me in particular he announced, "General, it seems that while the Gomers were landing around Washington and Richmond, they were also putting a much larger force down in Greenland."

"Say that again?"

"General, the Gomers landed en masse in Greenland. We're only hearing about it later because the USS Springfield's ELF/VLF is up the spout. They took one helluva chance by sending this VHF."

"Son of a bitch! So, were the Washington landings a feint, or were they here just trying to take us out of the game early?"

"Seems that either option would fit."

"Okay, why the hell did the USS Springfield's radios not work? Jamming? Electronic fault?"

"Sir, they didn't say, but they did say they were working the issue and heading back on station."

"Dammit. Okay, Admiral Lynch, do you have a submarine you can send to back up the Springfield?" With that, Admiral Lynch identified two back up submarines to immediately dispatch in the direction of the USS Springfield, and he headed over to make sure there was no confusion about the movement orders. While he was making those adjustments, we were still contemplating the status of our ELF/VLF systems, hoping they had not been compromised, when we received more bad news.

"General. Reports are coming in from Mexico that indicate the original fleet of Gomers, the one that dumped the troops in the Washington and Virginia area, just began with their tactics of blazing away at anything suspicious."

"Same as in the James River areas in the last war?"

"Yessir. It is also being reported that a portion of that fleet is turning north, and heading towards the California area near Vandenberg, doing the same stuff."

"Dammit, if they hit Vandenberg, we've lost our ability to reach way out and touch anything coming our way. Admiral Lynch, what do we have out there to attract them away from Vandenberg?"

"Sir, I've got the USS New Jersey and USS Nimitz task groups right off the coast of Vandenberg, and the USS Greenville and USS

Cheyenne are a couple of attack submarines in the same general area."

"Okay, send them a FLASH message priority IMMEDIATE. Strategic priority dictates that they have to take the heat off Vandenberg. Use whatever means to attack and destroy Gomer Fleet heading towards California, prior to their arrival to the Vandenberg area. You are further cleared to utilize all technologies available. Gomers using 'slash and burn' tactics that place strategic assets in grave jeopardy."

General Whitney immediately ran the message to the Communications Center, and on the way, he added a paragraph that indicated that our ELF/VLF could be compromised and/or jammed by the Gomers. As soon as General Whitney departed with the message, Admiral Lynch briefed me on the status of our task force that was in the area of Vandenberg.

"Sir, I'm concerned that even though the USS Greenville can start her decoy messaging to draw them off, if the Gomers are doing their random 'slash and burn' that they will slash and burn their way across our Task Groups."

"I agree, so send via ELF/VLF, and if necessary over the HF, UHF, and VHF, through our remote sites, the following message: Commander Nimitz Task Group to clear the area northward, launch supporting aircraft on request from Commander New Jersey Task Group, otherwise, stay clear of the coastal areas."

"So, you'll leave the New Jersey in the thick of it?"

"Yes. It isn't like I have a choice. We have GOT to protect Vandenberg, and that makes the New Jersey expendable. I don't like it worth a damn, but there you have it."

"Aye, Aye, Sir. I'm just glad I'm not in your shoes right now."

"Thanks, Admiral, I find that extremely damn comforting......
Now move your ass, if Vandenberg goes down, then you won't need to worry about that secret you were asking about!"

USS New Jersey Task Group, near the Northern Coast of Mexico:

Admiral Parks was new at this, but he wasn't new to fighting Gomers. He had been the Executive Officer onboard the New Jersey when they had taken on the really huge Gomer near Tierra del Fuego, so he understood the tactics. He also understood the tone of the message. He was expendable, along with the rest of his group, and that just sucked. The USS Nimitz was now hauling ass north, and while she was available with an Alpha Strike package, it wasn't what he wanted to hear. He passed on the message to Admiral Hammer with the Nimitz group that he was to send the package as close to Vandenberg as possible, to defend against any Gomers that might still head his way. He knew this left him without air cover, but it was the clear choice to make. Admiral Parks had been around long enough to realize that General Patrick was probably right. He also knew from the last war, and his reading of the top secret After Action Reports, that Vandenberg could be part of a bigger plan that would likely be their last best hope. Saying it mostly for his own benefit, "Hell, if we lose Vandenberg, we could lose more than just a few missile silos. It could be 'game over'."

"Chief of staff, get me the Captain on the line."

"Aye, sir!"

"Captain, I just got a message from the big kahuna, and we are to, and I quote, 'use whatever means to attack and destroy Gomer Fleet heading towards California, prior to their arrival to the Vandenberg area. You are further cleared to utilize all technologies available. Gomers using 'slash and burn' tactics that place strategic assets in grave jeopardy.' We also have to worry about possible jamming of ELF/VLF stuff, and we are without air cover."

"Goddamn, sir! That means we're..."

"Yeah, we are! Now take whatever steps you need to carry out those orders!"

"Aye, Aye, Sir."

Down on the bridge of the ship, the Captain had just hung up from the Admiral and he, too, now knew the drill. The Captain was contemplating his fate when the XO ran up, "Captain, CIC is picking up a large number of Gomer Carrier Class ships. They appear to be launching their Fighters as they move northward towards California."

"Excellent, you know the drill. We'll wait until they have passed, and then hit'em in the ass. Any other targets following them?"

"Nothing so far."

"Advise the Admiral, and keep me posted. Do a damn good search. I don't want something else to sneak out and pop us in the ass."

"Aye, Aye, Sir." As the XO stepped back into CIC, the Admiral entered the bridge with the Captain. With a brief exchange of nods, the Captain ordered the New Jersey to General Quarters, on all weapons. "Admiral, you sure we're cleared to use that spooky ass thing on our fantail?"

"Absolutely, but wait until I tell you to cook that damn thing off. I've seen it fired just one time and, frankly, the side effects were almost as scary as what it could do to the assholes on the other end."

"I know, sir, it ain't pretty." As he finished his statement, the XO reported that they were closed up at battle stations, and that their escorts were in the anti-Gomer formation. They could now see the Gomers, and watched as the formation began to split into two groups. The largest was still heading north, firing at everything on the ground, while a smaller group was headed in their direction. This smaller grouping continued the 'slash and burn' until it cleared the beach, and was now on the way out to sea to investigate the signals being sent by the decoy submarine, the USS Greenville.

"Well, Admiral?"

"Captain, let that smaller group get clear of us to the west towards the Greenville, and the main force get a little further up the beach, before firing. We're lucky these guys coming our way aren't still blasting at everything on the water, too, so we'll take advantage of it."

"Aye, sir." They watched as the smaller group cleared the ship when the Admiral looked at the Captain and repeated what he knew could be a real dangerous Order. "Captain, aim for the Northbound Fleet, and we will let the outer escorts tackle the ones that just went overhead. Good luck, and good shooting." Within seconds the Main Guns fired their first broadside of their 16" Sulphur shells at the Northern Fleet. They were at a slightly oblique angle, but their shots counted on the larger ships. The bulk of them went down, and the remainder turned towards the USS New Jersey, launching their Fighters as they turned. Thereafter it was a game of numbers, and it was a game that the New Jersey would eventually win, but only barely. Unfortunately, the same couldn't be said for several of her escorts.

Within seconds of the first broadside, the group that had passed overhead just moments prior began to turn back towards the New Jersey. They apparently couldn't see her, but they could see that there was firing from a pretty limited location. As the Captain maneuvered his ship in various 'shoot and scoot' turns, firing as she went, the other Gomer ships were narrowing down the area to focus their wrath. As the Gomers narrowed the area coming closer to the USS New Jersey, several of the escorts were also firing at both the Gomer Carrier ships and their smaller Fighter ships. The escorts were also scoring fairly well, when the USS Howard exploded from a direct hit amidships from one of the Carrier ships. Similarly, a smaller Littoral Combat Ship or LCS, the USS Freedom, was hit by several of the Fighters before she, too, exploded in a huge luminous fireball. As the fight continued, the Admiral could tell that it was about to become far too one-sided for the New Jersey or the remains of his Task Force to ever survive the onslaught. Noting that it was becoming a matter of sheer numbers, he told the Captain. "Okay, Bert, unleash the hounds." With that command, the New Jersey unleashed her secret weapon from the fantail. It was Gomer technology with a decidedly human twist and when it fired, it also launched humanity into a whole new world.

Like the most powerful Gomer weapons from their own Battleship Class or Mountain Class ships, this weapon was powerful and very indiscriminate in what it would accomplish. Unlike their weapons though, this human variant of the weapon released a burst of TeraHertz Radiation that went up, and then fanned out in almost an umbrella pattern to form a bubble around the task force. As the TeraHertz Radiation, or T-Rays, produced by the new and improved weapon enveloped the New Jersey and her remaining escorts, the Gomer fleet literally came apart from the burst. Those Gomers that did survive were well away from the Task Force, and they did not linger in the area. As for the Gomers that were still wandering up the coast towards Vandenberg, they stopped any 'slash and burn' firing and made an immediate turn out to sea, wasting no time in getting away from the area. Fortunately, the number of escaping Gomers was very few and only of the smaller Fighter class ships.

The USS New Jersey was not completely unscathed, since some of her protective gear for the crew and the after portion of the ship failed. She had also taken a few hits from the Gomers and, at the end of the battle, she was only about 65% effective as a combat asset. The damage control efforts of her crew made the difference, and she was underway with what remained of her escort group and headed to San Diego within an hour of the cessation of the attack. Clearly, this was not the way to fight the Gomers, but sometimes the strategic need outweighed the more basic tactical considerations. The two largest pluses to this battle were the protection of Vandenberg AFB and the actual combat testing of the "Gomer Bubble". There was no question about it now. The gloves were off and things were about to get very ugly!

Supreme Allied Headquarters (SAHQ):

The news about the "Gomer Bubble" traveled through our headquarters with almost the speed of light. As for our ships at sea, the news was only slightly slower. The confidence that it garnered was exactly what everyone needed, and for the men and women serving on our battleship and aircraft carrier battlegroups, the news was more than your average tonic. It meant that there was at least a way out of a real bind. Hope was springing eternal. Admiral Lynch approached me, with a rather astounded look, and asked, "Was that the surprise, because I sure as hell wasn't expecting it."

"Carl, that was the surprise, and it was your idea, too."

"How do you figure that it was my idea?"

"You made a passing comment to Dr. Abramson in front of Admiral Steadman, where you said it was a shame we couldn't put up a giant lead umbrella over a fleet at sea."

"You know damn well it was just that, a passing comment, and it was lead to keep them from seeing us."

"Maybe so, but tell that to Dr. Abramson. He dreamed it up, found a way to diffuse the T-rays, and now, Voila! You got yourself an umbrella with a bite. Admiral Steadman swore me to secrecy, since he wanted there to be at least one surprise for his buddy."

"That old bast...... never mind. Good thing it worked."

"I know, we weren't sure, and even Dr. Abramson was nervous about it. Still, it is a last ditch weapon, since it doesn't play nice with the persons firing it off, and the range limits are a still a real problem. Part of the New Jersey's damage was from that damn thing, and not just the Gomers."

"Yessir, I get that point. Still, it gives the boys a fighting chance, and that is all they've ever really wanted."

"Glad it works, but we've got a somewhat larger fish on the plate, and it is time to figure out what to do about it."

The situation was oddly quite simple, Gomer ground troops were now in Greenland, and they were there in force. They brought their own air support, and they were using the area to base their Carrier Class ships and Fighters. Thanks to the USS Springfield's ELF/VLF issues, they had been there unmolested just long enough for them to get fairly well established. Dr. Abramson and Dr. Clarkson were both convinced that they probably were attempting to rebuild an array and that, like last time, they were also using our own polar regions' darkness periods against us. They were also smart enough this time to put a base on land in the northern polar region, as opposed to the last time when they landed on the icepack where we actually were able to get right underneath them.

After our experiences in Tierra del Fuego, nobody in our headquarters was very excited about the prospect of having to pit our ground forces against a well dug-in enemy force. We also had the problem of how to maintain a buildup of our forces, when we had two additional Moon Class ships waiting in the wings around Mars. We had mathematical estimates of the strengths and types of ships each Moon Class ship carried, and these numbers alone were staggering. It was time to discuss strategy, and to prepare for what we knew was still coming. In the meantime, we were doing our best to get our scientific brain power set to counter these threats, and our ASOC boys to assess it. We also had a few prisoners to interrogate, or at least study.

CHAPTER VI

Supreme Allied Headquarters, (SAHQ):

The submarines we managed to get in the area of Greenland were reporting in hourly, via ELF/VLF. We were quite pleased to discover that the radio fault onboard the USS Springfield was the result of wire chafing, as opposed to some more insidious reason. Apparently, during the last maintenance period, the ELF and VLF radio Antenna Arrays were routed through the wrong point on the ship's frame leading into the communications center. As a result, a simple wire was the cause of our reconnaissance failure, as opposed to jamming by the Gomers. Taking this as a good sign, we had at least resolved one mystery. As for the Gomer buildup, it was clear that they had made themselves at home in the most northern part of that country. We also learned that the Gomers themselves were pretty impervious to cold or heat, which gave them a huge advantage over the people from ASOC who were attempting to discover their strength and intentions.

Major General Daniel Greene, as the Chief of the Allied Special Operations Command, was juggling a number of glass balls at once. The toughest of these to keep in the air was the selection and assignment of special operations forces from around the globe to get on the ground in Greenland. Naturally, a member of the Saudi Arabian Special Forces would not be a good choice for Greenland, anymore than someone from Norway would be comfortable in a sub-Saharan climate. As he pulled from forces around the world, it was also necessary to pull individuals with the necessary communication or language skills to be transported, fed, maintained, equipped, and integrated into the wider force structure. In other words, NATO special forces were the best starting place, along with other forces that routinely trained in Arctic weather. The Russians were out, since they were playing their own game, quite apart from the rest of the globe. As a result, there was a high percentage of these special operators drawn from the UK, more specifically the SAS and Canadian SAS, Norway, and the United States. The balance of these cold weather specialists were then drawn from the military forces of Japan, China, Argentina, Chile, Iceland, Sweden, and Finland.

General Greene was also required to get his people into position, and he began this process by moving his command into position both in Iceland and in Newfoundland, Canada. Establishing his Headquarters in St. John's, Newfoundland, General Greene was attempting to balance these forces and be close enough to influence and coordinate their efforts. Unfortunately, this process was taking a lot longer than anticipated, thanks to the weather and the lack of cooperation by the Gomers. There were very few passes over the North American Continent, but the forces being relocated from Northern Europe were being harassed on a regular basis. As the Gomers were building up, they would send their ships down from the Moon Ship near the Moon, and they would normally enter the atmosphere somewhere not too far west of St. Petersburg, Russia. We had the option of sending in a few Sulphur Isotope weapons but, without decent targeting information, we were more concerned about our weapons stockage levels, production schedules, and all of the related issues over the remaining Moon Class ships that were now hiding in and around Mars. The one thing we couldn't do at this point was to waste or expend the special ordinance without having more in the logistical pipeline for replacement.

In simplest terms, we were stuck in a log jam with some lousy choices to make. We could rid the globe of the Gomers in Greenland, but to do so would require the expenditure of weapons that were hard to make and replace. The alternative would be to commit a number of our ground and naval forces, all using less specialized weapons that were easier to build and replace, but with a greater loss of human life. The third alternative was to do a little of both, and hope that the big guys near Mars would leave us alone. Unfortunately, we also were more than aware of the cost in human lives if we followed either of these latter two options. To resolve our dilemma, we could either increase production methods for special weapons; use the old stuff and not worry about the environment; or we could find a weakness to exploit that might give us an edge. Two of these options were the optimal for us, but we had to have time for either of them, and the Gomers weren't just sitting on their oddly shaped thumbs while we worked it out. It was time to take it to the President, and I was afraid I already knew what his answer would be to the whole thing.

New Washington:

As I stepped out of the helicopter, the Secret Service was there to greet me, along with the local Division Commander and his young aide. "Sir, welcome to New Washington."

"Thanks, General Henry, good to see you again. I see your Aide appears to be in good health."

"Yessir, we've been trying to take care of him."

"Oh, not what I meant at all. I was told by his Mom to check and make sure his arm wasn't broken, or that there wasn't some other impediment to him actually writing a letter to her once in a while."

"Hah! I'll make sure we fix that little character flaw, sir!"

"No need, hand him to CSM Clagmore for a few hours, and I'll promise you he won't forget to keep his Mom informed ever again."

"Damn, Sir, you would wish that on him?"

"Yep, good character building exercise, don't you think?"

"Yessir, I'll take care of it!"

"Great. Now, somebody lead me into the wolves' den, and let's get down to business." With that, the Secret Service Agents led me and my two Aides directly into the new 'Oval Office'. As usual, it was great to see Marty again, and after passing him the latest messages from his family, and getting through the 'hi, how the hell are you' part of the program, we got down to cases.

Marty was seeing the problem through his military prism and, like me, he wasn't too wild about tossing our forces into the frozen combat mode again. He also knew, like me, that allowing them to build up in the region was going to spell disaster for all involved. Unlike me, he did have one more option on the table, but diplomacy with someone or something that is intent on your destruction is hardly a viable option either. Especially where there was no common language or even anyone who could interpret the languages. No, what we both needed was a breakthrough from our scientists, either with the Gomer research or in the production process of our special Sulphur Isotope weapons. As a consequence, the strategy coming out of my meetings with the President was nothing more than a compromise that we hoped would lead to more time.

We would utilize our special operations forces, with the support of certain conventional forces, to do target assessments and, where possible, attack the Gomers to deny them the ease of establishing themselves in Greenland. We would keep our conventional forces, ground, sea, and air, on standby, but there would be no major commitment of forces until it was necessary, or unless an opportunity arose that would not cost us too dearly. We had to husband these forces, to prepare for the conflict that we knew was coming when the Mars portion of the Gomer Forces started their attacks. Such was the way of a war of attrition; little could be done unless or until it became optimal to strike in mass. The reins for these special operations were now in the hands of General Greene, and thankfully, he was an old Gomer fighter of the highest order. In the meantime, we focused the rest of the defense on scientific breakthroughs and the Mars contingent of the Gomers' forces.

ASOC, St. Johns, Newfoundland:

The forward headquarters was sparse but well equipped with ELF/VLF equipment. General Greene was setting a mission schedule, and making sure that everyone was in place, rationed, supplied, and fully equipped. He knew this was going to be a tight process, but he also knew that it was necessary. The latest observations from the Norwegians indicated that the Gomers were setting up their version of an air field and keeping their Carrier Class Ships working the Arctic Circle. From the observations being made by various teams around the polar region, the Carrier Class ships were not carrying as many small ships. Instead, the Gomers were leaving them at the "airbase", where the small Fighter Class ships were now set up to take off and land to provide air cover and defense to the extensive and growing Gomer facilities.

The Gomers were also working themselves into a routine, with the passage of their Carrier Ships being channeled through several choke points around the Circle, especially in the vicinity of the Bering and North Seas. The resupply ships would enter the atmosphere just shy of the North Sea, and then depart again on the turn-around to the Moon Class ship near the Moon in the Bering Sea several miles west of Dutch Harbor. It was also noted that the Gomers were careful not to send anything larger than a Carrier Class ship. Although the Battleship Classes were spotted, they were always well outside the 'mine field' in the vicinity of the Moon. These behemoths would often rendezvous with the Carrier Class ships, but seldom would they move very close, and it always seemed that they were being utilized to preserve both their Mountain Class and Moon Class ships from exposure. Clearly they were building up a large ground force, and they were making it more difficult to approach them, based on their assigned 'air cover'.

Once General Greene identified these patterns, he was on the horn with my staff, and within hours, General Whitney and I were on a plane headed to Newfoundland. As we landed, General Greene met us and we went to his Headquarters, which wasn't far from the landing strip. Naturally, we didn't waste a lot of time on the pleasantries, but I must admit it was like finding an old friend all over again. He and his staff started their briefings and laid out their findings and their proposed plan. General Greene and his staff were all convinced that the Gomers' air cover would need their attention first, especially since the lower light levels and short hours of daylight allowed the Gomers to stay in the air longer. At least one of his teams was discovered and destroyed by this air cover, and General Greene knew that this was the first threat he would need to attack. His priority was to eliminate the immediate threat, so that he could infiltrate more of his teams into place.

After several hours in deep discussion, Whit and I were convinced that they were onto something, so we began the serious planning for what started off being called Operation Greenburg. It was born of the more practical need to nail these Gomer Fighters, and it wasn't all that far off from a plan forwarded in the last Gomer War by a staff wag. When the Gomers were deep into Antarctica, some staff weenie had said all they needed was a crop duster plane with some Sulphur to drop on the Gomers. It was a moronic idea then, and it would be just as stupid now, except this time we had a slight twist to put on it that might make it more viable than first thought. Later, once approval was sought and obtained from the President, it was coined with a new name. "Operation Acme" was how the concept was eventually laid out for the President, since it clearly arose from that "damn *Road Runner* cartoon." In fact, "Wiley E. Coyote" was the code name to be sent to initiate the Operation against the Gomers.

Operation Acme was to be painfully simple. Thanks to the advances of stealth technology, especially after we had liberated the Mountain Ship, it was decided to try and use the skin of a former Gomer ship to fashion into a stealth type drone. This drone was completely filled with almost 1500 gallons of Sulphuric Acid. It wasn't a healthy or environmentally friendly option, but it would work in a pinch, and at least it wasn't on the ice pack itself. The Special Operations 'Zoomie' Brigadier General was first sold on the idea by General Greene, and the Air Force Special Operations specialists involved in transforming a few of their huge stealth drones were able to make it a reality. At the end of the day, there weren't a lot of them, nor was there a way to replace them once they were lost, but there were just enough to make this part of the operation viable.

General Greene wasn't done with the idea either. He wanted to use daylight for the raid, since it was the only time the Gomer 'air force' would be on the ground, and he wanted to hit them as the twilight line passed over the North Sea. His hope was to put the resupply ships in the sights of a Battleship Task Group before they got to their Greenland base. It took some time to set it up, but we did manage to get the USS North Carolina Battlegroup and the USS Wisconsin Battlegroup nearer to the North Sea. Meanwhile, the USS Alabama Battlegroup was now on station in the Bering Sea near Dutch Harbor, Alaska. As these battlegroups were getting on station, several of General Greene's special operators were taking position to observe the main Gomer air field. As the H hour approached, it was a monumental event in both General Greene's headquarters and at the SAHQ. The way it unfolded was a thing of beauty.

USS Wisconsin Battlegroup operating in the Denmark Straits:

Admiral Chandler was the senior Admiral on site, and it fell to him to coordinate the attacks by both the USS North Carolina and his own battlegroups. He was a student of the previous war and the tactics that had worked for Admiral Becker onboard the USS Missouri, as well as those tactics that didn't work, for example, for Admiral Morton onboard the USS Iowa. He had no intentions of going down the wrong road, so he massed his gunfire support and doubled the escort screen to permit for their use on any Fighter Class ships that might turn back on him.

He also didn't want to have to take the route that the USS New Jersey did in her battle near California. The New Jersey was still undergoing repairs, and the loss of life had been huge in the escorts. Here, the lesson was that Admiral Chandler was not going to risk an oblique shot, at least if he didn't have to risk it. Instead, he positioned his ships at or near where the intelligence sources indicated was the normal Gomer route, and set himself up to be just north prepared to run south, if the path appeared to be set up along that direction. He knew that the Gomers were being too routine, since they avoided Iceland and always took the route over the Denmark Straits. The irony wasn't lost on him either, since over this same stretch of water, the HMS Hood was lost here at the hands of the German Battleship Bismarck in the early days of World War II. As the twilight line approached, so did the tension in his battlegroup.

Gomer Air Base, 180 miles West of Daneborg, Greenland:

Three large Drones were making their way northward from Newfoundland and were about 30 minutes from target. As they engaged in terrain following, the drones were being driven northward using higher frequencies for control. The down side to these drones was that they had to utilize dangerous frequency ranges and, for this reason, an observation team had to confirm the results before the operations code word would be sent. General Greene was beside himself as he sat back and watched as the controllers did their work. The timing was critical, since this facility would have to be evacuated once the drones were recovered by yet another ASOC team that was hiding near Baffin Bay. The radio signatures were the weak point to the entire plan, and unless or until someone could figure out a way to make the ELF/VLF system work fast enough to drive flight controls, this was always going to be the riskiest part of using drones against the Gomers.

ASOC Team Thor near the Gomer Air Base:

The good news was that the individual teams arrayed around the Gomers' air base were all using ELF/VLF technologies. This helped quite a bit, since it was not something that would attract the bad guys. Aside from this good news, wandering around in the middle of Greenland's ice pack was treacherous if not nearly impossible for anyone except Arctic experts. This was where teams from Norway and the Inuits from Canada came in most handy. In this case, Team Thor was under the leadership of a very capable Norwegian who spoke English better than most Americans.

"ASOC. Team Thor is in primary position, and we have the site under observation."

"Roger that, Team Thor. Advise when the package is delivered."

"Roger." Within moments of that transmission, the team could see out over the 'air field' and see all of the Gomer Fighter ships lined up around their primary take off location. It was obvious that some runway was required, but it was minimal. Maybe about 200 feet was all that was needed, which made this terrain almost perfect for all involved. Most of the Gomer Fighters were dispersed but still within a fairly compact area, which again was good news. Looking over the 'air field', the team heard the brief transmission that indicated that the drones were finally within the area. Scanning the sky, they saw a brief glint from the sun reflecting off something, and then the liquid began to fall as if it were raining. This time though, the rain wasn't water- based, nor was it snow. Instead, it was the Sulphuric Acid as it rained down over both the Fighter Class ships and their little runway. Operation Acme was now officially underway. As they watched and reported, Team Thor was impressed with the impact that the acid appeared to be having on the Gomer Equipment.

"ASOC, this is Thor, the Coyote is Oscar Tango!"

"Roger that, Thor, advise when Gomers begin their scramble." With that command, the Team Leader clicked his microphone twice, to indicate that he heard and understood his last directive. Now it was a matter of waiting.

USS Wisconsin Battlegroup operating in the Denmark Straits:

Admiral Chandler was intently listening in on the ASOC frequency and was at least aware that a Team Thor was observing the Gomer air field. Not really clear on 'oscar tango' until his Aide explained, "That means On Target, sir." The Admiral was still watching for the twilight line and trying to gauge whether he would need to make a run further south, when he got the simple message from SAHQ. "To Commander Wisconsin Battlegroup. Wiley E. Coyote, execute! Patrick." Looking over at his Chief of Staff, the Admiral just nodded his head, and the message was sent across both of the Battlegroups to come to full alert. Darkness approached, and along with it, so did the Gomers. The Gomers were spreading out some, and it appeared that their path would take them directly over both the USS North Carolina and the USS Wisconsin. Unfortunately, there were other ships that were going to pass to the south. The Admiral was cursing himself for being too far north, but then he realized that he wouldn't be able to get them all anyway. Taking it all in, he decided to remain that hole in the water rather than risk the run to the south.

The Range information, along with altitude of the Gomer formation, was continually fed to both the Admiral and each of the guns. Loaded with Sulphur Shells, each of the 16" guns was now following a Carrier Class Gomer ship, while the 5" and smaller caliber guns were following the Fighter Class ships. The gunners were also prepared to continue rapid fire and to shift targets the second they scored hits on their initial targets. At the same time, the escorts were closing in to their charges and were prepared to employ all of their anti-aircraft skills against any Fighter Class ships that might approach. As in the various other confrontations, when the formation of Gomers was cleared of the ship, the order was given to fire. The results were spectacular, and it was a quick strike on most of the larger Carrier and Transport Class ships. The Fighter Class ships did react, but with the additional escorts present, these, too, were destroyed in fairly short order. Sadly, one third of the Gomer fleet continued towards the 'air base' 180 miles west of Daneborg, Greenland. As they continued, things at the Gomer air field were about to get interesting.

Gomer Air Base, 180 miles West of Daneborg, Greenland:

As the members of ASOC Team Thor watched in rapt fascination, a number of Gomers were seen headed to their Fighter Class ships. The crew of three for each ship got as far as their entry points into their ships when many began to collapse. One of the Fighter Class ships, apparently on more of a ready status than the others, began to take off. Picking up to a slight hover, it maneuvered onto the short 'runway.' Nosing over, it began picking up speed and lifted to almost 1000 feet before it simply came apart. Team Thor watched, and not a single Fighter Class ship was able to lift off or to provide any escort work for the approaching survivors of the attack by the USS Wisconsin and USS North Carolina's Battlegroups. This would prove to be valuable news to one other observer.

The twilight approached, and along with it, the balance of the Gomer Fleet. Maintaining observation, the Team realized that this Gomer Fleet was not landing a single ship. While it was a wild guess, the Team leader theorized that nobody was going to land here, unless or until they could figure out what nailed their Fighter Class ships.

With the balance of the Gomer Fleet heading west, the Team Leader passed on his second message. "The Road Runner is headed your way." This latter message was sent in the clear, and Admiral Chandler was completely lost as to who the recipient might be, or what it meant exactly. Such was the art of security and compartmentalization. Only a small handful of people knew the whole plan, and Admiral Chandler just didn't have a need to know.

The Northern Davis Straits, off the west coast of Greenland:

The huge gray monster was lurking off the coast and was maintaining bare minimal steerage way as she held her same general position. She was remaining silent, but watchful, as the news of the previous events was reaching her. With the message about the "Road Runner", the Captain brought her to battle stations, while her lone escort, the USS Morton, eased to her west and took position just ahead of her port bow. There were no transmissions either in or out, and she remained even more of a hole in the water than either of the earlier battleships that encountered a Gomer Fleet. This time the USS Montana was going to have her crack at the Gomers. This was why she existed, since she was built with the express purpose of handing out punishment to Gomers. Now would be her very first test under fire, and everyone was ready, willing, and more than a little excited about it. Now it would be 18" guns, with Sulphur based shells that would blossom as they punched. There was even an extra turret, with three additional 18" gun tubes for killing bad guys.

Aside from sheer size and main weapons, what really separated the USS Montana from her smaller battleship sisters was that there was an as-yet-untried, at least in combat, weapons system that was even more innovative than the 'Gomer Bubble' used by the USS New Jersey. This time, the Terahertz weapons were quite similar to the Gomer main weapons batteries from their Mountain Ship, only they were made by what Dr. Abramson and Dr. Clarkson believed were even better materials. On each of the 18" turrets was mounted a "Gomer Gun" turret, and they were manned and ready by crews who were not only familiar with firing them, but were familiar with the theories behind them. Obtaining power from two relatively local sources, which were in essence two small self-contained nuclear reactors, these weapons were capable of generating significant output values in Terahertz radiation waves. The smaller reactors were located well beneath the weapons, almost in the bilge, and were designed to power two weapons located far above on the aftermost turrets. In a pinch, the power from these reactors could also drive the ship, as well as be re-routed to control all four Gomer T-Ray weapons on board.

The only restriction for the use of the weapon was that no personnel could be on deck when it was fired, and personnel on the bridge had to wear specific protective goggles as each was fired at a target. The Graphene panels or sheets were basically antenna utilized to focus the power emitted from the weapons. This system had undergone extensive testing and there was no question that it would work in theory, but combat was something else again. Today, they would get their work-out, since today they were going to be the primary weapons system against the Fighter Ships. Similarly, the USS Morton was set up with a smaller version of these weapons, and she was also cocked, locked, and loaded.

The Gomer Fleet was bypassing their airfield and heading on westward when Team Thor reported in with their "Road Runner" message. As the Gomer fleet approached the USS Montana, it was clear that the Gomers were now quite nervous about being over water. Ahead of the fleet flew a number of Fighter Class Ships, and they were firing at anything they could detect or even suspected as being a threat. This had been anticipated, and General Greene made sure that the Gomers had something to be nervous about, aside from the USS Montana. In what was probably one of his better deception operations, General Greene had several fishing boats adrift to the north that were transmitting remotely within the VHF radio band. The Gomer Fighters that were blasting at anything turned northward and headed to the decoy targets, while the Gomer Fleet itself remained southward as they crossed the area on the northern end of the Davis Straits.

Passing overhead, the weapons systems tracked them without sound, without signal, and without any fanfare. When the last of the Carrier Class ships passed, the USS Montana employed the time honored 'turkey shoot' method characterized by Sgt. York during World War One. Starting at the back of the pack and working her way forward, the USS Montana's Gomer weapons, by focusing the T-Ray beams in a tighter pattern, wreaked complete havoc on the remaining Carrier Class ships. Moreover, when the few stragglers passed almost out of Gomer Gun range, they were still well within the area where an 18" gun could do fatal damage to the Gomers' ships. The Fighter Class ships decoyed north realized what was happening and turned back towards the position of the USS Montana. This was their downfall, since the USS Morton was alive, well, and waiting in their path. Equipped with two smaller and less powerful

"Gomer guns," the USS Morton began firing at the Fighters as they approached the position of the small task force. When the Fighters got within range, the USS Morton began firing both her Gomer guns, as well as her Phalanx weapons systems that were equipped with high velocity and quite accurate Sulphur ammunition. The main difference with the USS Morton's Gomer guns, aside from the lower power available, was that their T-Ray beams were not as focused as those of the USS Montana. Here the Graphene sheet or panels were set to provide a wider area of coverage, and therefore the amount of sky being covered with the weapon, while not as powerful, did allow for a wider targeting area. In short, this was perfect for denying air space around the ships to anything that might try to approach.

On this night, the Gomers were completely stymied. Their massacre was complete, and this time there would be no resupply, nor would there be any immediate threat of Gomer air cover in Greenland. More to the point, it would be several days before the Gomers sent supplies, and it would be even more days before air cover would be partially restored in support of the Gomers. The success of this operation allowed us to examine the Gomers' methods, to include their need to resupply both material and Fighters from the Mars-based Gomer Moon Class ships. This was a great sign, since it depleted assets that could ultimately be used against us, and because it meant that we made a dent in them. It also meant we had almost 48 hours to set into motion other teams that would be in place to assist with future targeted operations.

Supreme Allied Headquarters, (SAHQ):

The War of Attrition was beginning to have other results for us. Throughout, we tested new weapons, we put into place new procedures, and we learned even more about our enemy. Like us, they were working a learning curve. With each new innovation, they worked hard to counter it. They certainly had great intellect, and they were not without their tricks, too. What I don't believe they suspected is that we were quick studies, and that we would make the most of what we were handed. One such example came about three weeks after Operation Acme. In an effort to increase their firepower in support, aside from their increase in Fighter Class ships, they attempted to send in one of the Battleship Class ships. It came in straight over the northern polar region, avoiding a normal passage from the Moon, and avoiding any passage over open water. We had watched and tracked her movement almost from the moment she pulled from around the Moon and headed inbound. Like many of her predecessors, she came out initially in what we thought would be a routine rendezvous with one of the Carrier Class Ships. Instead, she took a sharp turn to the north, avoiding the normal route. Clearly they had found, or at least come to grips with, the mine field we'd established along their normal route.

Taking this new course, she was beginning to descend to a point over Greenland when a single X-51A1 Waverider missile (now improved with lead and sulphur materials), traveling at over 3,500 mph, found her. The explosion was dramatic, but not completely fatal. She crash-landed near the 'air base', where another Waverider found her and completed the job. While not spectacular, at least not by earlier standards, the resulting damage rendered her inoperative and susceptible to subsequent ground operations by several ASOC teams. Together, these operations all made very sure that she was no longer an issue for us as an offensive weapon we would need to worry about.

A few weeks after the Battleship Class incident, another Mountain Class ship attempted to infiltrate using the same path as that first Battleship Class ship. This time, we'd replenished our mine field and expanded the layout of the pattern of mines to cover this angle of approach. We'd also done the same in the southern polar region, and a few weeks later, this pattern was tested by the Gomers with the same results. In both cases, the Gomers lost two Mountain Class ships and at least another three Battleship Class vessels. None of this could be construed as a huge victory for us, simply because they had the potential to overwhelm us in sheer numbers, but it had to be making a dent in their psyche. In fact, it was enough of a dent that they were starting to mass more and more Fighter and Carrier Class ships in reserves near the Moon. The traffic from at least one of the Moon Class ships near Mars was virtually in a constant flow.

Finally, the Gomers pulled together what appeared to be almost 3,000 of the Carrier Class ships, and they were staging in an area within a relatively short distance of the Moon itself. When we saw this concentration of ships, we were beyond concerned. In fact, the use of the term "concerned" was clearly an understatement, and the more we considered it, the more the serious wheels began to turn. This could be their breaking point, or it could be that they were finally set on initiating their main attack. In either case, we knew we would be very busy.

Near Bozeman, Montana:

The firing Order, if it ever came, would be anything but routine. Ever since the Gomers showed up the first time, this relic of the Cold War was now officially back in business. New weapons systems, to be sure, and the targeting was all-together different, but this facility had seen a lot of traffic and history. Closed down in 2002, she was the command center for one of the systems of missile silos that was about to be auctioned off as 'cheap' government excess property. Some potential buyer had actually bid on the land, but when the Gomers showed up, he disappeared somewhere near St. Louis, Missouri. When the dust settled after the first Gomer War, relics like the battleships were dusted off and re-evaluated for their potential usefulness. In this case, it was decided that Vandenberg, AFB, should not be the main or only place for outbound missiles, and several sites around the country were put back into service. This time they were missiles of a different ilk, and they weren't your typical ICBMs, either. Instead, they were designed not to reenter Earth's atmosphere like an ICBM, but were set for shots that would travel outbound, and then continue to strike a well-placed target or group of targets. The only change now was that the warheads needed a little hands-on preparation to facilitate the process of isolating the appropriate Sulphur Isotope 35, but once a firing warning order was sent, the missile's warhead could be prepared within an hour and had a shelf life after preparation of about 2 weeks.

This time, when the warning Order came into operations, it was sent to three of the 18 silos scattered around the area. The warheads were prepared, and the three missile crews got ready for the firing Order that would be sent along with the authorization codes for release by the President. They didn't wait very long, with the total time from the warning order to the firing order taking about 1 hour. The Target Coordinates were sent, received, and programmed into the guidance system. The warhead was activated, and the process was in place with the firing crews being given a green light across the board. Once they got the authorization codes, they compared notes and triggered the firing mechanisms by turning their keys on the appropriate countdown. As the missiles departed their silos, almost in unison, the main blast doors were sealed, and the silos were again hidden away. The crews felt a little comfort knowing how deep they were into the ground but, given the pictures of Diamond Head after the last war, most of them knew it was probably an illusion.

In this case, three Titan missiles, covered in a lead coating and concealing their deadly Sulphur Isotope payloads, streaked towards the gathering of Gomer Carrier Class ships that were near the Moon and amassing for a probable attack or heavy reinforcement of the Greenland Gomer base. Unlike the warheads used on Earth and in the first Gomer War, these warheads were about 100 times greater in kilo-tonnage. They were designed to not only spread the Sulphur Isotope 35 to maximum range, but to release sufficient energy in the vacuum of space to hopefully destroy anything within several thousands of miles of the burst. It was hoped, and it was at least theoretical to this point, that the blast would eliminate a large part, if not all, of the Gomers' attacking force.

The risks were huge, especially launching Strategic Nuclear warheads with that kind of power at a target anywhere near the Moon. The discussions leading up to the decision were several, and almost all of them were quite heated. Ultimately it was the President's decision, but the opinions were all over the board. Dr. Abramson and most of the Cabinet were in favor of it. Myself, most of my Staff and Service Chairmen, and Dr. Clarkson were not hugely thrilled about it, based on the potential impact on tides with the Moon, and the tipping of our hands for targets that might approach closer to us. Don't get me wrong, we liked the idea of what it could accomplish with the Gomers, but we were more than a little concerned about how it might create as many problems as it would solve. By way of contrast, most of the Congressional leaders who were consulted were just down-right hostile to the notion, which actually gave me more faith in the idea. It was finally an eleventh hour decision that the process was pushed forward. Taking out that size of an enemy force, for the price of a few of our strategic missiles, was finally making the math work in our favor. Regardless of all the wrangling, the die was cast, and those missiles were now within minutes of striking at or near the targeted concentration of Gomer ships.

Unlike most military attack situations, this one was given a little more media coverage than normal. The net result was that there were a lot more observers for this event than for just about anything else we'd ever done against the Gomers. It was felt by the President that people should not panic when the explosion took place, and they should also know it was us, as opposed to something coming from the Gomers. The President also took the unprecedented step of "spreading the word" so that people could remain sheltered for the whole attack. Naturally, this set off more gawkers than anything else, but it was thought to be a good idea at the time and, fortunately, the consequences were not so immediate that people didn't take cover once the stellar light show was concluded.

The strike was really another pretty simple plan. One of the three fired missiles was targeted to hit at the center of the Gomer formation, while the remaining two missiles were targeted to hit to both the left and right of center equidistantly from the mid-point. The idea was to spread the impact and to focus most of the destruction at the center of mass for the overall target. In this case, like in horseshoes, close was what would count, since a direct hit on any particular target was not really necessary. This was a 3D attack, since the center of mass was not just horizontal placement, but it had to consider the vertical and the yawl axis of the mass. No easy trick, these missiles were being targeted almost like the smart munitions we'd used some years ago in other wars. Again using remote message sites, we were able to make minimal adjustments to the target path as the missiles headed towards the targets.

Each of the missiles arrived in their target area at roughly the same instant, and the command for detonation was sent to all three missiles at the same time. The explosions were visible from Earth, as were the emitted shockwaves that overlapped in their passage in and around the Gomer Ships. Observers, utilizing old-fashioned visual telescopes, reported that the force of the blasts caused a large number of Gomer Ships located near the center of the fleet to simply explode. In some of the more distant portions of the gathered fleet, the blast and shock waves caused much of the gathered Gomer fleet to either crash into one another, or to simply crash into the surface of the Moon itself. Taking the more sophisticated view of the marshaling area that we had attacked, there was little sign of movement from any of the ships that were present in the initial fleet. It would be several hours, but eventually other Carrier Class ships came from behind the Moon to begin what could only be described as a search and rescue mission.

The overall view of the mission by the public was that it was a huge success. Media reports contained classic photographs and video footage of Gomer ships flying apart or crashing into the surface of the Moon. Some even went so far as to opine that this was such a huge victory, the Gomers would have to leave us alone. With such success, it would be easy to catch that 'victory bug' and to believe that hype. Most of the population did, and it was clear that the mood around the shelters was greatly improved. The President was thrilled, as were the formerly dissenting members of Congress. For me and my staff, our feelings were more mixed than ever, since we had a feeling that what was coming might not be nearly as pleasant. In fact, we were guessing that the retaliation would be huge, and would maybe make our brief victory somewhat pyrrhic.

The entire event brought to my mind the Doolittle Raid on Tokyo and Japan during the darkest days of World War II. While it was great for morale, it wasn't a huge victory from a purely military standpoint. Damage to the Japanese ability to wage war was minimal, and the only really substantial value was that it boosted American morale. Historians later would determine that the Doolittle raid led the Japanese leadership to make their greatest naval blunder of the war near Midway Island, thus elevating the attack from purely a strike for morale, into something that was far more strategically justified. I was in the same position as the senior military leadership of 1942 had been. While I was personally thrilled that it was a victory, I was still a little concerned that it would boomerang on us. I was also worried that our 'Battle of Midway' would be a lot more costly and dangerous than the one fought in June of 1942. In our present situation, we knew that the 3,000 destroyed or damaged Gomer ships sure sounded like a huge number, but when they were capable of massing at least three to four times that number to still attack us, it took on a slightly different color. So, instead of feeling euphoric, our emotions were far more restrained. We later figured out that our original guess about the huge retaliation was probably closer to correct, since what happened next was to be the proverbial snowball headed down hill.

CHAPTER VII

Supreme Allied Headquarters, (SAHQ):

The War of Attrition was now over, and we'd lit the fuse for the much larger bang with our strike on the Gomers' ships massed near the Moon. As was predicted, the strike worked, and from a purely military standpoint the impact was even better than what we'd originally hoped. Our Battle Damage Assessment, or BDA, revealed that most of the 3,000 plus Gomer Ships massed near the Moon were either vaporized or crushed when the force of the three blasts sent them hurtling into each other or into the surface of the Moon. Our observers had watched the Carrier Ships, with their countless Fighter Class ships still inside, all be destroyed with those three simple flashes of atomic energy. Fortunately, the Moon itself did not appear to be overly impacted, although the estimates were that we'd knocked the Moon about 20 feet further out in her orbit around the Earth. The observers were also reporting that the Moon's surface was covered in quite a bit of Gomer Ship wreckage and that movement on the surface of the Moon was virtually non-existent.

We saw only a few Carrier Class ships coming from the other side of the Moon in the apparent Search and Rescue operation, but it was definitely not the only movement of Gomer assets. The scientist observers monitoring the Gomers near Mars all reported the first most noticeable movement within a few minutes of the attack. As each station reported in to our Headquarters, they all agreed that once the impact of the blasts subsided, there was almost an immediate reaction of the remaining Moon Class ships. Both of them were now beginning the process of moving closer to the Moon, and both were deploying more of their assets to support that movement. They didn't come on quickly, but there was no question that they were moving our way. Very few of us harbored the illusion that they were just coming to pick up survivors and then go away. Most of us knew better, and we were not off center in that assessment. There would be no more waiting, and conversely, there was now no more time. We had to be ready, and we predicted that the onslaught would no longer be piecemeal.

Putting our main assets on alert, our initial plans called for us to send more missiles to intercept anything as large as or larger than the Mountain Class ship that might approach within range. Similarly, we were going to try and target any Battleship classes that might make it through the minefield, with our medium range missile assets, as soon as those large ships came into range. As for the Carrier Class Gomer ships, we knew they each had a punch both with weapons and the Fighter Class ships they carried. Our real problem was that there were still plenty of both the Carrier Class and Fighter Class ships to go around.

Now it was a matter of getting their fleet to commit to a particular course of action that would bring them to our forces and on our terms, so we could kill them. For one thing, this meant taking a portion of our force and sending them into Greenland to ferret out the Gomers in their holes. Personally we hated this, but knew from experience that it was necessary to draw the focus of the Gomers to a battlefield where we could hurt them. The only good news we could hold dear was that no Mountain or Battleship Class ships were in our atmosphere, at least they weren't here yet, and so there would be few, if any, of those surprises. That isn't saying that they couldn't get one or two on top of us, but we were at least now aware that they existed.

Almost instantaneously with the warnings that the big ones were moving towards our Moon, we began our operations to deploy our ground based defense net. This time we had the combat experience of the USS Montana and the USS Morton as a guide for the placement of our fixed assets. Within hours, the first Gomer Gun Batteries were in place and operational around New Washington. Adopting the same size and characteristics as those employed by the USS Morton, these weapons were designed to tackle the Fighter Ships. Intermixed with every three of these batteries was one Large Gomer Gun Battery, similar to the weapons carried on the USS Montana. Along with the grouping of the four Gomer Batteries were two separate power sources. One was to provide the primary power, while the second was to act as a supplement or back up power source should the need arise. In several locations, nuclear power was provided from the normal civilian sources, but in all cases, these reactors were supplemented with other back-up systems that could produce an equal amount of sheer voltage.

Finally, all of these Gomer type assets were supplemented by the placement of multiple Patriot Missile Batteries equipped with Sulphur based missiles. Three hours after the Batteries were made operational near New Washington, the New Pentagon and our own Headquarters both had these same type batteries in place. Eighteen hours later, all strategic targets and main population shelters on both coasts were similarly equipped. In each instance, all these weapons were fully readied and put on standby with ground crews that could operate these systems on a moment's notice. Thankfully, we had pre-positioned what we needed, and spent a fortune on training these crews, because within 24 hours, they were going to be fully employed.

I was headed back into operations after a short nap, when I got the 'green light' indication that all the batteries we could get into place were operational. As I settled into my seat to get an update on the operational movements related to our ground forces, I was advised by our observers that Thunder Mountain had just observed approximately seven Mountain Class ships and their escorts be destroyed in their attempts to cross the minefield prior to their entry into our atmosphere. It was believed that at least two such Mountain Class ships were still on the way, and that they were being escorted by multiple Carrier and Battleship Class ships. As we got the word, we began tracking their battlegroups to obtain an estimate of their speed, direction, and possible final points for entry into the atmosphere. We knew that two such groups were roughly twice the strength of the original two fleets that terrorized the Earth only a few years ago. We also knew that in the face of such numbers, we were going to be fighting the toughest battle in the history of mankind. As it became apparent that the entry point for both of these massive Gomer Fleets would be over Russia, the Russians suddenly became extremely cooperative with our State Department.

The call from the President and the Secretary of State came only minutes prior to the attack on Russia, and unfortunately for the Russians, it came about three months too late to do them a damn bit of good. We didn't have a single asset near them, since they had made it quite clear that we couldn't violate their territorial waters, their air space, or any of the territory under their control. In other words, we'd been told to go away, and they refused us the use of any of their other assets, some of which would have been very useful during our Attrition Campaign above the Arctic Circle.

The Gomers entered Russian air space and immediately began to fire with their largest weapons. Just like the last war, the Russians launched all they had left in their arsenal to either wound, destroy, or preclude the advance of the Gomers on their territory. This time they at least had some Sulphur weapons, thanks to our giving them a number of the Sulphur based rounds, but in the face of these sheer numbers it was not doing them much good. While some of the Carrier Class ships were destroyed, the big ships were completely unscathed, as the smaller caliber weaponry did little in the way of damage to these behemoths. In short order, St. Petersburg and large swaths of the western portions of Russian territory near Poland were simply destroyed. Similarly, the destruction was continued into Germany, where assets from our Allied Seventh Army, comprised mostly of German and French forces, were now engaged in a defensive retrograde operation. Heading for cover, their mission was to preserve as much as they could, while giving the enemy a black eye along their route of retreat.

In this mission, they were fairly successful. The Seventh Allied Army got hurt, but it wasn't destroyed. As in the first war, they had moved to their retrograde defensive positions, where they were at least partially protected, and they arrived there with far greater forces intact than in the First Gomer War. The Mountain Ships did do some damage to their mountain hideouts, but they didn't stick around to finish things off, and most of the attacks were similar to the elimination of Diamond Head. Thanks to that experience, most of the new shelters were hardened, and deeper away from the more obvious targets.

After completing their attacks on the Continent, the Gomer Fleets then crossed the North Sea and over the northern end of the UK, where they began to allow their courses to drift a little creating space between two distinct 'fleets' as they continued to move westward. It was clear that they were going both to the north and south of Iceland, and as we'd hoped, they were going to bypass the entire island. This did not mean Iceland was out of harm's way, simply given the stand-off range of the largest Gomer weapons that were onboard their Mountain and Battleship Class ships. Iceland did receive hits, but they were not as effective, and damage to actual assets and the population were definitely minimal.

During this entire movement out of Russia, into Europe, and then around Iceland, several of our assets were knocking out as many ships as possible along their route. The real problem for all of us was attempting to get the right asset, onto the right target, at the right location. We just didn't have enough Battleships of our own, nor did we have enough other missile or attack assets to cover the massive force that was now transiting the globe. Our damages to the fighting forces that did encounter and attack the Gomer Fleets were actually a pretty mixed bag of success and failure.

Charleston Naval Shipyard, Charleston, South Carolina:

The new USS Iowa was rushed to completion after the main missile strike on the Gomers nearest the Moon. Some of her systems still were not operational, but there simply wasn't time to worry about it. Setting out of the harbor, it was felt that she stood a better chance at sea with some maneuvering room. Just like the Montana when she was launched, the Orders for the crew of the USS Iowa were simple. 'Avoid all contact, and remain a hole in the water. Testing of all weapons systems to be conducted ONLY in daylight hours, and remain at or near the northern coast of Florida if possible.'

Shortly after leaving the harbor, the crew of the USS Iowa was quite gratified to see two armed escorts pulling up beside her. One was an older Destroyer, the USS Inoye, and although she was launched and commissioned only a few years ago, she was still a pre-Gomer war ship. The other was a brand new sister ship to the USS Morton. The USS Gregg, DDG 1101, was named for the General killed near the James River line during the last war. She carried the latest in weapons systems, to include the identical Gomer Gun system as the one on the USS Morton. Unlike the USS Morton, she even carried her own version of the "Gomer Bubble" system. As this small group formed, they turned southward out of the harbor, and began the process of becoming holes in the water.

Bremerton, Washington:

The new USS Alaska was a third sister to the new USS Iowa and USS Montana. She too wasn't completed in all respects, but her weapons weren't the issue. Instead, she was still missing a number of other systems related to communications, power for the Gomer Guns, propulsion and, added to those issues, there was a real dearth of personnel trained to operate some of the systems that she did have onboard. With the USS New Jersey still out of action, at least temporarily, Admiral Lynch was pushing for the USS Alaska to be completed almost two years ahead of schedule. A very daunting task, especially since the USS New Jersey was now two berths away being worked on almost 24 hours a day. With the onslaught that was unleashed by the Gomers only hours away from Bremerton, the Admiral sent an urgent message that was co-signed by the CNO, Admiral Steadman.

FLASH IMMEDIATE

TO: *Commanders USS New Jersey;*
        Commander of prospective Alaska.
FROM: *SAHQ, Chief of Allied Naval Operations*
THRU: *CNO*

1. *YOU ARE IMMEDIATELY TO PREPARE FOR GETTING UNDERWAY.*
2. *YOUR SHIPS ARE TO BE TOWED OR OPERATE UNDER THEIR OWN POWER TO A POSITION OFF THE COAST.*
3. *YOU WILL PROCEED TO MAXIMUM DISTANCE AND ASSUME SILENT OPERATIONS PROFILE.*
4. *YOU WILL NOT, REPEAT, NOT ENGAGE THE ENEMY.*
5. *IF UNABLE TO COMPLY, ADVISE THIS HEADQUARTERS IMMEDIATELY.*

S/ Carl Lynch   *S/C. H. Steadman*
Admiral, CofANO   *Admiral, CNO*

When the Commanders received these messages, it took a herculean effort, but they were able to get their ships moving, hopefully to be out of harm's way. The USS New Jersey was able to get out of port under her own power, and she turned towards the south, in an effort to hide in the vicinity of the coast off Oregon or Northern California. The Alaska, which still had not actually been commissioned into the US Navy, was taken by several sea-going tugs as far out to the southwest as they could get her from the Bremerton navy yard before nightfall.

Supreme Allied Headquarters, (SAHQ):

Admiral Lynch approached me to advise that he'd try to move what he could out of harm's way, and that he was trying to get our larger assets concentrated again in the Denmark Straits. The USS Montana was the exception, and she was now off the coast of Newfoundland, nearer the ASOC headquarters set up by General Greene. This was going to be interesting, since the ASOC was also covered by a number of the Gomer Gun Batteries of both types. The Gomers did stop for a period at their Greenland base, and our observer ASOC Teams all reported that it appeared to be a resupply mission, with some movement of force to reinforce the base itself. During this process it appeared that we lost one of our ASOC teams when a large Mountain Ship landed virtually on top of their hide/observation position. It would only be after daylight again that we would learn that at least a few of the team members survived. Unfortunately, the Mountain Ship remained in that position, and did not leave when the balance of the Gomer fleet moved off on their westward course.

The one thing that differentiated the North from the South Pole was that in Greenland, and throughout the Arctic, there were indigenous people. A population that was tuned to the harsh conditions of their surroundings, and we were lucky enough to have quite a few of these people join our Special Operations community. From the Scandinavian regions, there were forces from Norway, Finland, Sweden, Denmark, and on Greenland itself. Canadian and US Forces also had Inuits, some of whom were actually from Greenland and the coast of Canada adjacent to Greenland. These men and women were born and raised in this very part of the world, with a deep understanding of both the land and the animals. In fact, the Inuits had a number of teams in place, often as joint affairs with some of our Special Forces, who lived and trained in these areas quite frequently. One such team, Team Tornit, was the victim of the landing Mountain Ship. They observed it coming, but could do little to get completely out of the way. When the sun rose again to the level of the Polar Twilight, the survivors moved away from the giant and contacted us with the intelligence they had gathered.

Several of our ASOC teams were monitoring the movement of the Gomer fleet as it moved off from the Gomer base, and we were advised that the movement would take their fleet over the Davis Straits again. We had a short debate about whether to use the USS Montana Battlegroup again, or whether to allow for the new assets assigned to ASOC to take their crack at the bad guys. After a few minutes, we opted to advise the USS Montana to monitor movement, and if the Gomers were to take a more southerly approach, then they could engage. Otherwise, we were going to let the ASOC Gomer Guns take a crack, especially since General Greene apparently had something up his sleeve.

The Southern Davis Straits, off the west coast of Greenland:

The Captain of the USS Montana was handed the message from SAHQ, and then turned to his XO saying, "Okay Bob, here's the deal. We are to keep it south, monitor the bad guys, and report movement as necessary. We are only to engage the Gomers if they get south of the line at 65° North."

"Sir, what about north of that line?"

"Ours not to reason why, but my guess?"

"Yessir, I'd love a guess."

"Okay, you know that crap that we escorted northward to Baffin Bay?"

"Yessir."

"My guess is that it has something to do with Baffin Island, and they don't want us anywhere near it. Just in case."

"Sounds good to me, sir. Do you want to come to General Quarters?"

"Yes, let's do it. Make sure we're buttoned up for the Gomer Guns, too. I don't want anyone aft to get fried."

"Aye, Aye, Sir."

Baffin Island, Nunavut Territory, Canada:

In a line that stretched from Hoare Bay northward to the Admiralty Inlet, there were a string of a dozen Gomer Gun Batteries now in place. Each of the main guns was supported by three Anti-Fighter type weapons. These twelve main guns were also supported with 6 Patriot Missile batteries that were positioned more inland to allow for some coverage in any zones that were not covered by the Gomer Gun Batteries. This put everything above the line of 65° North and for south of that area, the USS Montana and her escort, the USS Morton, would have to pick up the slack. To sweeten the pot, General Greene had placed a relay station for VHF/UHF/HF transmissions on Prince Charles Island, which was centrally located just off the coast to the west. These transmitters were controlled from two locations, one on Air Force Island, and the other on Foley Island.

Inuit and other ASOC teams reported on the Gomers' movements leading off the coast of Greenland, and right before departing Greenland itself, General Greene gave the Order to activate the 'bait'. With his Order, the transmitters began a steady stream of transmissions, but this time it was transmissions that were sent using the native Inuit language, with some Norwegian thrown in for good measure. The Inuit transmissions were nothing more than the recounting of a number of their legends, while the Norwegian operators were enjoying the recounting of their own Norse mythology. Shortly after beginning transmission, both of the Gomer fleets that were leaving Greenland turned immediately on a course that would converge on the Prince Charles Island location. As they came over the various ridges or depressions in the north and south of Baffin Island, the Gomer Guns were waiting on the reverse slopes. Before the Gomer fleets arrived, General Greene had already issued the command for 'weapons free' for every Gomer Gun Battery on Baffin Island. The resulting combat was probably one of the greatest Gomer battles since the First Gomer War.

Allowing a number of the Gomer Battleships to pass over the ridges, the Gomer Guns unleashed their high impact T-Ray weapons at almost point blank range. Within minutes, all twelve batteries were not only engaged, but they were being swarmed from every direction. The resulting weapons fire, all on target and very effective in the destruction of the larger Gomer assets, reached a crescendo when the surviving Fighter Class ships all turned for the attack and the smaller Gomer Guns unleashed their fury. This was not a one- sided battle, and our losses in Gomer guns was becoming an issue as several of the Batteries were simply overwhelmed by sheer numbers. As the Patriot Batteries became involved, with their Sulphur tipped munitions, the din of battle was incredible. The T-Ray explosions, coupled with the more conventional strikes, were most devastating for both sides. The heart of both Gomer fleets were being hurled to the ground and into the sea, with both their Battleship Class and Carrier Class ships going down in droves. Against this destruction, a large contingent of the surviving Gomer craft began a retreat off into a more southerly direction to the south of the Island, right into the waiting arms of the USS Montana.

USS Montana, Davis Straits, near Hoar Bay, 65° North:

Watching the battle from a distance, the flashes against the night sky were almost blinding to the lookouts on board the mighty ship. Sensing, rather than seeing, the approach of the Gomer fleet that was escaping to the South, the Captain of the ship brought her broadside to the direction of the battle to his north. At the same time, the USS Morton moved to his port side and forward to take up a position that would allow her to bring all of her weapons to bear, without having to fire over the USS Montana. The blue, green, and red colored flashes streaking into the night sky were more vivid than anything anyone had ever seen before. Even the Northern Lights would pale in comparison, especially since those lights sing, and the lights they were witnessing now were often accompanied with thunderous booms several minutes after the flashes. Crawling along at just enough momentum to keep her steady, the USS Montana and her escort waited. Their wait would not be long, and it would be a night that nobody on board either ship would ever forget.

"Skipper? CIC. Those damn things are coming this way, but their Fighter Class ships are turning to the west again to move around to the Hudson Strait."

"Say again?"

"Sir, the Gomers are trying to flank the boys on Baffin Island, by cutting around and up through the Hudson Strait."

"Okay, sounds like they are hell bent to get to Prince Charles Island."

"Signal from the Morton, Sir. Seems she is picking up the heavies and they appear to be following the Fighters around the south side of the Island."

"Okay, XO, bring us in a little closer to where they are making their turn."

"Sir, recommend Course of 2-8-0°!"

"Do it, and all ahead full. Signal the Morton our intentions, and tell ALL Batteries to standby to commence firing once we are in position and they have a target."

"Aye, Aye, Sir!" With these orders, the USS Montana surged forward onto her new course, which would place her at a point that would allow her main and Gomer batteries to fire on the flanking Gomer fleet. As she started moving forward out of the darkness, there was no apparent detection by any of the Gomer ships, at least until she reached her optimal firing position.

"Captain, we have a firing solution on all main guns."

"COMMENCE FIRING!" With that command, the USS Montana and the USS Morton unleashed their collective fury on the portion of the Gomer fleet that was attempting to flank the line along the south side of Baffin Island. Again, the battle was intense, with the USS Montana taking out at least one Mountain Class ship and two Battleship Class ships. She was also firing on a number of the Carrier Class ships when the USS Morton was forced to release the brand new, retrofitted "Gomer Bubble" and the USS Montana had to cease fire. The USS Morton had simply been overwhelmed by the Fighter Class ships. In this instance, it wasn't about the amount of firepower, it was the sheer numbers of attackers. What made it particularly bad was that the Fighter Class ships attacked in swarms. As each of the wide band Gomer Weapons fired, a number of the Gomer Fighters would fall from the sky or explode, then as the weapon recharged for the next shot, two more waves of Gomer Fighters would take their place. This continued until the firing from the Gomer Fighters was beginning to cause casualties and damage to the ship. With a brief signal to the Montana, the Morton took the same steps that the New Jersey had to take during the battle off California.

The USS Morton fired her "bubble" which surrounded both the USS Morton and the USS Montana. This time the Gomer Bubble did not cause any damage to either ship, but when it expanded to form the umbrella or dome over the battlegroup, the Gomer Fighters were swept away like flies in a cloud of bug spray. As the residual THz Radiation dissipated, there was nothing in the air around either the USS Morton or the USS Montana, but there was a great deal of wreckage of Gomer vessels in the water. More interesting was that there were Gomer survivors clinging to some of the wreckage. Faced with the new moral dilemma, the Captains on both ships were at a loss over what to do about it. Sending their messages to SAHQ, it was only moments before we advised them to pick up survivors, treat them as POWs, and to turn them over to the ASOC personnel in Newfoundland once the dust settled. In an effort to assist, we also dispatched another escort to take the USS Morton's place, so that she could transport these new prisoners to Newfoundland, and maybe then move on to a location where she could be repaired. Within hours, the USS Ignatius, DDG 117, was on the way to relieve the USS Morton.

Lancaster Sound, Baffin Island, Nunavut Territory, Canada:

While they had no Gomer Guns or fancy Sulphur Weapons, Team Nanuq was capable of assessing the damage and movement of the remnants of the Gomers' fleets. They were also capable of putting some serious fire power on a stationary or slow moving target simply by contacting a nearby attack submarine, equipped with the conventional sulphur form of Cruise missile. Watching several Gomer Carrier class ships and the accompanying Gomer Battleship Class ship rounding the northern side of Baffin Island, Team Nanuq realized the same thing as the Captain of the USS Montana. These forces were simply attempting to flank the ASOC forces working the Gomer Gun Batteries to their south.

The Inuit commander of this team, Lieutenant Nathan Shiwak of the Canadian Armed Forces, was proud of the fact that one of his ancestors was a famous sniper in World War I. He was also proud of the fact that his Team Nanuk was entirely Inuit. Feeling his heritage strongly, he knew the legends of the region and felt that these flying creatures were more about his history than anyone would ever care to admit. It was his deep rooted feeling that these things were actually Kigatilik, which to him meant that they were a vicious or violent demon that some might even call the 'claw people.' There was no question in his mind, these things had to be driven from his lands. It was also this deep rooted gut feeling that made him know that they were evil and had to be eliminated without quarter. Against this background, he personally made the call.

"Ice Bird. This is Nanuq"

"Go ahead, Nanuq."

"Fire Mission, over."

"Go, Nanuq."

"One Battleship Class, two Carrier class ships, in the open at 2500 feet AGL and 250 yards to the north of point 1 -5, we are lazing the targets. Over."

"Roger, Nanuq, standby........" Waiting for a few minutes, the young Lieutenant got the call he was waiting to hear. "Nanuq, Shot out! Get LOW in your holes." Hearing this last part of the statement, Lieutenant Shiwak took the advice of the radio operator from the USS Springfield. He and his team, while still lazing their targets, got very low in their holes. Within seconds their wait came to a close with a series of three explosions that took place at the end of the three laser beams that were all focused on their three main designated targets. Unfortunately, the lazing process brought some of the small Fighter Class ships back to their positions. Knowing they didn't have long, nor could they completely escape the impact of the Gomers' Fighters, they simply waited.

As Team Nanuq cowered in their positions in the shallow tundra, the Fighter Class ships began blasting all around them. It was pure luck that they were not hit that hard by the Gomers. In fact, Lieutenant Shiwak would later confirm just how lucky they really were to only lose a few men, when they moved away from the position and saw the huge number of Gomer hits that encircled precisely where his Team Nanuq had been hiding. He was sad for the loss of the few men, but he knew that he might have lost up to 24 men, along with their animals and equipment. Given what they had dished out, he felt that just maybe something was looking after them.

Prince Charles Island, Nunavut Territory, Canada:

The remnants of the Gomer fleets, now consisting of One Battleship and three Carrier Class ships, converged from both the north and south around Prince Charles Island. Coming to a full stop, they waited over the island as several smaller Fighter Class ships descended to the island itself and approached the position where the antenna arrays were broadcasting their messages. The only observers to this odd ritual were too far away to determine exactly what was taking place, but it was obvious that no weapons were being fired by the Gomers. This was definitely out of character, since normally transmissions in these frequency bands were met with the immediate destruction of the source.

Finally, after waiting for almost an hour, the Smaller Fighter Ships were seen returning to their Carrier Class source, and a lone shot was fired at the antenna array by the Battleship Class Gomer. Concurrent with that shot and the Gomer Fleet's starting their movement towards the west, the Sulphur Isotope 38 weapon was detonated right beneath their positions on the island. The release of the Sulphur Isotope had an immediate impact on all of the Gomer ships in the area. Within seconds, all of the "capital" Gomer ships and most of their Fighter class ships were crashing around the island into the Foxe Basin, just to the west of Prince Charles Island. Once the impact of the explosion began to settle, the few surviving smaller Fighter Class ships returned back towards Greenland. A few made it, but most of these remaining craft crashed en route to their base.

As the survivors from Team Tornit surfaced again at a safe distance from the Gomer Base, it was learned that the Mountain Class ship that landed on their position was actually damaged to a degree that the Gomers must have crashed it deliberately. Now it was probably going to be repaired, and/or serve as a fixed gun battery for the base. The latter theory appeared to be confirmed by the remainder of Team Tornit when the massive Mountain Class ship began firing at a flock of Iceland gulls that flew near their position. Clearly, the bad guys were nervous about anything in the air, and we took some comfort in knowing that we were making an impression.

Supreme Allied Headquarters, (SAHQ):

The BDA, or assessment of the damages, we caused the Gomers was extensive and rather complicated. We knew that a number of them were destroyed before they ever entered our atmosphere, but as to what types or how many, the best our observers could give us was an estimate. The numbers we got from that approximation included almost 18 of the Gomer Capital type ships, which we used as a generic classification for the Battleship and Mountain Classes of Gomer ships. Similarly, the composition of the fleets as they entered over Russian air space and then began their division into two complete fleets was also a difficult assessment. Here the damage caused by the Russians was minimal in the area of the Capital types and was very modest for the Carrier Classes that were crossing their territory. Those estimates, which we believed were inflated by the Russians, still only added up to about 10 Carrier Class ships.

Most of the more accurate numbers we were able to compile started with the count of downed Gomers after they entered European airspace, and then continued their route as far as Greenland. We also know that the furthest west any of their ships traveled was maybe 15 miles west of Prince Charles Island, in Canada. The count in this department was extraordinarily high, with 7 Mountain Class ships destroyed, 1 damaged and landed near their base; 12 Battleship Class ships destroyed; and 56 Carrier Class ships destroyed. These latter numbers were confirmed by at least two sources and simply added up to a resounding defeat for the Gomers.

Although nowhere near the numbers of destroyed and dead Gomers, the Allied casualties were still rather high as a percentage of the forces engaged with the enemy. The Allied Forces in Europe lost almost 13,500 soldiers, along with their equipment, in the initial Gomer assault as it approached Europe out of Russia. The major equipment or weapon system losses were also heavy, with the loss of two destroyers, one Cruiser, and about 450 aircraft, mostly from the UK and German Naval forces. The Naval losses for the US Navy in the Denmark Strait, and in the Davis Strait, were approximately 25 dead, with 80 wounded. The losses in our ASOC teams that were inserted into Greenland totaled 15 men, 12 of whom were with Team Tornit, and 3 from Team Nanuq. Finally, our losses within the Gomer Gun Batteries on Baffin Island were approximately 800 men. We also lost 10 of the 12 Main Gomer Guns and 20 of the 36 Smaller Gomer Gun Batteries. The losses within the 6 Patriot Missile Batteries was minimal in comparison. Here we lost only 150 men and three of the actual missile launchers.

The truly horrific loss numbers were filtering out of Russia, where our people in the State Department were completely astounded at the sheer enormity of it. The losses near St. Petersburg alone were in the millions, as were the losses at or near Moscow and to their west towards Poland. The best estimates coming through our diplomatic sources indicated that the final count could well exceed 15 to 20 million people. The Russian military was equally decimated, with estimates that their forces were now less than 10 percent effective. There was absolutely no offensive capability left within their control. Even their nuclear capability was down to virtually nothing. This was all despite the fact that they were given access to our sulphur technologies and had spent quite a bit of time trying to rebuild their military forces that had been decimated in the previous Gomer War.

The most frustrating thing for me was the fact that we'd tried to incorporate them into the Global picture. Despite their losses and resounding defeat at the hands of the Gomers, the Russians were still refusing us overflight privileges and were not allowing us entry into their territory for any purposes, to include any possible assistance for the St. Petersburg area. I personally was having to come to grips with the notion that some people are just incapable of learning from their mistakes. Despite their precarious position, they simply refused to let anyone help them out of the hole they had dug for themselves. I wasn't alone, either. Our President was even more upset about it, especially since he had been the one soul to offer them an olive branch after the last Gomer War. This was no mean feat, especially given the treachery exhibited by their General Zhukov during the first Gomer War.

The lessons learned were to be on both sides, since we were not out of the woods when it came to Gomers coming back into our atmosphere. We repaired, repositioned, and resupplied our key forces, taking into account their previous tactics and patterns. We restocked our 'stellar mine field' and rearmed and built as many of the Gomer Gun systems as possible to replace and supplement our losses. At the same time, the Gomers were preparing, too, and their preparations and planning were perfectly set to take advantage of our geopolitical divisions. This time around when they came, they not only came in over Russian airspace, but they learned that it was a perfect place to stick a thorn into our backsides.

Naturally, after this recent defeat, the turmoil within Russia was horrific. Dissidents were taking root and with the loss of their key leaders, some to the Gomers and some to the typical Russian ailments that often lead to turnover in that part of the world, they now were having to do some of the things we did during the First Gomer War. They were moving people around, supplementing their former leaders and, in one case, were forced to bring back from retirement someone I had known from his days with the KGB. Their new President, and apparently Prime Minister as well, was a notorious field agent and cut throat I had known back in the bad old days. More like a pirate than a leader, President Yuri Dubronin was reportedly the new man in charge. This fact alone was not particularly comforting to me, but it was something that I considered as a possible card I could play. One thing was sure, at least I could try to talk to him if it became necessary. What I didn't know for sure was whether he would have me shot on sight before I had a chance to speak my mind. After all, the last time I had been around Yuri, we were not exactly on the friendliest terms with each other. In fact, the bastard had worked very hard to try and kill me. Then again, and in the spirit of complete disclosure, I was doing my best to take him out, too.

CHAPTER VIII

Supreme Allied Headquarters, (SAHQ):

As the information coming out of Russia was sifted and examined by our experts in the Russian psyche, it was very clear that Russia as a nation was no longer an entity that could project any power, even within its own borders. It was also quite evident that they were now grossly limited, or just plain incapable, of being able to even protect themselves. Our diplomats were burning up every contact and phone line with their remaining leadership in an attempt to assist, and yet the Russian 'government' still refused us entry and would not allow us to provide them with even a modicum of humanitarian assistance. They refused all defense discussions with anyone, not just the United States. They were even stonewalling their other neighbors throughout Europe and Asia with adamant refusals of any type of mutual defense agreements or assistance. Adding to their predicament was the complete collapse of their economy and the overwhelming hatred directed at the government by their own citizenry. The refugees leaving Russia, in almost every direction, were a huge indicator that the rats were leaving the ship, and that it was going down rapidly into some very deep water.

Whether the Gomers were aware of these facts, or perhaps it was because it was one of the few places in the Northern Hemisphere where they hadn't received a serious bloody nose, we'll probably never know for sure. What we did find out, much to our horror, was that the

Gomers were going to exploit the Arctic region by using nothing but Russian and/or Siberian air space. The next Gomer fleets to come to Earth began and ended their trips almost exclusively in Siberia, and there was absolutely nothing the Russians could do about it. This left us in the position of finally having to consider flushing the traditional concept of Russian sovereignty. Instead, the State Department was actually giving serious thought to recognizing a dissident group of Russian Refugees that had formed their own government in the area of Kiev in the Ukraine, as the official government of Russia. Sadly, this latter group was more stable and appeared to control more of Russia than the original government that was still attempting to run things out of what was left of Moscow.

Now our immediate problem was the infusion and approach of the Gomers who, for all intents and purposes, appeared to be attempting to colonize the most northern portions of Siberia. This geopolitical turmoil was making our lives far more difficult, and it was against this backdrop that I gave consideration to my next serious move. As if the Russian situation wasn't enough, adding to our woes, the Gomers that were still camping out in Greenland showed no signs of leaving. They were clearly not being resupplied or visited by any Gomer ships, but they did still have some Fighter Class ships and the one damaged Mountain Class ship. Whether we liked it or not, we were finally going to have to put some boots on the ground, beyond our ASOC teams, to eliminate this pocket of Gomers. I was also faced with trying to take up the reins where the diplomats were failing. This was a completely new role for me, but one that my predecessor, General of the Army Eisenhower, had faced when he was trying to cobble together a working group of Allies prior to June 1944.

In the last Gomer War, I had been thrust initially into a role that was well beyond my pay grade. I had little to work with in the way of forces, and I was forced to rely on my knowledge of history to make things work. When my role expanded to deal with global forces, again, I was stuck in a role that was even further from my pay grade. I would like to think that my own personal development helped, since things like the Naval War College were by and large only useful to a point, but I can tell you that I wasn't running things quite the way the most recent playbook demanded or expected. I turned back the clock in more ways than just unit strength and the military formations involved. In the First Gomer War, I had to think tactically based on the available assets. In other words, it was necessary to organize and think in terms of the battle, as opposed to a campaign, which wasn't the best way to operate. As the role expanded, so did the thinking. I went from trying to put Divisions together and then send them into battle, to managing assets at the Army and Corps level. Policy was a sideshow but, as I learned from President Blanchard and the California attack, it was a damned important one. This time around, the division was the furthest thing from my mind, and so were Corps. Now I was trying to operate Armies, while also sticking my nose into international relations. Not a fan of the Russians, it was now falling to me to try and get them to play ball.

Another glass ball that was still hanging in the air was the need to develop more scientific intelligence. This required asking questions, poking at the scientists as often as possible, and making sure they had the assets and personnel to make this happen. I had to know what the Gomers were thinking, doing, and what might make them tick. Certainly, understanding your enemy will be critical to the plans you make to defeat him, and we actually knew very little about the Gomers we were fighting. Oh, we were learning things about their physiology, technology, and maybe even how they might communicate with one another, but at no point could anyone tell us the critical answer to the most important question. Why? Why were they here, and what the hell did they want? Lots of answers were postulated, but none quite fit the facts. Until we had this answer, our only plans would have to be about just killing them, and hoping we got them all. That was actually a hell of a position to inflict on any Army. There was just still too much we didn't know, and not being able to communicate with the Gomers or ascertain their ultimate goals made our jobs a whole lot harder.

The key to strategic thinking isn't just on how to beat the enemy, but to ask the next question, "Now what?" In other words, what the hell was the end game? In most instances, you should be able to answer the question. It was the failure to answer the question on the front end that ultimately got me my first star, since as things morphed during the War on Terror, it would be the end game that would give us fits. I won't rehash that history, but it did have a lot to do with how I would approach things in the here and now. Looking back at the wars thrust on us, it should be simple to compute the end game. You had to win, and you had to do it totally and unconditionally. We learned with World War II that even then, it was a problem that required more thought, but it wasn't a question for the front end. For example, with World War II, it was necessary to rid the world of evil from within, and as the prospects for victory started to appear, it required our leaders to then ask the question of "now what?" We needed a serious post-war plan for how to deal with those issues, and hopefully keep it from happening again, which meant that during the war that ground work had to be developed.

The only real difference between World War II and both of these Gomer Wars was that with the Gomers, we are dealing with external threats. The desired outcome was the same, losing was just not an option, and when this war was over, we were going to have to be concerned with the "after." History has taught us, or should have taught us, even victory requires a great deal of thought about how to set it up, and then rebuild, to preclude as many future issues as possible. Knowing this, I approached the President and finally got a very reluctant approval to travel to what was left of Moscow, to meet with their latest President. It would be a 'long shot' kind of trip, but I knew this guy from years ago, and while we were anything but cordial, we did have a professional understanding of each others' mind set. Hell, we had a history, one forged in the later fires of the Cold War, that hopefully would allow me to reason with him. One thing was sure, I had some very serious misgivings about having anyone at State recognize a group of dissidents that would likely force things to a Russian Civil War after the Gomers were gone.

When I advised my staff that I was going forward to Moscow, the wailing and gnashing of teeth was monumental around my Headquarters. The Staff wasn't happy about my decision, and the thought of my going that near to a location where the Gomers operated with almost complete freedom at night caused several of them to blanch. Despite being the boss, I entertained their objections right up to the point where I finally made it clear that this was no longer an idea susceptible to discourse. In other words, "GET ME THE DAMNED AIRPLANE!" Once they realized that there was no changing my mind, the Staff did their best to stack the deck with as many 'strap hangers' as possible. When I again made it clear that it would be myself, my Senior Aide, Captain Randy Bowen, USN, who spoke passable Russian, and two security men only, the objections poured in yet again. Finally, when the staff processed the notion that I meant business, we set our itinerary and were off within 36 hours of my having approval from the President.

I realize that this is an aside, but the real interesting thing about staff is that at all levels of command, you have to have a good staff to assist in the planning and execution of any operation. For me, the key was always finding the right people and putting them in the right position. The other key was to follow the KISS principle, of "Keep It Simple, Stupid". Unlike many of my predecessors, I preferred fewer staff members, and even fewer people on the personal staff. One thing I had always observed, even when I was a young enlisted trooper, was that General Officers moved with more people than a damned three ring circus. Just like the three ring circus, there were just way too many clowns and "yes men" to suit me. There was also a huge sense of entitlement that seemed to exist before the Gomers showed up, and honestly, the elimination of such behavior became somewhat of a priority to me when I was put into a position to fix it. A friend once told me, "The biggest mistake a man can ever make is to start believing his own bull shit."

Around our house, my wife still cooked, cleaned, and I still polished my own shoes. Either my wife or I would wash and iron my uniforms, we answered our own telephone, and we always did all those mundane things that remind you that you're a human. When the Gomers came to town the first time, the luxury of such high on the hog living was swept away out of necessity and attrition. After the First Gomer War, several of my General Officers tried to rebuild their fiefdoms, only to discover that it royally pissed me off and I wouldn't allow it. Now the personal staff was limited to two Aides and two Drivers. There were no more personal aircraft, personal chefs, or other personnel to be wasted on doing what a General could do for himself. My philosophy was simple; if a Lieutenant or Sergeant had things to do to get ready for the next day, then you can do them too. Was I being unfair? Perhaps, because there were times that a little extra help was necessary. In those instances, you could draw from experts to assist, as opposed to tying them up as personal staff members who would sit on their asses waiting for you to use them. My trip to Moscow would be a prime example of this ideal. I didn't need a full time aircraft with flight crew dedicated for my occasional use, but now I had to have one for the immediate mission, so I tasked the Air Force to get me one with a crew.

Now seated in a VIP aircraft normally tasked for the use of our civilian leaders, Captain Bowen and I were racing the Twilight line into an airbase in the Scottish Highlands. This would be the first leg of the journey, and it permitted me to meet with my Deputy Commander, Field Marshal Sir William Fuller, UK. The idea was to take advantage of the layover for the night by consulting with both Sir William and the Prime Minister about the best way to approach the Russians, and about possible strategic planning. Certainly they had tried to obtain permission to enter Russian airspace, but for some reason, the Russians simply were adverse to the notion of anyone coming onto their territory, regardless of the reason and despite their Gomer infestation. After several hours discussing the problem, Captain Bowen and I decided to grab a few hours sleep. The next leg of our trip would be tough, and we thought rest would be a good way of preparing for it. We were dead right.

Moscow, Russia:

As dawn appeared overhead, we lifted off to Moscow. Racing against time, the plan was to be dropped outside Moscow, with the Russians taking us into the location where their Government was now operating under cover from the Gomers. We then had to allow for our aircraft to immediately head back southwest, to the safety of a base near the Carpathian Mountains. I would be stranded with the Russians until our aircraft could return the next day to pick us up. This was obviously a leap of faith that all these moving parts would come together, and it relied on the Russians to allow it to happen in the first place. When I thought about it, I could see why my staff went a little "bat shit" about the idea. I guess what they didn't know was that my meeting with President Yuri Dubronin was not the first one we ever had, nor was it our first rodeo together face to face.

Our aircraft touched down, and we taxied over to what was left of a hanger, which had clearly seen better days. From the air it looked as though Moscow and the airport had both been hit hard, fast, and repeatedly. Gomer 'holes' from their weapons were virtually everywhere, and I genuinely questioned how the hell the flight crew was able to land or take off from this facility. When the stairs were lowered, I looked out of the doorway of the aircraft and saw three men on the ramp with a Russian Hind-D, MI-24, helicopter about 50 yards away. Stepping out, followed by my Aide and the two security agents, we stood on the ramp as the three men started toward us. As they got closer, I immediately recognized the shortest of the three men and saw that the other two wore the uniforms of the Russian Army. Stopping about 5 feet away from us, the shortest man took a step forward and yelled something at me in Russian. Turning to my Aide, I said, "Did you get that?"

"Yessir," he said, "welcome to Russia, you old son of a bitch!'"

"Great, tell him that, 'it is good to be here, you loathsome bastard'."

"Sir?"

"Yeah, just say it, exactly like I told you with no deviations whatsoever."

"Yessir." As he repeated my message to the Russians, you could tell that the General Officers with Yuri were shocked. You could also tell that Yuri was the same old Yuri, when he burst out laughing, and we greeted each other with the typical bear hug. He then turned and waved us over to the waiting helicopter, as our 'ride' taxied away from the ramp and got into the air. We climbed into the helicopter, and Yuri handed me a headset. Conspicuous was the fact that neither my Aide, nor his entourage of General Officers, were handed a headset. As the old Hind-D lifted from the ramp, Yuri spoke to me in perfect English.

"Michael! It is good to see you, and your arrival is none too soon."

"Why is that, Yuri?"

"You might be about to save both me and my country. If I seem difficult over the next several hours, please know that this is a high stakes game. If we both play it right, we can help one another."

"Okay, how do you want to play it?"

"Simple, I'll be the son of a bitch, and you be the bastard. Don't be afraid to dig in your heels, and I'll dig mine in, too. At the end, we will both relent a little, and we both will walk out with what we want."

"Geez, Yuri. Who is the audience?"

"Bastard Generals. These two are okay, but the others you will meet are hard-headed."

"So, you want to play this like Berlin?"

"Yes, just like Berlin!"

"Allright. Let me ask this then, will our quarters be wired?"

"What do you think?"

"That's what I thought, or assumed. Okay, game on."

"Da! Good! Now look angry, and we will get the show started." With those words, I yanked my headset off, tossed it to the side, and proceeded to ignore Yuri for the rest of the trip to their headquarters. When we landed, Captain Bowen and my two security men were escorted to our quarters inside a rather extensive underground complex. A complex, I might add, that I'd tried to find for years during the Cold War.

The meetings went as Yuri intimated they would go with his General Staff. The Generals, concerned about the impact of our fighting on their territory and the loss of sovereignty for Mother Russia, were digging in deeper and deeper. The discussions went back and forth about the use of the Gomer technology, our using this as an excuse to destroy Russia, and our discussions with the dissident movement in the Ukraine. With this latter revelation, I told them that if they didn't play ball, then we'd have to just stick the bat up their ass. We were prepared to make a deal with their dissidents in the Ukraine, or do whatever hell else had to be done, to get at the Gomers. Finally, I disgustedly got to my feet and held up my hands, "Gentlemen, really the problem has a simple answer. If you want to maintain your sovereignty, save your Mother Russia, and regain that which you have clearly lost, you will join us. We have no desire for your territory, anymore than we wanted the territory of Germany or Japan. We have no desire to tell you how to govern, how to live, or how to die. If you choose to die as old men, then we wish you health until that day in the future when you can die in your own bed, in your own country, as Russians. Right now, if you do nothing, you will die homeless at the hands of the Gomers, AND you will lose your Nation. Trust me, the rest of the world will ultimately prevail, either with or without you, so now it is up to you to make that choice! Join us and fight for YOUR land, or stay alone, and die alone!" With those words, I motioned to my Aide, and we both started to head for the door.

With my last words, the silence within the room was palpable, but as luck would have it, the Gomers would provide the real punctuation. As we stood up to storm out, the whole room was rocked by a blast the likes of which I hadn't felt since the Gomer Battleship took out Diamond Head, almost four years before. The Russians, not following our normal protocol, were still using VHF/UHF channels for some of their communications. We had warned them, but as usual, it was seen as one of our 'tricks' to gain control over them. Yuri and I both understood these issues of the Russian mind set. They trusted no one, and historically, they had good reason not to trust anyone. Starting with the Mongol hordes, to Europeans, such as Napoleon, the Kaiser, and then Hitler, the Russian psyche was built on being invaded and mistreated. Now that the Gomers were here, they still had the mindset that they would ultimately prevail, even if all they did was nothing. What they didn't fully comprehend was that this was a foe that didn't give a damn about the bad weather, lack of food, or sheer size of the geography. Instead, the irresistible force was now striking an immovable object that, well, could be moved.

The explosion was close enough to make for some internal damage to their command center. Walls collapsed, dust and rebar fell, and it was very reminiscent of my personal experience at the Aliamanu Crater. Unfortunately, it wasn't the blast alone that reminded me of that event, it was the casualties, too. One of my own security men, in an effort to protect me and Yuri, was severely wounded when a large piece of concrete fell from the ceiling. He was shoving me and Yuri out of the way when the chunk of ceiling fell, crushing his left leg underneath. One of Yuri's largest detractors was also killed, although Captain Bowen believed that it wasn't the blast that got him. We didn't discuss this point until we were well on our way home, but Randy thought he saw someone reach over and snap the old man's neck. When I asked him who he thought it was, he just grimaced. At that point, I knew exactly who did it, and didn't doubt for a second that Captain Bowen was probably correct in his observation.

Once the dust settled, the survivors in the room had a brief discussion where they made it clear to Yuri that he needed to make a deal with us. There was still some reticence, but either my speech, or the Gomers, or all of the above, finally made our point. With the approach of dawn, we had inked a deal that allowed for a wider exchange of information, the utilization of Russian Forces to be exclusively under MY command, and complete access to Russian soil for the duration of this, the Second Gomer War. The Russians made it clear that they would ONLY offer their forces to serve under the Allied Command, so long as the Command was held by me. If another nation or unacceptable commander were put into place, then all bets were off. This was not my idea, but that of Yuri and of his General Staff, who placed their trust in me, as opposed to a particular nation or nations.

While I might have some of their trust, it would appear that this trust was somewhat personal and still quite conditional. Not a complete deal, but it was a start. Eventually, our President was able to convince Yuri that he could be trusted to the same degree, but it would take a while, and in the meantime, I would be roundly criticized by some in New Washington as attempting to usurp power as a result of my position. This was complete bull, since the one thing I never wanted was power or position. I think honestly that is why the Russians were going to trust me, since Yuri knew damn well I'd rather be a small town lawyer living quietly away from all of this crap. I also knew that Yuri didn't want to be drug back from his farm along the Volga to serve his beloved Russia. Neither of us wanted the jobs we had, which is maybe why we were still able to communicate.

As we were getting ready to fly out of Russia, I was pondering how funny life can be sometimes. Before this latest meeting, the last time Yuri and I had seen each other was almost 30 years earlier, when we'd exchanged a great deal of gunfire in a remote corner of Berlin. Yuri had been working with the KGB, and I was on a quickie assignment into Berlin as part of a relatively straight-forward training exercise. Thanks to a huge misinterpretation of what was going on, poor espionage, and a HUGE glitch in a simulation, things had gotten out of hand and very ugly. The problem was bad enough that both sides were actually staring at a full blown nuclear exchange. It was the first time we'd made a deal, and on that day, just like now, we'd managed to save a few lives and kept things from blowing up by 'talking out of school' and putting on a good show.

Yuri personally went with us to the airport for our pickup and with him was a young Captain in the Russian Army, who was standing with a young woman holding a small child. The young Captain was staring at his feet, and I suddenly realized how much he looked like Yuri. Turning to Yuri, I whispered, "Yuri, is that your son?"

"Da, and his wife and baby."

"Yuri, why don't you let me get them out of here?"

"I was hoping you would say that, but how to do it without it seeming like you are doing me favor? Others can't leave."

"Don't worry, I've got it."

Turning away from Yuri I grabbed my Aide, and told him in a much louder voice that could be overheard by Yuri's Generals, "Dammit, Captain, we are going to need a special liaison, and we don't have anyone..... Wait, what about him?"

I then turned back to Yuri, and said, "I need a personal liaison officer for communications to your Generals. He needs to be a Captain, and someone you can trust. Since we are minutes from leaving, how about this young man?"

Yuri shrugged his shoulders and said, "But he has family."

"Don't worry, he can bring them along, but we're leaving here in a few minutes, and this guy looks as good as any for what we need. Can you trust him?"

Captain Bowen repeated this in Russian just loud enough that it could be overheard by the Generals that were standing nearby. Yuri smiled and said, "Da, he is son. I think I can trust him."

I asked, "Can you get him and his family ready to leave in about 5 minutes or less?"

The response was a simple nodding of the head, and I was then officially introduced to Captain Alexander Dubronin, Mrs. Irina Dubronin, and their two year old son, Yuri. With only the clothes on their backs and a bag of things for the baby, they were ushered onboard our airplane for the flight out. The injuries to our security man were sufficient that he was not going to be able to travel right away, so he was left behind in the care of Yuri and his medical staff.

Once he was able to travel, we were going to make sure he got home as quickly as possible by sending in some medical personnel and evacuation assets. It was obvious that Moscow was a rough place to be for the moment, and I wanted our man out, almost as much as Yuri wanted his own son and his family out. We also wanted to start supplementing the Russians with humanitarian assistance to go along with some higher tech support, if nothing else, as a sign of good faith.

When our aircraft touched down in the Scottish Highlands, I had a brief meeting with the Prime Minister and Field Marshal Fuller, and I was finally able to advise the President what had taken place. In a conference call, we all agreed that we needed to get medical personnel on standby, and that food and basic sustenance was also going to be critical. As we finished refueling, we departed with at least a framework of a plan for the defense of Moscow, which was as good a place to start as any. If we could take the pressure off Yuri Dubronin, then we could assure ourselves of a partner for down the road. While the State Department wasn't thrilled with our move, there was little they could do but go with it, especially given the President's obvious delight over our new deal. On our arrival back in CONUS, I made arrangements to brief the President and his Cabinet, while turning our new Russian Liaison and his family over to my bride, Leah, to get settled. Fortunately, Irina and Alexander spoke flawless English, so it didn't take long to get them settled. Leah and Chris helped them get clothing, food, pots, pans, and all the sundry stuff to start building their household. In the process, they actually made some new friends that would help down the road.

After briefing the President, Cabinet, and some Congressional leaders in New Washington, I returned to SAHQ with my marching

Orders. We were to finalize the planning and start our campaign to clear Greenland; immediately start getting relief to Moscow; and begin the planning process for what would hopefully be the final campaign to completely rid our globe of the Gomers. Against these priorities, I gathered the staff, and we began the process of sifting through the assets available, and the best way to feed those limited assets into the process.

Supreme Allied Headquarters, (SAHQ):

Naturally, my first call was to General Greene with a request for some of his Gomer Air Defense assets to be forward deployed into Moscow. We couldn't put up hospitals, or distribute food, clothing, or other humanitarian assets without being able to defend them. We also needed to find more ELF equipment for them to use, along with sufficient forces to defend our Gomer Air Defense assets from both the Gomers and anyone else trying to steal the technology. The ball was rolling, but it would take time to get those assets in place. Unfortunately, time in Moscow was a premium, and everyone knew it. With each passing night, the Gomers were putting a hurt on the civilian population of Russia around Moscow. I was also concerned that perhaps we were putting too much on General Greene, and with this assessment, I was about to shake up the leadership with another fairly major change.

Going back to history, when faced with trying to manage a great deal of global and international assets, it was necessary to organize the various field Armies, of all the allies, into what was then known as an Army Group. Taking this form of organization would put the Army Groups under a theater commander. In turn, each Army Group would command several Allied Field Armies, who then controlled several Corps level organizations. Each of these Corps would then control several Divisions of various types. As the overall Allied Commander, it would now fall to our staff to locate, recruit, and put into position the most qualified commanders at the upper levels of the Theater, Army Group, and Field Army levels, so that they in turn could do the same through their own areas of control down to the Division. I was no longer in the business of moving a Field Army's assets around on a map. That concept was for an earlier time and place, when our assets were too limited to allow for the more global command approach. Now we would move the Army Groups and their Field Armies.

After some discussion, and several fits and starts, we initially combined the Theater Command with the Allied Army Group Commands. The final form of the flow chart created two central areas for concern. The first was to be handled by the 21st Allied Army Group, commanded by my Deputy, Field Marshal Sir William Fuller, who would be responsible for the Atlantic Theater. The second was to be the 42nd Allied Army Group, commanded by General Richard Davis, USA, whose area of responsibility would be the Pacific Theater. ASOC would be used to handle the special areas that needed to be resolved, which included support for both the Greenland and Siberian campaigns. I made it quite clear to the Allied Army Group Commanders that ASOC was my asset, and it would fall directly under my direction and guidance. Similarly, the Naval Assets would be the responsibility of Admiral Lynch, with task organization flowing from our headquarters. Finally, the Strategic Reserves, to include all naval, air, and ground, would be directed from our headquarters, using task organization as required for a particular mission.

With the addition of these new headquarters, there were a few growing pains. Coordination for the movement of the Air Defense assets took priority, and finally, after almost two weeks of more movement, with additional fits, starts, and much wailing and more gnashing of teeth, we had forces on the ground in and around Moscow. Within a week of their arrival, there were several significant battles for the air space that permitted us to begin the flow of assistance and medical support. We were a long way from taking back the night in Russia, but we were at least in position now to permit for the distribution of relief to the people that needed it around their Capital. Buying us this time was critical, since the forces we needed to retake Greenland were also beginning the process of completing their preparation for movement. The overall strategy dictated that we take Greenland first, since we would need that air bridge to complete the encirclement of the Gomers in Siberia, and we couldn't leave that many Gomers with a Mountain Ship still operating in our rear.

I had waited, in hopes our scientists would give us something that might keep this from having to be a hole to hole removal of the Gomers in Greenland. Unfortunately, without anything concrete coming from our scientists, we were finally down to where it was time to either fish or cut bait. Flashing the green light for the operation, Field Marshal Fuller and General Greene began what we feared would be the costliest campaign to date.

CHAPTER IX

Thule, Greenland, at the remains of the former US Air Force Base:

The 21st Allied Army Group tapped the Third Army, under the command of Lieutenant General S. L. Simpson, USA, to assume responsibility for the re-taking of Greenland. Lieutenant General Simpson then turned to the XVIII Airborne Corps to open the door for his forces through the old US Air Force Base at Thule, Greenland. The plan of attack for the Corps was lead by the 82nd Airborne Division, who were the first arrivals at the old airbase. They were followed closely by the 101st Airborne Division, who landed on the captured airfield along with their assigned aircraft. It fell to these Divisions to secure the 'air head' position, which would allow for the landing of other forces into the area, to include the infantry and very limited armor forces that would follow up with the VIII Corps through the old Thule base. Meanwhile, in an amphibious operation, VII Corps would land two infantry divisions on the eastern coast of Greenland near Daneborg, with the support of the Naval Task Force, TF - 25. Overhead, the First Air Force would be flying additional air support missions to assist in both the Airborne Operations and with the tactical air support as required.

Shortly after the initial landings were to take place, the 17th Airborne Division was set to jump literally on top of the Mountain Ship's position, and hold until the 82nd Airborne could reinforce them.

Armor units were almost useless in the terrain, except for defensive positions around the very edges near the coasts or at Thule, so the worst of the campaign would fall on our Infantry and Airborne units assigned to hit the enemy directly. Once Thule was retaken, the Air Force was going to try to provide tactical air support from that location, while the naval assets supporting the landing were to provide their tactical air support as was consistent with the defense of their respective fleets.

Within hours of the first landings on Thule, we were back in control of the airbase, and men and equipment were pouring in to expand their area of influence. At the same time, the amphibious landings were completely unopposed, and even later that night when the forces expected an attack from the Fighter Class ships, there was absolutely no activity coming out of the Gomer-held areas. As assets got closer to the Gomers and brought Sulphur fire power into the Gomer zones, there was still very little resistance or overt reaction towards the attacking forces. The only major battle developed when the 17th Airborne Division dropped onto and around the Mountain Ship's position. With the first air drop of forces, the local Inuit Teams assigned to our ASOC forces were able to guide the 17th Airborne Division personnel into positions from which they could attack. The Inuit Reconnaissance teams had done a superlative job of locating and identifying the key locations of the Gomers. They had also registered each of these locations and done an excellent job of designating the primary targets for the air support.

Throughout the area of the main Gomer occupation around the Mountain Class ship, the Gomers put up a monumental fight. Initially, our casualties were starting to mount significantly, with the dead and wounded personnel from the 17th Airborne Division almost representing the equivalent of the strength of a Regiment. This changed almost to the second the 82nd Airborne Division dropped into position to reinforce and support the 17th Airborne Division. The infusion of their additional Sulphur based weapons and the aerial insertion of several mobile Gomer Gun Batteries quickly changed the face of the fight. The casualties now favored the attacker, with the outer and then inner perimeters around the Gomers' positions crumbling in the face of the increasing fire.

Instead of a month, or even a week, the conclusion of this battle was really decided in a matter of hours, and it ended in a way that nobody ever suspected would be possible. The Gomers began to come from their holes, without weapons, and without aggression. To the amazement of several thousands of our Airborne troopers, the Gomers were actually surrendering en masse by leaving their holes and lying face down in the snow. The only thing to mar this success was the fight that was still taking place immediately adjacent to the damaged Mountain Class Gomer ship.

This last bastion of Gomer defense was decidedly a tough nut to crack. As our forces landed on top of it, or at least very near it, they were quickly destroyed by highly accurate Gomer fire. The Sulphur tipped Cruise missiles fired in support of these troopers seemed to slow the Gomers down but did not stop their overwhelming rate of fire. Several of these missiles actually struck the ship directly without having too much effect. The weapons continued to fire, from both sides, until an enterprising young trooper and an Inuit guide found a way into the Mountain Class ship through a large open portion near the worst damage. It was a back door to be sure, but it was at least a way inside that would allow the troopers a chance to clear out the Gomers. This battle would rage for three more days, as troopers had to engage in street fighting to take each compartment one at a time. Finally, when both sides were almost too exhausted to continue, the final few surviving Gomers also gave up by just lying face down. Still astonished, the troopers took them prisoner, and we began the process of shipping them back to the facilities set up by General Greene in Newfoundland. Here they would meet some of Dr. Abramson's personnel, to include Dr. Marvin, who was by now most interested in the potential for finding a language for communications with the Gomers.

ASOC Headquarters, Newfoundland, Canada:

Gomer prisoners, while not exactly a new twist, raised a whole new set of issues for us, since what do you feed them? How do you feed them? Just how in the hell do you treat them in a humane manner, when they aren't human? We knew to keep them away from Sulphur, and we knew they liked fresh water, but other than that, we had little to go on. The eggheads argued, debated, and otherwise had their own opinions, but it would be just a simple matter of setting out a number of items to see what they went towards as food. It ran the range of fresh water, to dirt, to rocks, ice, to various raw elements, to food as we know it, and finally to things such as Sun lamps, regular lights, UV lamps, and finally just an electrical line. What we learned was astounding. They were like plants. They wanted water, mineral infused potting soil, and a few mild UV rays to keep them happy. It wasn't much, but it was a start.

Once our eggheads got past the feeding process, and the keeping them out of the sun or away from Sulphur, they started the process of observing the Gomers and their own interactions with one another. There was little in the way of what we would think about as overt communications, but their body language sure looked like it was happening. Some theorized that it was ESP, while others were convinced that it was sign language of sorts. The truth was even stranger. As the USS Morton was limping back towards Newfoundland with some of the original Gomer prisoners onboard, a radioman had noticed that the static on the UHF receiver was bursting with what sounded like waves of interference. Not knowing what it might mean, he wrote it up, and naturally this report was promptly buried until someone else noticed the same thing.

In the POW lock up now established in Newfoundland, the UHF/ VHF frequencies that were being monitored by the staff began to blow up with noise that wasn't quite static. With the population increase in the lock up of Gomer prisoners, this seemingly random noise on the UHF/VHF bands expanded exponentially. Finally, when the last of the prisoners were finally brought into the area, the UHF/ VHF bands were virtually jammed with these signals. When this information eventually made it to Dr. Marvin, he began checking these random UHF/VHF frequencies and comparing them to the sine waves of the earlier signals he had intercepted on the Terahertz frequencies. It took a while longer for Dr. Marvin to piece it all together and then confirm his theory, but when the light bulb finally went off in his head, it was a doozie!

Dr. Marvin finally had an answer for how to "jam" or disrupt the Gomers' lines of communications. It wasn't necessary to approach it from the Terahertz side anymore, now he could jam the communications literally from their source of origin. While not exactly something recommended in the handling of POWs, several of the prisoners were placed in facilities where tests on jamming their ability to speak were conducted. After some trial and error, Dr. Marvin was able to confirm that the jamming on certain UHF/VHF frequencies could actually preclude the Gomers from being able to 'speak' to each other or otherwise communicate. This would be something we could use, and production began on the necessary equipment we would need to jam these frequencies. What we were hoping to find, and what would be the real leap forward, would only take place when we could decode or learn their language, and this process was clearly going to take a lot longer. Still, we at least had a starting point, or a point of reference for what to observe and to monitor. Hopefully, we'd be able to discern patterns and/or maybe even words to be able to communicate with the Gomers themselves.

Supreme Allied Headquarters, (SAHQ):

Against these scientific breakthroughs, we were still dealing with some pretty major elements of a global conflict. The amassing of forces on both coasts of Russia was taking time. We were also trying to gather foreign forces along the southern border between Russia and China. Our navies were attempting to get set up in the adjacent waters around the area on both coasts, and this was all taking time. We had to determine how best to exploit our ability to completely encircle the portions of Russia where the Gomers were still operating to set up their colony. The flights into and out of this part of Russia by the Gomer Fleet were yet another issue that had to be resolved, since their firepower was considerable. The more individual fighting was becoming a little more sporadic, as it appeared that both sides were waiting on an opening from the other. Like two boxers waiting on someone to drop their left before striking with their right, we were now doing this same dance with the Gomers.

Moscow was still not completely secure since raids against some of our positions, along with other key positions in western Russia, were still happening. Our only real success was that such Gomer raids were no longer on a nightly basis, and when they did take place, they were still largely ineffective. Looking like we were heading back to a war of attrition, we felt that the situation required that we take more of an offensive stance. With this in mind, the staff began the finishing touches to their vision for the larger master plan for a simultaneous attack from both the west and the east coasts on the Gomer enclave in Siberia. Within three minutes of the start of the briefing, I sent them back to the drawing board.

Supreme Allied Headquarters, (SAHQ):

With the infusion of Russian Forces and the geopolitical considerations for any end game after the war, I made sure that whatever plan the staff finally put together would balance all of these considerations. The idea of a simultaneous attack was too far outside the realm of logistical and manpower capabilities, and it relied on forces that would not play well together to get it accomplished. It was aggressive, audacious, and in a perfect world, it would be brilliant. Unfortunately, a perfect world was not our area of operations. Moreover, the intelligence we had on the exact location and disposition of the Gomers in Siberia was minimal at best. Looking at it from the broader perspective, I realized that we would have to go back to building boxes and denying the bad guys the turf in smaller pieces. We also needed a better handle on patterns, pathways, and tactics being used by these 'smart' Gomers. The last thing I wanted was for the Gomers to just drop in from space onto a massing field army, or on any concentration of forces, and wreak havoc. We had to build ourselves a buffer area somewhere adjacent to the Gomers where we could stage our attacks, otherwise, we would invite trouble. With this guidance in mind, it was my decision, after consultation with the political leaders for the nations impacted, to set out the priorities and direction from which we would proceed.

Knowing what we needed, I initiated some shuttle diplomacy that required three more visits to Moscow, and countless consultations with our own President and his Cabinet. After two weeks I'd logged more flight time than a migrating duck, especially with all the intermediate stops in the various Capitols around the world. In each case, it was to sit down and consult with the civilian leadership to discuss the implications of what we could, or might, try to accomplish. During this time, the Gomers were not idle either. On a nightly basis, they were sending ships to the surface of Earth and building or supplying several enclaves of Gomers in the more northern reaches of Siberia. Finally, after several conferences to include one face to face meeting involving both President Blanchard, United States of America, and President Dubronin, Russian Federation, I gave the following written guidance to the Allied Staff to get the process moving in the right direction for their planning:

MEMORANDUM

FROM: *Supreme Allied Commander*
TO: *Allied Planning Staff*

Re: Planning Guidance for Summer Siberian Campaign 17-1

After consultations with world leaders, the following instructions are being provided for your consideration in the planning of the future operations to eliminate the Gomer Presence:

1. *We must retake and secure the western portion of Russia to the west of the Ural Mountains;*

2. *We must initiate and pursue intelligence gathering to include any information about tactics, patterns, positions, weaponry, etc., that are available to the Gomers;*

3. *Once the line to the Ural Mountains is secured, we will need to establish marshaling areas that can be defended, while we prepare forces for the initial attacks into the Siberian region from the west;*

4. *Simultaneously, we will establish and secure marshaling areas along the Pacific coast of Russia, relying on available ports, etc., to allow for the build-up of those forces that will be required for the additional phase of an attack into Siberia from the East; and,*

5. *We will utilize any available forces from China and Japan to secure the Southern Line and the Eastern Flank of the areas surrounding the Gomer enclaves within Siberia.*

Only after the accomplishment of the tasks listed above, will an attack into the Gomer areas of Siberia be initiated on the two fronts provided in the earlier Allied Staff Plan. The above priorities were acknowledged and ratified in a written document by and between the United States and the Russian Federation, on whose soil we will be operating.

S/ M Patrick

Michael Patrick
General of the Army
Supreme Allied Commander

The above document became the initial road map, and it would take almost a month before the first phase of the Campaign could begin. From the outset, even though it was designed to methodically build a box for our Gomer enemy, it was a logistical and personnel nightmare. As March turned to April, we were just beginning the fight for the line around the Ural Mountains. What had originally been envisioned as a summer campaign clearly was going to turn into something much larger, and one helluva lot more difficult.

Field Marshal Sir William Fuller was not only wearing the hat of my Deputy Allied Commander, he was now taking to the field in Command of the 21st Allied Army Group (Atlantic). At his disposal were Lieutenant General Daniel Mickelson, commanding the First

Army (US); Lieutenant General S. L. Simpson, with Third Army (US); Lieutenant General Karl Kessler, German Army, commanding the Seventh Army (composite); and, General Sir Edward Fitzhugh Mallory, commanding the British Eighth Army (UK). General Vladimir Petrofsky, of the Russian Federation, was commanding the Russian Army Group, which was composed of 10 field Armies.

In this latter group of armies, one Russian Field Army (the 11th Army (RUS)) was in the vicinity of Moscow, while another four Field Armies (the 12th, 14th, 15th, and 16th, Armies (RUS)), were attached to Sir William Fuller's 21st Allied Army Group. This latter attachment was tenuous, and as a result, General Gerald "Jerry" Larkin, (USA), was brought in as the nominal Commander of a provisional 25th Army Group, formed for the sole purpose of leading the four Russian Field Armies into the Campaign. General Petrofsky focused his attentions primarily to the defense of Moscow, and was not slighted in any fashion about the arrival of General Larkin. He WAS slighted at the prospect of being under the command of anyone from Europe, especially Field Marshal Sir William Fuller. It was this animosity that led to the creation of a separate Army Group, under a hand-picked American commander, to control the Four Russian Field Armies that were needed to assist in and around the Ural Mountain defense line.

Similarly, the Pacific areas were to be even more of a challenge. In this Theater, General Richard Davis, USA, a hero in the First Gomer War, assumed command of the 42nd Allied Army Group. Assigned to his Group was the Sixth Army (US), commanded by Lieutenant General Manuel "Manny" Ortiz, USA; the Eighth Army (US), commanded by General Winfield David Smith, USA; and, the Tenth Army (US/Composite), commanded by General Roberto

Guzeman, USA. This latter army had two of its Corps coming from several Allied Nations, one being provided by Australia and New Zealand, and the other by Japan. Other nations contributed a number of units to the mix, and they were also assigned to the Tenth Army to supplement various Corps and Divisional assets. A prime example was the provision of several Separate Brigade size units from Taiwan that operated within the Australian/New Zealand Corps (since they refused to operate within the Japanese Corps or any forces coming from China).

Aside from the two Army Groups with control of the Atlantic and Pacific Theaters, there were other strategic commands for ground forces. These elements consisted of the Chinese Army Groups (composed of approximately the strength equivalent of six US Field Armies), under the command of General Xi Jintao, PLAGF. These Chinese Army Forces were to operate as semi-autonomous elements, with the single mission of securing the southern part of Russian Siberia. Simply stated, they were there, on their own soil, to act as a blocking force and would not, unless conditions warranted and only on my order, ever actually enter into the territory of Siberia. Outside of China, these forces acted solely on my order, but within their own assigned areas in the protection of China, they would continue their normal mission. These forces were all to report to General Jintao, with the key allied mission of preventing any Gomers from leaving our eventual kill zone within Siberia. This rather convoluted mission statement was a direct result of the desire of the Russians to keep the Chinese Army out of Russia if at all possible.

Similarly, the remaining five Russian Armies, the 21st, 22nd, 23rd, 24th, and 25th, were assigned to me directly for use in the initial part of the Siberian Campaign on the Pacific side of Russia. Again, to simplify these command relations, I appointed the commander of the Russian Airborne Forces, General Igor Sevitch, to act as their nominal Army Group Commander, which was later identified officially, on the eve of the actual campaign, as the Provisional 48th Army Group. Each of these latter issues all arose from the desire to keep things out of the hands of foreign forces. Requests to keep the Japanese Army out of the Kuriles and Chinese Forces out of their southern territories clearly were part of the historical scores that existed way before the arrival of a Gomer. After all, the population of China, before the Gomers, was over 100 million, and the population of Russians within the entire eastern part of Russia, was probably less than 7 million. Of course, the Gomers had handled many of these population issues, but the Russians were not exactly noted for their flexibility in mind set and were still quite convinced that while Americans might go home, neither the Chinese nor the Japanese would ever leave. I couldn't refute their argument, but I was able to get permission to use these forces, IF the tactical or strategic situation forced me to use them.

Personnel and geopolitical issues weren't the only things having huge impacts on our planning. In fact, the personnel re-organizations and movements were the easy part. Logistics were the real problem. General Clark, who had been by my side since my arrival at the New Pentagon during the last Gomer War, was pulling the last three of his hairs out. Pushing strategic weapons by rail, by air, and by sea to key locations; getting the 'recipe' for munitions distributed to manufacturers, both here and abroad; overseeing the manufacture and distribution of Gomer Guns; dealing with the 'beans and bullets' issues for each of the Armies, both foreign and domestic; and keeping everyone moving in the right direction was virtually a 28 hour a day function. I assigned more personnel to him, and made sure that the various services and foreign nations put what assets they could at his disposal. It wasn't easy, but he was able to put into place at least a workable plan for each contingency as it arose. Things like this took time, but with everyone clamoring for supplies to support their operations, the priority system was the only saving grace. Working from my first memorandum, General Clark developed his priorities, keeping in mind that some places, like Vandenberg, Bozeman, and SITE X, were always number one, he worked his way down the line to the units that would be entering combat last. Not an easy process, it was only short of a miracle that it was ever completed in time to keep us on a workable timetable.

Movement of troops and supplies was set on a convoy schedule, which was another logistical nightmare, especially where assets had to be identified and protected throughout any movements. This was why it was vital that we establish defensible safe zones within the actual areas we were to operate. These depots of supplies, food, ammunition, fuel, etc., had to be set up, manned, and stocked, in advance of any offensive. They also had to be defended, and while they all maintained low profiles, were set up in safer terrain, and armed with Gomer Gun support, they each had to be selected to take advantage of the routes into and out of their locations. At several points, fighting units were pulled out of training to facilitate certain functions, and it was finally necessary to utilize two entire Armies, (US), to perform logistical, defensive, and training functions on a rotational basis. None of this went smoothly, and more to the point, some of it didn't go without Gomer notice.

Murmansk, Russia:

The supply and troop depots at the Port of Entry, or POE, were running at capacity. As night approached, the arrivals were all hustled to their shelters and locations away from the main port facilities. As with all things logistical, sometimes it was a tough choice to leave things unattended or to risk trying to move them where the enemy might see you. The Officer in Charge of these Port Facilities, Colonel Melvin McNamara, of the Royal Army, made his decision and opted to keep several crews working even after night fall to clear the ammunition from the docks and move it off towards the Ammunition holding areas several miles away. This was a mistake.

"Hey, George, what do you imagine that thing is?" Turning and looking, the Sergeant in charge of the detail peered into the dark sky, but couldn't see anything. Turning back towards the Corporal that had called his name, he said, "What, I don't see a bleedin' thing!"

"Serious, George. Right there, next to the Moon." Looking again, the Sergeant finally saw the glimmer of something in the very pale moonlight. "Gore, I got no clue, but it is hu......."

As the Sergeant uttered his last word with his last breath, the Gomer Battleship cut lose a salvo of its main weaponry. Within seconds, that portion of the dock holding the ammunition and the off loading crew was simply gone. There were some secondary explosions, as the Gomer Battleship continued its rate of fire into the Harbor area. With each shot from the Gomer, more of the port facility was being destroyed. The Fighter Class ships were also sweeping over the harbor area, firing their weapons in the 'slash and burn' style we'd seen earlier in the last war. As they made their second pass, the Gomer Gun Batteries around the area began a rather vigorous defense. The firing was constant from both sides, and a number of direct hits were made on the Gomer Battleship. After approximately 15 minutes, the Gomer Battleship had gone down, and quite a few Gomer fighters were eliminated before they turned and fled back to the east. It was an extremely bad night at the port, and it would lead to the UK having to replace Colonel McNamara. Field Marshal Fuller not only had him relieved and replaced, but he was in the process of having the Colonel tried by a court-martial for dereliction of duty.

Supreme Allied Headquarters, (SAHQ):

I wasn't happy about this type of poor judgment, but if we had a court-martial for everyone who made a mistake, then half of the Army would be in jail. I understood what the Colonel was trying to accomplish, but I also believed that it was best for me to stay out of the mix. I would probably have relieved him, there is little question about it, but putting him on trial was a little much. Sure, he'd made a mistake, but he was trying to accomplish the mission, and he just bet wrong in his risk analysis. In another place on the battlefield, he could just as easily be a hero for exercising that kind of judgment and being successful. My biggest concern about this particular fiasco had more to do with the delay by the Gomer Guns in responding to the attack, and them not spotting the enemy before they struck. This to me was the main failure, and Colonel McNamara wasn't the person who dropped that ball.

Still, far be it from me to second guess the UK and their Army, but that was something I did not want to see in ours. I did relieve a number of commanders during this phase of the war, but it wasn't for exercising initiative and making a mistake, it was for not moving fast enough, or failing to take timely action in combat. If the reason for not moving fast enough was from lack of confidence or training, then we got them to a training situation to cure the problem. If it was for incompetence or just plain being sorry, then they wound up doing whatever might be useful to the war effort, regardless of how menial. As usual, the key was finding the right person for the right job. I did send a memorandum to Field Marshal Fuller about the failure of the Gomer Gun Battery to timely perform their function, and eventually the idea of the court-martial for Colonel McNamara was dropped. The relief of the Battery Commander, on the other hand, was finally accomplished, after a second smaller raid by the Gomers demonstrated clearly that he was unfit for command.

Other more mundane issues were every bit as important as the big ones. For example, we were approaching summer, but our training had to still be for winter operations. The weather was warming in most of our training areas, so we had to begin rotating our units northward into Alaska and Nova Scotia to keep them at their edge of training for the conditions they would face in Siberia. As units were identified and starting the deployment process, they were first rotated through the applicable training areas prior to embarking for their respective Points of Entry into Russia. Their equipment was also going through the same process, and since I had a feeling we were in for a long campaign that would lead eventually into winter, this was all a huge factor in both the training and equipment preparation. Cold weather gear, especially with the limited availability in stockage around the world, was just such an issue.

Shipping, tonnage, escorts, aircraft, fighting ships, tanks, missiles, beans, and Sulphur bullets, were all swirling around in my head, along with the political, geopolitical, tactical, strategic, and basic functions of life. I was concluding that sleep was for sissies, and that a pack of cigarettes might last for 8 to 10 hours, if I was lucky. Coffee was being consumed by the gallons, and the one meal of cardboard rations and the four hours sleep on a canvas cot were all taking their toll. Finally, after two solid months of this schedule, I took a day off to see my family. Naturally, it was interrupted by several phone calls, but I at least got a decent hot meal, and more than four hours sleep. Our standard joke was that I had been gone so long, that I might have to show my ID card to my wife at the door, just so she would recognize me. The brief break was fantastic, and I truly hated that it was ending. As we stood in the door to say goodbye, she gave me her funny look, and just said, "Be careful!" It was her look, coupled with those words, that for the first time in over 36 years of military service, scared the living hell out of me.

Arriving back to my War Room after that brief 24 hour break, the briefings of what I'd missed seemed endless. I was back on the coffee and cigarette diet, and munching on the cardboard sandwiches that were being tossed around, as we plowed onward to the completion of the planning and execution of our Phase I in Russia. It was nearing the time when we would have to forward deploy the entire Headquarters. General Whitney and General Greene had departed and were in the process of finding us a suitable location as far forward as possible. Once the word arrived that such a location was found and improved, the rest of the Headquarters began the deployment of their own staff personnel, along with our other assigned support personnel. There were many tearful goodbyes as we all left family behind, and our establishment of a rear guard headquarters to handle those things that always arise after the main unit's departure. It was official. We were going to the battlefield.

Brasov, Romania, in the Carpathian Mountains:

"Geez, Daniel, you have one seriously sick sense of humor."

"General Whitney, this is perfect. The tunnels and the area are defensible, and a Gomer has never been to this side of the Mountain before."

"Dude, this is Dracula's frickin' Castle!"

"No, it is Bran Castle, and somebody was kind enough to put in a bunker system right adjacent to it. This is perfect, and General Patrick will love it."

"Yeah, he might, but I personally hate it." General Whitney then threw up his hands, and walked back to their vehicle and the security team. With that acquiescence, the new location for the Supreme Allied Headquarters, (SAHQ - West), was officially found. It was only a matter of days before the initial and advance headquarters elements began the process of turning it into a home. Within three weeks, it was occupied full time and on the last day of that month, the place was fully operational, manned, and ready. It would be from here that the initial battles would be directed on the west side of the Gomers. The east side was another story, but that headquarters had been identified and started some time ago. On that side of the future Siberian battlefield, the Gomer traffic wasn't nearly as frequent; on this one, the traffic was heavy enough that things moved just a little slower.

At this stage, we were still dealing with how to protect the western portion of Russia from the nightly Gomer incursions. Each night, the western portions of the country were being hit, much in the same way as the United States had been hit during the First Gomer War. In this case, Carrier and Fighter Class ships, with the occasional attack by a Battleship Class ship, were traveling around the western side of the Ural Mountains and heading as far south as the Caucasus Mountains, then west to the Carpathian Mountains, before turning north again towards the Baltic Sea. From there they would continue due northward to the North Pole, where they would then swing back to their starting points in Northern Siberia, after passing over the East Siberian Sea, and entering the far Northeastern portion of Siberia near the Kalyma River. They ran this cycle, or various modifications of this route, on a nightly basis, with often devastating results in portions of Eastern Europe and throughout Russia. During the day we were trying to build up our forces and stockpiles of supplies, and at night, the Gomers were trying to find and knock them out. When my Headquarters moved forward to the Carpathians, we were still being attacked regularly in areas that were literally just on the other side of the 'hill'.

One such attack had a devastating impact on our plans and our forces now in Europe and Western Russia. It was fairly soon after the twilight line had passed over the Headquarters for the 21st Army Group, and it involved not one, but two, Battleship Class ships being brought in for a major attack. We would later learn that there was a communications break down, and that someone had put the deception transmission facilities far too close and in a pattern around the Headquarters for Field Marshal Sir William Fuller. The Gomers were able to do two things. They were able to identify the pattern, and as a result, the location of the actual Headquarters. I also learned, well after the fact, that the positioning around the Headquarters had been the actual decision of Sir William himself. We may never know why he had insisted on the pattern, but the clear impact was on himself and almost all of his Headquarters staff.

Within minutes of the passage of twilight onto the area, the two Gomer Battleships unleashed a salvo of their main weapons. They were perfectly on target, and they laid down such a pattern of devastating fire that within seconds, the 21st Army Group Headquarters element simply ceased to exist. There were no survivors, and there was nothing to salvage. The destruction was complete, and the impact on our operations had the potential of being a huge setback. Initially, we assumed the role of directing the 21st Army Group, but it was clear that we would need to reconstitute the Headquarters and find a new Deputy Allied Commander and a New Group Commander. This time, I decided not to use the same person for each job, opting instead to diversify matters. I probably should have done that originally; however, geopolitical considerations dictated the use of a foreign officer as my Deputy, and given his experience with the Gomers in Tierra del Fuego, Sir William was also an excellent choice to lead the Army Group. This time, I was going to toss out geopolitics completely, and find someone who could do each job with no distractions.

Doing the soul searching necessary to see which peg would fit into what hole, I decided to have a conversation with General Whitney on the subject. "Whit, what about you? Want the job over with the 21st?"

"Sir, you know I've been on staff ever since I pinned on the first star. I'm not qualified to lead at that level. Hell, I've never even commanded a division."

"Whit, not to belabor the point, but neither have I, at least not in combat."

"I know, sir, but you've got this experience, and experience from the First Gomer War. Besides, you commanded a division and a corps, before the First War."

"Whit, I commanded the 11th Airborne Division on paper, as a peacetime contingency or a 'what if.' It wasn't even an active division then, there were no real troops, equipment, or ideas. Same with the XXIV Corps, it was just a place marker job, with the inscription 'in case of war, break glass' emblazoned on my forehead. Neither of these units actually was active at the time, and they both only still existed in history books or at the Center of Military History, in some annex for 'what units to call up or activate first.'"

"Still, you at least studied the concepts. Me? I've helped move them around and even gone so far as to decide which one goes where, but as for what to do? Hell, I was a Battalion Commander the last time I commanded anything."

"True, Whit. Still, how many of our Generals today could say the same thing? Most wouldn't be Generals today or ever, for that matter, if it wasn't for the Gomers. Now, I'm going to ask you, do you want the Group or not?"

"Damn, sir. You're putting me on the spot. I've been with you since the beginning, and honestly, I'm comfortable here. I'm not sure that having been an Intelligence Battalion Commander is going to permit me to do something as complex as an Army Group. Geez! As much as I would love to try, I'm not sure I'm even remotely qualified, so I guess........"

"Okay, Whit. I get it. You've never considered it, and now you're nervous. I also know you want more time to start getting ready for such a job. So, I am going to make it easy on you, but only for a little while. Right now, I'm making you my new Deputy Commander, and I'm going to give the 21st Army Group to Jerry Larkin. Now, let me make one thing real clear to you. From here on out, you are going to take every free minute to consider how you would command that Group, or a Field Army, as we move forward. If I lose another Group or Field Army Commander, your ass will be in the breach. Got it?"

"Yessir, and thanks. I won't let you down as the Deputy, either."

"Damn right you won't. Oh, and Whit, if something happens to me, then you're going to be in a worse position than an Army Group Commander, so truly, you need to loosen the bolts holding your ass in place, and start getting ready for the worst."

"Yessir!"

"Now get a hold of General Larkin, and tell him I want to see his ass HERE right after first light tomorrow. Also, you're going to need to scrape around here and in the First and Third Armies for some staff guys. We have to get that Group back up and running, and we need good guys, not just some pulses filling slots. DO NOT be afraid to stack the deck, and screw politics, right now we need doers, and not ass kissers from the United damned Nations."

"Yessir!" With that, General Whitney started the ball rolling to get things back to normal. I was taking comfort that the Russian Armies would respond to Jerry, and that much of what he needed already existed in the Provisional Army we'd created for his Russian Armies. This time, we could consolidate things without worrying too much about the geopolitics involved. For some reason, I found this extremely comforting. Within two hours of first light, I was meeting with Jerry Larkin.

"Giant, how are the Russian Hordes treating you?"

"Fine. Once we got past the language, the tactics, and the hubris on their part, it started to fall into place."

"Did you hear about Sir William yet?"

"Heard a rumor, and since nobody there is answering the phone, I figured it might be a good rumor."

"Well, I'll confirm the rumor. I need you to do a couple things. The first is that I need you to find out what the hell happened at that headquarters. The second is that I will need you to cherry-pick the best from your provisional group staff, and then round it out from my staff, to put together a new headquarters element for the 21st Army Group. The third will be a damn sight easier, but I'm going to need you to pass on the word that your Provisional Army Group is being abolished, and that everything will be now under the control of the 21st Army Group..."

"Sir, the Russians will not stand for it, they do NOT want to work for anyone who ain't American or Russian."

"Well, if you hadn't been such an ass, you would have heard the last thing I had on my list, but since you're going to be an interrupting jerk, maybe I won't tell you. Maybe I'll just change my mind, or maybe I'll just tell you that I am officially making your sorry, loud mouthed ass the Commander of the 21st Army Group."

"Sir. I'm humbled in your presence."

"You sucking-up bastard. Figures you would say some crap like that.... Okay, here's the deal. General Whitney will be my Deputy Commander. You can bitch, rob, steal, or otherwise annoy him with what you need to get that Headquarters back up and running. If you DO steal much from my staff, I want to at least know about it, otherwise I'll sneak into your tent with a trench knife. Got it?"

"Sir! Yes, sir!"

"Good, now get the hell out of here and get to work. We need this to happen, and damn fast. Check with Whit, he knows the deal, and he is prepared to do whatever it takes to have you a working headquarters within the next 48 hours at the latest. Be careful!"

"Yes, sir." Jerry almost ran from the room, and went straight to find General Whitney. I was definitely pleased, since between the two of them, the 21st Army Group was back in business within 36 hours, and this time around, they were smart enough NOT to leave a calling card that the Gomers would find to exploit in their targeting information. The flip side to this was that I was feeling a sense of real loss. Sir William and I had fought the Gomers together throughout the Southern Hemisphere in the First Gomer War. We'd even been blown up together when they took out Diamond Head, and we'd had so many meetings, dinners, and social events over the last several years, we forged a true friendship. There wasn't a thing I wouldn't entrust to Sir William, and I always knew that our feelings were mutual. Sure, we sometimes called each other names, but they were actually the kind of things that friends exchange as barbs. I was that Bloody Yank and he was my Lousy Limey.

Our families had shared things too, and had become rather close. I knew that when word of this filtered back to Leah, it would hit her especially hard. I think Jerry's wife is the one who ultimately broke the news to her, but unfortunately, it was while she was telling Leah that Jerry was now commanding the Army Group. When Leah dug further asking about the "why and when," Chris finally explained what had happened. I could imagine Leah's feelings, because my own were pretty close to them. Personally, I was crushed. Professionally, I couldn't let it show, nor would I let it impact how we fought. Instead, I had to find out why, not for personal reasons, but to keep it from happening to anyone else.

The other thing that kept me focused was that we were taking casualties across the board, at every level of command from the squad to the top. Such is war, and when it is a total war for the entire species of man, these losses were inevitable. With each individual loss, I think there was a loss for all of mankind, but we couldn't let it stop us from our mission. Instead, each loss drove home the point that it really was about saving mankind. This wasn't propaganda; it was literally about preventing genocide, or more to the point, the complete extermination of all man.

SECTION 3

GLOBAL OFFENSIVES AND INTRIGUE

CHAPTER X

European/Russian Theater:

Using the daylight, just as we had in the Southeastern Campaigns of the First Gomer War, we got our forces in place to begin that part of the campaign to deny the Gomers access to anything west of the Ural Mountains. Using various choke points along their nightly route, we stacked the deck, used radio decoys, and took our time in obliterating anything that came near our forces. The Gomers made nightly runs, and we had nightly ambushes on their ships. Starting at the very top of the Ural Mountains, in the narrow passage over the low lands near the coast, we were able to direct a lot of fire, with excellent results, on the ships as they bunched up to transit the area. Our gauntlet continued throughout their pathway, to include ambush points near key energy sources that mirrored the use of ERWs and Sulphur Isotope weapons we'd employed at the SRS. At each and every point where the Gomers would bunch up to move around various terrain features, we had something to pop them. As we would find a choke point and exploit it, the Gomers would modify their routes or tactics. Each time, we would try to anticipate their moves, and counter them with our own.

This cat and mouse activity continued for another week or so, until we decided to liven up the process a little. We placed Gomer Gun Batteries on mobile platforms at each of the key choke points, and then began our attacks even before the twilight line enclosed us.

In essence, we were firing from the light, and firing into where they thought they were relatively safe. We would shoot, and then scoot to a location that was not where they could locate us. Often times, the alternate firing positions were set on the other side of a lead based or stone obstruction such as a ridge, where the Gomers would not see us when they passed over. In some cases, the same Gun Crew would be responsible for both Day and Night hits on multiple Gomer targets. After a while, they would wait until much later after the twilight line passed before they began to make their runs. Once that took place, we simply let them pass before popping them from behind out of different positions that were already prepared for just such an occurrence.

After several weeks of these type attacks, the Gomers finally ran two of their Battleship Class ships up to use their standoff range in striking suspected Gomer Gun positions. They were firing from their side of the twilight line, into the day light side of the line, in an effort to blast at any suspected Gomer Gun positions. We had hoped this would happen and were ready for this tactic from the Gomers. When the Battleship Class ships were spotted and reported on their way to the twilight line, our two standby B-2 Bombers launched and detonated their two Sulphur Isotope 38 Cruise missiles with direct hits on both of these large targets. This was the last time their Battleship Class ships would run anywhere near the Ural Mountains, or into western Russian, or even into parts of Eastern Europe. We were making our point, and the Gomers were beginning to curtail their sorties much past the Ural Mountain line. It took us almost 9 weeks, but we had finally mostly secured our side of the Ural Mountains.

The loss of life was horrendous, but we had made enough headway that the City of Moscow was no longer being attacked with any frequency, and life even began to stir again around St. Petersburg, where we established another more accessible area for bringing in the much needed supplies and replacement personnel we needed to get the 21st Army Group ready for the next phase of the war. With the increase in size of the areas that were not subject to nightly attacks, local production was again beginning to take place, and the logistics issues that plagued our early planning were now finally starting to come together. Locally produced artillery shells do not have to take up space on transports, nor do locally produced rations for food stuffs such as coffee, bread, etc. This naturally left more space for the other more specialized equipment, such as Gomer Gun Batteries and the new Gomer Gun tank and self-propelled artillery platforms. In fact, the Russians were delighted to begin producing the armor chassis for our mobile weapons, which meant we could ship the weapons system, as opposed to the entire assembled unit, which in turn saved us even more shipping space. This allowed production facilities in the United States to shift their focus and produce those items in mass for use with our Pacific Forces.

Despite these successes, we were still struggling with questions about the Gomers themselves. Yes, they learned from their mistakes, and they had a nasty talent of making us pay for their advances in their own learning curve. Part of the time we could guess what their next move would entail, and other times it was so out of left field that we were left reeling. This happened the first time they tried a new approach in direction. Shortly after our denial of access to the Gomers west of the Ural Mountains, they tried to arrive using a course above the Arctic Circle into Murmansk and the Archangel areas. Their sole mission appeared to be a strike at our port facilities. They caught both locations a little flat-footed, and both positions were left with a great deal of damage, with little return for us in downed Gomers. A second night was only a little more productive to our defense forces, but the damages again were substantial to the facilities and supplies that were still awaiting transport. The third night became a resounding victory, mainly because of luck, timing, and the United States Navy.

The 2nd Fleet, United States Navy, was in the process of providing escort services for a rather large convoy of Merchant vessels headed into those main Russian ports. With the repeated attacks over the Arctic Circle threatening to cut off these ports, the Fleet Commander dispatched Task Force-20, or TF-20, ahead of the convoy into the waters just north of Murmansk and Archangel. This Task Force consisted of the USS Montana (TF-20.1), and the USS Wisconsin (TF-20.2), along with their escorts. For good measure, the Commander of the 2nd Fleet had also sent the USS North Carolina and several of her escorts from TF-25 to act as an additional gun platform just outside the harbor of Murmansk. Forming in essence three anti-Gomer battle groups, these ships were in position on the third night. Back in the fold, the USS Morton was the picket ship that spotted the oncoming Gomer Fleet, and she, along with the USS Inoye, were waiting as holes in the water to catch any returning ships or stragglers. After the Gomers passed over the USS Montana, USS Wisconsin, and USS North Carolina battlegroups, the fight that ensued was short, brutal, and extremely violent.

With no losses to any of these naval assets, an entire attacking Gomer fleet consisting of a number of both Carrier and Fighter

Class ships was eliminated. These Battlegroups remained in their relative positions in and around these key ports during the entire period that the Convoy was in the area. There was only one other attempt to attack the ports, and it ended just like the first one with the total destruction of the attacking Gomer force. Thereafter, these ports were completely unmolested, and the Gomers were no longer traveling over water. They didn't mind ice, but if there was water involved, they were not going to chance it. They learned, as did we, that the water was a great place to hide things you wanted left alone. Moreover, they didn't use their typical slash and burn tactics over water, simply because they could not be sure if they were effective or not, and there was this little problem of getting their weapons to work well after striking the water. We filed this information away, and would rely on it heavily on the Pacific side of the war.

Several European and Russian Theater lessons were actively implemented in the strategy for the upcoming joint offensive, especially in technology and manning for the Pacific forces. One of the first things I did, after the shift in leadership in our Atlantic forces, was to divide out the Theater and Army Group responsibilities on the Pacific side. I gave General Davis a choice, and he opted to stick with his 'boys' and the 42nd Army Group, so I appointed General Stephen Richardson to take over as my Deputy Commander for the Pacific Theater. This was a comparable position to my Deputy Commander for the Atlantic Theater, General Whitney. General Richardson had commanded First Army in the First Gomer War, and had actually decided to retire just weeks before the first alert was sounded this time around. Frankly, I hated to drag him back, since like me, he was probably a tired war horse that would love to be elsewhere. As I thought about it, that probably made him the perfect choice for the job. It would be through the efforts of General Richardson, along with some help from General Greene, that our SAHQ forward command post would be completed and opened in Dutch Harbor, Alaska. This particular command post was one we'd started building during the First Gomer War, just in case things shifted from the South to the North Polar regions. We'd never actually used the facility, but it did come with some state of the art features that might even have made it better than our Headquarters at the former 'new Washington' facility.

As we were finalizing our plans for what we hoped was a dual campaign, General Greene and his ASOC teams were working their way through every corner of Siberia in an attempt to map out targets, locations, and the habits of the Gomers. The information was staggering. There were entire settlements being constructed, and at least two arrays similar to the ones they were constructing in Antarctica during the First Gomer War. These were a little more complex, but they were there, and ripe to be hit. As the campaign to secure Russia was approaching closer, we decided to take the conflict to these arrays from a distance. General Quentin J. Thayer, Jr., USAF, was commanding all of the Air Forces, to include our Strategic Bombing assets. Taking the gloves off for these types of operations played right into his wheel house, and once he had a green light from the President and me, he began putting the right assets into the right places to make it happen. Within one day of our having photographs in place, we had launched a strike to work with the daylight in the region. With the sun came multiple Sulphur Isotope 35 cruise missiles, which not only took out these new antenna arrays, but also did considerable damage to the areas that were contiguous to these Gomer compounds. There were holes to be sure, since Gomers seemed to love their holes, but if it was above ground, it was now destroyed or taken out of play. Our ASOC teams and more daylight aerial reconnaissance confirmed the damage as significant.

The reaction to this strike was for the Gomers to send in more assets, which we took great pains to destroy prior to them entering the atmosphere. The more they pushed, the more we took advantage of the weather and daylight to destroy. A similar strike was conducted on the base for the Gomers' Battleship Class ships. Locating five of them in the open was enough for one ASOC team to call in all the tactical assets they could find. In this case, it wasn't just the Air Force, but even assets from the Navy that were able to get some ordinance on target. In a strike that was extremely well coordinated by the ASOC teams, the Gomers either lost or had severely damaged all five of those capital ships. As we continued reducing their strength in their Gomer Areas, we also were putting together the finishing touches for our ground offensive. In some respects, it was almost going too well, while in others the getting there was more than half the battle. The terrain was the worst enemy, and so the initial striking force would have to be more about the Infantry, and a lot less about the Armor and other support.

This time the plan called for our newest Airborne Corps, the IX Airborne Corps, with the 11th, 13th, and 108th Airborne Divisions, to lead the way into the heart of Gomer controlled territory. Still, before this could take place, our Marines and other Army elements had to invade and control the coastal areas on Kamchatka Peninsula. Then we could take control of the terrain that would allow us to move our Armor and Mechanized Infantry into place for the more rapid advance into "bandit" country. As a result, the first strike of the Pacific Campaign was now on the shoulders of General Davis, of the

42nd Army Group, and specifically on Lieutenant General Manuel "Manny" Ortiz, USA, commanding the Sixth Army.

Moving back to my earlier Memorandum to my planners about how this would have to work, we were now on that paragraph that required us to get our forces safely into the Siberian area, built up, supplied, and ready to move into the heart of the Gomers' several enclaves. Everything else on our check list was completed, up to and including the Chinese and Japanese Forces, who were now securing the southern end of the Siberian Box. Even the Russian Field Armies were in play, and their mission was to also work the southern end of the Siberian Box ahead of the Chinese forces. The thought was to put on the "squeeze play" so that the kill zone for the Gomers would keep getting smaller, at least until we could wipe them out from the key three sides. Thanks to the ice and space variables, that fourth side and overhead were far more problematic; however, we now had the ability to extend air power into the region, along with some naval assets, to at least deny the Gomers certain key avenues of approach for resupply. Kamchatka was the key to our Pacific planning, for the same reason that Murmansk and Archangel were key to the Atlantic portion of the Campaign. We had to have the physical presence that would permit us to get our proverbial "stuff together" before starting the fight. We also needed a point directly underneath the most common Gomer flight path from space to the region. Kamchatka was just the right spot, and it would be here that we would build up our forces.

As these elements were finally coming together, apparently so were some other great pieces of information. It seems that Dr. Marvin was finally having something of a breakthrough in the THz communications area, and he felt it was significant enough to ask that

I get back to my rear headquarters to be briefed on the subject. This summons was somewhat fortuitous in timing, since I was already in the process of preparing to shift my key staff to our Pacific Forward Headquarters. I had made the decision early in the planning process that this shift would be necessary, mainly because most of the exposed offensive would be coming from the Pacific side. This was for several reasons, but the main one for me was the flight path taken by the Gomers as they entered earth's atmosphere. As we started the offensive we would be vulnerable on two levels, given the twilight line, and I felt that my presence on this side of the campaign would be more critical to the strategy and to the forces facing this type of advance. Once past Kamchatka, our soldiers would be fighting across Siberia, with the Gomers potentially coming at them from both forward and to the rear. This was a lot to ask, and I wasn't about to let them down by sitting on my ass on the 'safer' side of the battle. We would use the daylight to our advantage, but in this corner of the world, that was a pretty small operational window.

Airspace above the Atlantic nearing Canada:

We had lifted off at dawn. With the bulk of my staff following in a C-17, the VIP aircraft was hauling it to keep in the daylight, just in case. The plan was to get me back to my rear headquarters to meet with my scientists. We were almost to the coast of Nova Scotia, along the northern route, when the oil pressure light on the "master caution" panel went off. It didn't take long before the starboard engine flamed out, and the power loss reduced the flight characteristics considerably. Calling it in to the Air Traffic personnel as an emergency, we were on short final into a small airfield when the other engine began to sputter and then flame out about a quarter mile from the runway. It was a long glide, and as luck would have it, we were just short of the runway when the aircraft bellied into the ground at around 120 knots. The ride was damn sure "E-Ticket" and the impact was tremendous. As the starboard wing sheared off on a runway marker, we went through a fence and came to rest inverted near another border fence line that was off to the right of the main runway.

I only know this because when I regained consciousness, I was in the grass near the now burning airplane with Captain Alexander Dubronin standing over me. There is little doubt in my mind that he saved me by dragging me out of the wreckage before the fire completely consumed it. Sadly, he and I were the only survivors. I'd lost Captain Bowen, USN, and my new Chief of the Allied Staff, General Anthony Stephenson, USAF. Captain Dubronin and I were both burned, not horribly, but we each had second degree burns on our arms and legs. The rest of the passengers and crew either died on impact or in the post-crash fire. Either way, my trip to the Pacific was now going to be delayed, as would my briefing from Dr. Marvin and Dr. Clarkson.

The local Crash Crew found us, and we were taken to a nearby civilian hospital. I was still in and out of consciousness, and the fact that Dubronin was not your normal "English" speaking individual, it took a little while before the local authorities figured out, or finally understood, who or what we were. In the meantime, the C-17 landed at Andrews and was preparing for the next leg of their journey, when they realized that we had not arrived. My staff went nuts, delayed their flight, and spent the next 24 hours trying to find us and then get us home. I do know that the first 24 hours while they were rounding us up was probably the worst 24 hours of my wife's life. When we finally got back home, despite being sore as hell and with a couple of broken ribs to go with the burnt legs, my wife put me in a bear hug that still makes me wince to think of it. It hurt like hell on one level, but on the whole, I still wouldn't trade that hug for all the gold on the planet.

As a result of the crash, I was forced to find a new Chief of Staff, and I picked my former G-3 from the first war, Lieutenant General T. James Roberts. His first official act was to gather the staff and get them going to set up operations at our Pacific Headquarters. I'd made the decision that I would head out after a little time to recuperate, but in the meantime, they were to hold off on nothing. General Richardson and General Whitney would call the shots in their areas, and if anything came up, I'd be reachable through the War Room using the rear staff headed by General Clark. This would be a really crappy way to start a campaign, but it was my intention that it would still start on time. As for me, I knew it hurt enough that a few weeks to shake off the crash would be necessary, and I knew that Captain Dubronin wasn't complaining, either.

Supreme Allied Headquarters, (SAHQ-Rear):

On the morning of the fifth day after the accident, I finally felt good enough to stagger into the War Room to get updated on the daily events. After being in the room and turning a lovely shade of green in the process, I was approached by the Communications Officer with three messages. The first was that the President wanted to talk to me as soon as I was able to manage it. The second was from the Russian President, who was wishing me well and thanking me for making sure that the message from his son, saying he was okay, was given such a high priority. The third was from Dr. Marvin and Dr. Clarkson, who were chomping at the bit to get me briefed on their latest findings. I decided to take these one at a time and thought the President probably should have a slightly higher priority. With that in mind, I handed the list back to the Communications Officer and told him to get the boss on the line.

"GENERAL, are you alright?"

"Yessir, Mr. President. I'll survive."

"How bad is it, not that asking you will ever get me a straight answer."

"Sir, I'm in a lot better shape than most everyone else on the plane, and if Captain Dubronin wasn't there to drag my ass out, you'd be shopping for a new Commander to stick into this job."

"Yeah, I've read the reports from the local fire captain, who said that 'the Rushkie probably saved your ass.' He was also kind enough to point out that he never thought he would live to see the day that such a thing would happen."

"Honestly, I'm not sure I would have thought it possible, either."

"Well, I'm going to decorate him with a Legion of Merit, Purple Heart, and a damned Soldier's Medal. Any objections?"

"No, sir. No objections at all, and I'm glad you're going to do it, since it would look like clear favoritism if I did it."

"Not at all, just because it was your ass doesn't mean favoritism!"

"Thank you, sir. I appreciate you looking out for him."

"Not a problem. Now on to official business. Just WHAT THE HELL were you thinking by being out there in Gomer Country in the first place? I keep hearing about these forward headquarters of yours, and I'm genuinely wondering what you are smoking. General Marshal kept his ass in Washington for most of that war, so why does your getting close to the gun powder matter in this one?"

"Damn, Sir. You're an officer, or were, so you should know exactly why I'm out there. I've got to lead from the front once in a while. Hell, Patton understood the concept. He said that he always drove to the front, and then flew back, so that the troops would NEVER see him going towards the rear. General Wainwright did the same thing on Bataan, in a big old red Packard convertible, just so his boys would see him to bolster their morale."

"That is why you have Generals like Davis and Larkin. Let them get their asses out there for the troops. You're not a damn spring chicken, and neither am I. Do you see my ass at the front? I've been there before, so it isn't fear, it is just getting in the way."

"Sir, with all due respect, it wasn't me pestering the hell out of a division commander outside New Washington a few months ago."

"Exactly, and in fact, if I recall correctly, a certain Sergeant Major we both know reminded me that old guys should be someplace else.

He said it was bad enough that they had to deal with the Gomers, without having to look after the 'boss of bosses', too."

"Sir, are you ordering me to stay here and run the war?"

"Dammit! Mike, do you have to make this official?"

"Well, sir, we both know that if I have to sit on my ass here, then I won't feel like I'm doing my job. So, yeah, if you're going to tell me to stay here, then I would prefer it be stated in a rather public order."

"Now you know I can't do that, but one thing I can do!"

"Yessir, what's that?"

"I can tell your doctor to not mark you fit for travel OCONUS."

"You would, too, wouldn't you!"

"Yes, I would, which means you might as well plan on hanging around a little longer."

"Mr. President. I can appreciate your concern, but really, you know damn well I need to be out there."

"Mike, I only know that right now I want you here, and here is where you'll stay. At least for the next few weeks. Now get your ass back to your quarters, and let your staff run this war. The invasion is a few days out anyway, so go!"

"Yessir, I'll take that under advisement."

"Advisement, my ass. GO TO YOUR DAMNED QUARTERS!"

"Yessir." With that the President hung up the phone, and I continued to feel like real crap through a strainer. I started to get up to do what the President asked, not because I was in the mood to follow orders, but because I was hurting that badly. Before I even got to my feet, the Communications Officer approached and told me that Dr. Marvin and Dr. Clarkson were literally foaming at the mouth to get to me. Knowing that Dr. Clarkson usually only got demonstrative when there was something big going on, I decided to sit back down to hear what they had to say. I'm damn glad I did, because what was coming was probably a turning point in our war.

"Doctor Clarkson, I feel like hell, so can I at least get the Readers' Digest version?"

"Yessir, we've broken a part of their code, figured out how to jam, and better yet, we have a new weapon idea that could save a lot of lives."

"Jesus, that was a short version alright! Okay, can we take that one at a time?"

"General, the code is wild, and operates in the Terahertz band. We figured out that they speak or communicate at the UHF/VHF frequency levels."

"Yeah, I read your paper about that, and I know you were trying to use that information to get patterns, so what have you found?"

"Well, sir, they are speaking at the lower frequency levels, and then transmitting that at the Terahertz levels."

"Sort of like using a radio signal to send another radio signal?"

"Yessir, something like that, and in fact, that is how we were able to actually start trying some rudimentary communications with them. We also discovered that among the prisoners, they had almost a chain of command, with some Gomers clearly in charge of other Gomers."

"We've suspected that since the first war. It was clear to all of us that they were communicating various orders and formation changes. So, that isn't new."

"NO, this is new, because now we have identified and isolated a few of these leaders."

"Okay, go on."

"Well, we now can at least come up with a base set of words and damned if it doesn't sound like some of the Inuit stuff we heard before from General Greene's guys."

"You are kidding me. Really? Inuit?"

"Yessir, in a modified form, but it had the same patterns. Doctor Marvin got a linguist in from a university in Canada, who knows both the Inuit and some other Native American languages. These Gomers are speaking essentially a rather ancient form of the same thing!"

"I'll be damned. What have you learned?"

"We aren't sure yet about being able to communicate on any diplomatic level, but we have been able to expand our knowledge a little about them."

"Like what?"

"We know now how they eat, how they sleep, what they do for speech and communications, which I guess is a good start."

"Okay, will we see this information in a report we can disseminate?"

"Yessir. Of course, the real things we've learned are how to disrupt or jam their signals, and while we were developing that equipment, we discovered the idea which should save a lot of our boys' lives."

"I'm listening."

"Okay, you remember the old HARM type missiles?"

"Sure, they were designed to follow a Radar beam back to the target. We used them a lot in Viet Nam to take out Anti-Aircraft

Radar systems, which were being used to guide the bad guys' missiles towards our aircraft. They were anti-radiation...... I'll be damned! I get it! You have a way of tracking a missile back to the source of the damned Terahertz Transmission!"

"Yessir!"

"That, Doctor Clarkson, is a good day's work. Congratulations, you have just found another Eureka moment!"

"Thank you, sir, and we've also found a stockpile of these missiles that we can modify to incorporate Sulphur technologies and Lead coatings."

"Okay, how long before they are ready, how many, and what will be their ranges?"

"Sir, I've been going through this with both General McDaniel and General Thayer, and we think we can reach out and touch them from several thousand miles away, and in some instances, maybe even to the Moon."

"How long?"

"Give us three weeks."

"Doctor, we don't have three weeks, we start our combined front operation in less than two days."

"Sir, we would strongly recommend that you let us put together this package for you, since we honestly believe it will save a ton of lives."

"Crap! Gentlemen, we're on a time table because of the weather. If we roll your dice, then it would be almost another 9 months before we could start the operation if it didn't work. We also don't know if your new weapons would get us where we would need to be with the Gomers, so if it doesn't work totally and completely, we've got to worry about how much the Gomers can do to settle in before we can dig them out."

"Yessir, we know the dilemma, but we still believe that this way will get the job done, at least enough to maybe get them talking."

"Doctor Clarkson, Doctor Marvin, hang on a minute." With that, I waved the Communications Officer over to me, and told him to, "Contact the Senior Staff at Dutch Harbor, and tell them to mount up and get their asses here ASAP. Once you've done that, tell Generals Davis and Larkin to delay operations for ..... 72 hours. Then tell Generals Whitney and Richardson they are to proceed to this headquarters, fastest transportation. Finally, using the respective time tables for their arrivals, please set up a conference with the President, Doctors Clarkson and Marvin, General Whitney, General Richardson, and me either here or in New Washington at the convenience of the President." Turning back to Dr. Clarkson, I just nodded my head, and told him, "Well, Doctor, you've got at least 24 hours to get your 'dog and pony' show up and running, and about 72 hours to convince everyone, specifically the President, that we should hold off on the operation."

"Yessir." With those words, both Dr. Clarkson and Dr. Marvin almost ran from the War Room. When I looked back at the Communications Section, the Officer in Charge was burning up the ELF/VLF airways. As a wave of nausea crested over me, I told my Aide, Major Fellers, USAF, to get me if anything came up besides my lunch. Fighting the pain, I staggered back to my Quarters, and landed hard for some much needed sleep. Whether it was the pain killers or the fact that I was hoping that we'd found a major breakthrough, I slept deeply and longer than I had since the Gomers first arrived near the Moon.

CHAPTER XI

Supreme Allied Headquarters (SAHQ -Rear):

I wasn't really feeling much better, but there were some things you just had to fight through, and the pain was one of them. The burns on my legs had not become infected, but it was apparently a near thing. Either way, between the ribs and having to walk on a cane, I was pretty miserable. The President, fully aware of my condition, opted to have the meeting of the minds in our facilities. When I entered the Conference Room, the key players were all present. General Richardson, General Whitney, and General Roberts were present, and when I came into the room, they all sprang up either out of respect, or more likely, to try and help 'the old guy' to his seat. Within minutes of my arrival, the President came bounding into the room with his entourage. We greeted one another like old friends, and Doctor Clarkson took the podium. Going through his slide presentation, it was clear that our eggheads had started at least the rudimentary communications process with the Gomers. Each slide and short film clip gave everyone in the room something to ponder.

Dr. Marvin then entered the room with a young Lieutenant and two Military Policemen, who were standing on either side of a 'smart' Gomer wearing what looked like a Haz-mat Suit. This wasn't something I expected, but it was damned effective. The hush over the room, and the reaction of the Secret Service was pretty priceless. Clearly, Dr. Marvin and Dr. Clarkson were opting for the highly dramatic, and it certainly had an impact on those of us in the audience. Dr. Marvin began his dissertation with a brief introduction about why the Gomer was in the suit for his own protection from the Sulphur content in the stone around us. He then asked the young Lieutenant to step forward. Handing him a small hand-held VHF radio, the Lieutenant, who'd been introduced as an Inuit commander of an ASOC team, Lieutenant Nathan Shiwak, Canadian Armed Forces, began to transmit over the radio. At the conclusion of his sentence in the Inuit Language, the most incredible thing took place. The Gomer reacted, and the small hand-held radio began to emit a response from the Gomer to the Lieutenant. Turning towards the audience, Lieutenant Shiwak translated the message. The Gomer had introduced himself as a Commander Algatok.

The shock of what we'd just seen went around the room. It was even more shocking to note that the Gomer was actually communicating, and understood enough to bow his head. The President's jaw was literally headed to his lap. I asked the Lieutenant, "Son, how much are you able to really translate and communicate with the Commander?"

"Sir, they don't have rank like we do exactly, but Commander sounded to be the comparable position from his wording of things. He says that he was actually a captain of one of their Transports that we knocked down in the Davis Straits."

"Again, Lieutenant, how much of his vocabulary do we understand, and vice versa?"

"Sir. I am guessing that he is getting about every third word that I'm saying. He is speaking a twist of our language, but some of it is using words that are spoken in other places." Dr. Marvin broke into the answer and added. "According to our linguist experts, the language they are speaking includes elements of Ancient Inuit, Norse, and Hebrew. So, Lieutenant Shiwak is only able to get parts of it. We're working on trying to develop software that will allow for better communications. This prisoner, Commander Algatok, is one of the leaders we segregated from the others, and he has been more than cooperative in our efforts to try and find the common ground for communications."

"At any point, gentlemen, has Commander Algatok said why they are here on this planet?"

"Not yet." With this exchange the President appeared to regain his composure, and said, "Okay, if we can communicate with this one, is there any hope for diplomacy?"

Doctor Marvin looked at Dr. Clarkson, and it was quite clear that this was the question they had hoped to get from somebody at our briefing. Dr. Clarkson took up the reins, and said, "Mr. President. That is precisely what we think. The Commander here is quite reasonable, and we've never seen any threatening behaviors from him or any of the other captured Gomers."

The last statement got both General Whitney and General Richardson talking at once. In essence, they made it quite clear that they were questioning the amount of intoxicants that both Dr. Marvin and Dr. Clarkson had perhaps ingested prior to the briefing. I myself was beginning to wonder, but before things got out of hand, I asked, "Dr. Marvin, how do you explain their actions in Tierra del

Fuego, Greenland, and now all over Siberia, if they are reasonable and non-threatening?"

"Sir, they defended what they occupied ...."

"Bullshit! Doctor, they invaded before they occupied. They took out our leadership in a pretty cold and calculated way. Do you recall the James River? The slash and burn tactics? The raid on California? I mean do I really need to go on about their behavior this time around?"

"No, sir......"

The President was pondering the entire exchange and looked at me with that 'what do you think' look. I shrugged, and the President finally spoke up. "Doctors, he might seem to be reasonable and non-threatening now, but wasn't that after we'd taken them prisoner?"

"Yessir."

"Have either of you read much history?"

"Sir?"

"Yeah, history. Are either of you aware of how the Japanese acted when we took the few prisoners we did in the Pacific campaigns of World War II?"

"Well, yessir, I mean, well.... not really sir."

"Gentlemen, let me just say that they were cooperative, reasonable, and very compliant. I can also tell you that they sure as hell weren't cooperative, reasonable, or compliant before having their asses handed to them. Until then, they fought like tigers, and to the death where possible. Now doesn't that sound like what you've seen?"

"Yessir, but that still doesn't mean we can't use diplomacy to talk to them about peace."

"PEACE? For what? So they come down here, invade, and exterminate us? Again, history! Peace was the Japanese term for what they did starting in like 1931 and leading up to December 7th. Their definition of Peace and our definition didn't go together worth a damn then, and it won't match now."

"Mr. President, if we....."

"NO! This was interesting as hell, and I want you to have all the support you can get to communicate with these guys, but I'm not going to rely on some wild ass chance that we might someday be able to speak to these assholes. We can't have them raiding around sucking people's energy and terminating mankind, no matter what Goddamned language they're speaking."

Sensing that they were about to completely lose credibility, Dr. Clarkson nodded, and the MP escort and Lieutenant Shiwak departed with the Gomer Commander. Taking back the podium, Dr. Clarkson began the rest of the presentation which, honestly, is why I wanted to have the meeting. They were showing us a more strategic solution to the Gomer problem, and their version of the old HARM missiles was captivating. At the close of their presentation, a long discussion amongst the policy makers was about to begin. As we started to get down to cases, I asked the President if we could include two more people, and he readily agreed. Captain Dubronin was ushered in, along with our Russian Liaison Officer, Brigadier General Vladimir Karnaukhov, of the Russian Federation Army Ground Forces. I wanted them included for a couple of reasons, one was that we were discussing the offensive timetable that was to take place on their territory, and the other was to ferret out the attempted assassin. I already knew in my heart who it was, but the President wanted to see for himself, and it was important that we find the traitor before it was too late.

Several days prior, when the President was making it clear that I wasn't to leave CONUS again, he knew something I didn't know. The VIP airplane that was flying me back to CONUS had been sabotaged on the ramp at the airfield in Romania. The tampering had taken place before a flight that only my key staff knew about in advance. It had also come as a last minute sloppy attempt to take out the fuel and oil lines with an abrasive that would hopefully eat through those lines while we were well out over the ocean. In other words, it was a deliberate attempt to assassinate me. Intelligence and aviation experts were culling through the wreckage in Nova Scotia, almost before I was home at my rear Headquarters. They spotted the evidence within hours, and once the cause had been determined, the President was involved personally in the investigation. He not only knew what had happened, but he also had a very good idea about who was behind it. He narrowed it down to two main suspects. The Russian Federation or the Russian Dissidents.

The President's theory that it was the Russian Federation was pretty convoluted, but the case against the Dissidents was building rapidly. They had a definite motive, since it was my personally reaching out to Yuri Dubronin that had cut them out of the loop. Besides, no matter how many times I ran the various scenarios, I just couldn't see Yuri killing his own son to get at me. Our history alone kept me from thinking this was an option, otherwise, why did he save me from the crash? Then there was the obvious point that Yuri really doted on his only son, and would never consider using him as a weapon. No, the motive and opportunity were definitely on the side of the dissidents. The last piece of the puzzle came when we found evidence that General Karnaukhov was tied through a woman to the dissident faction. I would have suspected him immediately anyway, since he was the SOB liaison officer I had unceremoniously sent back to the Russians when we had our little confrontation during the last Gomer War. He had also been a disciple of that traitorous General Zhukov, who almost blew up the planet during that first war. Nope, I never did like the bastard, but then again, in the world of espionage that might make him as clean as a whistle. Now the President had a plan to find out for sure who was responsible, and acting on behalf of someone else. Now we would watch and see who screamed the loudest against delaying the attacks into Siberia, and who would think we should keep out for a little while longer. Then we would watch who went running to tell what he learned, and to whom he was telling it.

General Karnaukhov was the last one to enter the room, and with him in place, the President opened the discussion. In essence, the options were to begin the ground strike into Siberia along the lines of the original time table, or to put the ground campaign on hold, while we attempted to utilize the new technology to strike the Gomers. This latter option would extend the potential start date of the ground campaign for up to 9 months thanks to the weather, but it did hold the promise of lowering our potential casualties. This promise for lower casualties was just that, a promise, since during that 9 month delay, it gave the Gomers more time to consolidate and improve their positions. It also gave the Gomers the same time frame to resupply and/or make a move that could shift the offensive back to them. Not easy choices, but as the reaction and consensus around the room was taken, there was only one person who was vehemently asking for the delay. Even Dr. Clarkson and Dr. Marvin were not ready to say that the 9 months could lead to better results. Instead, General Karnaukhov was the only individual that argued that waiting was a good thing. When I glanced at Captain Dubronin, it was clear that he was seething. Not just at the idea of the delay to retake the land for his people, but at General Karnaukhov, who was too ready to allow his people to continue to be killed on a nightly basis in the more open parts of Russia. When we took a short break, General Karnaukhov asked for some time to consult with his government.

Captain Dubronin came to me during the break and made it clear that something was wrong with Karnaukhov. "General, this man is not looking after best interests of Russia!"

"Captain, is that just your bias in favor of Russia talking, or do you know something?"

"Sir. I am loyal to Russia, and to Russia's people. Karnaukhov is not. This is not some bid to buy time to keep soldiers from being harmed, he is looking after Karnaukhov."

"Alexander, what are you not telling me?"

"Sir. I believe Karnaukhov is traitor to our people. He is too quick to, as you would say, throw my country under bus."

"Well....." I was just starting to reply when a Secret Service agent came in to the room, along with my chief Criminal Investigation Division Commander. They approached the President and myself, and simply nodded. I excused myself from Captain Dubronin and said, "Captain, don't worry, I think this is going to work itself out rather quickly."

General Karnaukhov returned to the room, and started to speak when the President cut him off. "General Karnaukhov, I have just been advised that you did consult with someone, but it wasn't YOUR government."

"What? I speak with Government."

"Really? You spoke with President Yuri Dubronin?"

"Uh, no sir. I speak with his advisor."

"BULLSHIT! General, you spoke with Andre Stefinski, who we both know is the leader of the GODDAMN dissidents!"

"Da, he is advisor, and the real head of Russian Government!"

"You Bastard!" The room was silent as a tomb, when the President turned to the head of the Secret Service detail and simply pointed. It was then that I spoke up, "Captain Dubronin, you will advise your government that we have General Karnaukhov in custody and under arrest. You will then tell them why we have him in custody and under arrest. Finally, you will ask them what they would like us to do with him." The young Captain nodded his head, and left the room. The call was monitored, but it was directly to his father, President Yuri Dubronin. When he returned, we already knew the instructions from his father, and it was just about what we expected. We were to hold the General under arrest, until the Russian government could arrange for his transport back to Moscow.

Knowing how the Russian system worked, I had a feeling that General Karnaukhov was not going to have a pleasant journey or a happy arrival. It didn't take long, and the following day, a flight arrived from Moscow with a crew of two, and four security men to pick up the General. After verifying their credentials, it was clear that these men were handpicked by President Dubronin, and it was their job to make sure that the traitor was handled properly. Two days later, when the aircraft landed in Moscow, it contained precisely two pilots, and four security men. It seems that somewhere over the Atlantic, the aircraft encountered a problem that apparently forced them to jettison some excess weight. Again, knowing how these things worked, I wasn't the least bit surprised at the particular weight they chose to jettison.

Aside from ferreting out the ring leader, it was apparent that we'd need to find the other individuals that were working with Karnaukhov. I knew from experience, from seeing Karnaukhov in action, that there had to be at least one or more individuals working with him on our staff. I doubted seriously that he was the guy who actually put the acid on the lines of the aircraft. For one thing, he was too "important" to engage in getting his hands dirty, and for another, he would never have compromised his ability to obtain key information. As the investigation continued, Yuri Dubronin came up with the best solution. He rotated every single Russian on our staff, and replaced them with people who had been vetted carefully by his security forces. He knew that Karnaukhov had selected many of the people we had on board, so to keep it simple, he just replaced them all. This new group was superlative, and they made it a source of pride, indeed of National Pride, to do the best job they could do for us. There were no more incidents, nor were there any more discussions between our State Department and any of the known dissidents. The President made it a point of OUR National Pride that where possible, we would not only cut them off, but would be more than happy to pass their identities on to the actual Russian Government whenever possible. Our President took this entire incident personally and so did I. The men I lost on that flight were all men I trusted and cared about on both a professional and personal level. Frankly, I was glad that the Russian Aircraft had to jettison some weight, and my only regret was that I wasn't there to personally open the damn door.

Dutch Harbor, Alaska:

"General, why are we baby-sitting this mountain? All we've done since the damn Gomers showed up is baby-sit fucking mountains!"

"Sergeant Major, that mountain is where the Supreme Headquarters is set up, and ours is not to reason why. Right, Lieutenant?"

"Yessir! Although, I'm kind of with the Sergeant Major on this one. When the hell do we get to kill Gomers?"

"When General Patrick and General Richardson decide, and not one minute before! Understood!" With that, both Lieutenant Patrick and Command Sergeant Major Clagmore nodded their heads.

The Sergeant Major looked up at the sky at the falling snow and simply said, "To think, I USED to like that damn crab fishing show. Now I wouldn't hit a bull in the ass with this damned place."

Chuckling, the Lieutenant just said, "Yeah, my Dad used to watch that all the time too. What is it with you old guys?"

"Lieutenant, you are cordially invited to kiss my ass! Don't you have some dog robbing to do for the General?"

"Yes, Sergeant Major, I do. I was told to keep you out of trouble."

"BULLSHIT, son, you couldn't keep a petrified mouse turd from getting into trouble."

"Sergeant Major, I've got a question I've been meaning to ask you."

"Yes, Loo'tenant."

"Just where and how do you know my Dad?"

"L-T, that is so damned classified that by the time I could tell you, it would be about 15 years AFTER he and I are both dead."

"Sergeant Major, why did I know you'd say that?" The Sergeant Major just smiled, and headed off to find a Regimental Sergeant Major to gnaw on about the defensive placement of the Gomer Gun Batteries assigned to the perimeter. The Lieutenant turned in time to watch a C-17 head into the airfield. What he didn't know was that it was the aircraft carrying General Richardson and members of his key Staff back into the Theater. The big show was long in starting, but the pieces were now starting to move into place.

Supreme Allied Headquarters, (SAHQ - Rear):

The options discussed earlier were now being pushed together into a new strategy. We would begin consolidation of our positions in Siberia on the Pacific side, and start pushing until we had gone as far as we could based on the weather and terrain, with the purpose of establishing a Pacific boundary for the target or the more accurately called "Kill Box." This wasn't what we wanted, but time, weather, logistics, and those things that seem to always jump up were working to slow things down. Knowing this, we opted to make it a process of building that box and then, using the HARM-based Sulphur technology, we were going to keep the pressure up on the Gomers. We also were going to be using the terrain in the Pacific to get some larger variants of the Gomer Guns constructed, with the singular intent to harass or deny airspace to the Gomers as they entered the atmosphere over the far eastern portions of Russia. With this change in strategy, we knew we were going to be faced with a much longer war but once we'd made the call, there was some relief to know that by hitting them hard and often from a distance, we just might be able to keep things under our control.

Within 24 hours of the decision to move forward, the Marines who were getting well established on Kamchatka, and our other forces that were staged within the area, were pouring northward and then westward. Their mission was to occupy various mountain ranges and to begin setting up the Gomer Gun Regiments that were to deny the Gomers the use of key airspace entering into their Siberian enclaves. Unlike past wars, where we literally had to fight our way onto each mountain, here these key terrain features were completely undefended. It was a matter of using daylight and stealth to achieve our key objectives. Within two weeks, we had Gomer Gun Regiments set up from the East Siberian Sea to the Cherskiy Mountains, and then westward to the Verkhoyansk Mountains. These units had the single mission of denying air space and they employed a number of rather local, but innovative, techniques. My favorite was the use of small trains to move the Gomer Guns along rail lines, from tunnel to tunnel, which would employ the classic 'shoot and scoot' to hit targets, and then move rapidly to a new location. In other locations, self-propelled Gomer Gun units would move from the woods and their defilade positions, where they would fire and return to their hidden positions. These latter units would often have a number of primary and then multiple secondary firing positions to go along with their "hide" positions where they would recharge their weapons and take care of their more basic needs.

The XVIII Airborne Corps and IX Airborne Corps assets were withdrawn from both front lines and placed in reserve still in their respective front areas. Both of these Corps intensified their training, since they would be the primary assault troops on the actual Gomer enclaves during the next spring. For now, they would wait, train, and keep the rear areas secure. The Armored and Mechanized units were finally coming into play on both fronts, where they were providing both security for the forward Gomer Gun Regiments and moving to positions where they too could advance come spring. At the end of the Siberian Summer, we had in place approximately 90% of our ground strike force, and it ran from the East Siberian Sea, in a circle around the Gomers, to our western positions near the Ural Mountains. The Pacific Forces were as far west as Krasnojarsk, Russia, where their line met with the Atlantic Forces, who had extended from the Ural Mountains to the east. In both cases, the forces were at or in the closest mountain range to winterize, prepare for the next phase of the campaign, and to harass the enemy whenever possible.

As for ASOC, they weren't just sitting around. Their teams were as far forward to the Gomers as possible, with their primary positions located in the mountains near Noril'sk, Russia. Thanks to the Special Operations forces now included from the Russian Federation, a number of the Gomer Enclaves were under almost constant observation, evaluation, mapping, and, on occasion, harassing fire from either the Navy or the Air Forces. Once we were in place, we began the systematic process of keeping these forces under cover, fed, clothed, and still training as necessary. We weren't happy about the delay, but after the monumental task of getting them all into position for their final attacks, it was clear the delay was the smart thing, and it gave our future assault forces the time they needed to be fully prepared.

Mother Nature also never rests. Summer was turning to fall and along with the coming of bitter cold, ice, snow, bad weather, and the occasional earthquake, we were also faced with several volcanic eruptions that further delayed our advances throughout the Siberian Region. On one hand, the spewing forth of Sulphur gases kept the Gomers far away, but on the other, the loss of rail lines or the use of air space would sometimes set back a timetable or a movement for weeks. When you're trying to get this much material into position, these types of headaches could be huge. General Clark and most of his staff were beyond exhausted. They had kept the supply lines moving over the entire globe, and they were doing it while being handed different and, in some instances, completely conflicting priorities. This herculean effort was taking its toll, and I finally had to force General Clark to turn things over to his deputy and take a break. The notion that things were going to be delayed, even slightly, was about to force him into a heart attack. I guess, like me while recovering from the airplane crash, there just comes a point where a rest is mandated. When I brought him in and told him he was taking 30 days leave, he wasn't happy about it. After a very long and somewhat heated discussion, he finally got the same message the President had tried giving to me. Let your deputies run things, and get a fresh perspective. As I was recovering, I was making General Clark take a breather with me.

General Thayer, as head of the USAF, assumed the Allied Air Force duties for this phase of our operation. In conjunction with his counterparts around the world, they planned a winter Air Campaign that was designed to put as many of the HARM, Sulphur Isotope 35 and 38 Weapons, and conventional Sulphur ordinance on target as possible. These experts also were putting into place a great grid system and target identification system that would allow for faster calls for air support from our ground forces. There were few places within the Gomer Enclaves in Siberia that were not already pre-strike identified, with ordinance selection and targeting data available for both the end users and the flight personnel. Coordination with ground air support, such as our Army Aviation assets, was also completed, and the juggling of "incorporating foreign assets" into the mix was monumental. It was the accomplishment of these tasks, and a real credit to General Thayer, that it was done seamlessly on both major fronts.

While we were getting people in place around Siberia, and General Thayer was putting together one of the best air campaign packages known to man, the Navy wasn't just sitting on their backsides either. Working with the Air Forces, the Naval Aviation packages and gun packages were being pieced together. The strategic submarine assets were already in play, working with ASOC, but now so were the surface units and various Battlegroups. Taking their lessons from the Murmansk and Archangel battles, these naval units were planning and operating as freely as the ice would let them. The entire Allied Naval effort operated with the goal of getting into the best positions to support the Gomer Gun Regiments that were working their way forward. When the ice made it more difficult to get our troops in the right places, every effort was made to get them in place, regardless of what service would normally carry the ball. There was no room for inter-service rivalry, and to everyone's credit, the outcome was a rounded multi-service effort without friction. For once, everyone was learning to speak the same language.

When the winter arrived, in all her vengeance, we were almost completely ready for our spring offensive. We were also ready to start the harassment campaign against the Gomers, as well as their bases and possible settlements. As each asset reported that it was ready to engage the Gomers, we marked their arrival at 100% by marking the position on our central map and verifying the proximity to either the Gomers themselves or their highly routine route system. It was now late October, and we were seeing a lot of green on our maps. As the last positions came up in mid-November, we knew that we would be ready to begin in earnest by the end of the month. Getting our Orders, Policies, and Directives out in the field, we made sure that each of our theater commanders was in constant contact with one another, to keep them as fully informed as possible. On December 1st, we unleashed the first salvo of HARM munitions at the Gomer communications system. The results were fantastic!

When a Gomer transmission began towards their Moon Ships or a resupply vessel, a HARM would be released from the aircraft that were orbiting, waiting for just such emissions. The command within the system would literally home in on the beam and track it back to the source. Within the first day, we estimated that the Gomers' communications centers were reduced to less than 15% effectiveness. The few that escaped damage or destruction seemed to be because the atmosphere would sometimes preclude us from getting a solid lock on the signal. These HARM munitions were also highly successful against any of the Gomers that were communicating with each other or with one of their command ships. Several Carrier Class ships were destroyed by HARM missiles, and at least one Battleship Class ship was destroyed in spectacular fashion as it was attempting to land near the largest of the Gomer bases. At least three separate HARM missiles, fired from three separate directions, homed in and exploded against the sides of the Battleship Class, sending it in pieces to the snow and ice below. The ASOC observers were somewhat surprised, since they'd spent several minutes in an attempt to bring a laser designator on target to guide in some naval munitions. They still didn't have it targeted when it simply exploded in front of them, thanks to the HARM ordinance.

The Gomers obviously knew that there was something new going on, and as a result, they tried to step up their flow of supplies and forces into Siberia. This time around though, it wasn't clear sailing for them. Instead, it was about to get down-right ugly. We were waiting for them with more than a few surprises of our own, and these surprises would involve almost every service, every nation, and be on every front. For the second time in our recorded history, we were going to take back the night.

CHAPTER XII

USS Alabama, near Pevek, Russia:

The USS Alabama was one of three main Battleship Battlegroups positioned around the Bering Sea, Bering Straits, and as far north as the permanent ice pack would allow them near Russia. She was perhaps one of the oldest of the Battleships drug out of retirement, refitted, and sent out to hunt Gomers. She had missed the First Gomer War only because she was still being readied from her prior role as a Museum Ship. She was equipped with her main 16" guns and had onboard two Gomer Gun Turrets, with one forward and one aft, near the stern. Her Captain was one of the few survivors of the old USS Iowa, after she was sunk in combat with the Gomers, and he had learned his lesson the hard way. He was no rookie, but many on his ship were, which gave him a great deal of consternation at times. It would not be much longer before he and his ship would have to head towards more suitable waters and away from the ice pack. It was turning to winter, and the weather was becoming anything but friendly. His counterparts in the USS Missouri and the USS New Jersey were being bounced around quite a bit by the weather further out to sea, and he knew that, with winter, it would be a very hard place to work.

The Captain was closely following the HARM strike information around the Gomer Areas in Siberia, and when he got the green light to fire on anything that came within range, he had mixed emotions. He wanted pay back for the USS Iowa, but at the same time, he was still a little gun shy about having been on the Iowa when she went down. Setting the appropriate condition around the ship, they waited and watched the sky. They were near Pevek, Russia, for the sole purpose of busting a cap into the Gomers who were using Pevek as a point of entry over the planet. Further out to sea was the USS Missouri who, like the USS Alabama, was preparing to take her best shots. The USS Missouri had the advantage of being in seas that would allow for more maneuvering, but she was also hamstrung by the great ranges to consider in firing into the targets, since the Gomers were much higher in their approach arc to enter Russian airspace over the USS Missouri's position. The USS Alabama, on the other hand, would be firing at virtually point blank range with not as much room to scoot after the shots. As the darkness or twilight line approached, so did the Gomers. The rest of the package lay to the west in the form of several railway mounted Gomer Guns that were all set to deny the Gomers the use of this entry corridor over Russia.

True to form, the Gomer fleet arrived within a few minutes of the darkness. There was a pretty large formation of Gomer Carrier Class ships with at least one Battleship Class ship as part of their convoy. As the Gomers began to flare into the atmosphere along the Arctic Circle line over the Bering Straits, the USS Missouri took advantage of her position and angle. As the large Battleship Class ship was transiting the area, the USS Missouri began her destruction of the Gomers' Battleship Class ship with her 16" guns. When two of the Carrier Class ships turned to launch their Fighter Class ships, the Gomer Guns on board were unleashed, destroying both of the larger Gomer ships before they could launch their fighters. Once she had fired on these last two targets, the USS Missouri did as tactics demanded. She disappeared as a hole in the water, traveling at flank speed in a perpendicular direction, she would then turn back towards the USS Alabama's position to render what support might be necessary if the latter ship needed help.

The remaining 12 Carrier Class Ships were now at or near Pevek, Russia, and almost directly overhead of the USS Alabama. As the last Gomer passed overhead, the USS Alabama began her "turkey shoot" tactics of firing on the nearest one from the rear. Since the Gomer fleet had been deprived of its truly big gun support, the real threat facing the USS Alabama would come from the Fighters. As the old ship continued to fire at each of the Carrier Class ships, she was doing her best to keep her fires restricted only to rear of the pack. As a result, her score wasn't nearly as impressive as it could have been, but it was definitely respectable. She had reduced the Gomers fleet by another 5 Carrier Class ships. When the remaining Gomer fleet reached the Railway Gomer Guns, about 100 miles west, the other 7 Gomers' Carriers were dispatched with great speed. On this night, there would be no supplies going in to, and very few communications coming out from, the Gomers enclaves in Northern Siberia. The few transmissions they attempted that night were met with another HARM strike, which I'm sure discouraged the Gomers from wanting to use their communications equipment.

Supreme Allied Headquarters, (SAHQ-Rear):

Our HARM missile strikes on the Gomers weren't the only battles being fought. I was locked into a huge battle with the President about my moving forward to my Pacific Headquarters at Dutch Harbor, Alaska. The more I pushed, the harder the President pushed back against me. My doctors were dragging their feet, and every single time I would jump through one of their hoops, they would pull another one out of their bag of tricks. With each passing day, especially as the HARM campaign was intensifying, I was feeling more and more fenced in. I honestly tried sneaking out once, only to be busted by some well-meaning medical officer at Vandenberg, AFB. It seems that he sent a message back to the rear just to let them know that since I was visiting, he would need a copy of my medical records. So much for sneaking out. Within an hour, the President was on the line chewing my ass for leaving my rear Headquarters. It was during this time that I learned of one more break-through in Gomer intelligence, and it came from a rather unlikely source. My daughter, Chris!

After my return from Vandenberg, AFB, I was in my quarters contemplating how I was going to make my next great escape attempt to the west. Sipping a scotch, perhaps the first one in some months, I was taking full advantage of what it would do when mixed with the pain killer. The fun thing about pain killers and scotch is that even though you might still hurt like hell, you just don't seem to much care about it. On this particular evening, I was just mad enough that I was taking solace from the fact that at least I was with my family. Gathering for a dinner, Chris took the lead in the discussion. "Dad! Did you know that Holly is working on an algorithm for Dr. Marvin's software?"

"No, I didn't know. So we'll be clear, what algorithm?"

"You know. The one for Dr. Marvin."

"Crud. You're just talking in circles."

"No, you know, the software that Dr. Marvin is developing for the Gomers' language."

"Dammit. Chris, that is classified four ways from Sunday, and certainly not subject for discussion at this dinner table."

"Dad. Look around! Everybody here has a clearance, okay, everybody except Michael, but then he is 6 years old, so what do you expect?"

"Well, that is enough not to open up about anything. Now we'll talk later."

Chris was not to be put off on the subject, and so she sent Michael out of the room to go play. Then she said, "Satisfied?"

"Okay. So, what the hell is so important about this right now? You just kicked out the only member of this family that truly understands me."

"Funny, Dad, very funny!"

"Holly. Tell Dad what you told me before we came over here."

Holly looked at her sister, and then back towards me. Never really all that bashful in most instances, Holly seemed to be a little reticent to say anything to me. This was not too far out of her character, since she'd always been more talkative around almost anyone except me. This was a phenomenon I never understood, but letting it go, I just looked at her and waved for her to tell me.

"Okay. Well, you see it is like this. I have been working on the algorithm that will allow us to complete the software for deciphering the Gomers' language."

"Go on."

"Well, we've done a model, based on the few sounds and words we've been able to pull out of their conversations. Dr. Marvin got me working on the math end of it, while Dana worked on the language end of it."

"Wait. Who the hell is Dana?"

"Oh, sorry. Dr. Cobb. He is the linguist they found out of Canada, and he knows his ancient languages."

"Okay, go on."

"Well, we did our first major test earlier today, and it worked."

"What do you mean, it worked?"

"Well, we were able to go beyond simple communications, like what Dr. Clarkson and Dr. Marvin did for the President at your brief...."

"WHOA! Now how in the hell do you know anything about that briefing?"

"Come on, Dad. I don't live under a rock. They worked on that presentation for weeks before you got back from Romania."

"Geez. Isn't anything sacred around here?" Leah spoke up on that one with a typical comment. "Nope! Mister, when you walk in here, there are no secrets or clearances, and you sure as hell don't wear any stars!"

"Thanks, Angel, I appreciate your input. Still, sometimes..."

"Oh, HUSH! I heard about it from Toni before you even got back to our quarters, and just who do you think keeps the President informed about your crazy attempts to sneak out under the cover of darkness?"

"YOU?!"

"Hell, yes, me! And Chris! And Holly! Trust me, we know more about you than you do, and if you think you're going forward while you're still on pain killers, then think again. You're lucky I poured you the damn scotch, which I would note for the record is about the weakest drink I've ever given you."

"Gee, thanks, honey. You're such a sweetie."

"Damn right I am, mister. I don't see how you can drink that nasty stuff anyway. Tastes like camel pee that somebody poured through a dirty sweat sock."

"Okay, screw this! I'm going back to work." As I started to stand, Leah pushed me back down, and said, "No, you're going to listen to what Chris and Holly are telling you."

"Okay then. Holly? Speak!"

"Geez, Dad, I'm not a dog." With that crack I started to get just a little pissed off, but I kept silent, and she continued. "Okay, we had a pretty major breakthrough today, and Dr. Marvin isn't going to say anything until he gets it approved by Dr. Clarkson, and confirmed by at least two more independent tests. That could take weeks, and Dana and I thought it was more important that you know about it sooner than later. Dad, we learned some things today that you're going to absolutely need to know."

"Like what?"

"Well, for one thing, these Gomers and the meaty ones from before aren't from the same planet."

"WHAT? You've got to be kidding me!"

"Nope, and those crab Gomers aren't from the same planet, either."

"Okay, from the top, and go slowly for the benefit of an old guy on pain killers and scotch. WHICH by the way, Honey, this one is about empty, and believe me, I think I'll need another one."

Leah gave me a dirty look, but she got up and started to pour me another one. This time she wasn't skimping on the scotch, and I knew that what I was about to hear was going to dictate that I have the damn drink. While Leah was getting the drink together, you could see the wheels turning in Holly's mind. She sat in silence for a few minutes, and then with perfect timing, the drink and the thoughts in Holly's mind arrived together.

"Okay, Dad. Here goes, and I'll try to take them in the apparent pecking order." Looking around, she was met with complete silence, so she continued. "The Smart Gomers we're facing, and the ones we've been talking to over the last few weeks, are from a planet known as Glavanna. The Meaty Gomers are from a neighboring planet, and right now I'm not sure as to the name exactly, but they are further down the evolutionary chain. Their planet is in the same solar system as Glavanna, and it could be named Tornatik, although there is some debate over the actual name. Anyway, the Dusty Gomers are actually the Tornatik or Meaty Gomers, who have well..... This is the creepy part, Dad, so stay with me. The Dusty Gomers used to be Meaty Gomers, but, thanks to the Crab Gomers, they have lost enough energy that now they are just basically charged electricity. They have shape, some substance, but because they are charged electricity, loud sounds make them just crumble."

"Okay, I knew that about the Dusty Gomers, but you're telling me that they used to be Meaty Gomers? How the hell does that work?"

"Crab Gomers."

"Crab Gomers?"

"Yessir. Seems that the Crab Gomers are from a third planet in that solar system, and they are advanced ahead of the Meaty Gomers from Tornatik, but not quite as advanced as those from Glavanna. They are from a planet that the Smart Gomers call Tornit, and they are evil as hell. The Smart Gomers hate them, because they are at war with one another."

"Say that again?"

"Yeah, the Smart Gomers and the Crab Gomers are at war. Seems that the Crab Gomers were enslaving the Meaty Gomers from Tornatik and using them for 'food' or 'energy' sources for their long space voyages."

"No kidding."

"OH, it gets worse. Once they are almost consumed, the Meaty Gomers will become the Dusty Gomer, at least until they are completely used up."

"Damn, that is sick as hell. No wonder your Mom didn't mind giving me this drink. So, is there anything else?"

"Well, it seems that the Smart Guys are at war because the Crab Guys are trying to enslave them, too. Apparently, the ships we've got upstairs are some of the last Smart Gomers, and they are here to build a new colony on Mars."

"On Mars? Then why are they screwing with us here?"

"We apparently attract Crab Gomers because we keep sending signals out into space, which is what drew all of them here in the first place. You remember seeing something on the Science Channel a few years ago about our SETI stuff?"

"Sure, we watched it together about two weeks before they showed up the first time."

"Yeah, well, that physicist you know, Stephen Hawking, was saying he was afraid it would attract the wrong kind of attention, and he was right. All our signals being sent out to space are precisely what the Crab Gomers hit on, and precisely why our corner of the Solar System is about to get damned crowded." With her saying "damned," Holly looked around and said, "Sorry, mom." Chris rolled her eyes and said, "Geez, Holly, you're old enough to say Damn! You're just sucking up now." Chris' comment finally broke the tension, but it was certainly mind-blowing to realize that we might not be getting a good handle on these Gomers after all. I looked at Holly and said, "You know I'm going to HAVE to confront Dr. Clarkson and Dr. Marvin about this, don't you?"

"Yessir. I knew you would when I told you, but Dana and I think you have to know, and the sooner you have this information the better."

"Well, Kiddo, I hope this doesn't cost you your PhD with Dr. Clarkson. I will try to keep it low key, but if push comes to shove, I'm going to have to poke it hard."

"I know, and frankly, Daddy, if this will keep us from killing the wrong folks, then it is worth the PhD. In fact, the other thing that everyone really needs to know is that the Crab Gomers were leading the charge the last time, and they will be back."

"Why did I know you'd say that to me?"

"Well, according to the Glavanna or Smart Gomers, the Crab Gomers only sent a recon mission with their first visit, and it is highly likely that next time they will return with a fleet that will at least double or triple the size of the fleet currently overhead of us."

"How do we know that we can trust the information you've just handed me?"

"Well, we don't know that for sure. I can tell you that the arrays they are building here and on Mars are in fact huge versions of their Gomer Defense weapons, but they are all aimed upwards. Does that help any?"

"CRAP!"

"Yessir, I think Crap just about covers it." I looked at Leah, Chris, and then Holly in turn, and felt like I had been punched. Now what do we do? We've been knocking their stuff down faster than they could put it up. Was that the best thing to be doing? How could we trust this information? More to the point, how do we verify this information, and then based on what we verify, what do we do about it? Does this breakthrough offer us a diplomatic solution? Nope, Dr. Clarkson would have to let this run its course, because it was the checks and balances that got this kind of information verified. Then again, how the hell do I sit on this waiting on the eggheads to go through some protocol? We just might be slitting our own throats, and losing a hell of a lot of good boys in the process. One of those good boys is my own son, and how would I even live with the fact that he might be lost based on a bad decision. Despite the pain killer and scotch, all of a sudden I had the headache from hell.

The following morning, I was up and headed to the War Room. My only thought was that 'today we have to deal with the questions arising from these translations.' On entering the War Room, I asked for the direct line to Dr. Clarkson, and when he answered, I just asked him if he had any breakthroughs we could exploit. His response was guarded, but he did tell me, "Sir. We have had one pretty major breakthrough, and we're in the process of confirming it."

"Oh, what's that?"

"Sir, I think we've broken through their language barrier, and if we can confirm the information from more than a few sources, we'll get you the read out within the next day."

"Excellent! Anything really useful?"

"Well, sir. If we're right, then you're going to want to get the President back, and we're going to need to discuss our earlier diplomatic theory."

"No kidding?"

"Sir. I appreciate you trying to protect your daughter, but I knew Holly would come to you, and honestly, I knew it before she knew it."

"Well, Doctor, you can appreciate that a Dad doesn't want his littlest one to lose out on her opportunity to study with one of the finest scholars and scientists of our time."

"General. Are you trying to pump me full of sunshine?"

"Doctor, you can bet your sweet ass I am. I don't want my baby to lose out here."

"She won't! Hell, without her, I'm not sure we would have cracked the code so quickly. I might even have to give her Mom a Doctorate too, since she was working with Holly and Dr. Cobb on the algorithms and helping her go through the languages and the math."

"I am surprised that Leah was helping. Not because she doesn't know her stuff, but because she's been so damn busy spying on me....."

"Sir?"

"Never mind, Doctor. Thanks, and I'll await your report then. Oh, before you go."

"Yes?"

"Holly was telling me quite a bit about the Gomers and she intimated that there are more of a particularly nasty type on the way.

The second you confirm that, or have a timetable on it, I'd really LOVE to hear from you."

"No problem, General. I think that is the part that we will be verifying first, since it has kept me awake since hearing about it myself."

"Thanks, Doctor."

Having this in the back of my mind, I then advised my two main Commanders in the field, Generals Whitney and Richardson, to keep our activities limited to HARM strikes only. We were to lie low, and wait for our next major terrain denial mission. In the meantime, I figured that keeping their communications cut off, at least for the time being, might be a good start for what could well be the next step in all of this. The following morning, I had my confirmation and some more answers. Within hours of confirming the information, we'd set up another briefing for the President, and this time it would be more about diplomacy than killing Gomers. The eggheads had finally fine-tuned their plan for communicating with the Gomers and, knowing a little more about their motives, we felt like we were finally on the verge of putting things in the proper perspective.

It was the next day before the President could come to the briefing, and given the highly classified nature of what he was about to hear and see, he came to us. This time in attendance was the President, the Secretary of State, Secretary of Defense, most of the key scientific staff, and from my staff, it was Admiral Lynch, Lieutenant General Roberts, and the various members of the Joint Chiefs of Staff. When Dr. Clarkson began the briefing, he started this time with footage of the initial language testing sequences, and then moved on to the communications between several Smart Gomers and various members of the science staff. Then he pulled out the interview conducted by Dr. Cobb and Holly, and as it unfolded, the entire room was completely silent. When the lights came up, Dr. Clarkson, utilizing various members of his staff, briefed what they knew and how they knew it. He was also careful to keep the presentation balanced by stating what was confirmed and what was speculation. Okay, speculation might be an overstatement, it was probably better described as a "Scientific Wild Ass Guess, or SWAG," but Dr. Clarkson was very up front about it. He added some things that even Holly hadn't told me. For example, all of the Gomers were from a Red Giant star that was long on radiation, but low on light. They were all in different orbits around that sun, but their orbit patterns gave their home planets about the same energy/radiation levels as what can be found on our Mars or maybe further out in our Solar System.

The show stopper was the entire dissertation from one of the prisoners about the evilness of the Tornit, or Crab Gomers. The description, as it filtered through the radio receiver, was in their language, but the apparent emotion seemed very real. Once it was translated, there was no question that those emotions were at least plausible, since they described both fear and courage, loss and sorrow, and an undying hatred for the Tornit. The other very significant bombshell? The briefing pointed out that because we had some commonalities in our ancient languages that made up the Gomer dialect, then one of two theories was possible. Either they'd been to our planet before at some point in our ancient past, or that we had some visitors that were common to both our world and theirs. In either instance, it was a basis for some commonality that we did not think could ever exist. We all knew these Gomers were just a little different than the ones from before, but now we felt more assured that it was because there were some positive differences. Once the briefing was over, we realized that we had a new playing field, and that there was something else out there, far worse than these Gomers, that was going to be stalking all of us.

After Dr. Clarkson's people packed up their dogs and ponies, we as key decision makers were left in the room to ponder what we'd just heard. We were also left to start making some decisions. Dr. Clarkson, Dr. Abramson, and Dr. Marvin remained, along with Dr. Cobb and the young Lieutenant Shiwak, who were both the primary translators for these Gomers. Once everyone had cleared the room and we'd taken a short break, Dr. Clarkson stated that he had one more thing to cover, but would only do it for this select grouping. The President gave him the floor and Dr. Clarkson began, "Sir, one thing we didn't publish, and couldn't, based on some of the people involved, is that the Gomers, at least the ones we have in custody, have all indicated that their command will negotiate. We believe we made that clear in our briefing. What we didn't say is that their list of people for them to negotiate with is short, and, well, pretty specific."

The President responded, "What do you mean specific?"

"Sir. They know some of our key players, based on various intercepted transmissions, they realized that some of us were . . . well . . . in charge."

"Intercepted transmissions? Are they reading our ELF/VLF mail?"

"Actually, no, sir. They are not. Instead, if we went back to check on things as far as communications in both this and the last war, we do have some pretty key VHF/UHF signals that went out during emergencies. For example, General Patrick had a Tsunami Warning sent out in the clear when the Gomers had that ship in the Puerto Rican trench."

"Okay."

"Well, sir, they know of General Patrick by name. They also know General Greene by name, and they know who you are by name."

"ME?"

"Yessir. You apparently sent out some transmissions about the time of their trying to land troops in Washington, D.C."

"Damn. I did. I should have known they were reading our mail."

"I can't say that they understood your message, but they got your name."

"Okay, anybody else?"

"Yessir. President Dubronin and General Fuller, who of course is now no longer with us, and some Sergeant Major."

"A Sergeant Major?" As the President said this, he immediately turned towards me, and I just smiled and leaned forward, telling the President, "I've got $5 on who it might be!"

"Damn, you're probably right. Okay, Dr. Clarkson, care to settle our bet?"

"Uh..... I have no idea what you're talking about, but it is a Sergeant Major Clagmore. Do you know him?"

The President jumped into that one first with a rousing, "Damn right I do! Honestly, if they know who he is, then it is probably for all the wrong reasons!"

"I have no idea, sir, but some of the prisoners know of him, and think that he has some special powers. They were very specific about him and General Greene."

"What do you mean, specific?"

"The senior prisoners indicated that if there was to be negotiation, either you or General Patrick would be the only ones with whom they would discuss anything. They were very specific that President Dubronin, General Greene, and the Sergeant Major would not be our best choices for negotiations." With that latter statement, I burst out laughing, and the President just glared at me. In response to the glare, I looked at the President and just said, "Mr. President. If you want to get this ball rolling diplomatically, then I guess NOW you'll finally have to let me out of this damn cage. Either that, or we could just send in Clagmore and he could cuss them to death!"

Most of the military side of the room burst into laughter, and the President seemed to lighten up just a little. The smile finally began to play over his face as he considered the notion of us ever sending the famous, or infamous, CSM Clagmore on a diplomatic mission. Finally, even the President couldn't stand it, and he too, burst into laughter. The diplomats and cabinet members present didn't get it, at least until someone on the Joint Chiefs related the story of Clagmore running over the Marines in Tierra del Fuego. Finally, after hours of discussion, lots of argument, and more than a few heated tempers coming to a boil, we came from the meeting with a slightly new strategy. We would fight them as before, with one small exception, we would not focus on their antenna array construction, at least for the present. We left the option open, just in case it was a trap, and we were fully prepared to knock them out at a moment's notice on the President's or my own Order. The only news was that we also decided to see if we could get their attention via communications for possible negotiations. One thing the President and I finally agreed on was that my negotiation team, should we ever get that far, would consist of Lieutenant Shiwak, me, and the apparently much-feared Command Sergeant Major Clagmore. He was to be the little reminder of what we could and would do, should they decide to be less than honorable. Besides, we weren't going to let them dictate all the terms.

Still something, for some reason, just didn't quite ring true to me, and the notion was continuing to fester. I had been puzzling over it since my conversation with Holly over dinner, and since this feeling wasn't going away, I finally decided to hedge my bets a little. Contacting General Greene, we set about our own program to attempt to verify things.

"General Greene? Patrick here."

"Yessir. What can I do for you?"

"General Greene, I need you to set up one of your classic science plus ASOC operations."

"Sure, what do you have in mind?"

"Daniel, this has to stay between us, and whoever you drag into the mix. You remember all those data devices we retrieved from Tierra del Fuego?"

"Sure, I've got our folks in Cyber Command trying to break into them, but they haven't been able to get the language straight."

"Well, what if I got you someone that could speak Gomer over to help them?"

"It would help a lot! Who do you have in mind?"

"When I can bust her free, I'm thinking seriously about sending you either Holly or one of Clarkson's other math whiz types. My hope is that we can bust into their computer data and verify a few things. In other words, I need you to check the dog for fleas!"

"Can do. Send me a translator with math skills, and we'll do our best to see what the dog is wearing."

Wrapping up the conversation, I made a note to get someone out to the Rockies that could speak this Gomer stuff, and while Holly was my first choice, I realized that it would probably have to be someone else. Unfortunately, Holly was now going to be employed elsewhere, and as a parent, I didn't like it a bit. Then it hit me, why not put her on the project later and in the meantime, get someone else to get the ball rolling. Taking this thought to heart, I picked up the phone to Dr. Clarkson, and we found General Greene another math whiz from the Gomer Language project. Holly's project assistant in drafting the algorithm was the perfect choice and within two days, she was headed to the Rockies.

CHAPTER XIII

Supreme Allied Headquarters, (SAHQ-Rear):

Winter was becoming harsher by the day, and the Allied Meteorologist, Colonel Millicent Tucker, USAF, was making no bones about the fact that it was the worst winter we had experienced in over 100 years. The ground troops we had forward deployed were doing their best to stay warm, while continuing their training, and preparing for the Spring offensive. Our Naval units were also against the wall, since the oceans were even more hazardous. Our largest Battleships were being tossed around like toys in a bath tub, and the small ships were doing all they could to just maintain steerageway in the ever-increasing seas. Then there was the ice build-up on each ship throughout the entire fleet, which made a sailor's life even more dangerous and constantly demanding. As the Ice Cap moved southward, the danger to navigation was sufficient to force our surface fleet to maintain their distances from the normal Gomer approach to their Siberian enclaves. This made their usefulness in denying the Gomers the airspace into Siberia very questionable.

During the first part of the winter, the only good news was the launching and commissioning of the third Montana Class Battleship, the aptly named USS Alaska. After a brief shakedown and training period, she was to join the Pacific Fleet right before spring. As many a young soldier and sailor learned during this winter, the weather could be as fierce as and more dangerous than a nest of Gomers. Against this backdrop, we had to maintain pressure on our enemies, while at the same time try to begin some form of communications with the very things we were trying to destroy or eliminate from our planet. This required a balancing act, with just a little of sleight of hand. Naturally, when you needed a serious magic trick, you called on the boys at ASOC. Part of their business, at least under normal wartime conditions, was Psychological Warfare, or Psyops, and now that we were cracking the language barrier, it was time to unleash this new form of Gomer harassment. When General Greene found out that he was one of those specifically identified as being someone the Gomers knew, he was more than thrilled to get back into their heads as soon as possible.

Wasting no time, General Greene made it his personal mission to see that the 11th Airborne Division lost their Command Sergeant Major Clagmore, at least for some temporary duty. This was a compromise, since General Greene did all he could to convince the Allied Staff that he needed Clagmore full time. I guess, unlike the rest of us, General Greene had no idea of what he was about to receive. More than likely, if history was true to form, he would later thank us for just keeping it as a temporary duty assignment. At first, when the Sergeant Major got his Temporary Duty Orders, he was excited to be going closer to the Gomers. What he didn't realize was that it was actually going to be in a recording studio, along with General Greene and the egg heads responsible for the translation software. Saying that Clagmore was disappointed would be like saying that Napoleon was 'vertically challenged', and whenever Clagmore was disappointed, everyone knew about it.

"After almost 40 years of military service, those dirty rotten SONS of bitches have the unmitigated gall to make me a fucking radio guy? I ain't from no damned Hollywood!"

"Sergeant Major, I asked for you, and I'm General Daniel Green, the ASOC commander."

"Sir, with all due respect, I wouldn't give a damn if you were Jesus H. Mother Fu...."

"Dammit, Sergeant Major! Shut the hell up! General Patrick approved this, and you and I are going to make it work!"

"Make what work..... Sir."

"Sergeant Major, we're going to use our voices to talk to the Gomers."

"No Shit? We can do that? Hell, I've got a thing or two to tell those crab-faced bastards!"

"See, now that's the spirit! Sergeant Major, we are going to say the message, and this little box here is going to translate it. Then all you have to do is deliver it in that song bird voice of yours into this microphone."

"Screw that noise.... Sir."

"Sergeant Major, how would you like to be a private again?"

"General, again with all due respect, I've been busted by way better'n you. I ain't too worried, since there is plenty of war to go around, and my boys back in the 11th need me!"

"Sergeant Major, I'm only going to use you for about two weeks, and then you can go back to freezing your ass off with your boys. Is that okay with you?"

"Yes, General. That will work fine." As he finished these words, the team of 'eggheads' entered the room and started setting up their equipment to facilitate the translation. The head of this particular team was Dr. Dana Cobb, and a really cute little red-headed girl was the person operating the machine. As the Sergeant Major stared at the girl, it was obvious that he was almost immediately taken in by her. He stood there gawking like a school boy and was about to drop his chin all the way to his ankles when General Greene broke his stare with this statement.

"Sergeant Major, I would love to introduce you to Dr. Cobb, and Dr. Patrick. She is General Patrick's youngest daughter, and I have permission to summarily execute anyone who gets near her. You DO hear what I'm saying, don't you?"

"Uh, yeah ..... Yessir. Did you say General Patrick, as in THE General Patrick?"

"Yes, as in THE General Patrick."

"Now how in the hell did the Mouse get a daughter that looked like her? I've seen her brother, and well, let's say I'm just a little surprised."

"She takes after her Mother. Now then, Sergeant Major, if I hear you make one more comment about her, I'll have you shipped to the 'old man' so fast it would make your head spin!"

"Hell, no. I ain't afraid of much, but that man would gut me like a trout! No thanks, General, I'll be nice." With those words, the Sergeant Major began to cooperate completely in the operation. When it was completed, he was almost sad to have to say goodbye to Dr. Patrick. He didn't mind getting back to his 'boys,' but he realized that when they were freezing their asses off, he just might have something to think about to keep him warm. At least he would think about it to himself, since he knew if this kind of thing got out, his wife of 40 years would also gut him like a trout.

Within a few days of their departures back to their respective commands, the transmissions to the Gomers got underway. The message was fairly short and to the point, and it was sent out on a number of rotating frequencies, including the Terahertz bands.

> *Negotiate or die. You can reply on any frequency from 120.0 MHz, up to 243.0 MHz. If you continue to fight, we will cut you off from your friends, and you will die. Surrender or I, Sergeant Major Clagmore (or Lieutenant General Daniel Greene) will come for you!*

In conjunction with this rather repetitive message, the HARM missile campaign was ramped up to almost maximum capacity. This drove General Clark and General Thayer a little crazy, since it was up to them to keep them supplied and to fire them at the right targets. While the weather wasn't cooperating in a lot of ways, it did allow for sufficient sorties to keep up the pressure.

Supreme Allied Headquarters - (SAHQ-Rear):

Everyday, we monitored the frequencies, and with each day's passing, there was no reply. In fact, there were no communications on any frequency, even in the Terahertz band. Presumably, our HARM campaign made them a little gun shy to use their radios, so we started a more direct approach. We actually began to broadcast the message out on the Terahertz bands, to include the specific frequencies we knew they were using, and we were advising them how to reply without risking another strike on them. As a result, the communications centers were somewhat over-tasked by having to now coordinate the HARM strikes based on when a "surrender" message was being sent out. Still there was no response. With the weather beginning to lift and the Ice Pack starting to recede, we knew that we would have to push them harder, if we were ever going to get a result.

There was then one more try to get their attention. This time, I recorded the message, which was also pretty simple.

> *This is General Michael Patrick. We know about the Tornit, and we can work together, but only if you lay down your weapons, and come forward to negotiate. Only then will we all find a way to defeat them. Let us help one another. If you wish to negotiate, contact us on 121.5 MHz or 243.0 MHz, otherwise you give us no choice.*

Immediately after my message, a message was repeated as recorded by one of the Gomers themselves, Commander Algatok. Lieutenant Shiwak observed and translated, and the software system also confirmed, that Commander Algatok identified himself and stated my message verbatim. He also apparently gave them his identity for verification, confirmed that there were a number of prisoners, and that they had been treated fairly. I didn't trust him, so before the message was sent out, the entirety of it was reviewed at least several times, by virtually all of our experts in their language translations. Unfortunately, with the earliest hint of spring, we were still getting no response. We had waited long enough, and now it was time to act.

Dutch Harbor, Alaska:

The weather on the runway was brutal, but the Division Commander insisted on being there to greet the incoming VIPs. Lieutenant Robert Patrick wasn't too thrilled at the prospect, since it meant standing outside trying his best to keep warm, while also trying to keep an eye out for the approach of the aircraft. Standing with his back to the wind, the heavy fur collar and hood of his cold weather coat were now being blown into a full standing position behind his head. "What idiot would be flying in this crap?" He quickly turned to look around, hoping that nobody heard him and cursing himself for allowing that to slip out of his mouth. His wait was mercifully coming to an end, as he could see the C-17 turning from the runway and starting to taxi up to the ramp. Running back inside, he advised 'his' General that the aircraft was here and would be on the ramp within the next couple of minutes. As he stepped back to the ramp, the Division Commander followed him out of the nice warm building just in time to see the aircraft pull into position. Within a minute, the side door opened.

What came next was definitely something that Lieutenant Patrick would never have thought possible. Stepping out were two heavily armed Military Policemen, and Command Sergeant Major Clagmore. Immediately thinking that the Sergeant Major had finally done something bizarre, even for him, he quashed the thought on seeing the next three passengers. Next off were two more Military Policemen and something wearing a rather large hazmat suit. Finally, he recognized the next two passengers. It was General Greene and his dad, General Patrick. On seeing his dad, all Lieutenant Patrick could think was that the 'old man finally snuck away again.' He'd been privy, thanks to his Mom, to all of his dad's shenanigans and attempts to sneak away to the front, and he just assumed that this was one more such attempt. He'd have to say something to Mom, since he was even more afraid of her than he was of the Gomers and Sergeant Major Clagmore put together. Stepping forward, the Division Commander snapped a very crisp parade ground salute, and asked General Patrick and General Greene to step inside with him. As the party got out of the cold wind, Lieutenant Patrick got a good look at the 'guy in the hazmat suit'.

"HOLY HELL, is that a Gom......" Before he could finish the statement, the Division Commander whirled around on him and said, "Lieutenant, please refrain from any more outbursts, and yes, it is." Robbie wouldn't hear much more of the conversation, since he was completely mesmerized at the Gomer in the suit. He'd never seen one up close, and this one was alive. Not only alive, but apparently quite capable of movement, and maybe even communication. As he continued to stare, someone came up behind him and gave him a very swift kick. Turning around, he was face to face with his sister, Holly, and she was grinning like the Cheshire Cat.

"Hey, useless, are you going to help us with our equipment, or are you just going to stand here all in a stupor?"

"Hey, sis, so what the ....."

"Nope, need to know only, and YOU don't have a need to know. Just get some people out there to carry our stuff to the transportation."

"Sis, last I looked you aren't in the Army, and you can't...."

"The hell I can't, Lieutenant! While you were out being a door stop with your airborne buddies, I was getting a PhD, and I'm also now a GS-15 on General Patrick's Personal staff."

"I had no idea..."

"You should read Mom's mail more often, assuming you can read. You can read, can't you, brother?"

"Why, you little..... Okay, we'll get your stuff."

"Thanks, butthead, oh, my bad. Thank you, Lieutenant." As she turned away, the young Lieutenant got another shock. Stepping out of the cold wind was another redhead who was carrying two lap top computer cases, and an expression of abject fury. "My God, is this a family reunion?"

"OH, hey, Robbie, could you get someone to get me a hand with Dad's foot locker of files?"

"Sure, Chris, and I must say, it is truly a pleasure after seeing Holly to know you will be here to referee."

"Hah, she is a handful, isn't she. I always knew she would be dangerous if she ever decided she wanted to be..." As she was about to complete her sentence, Sergeant Major Clagmore stepped up, saluted, and smiled. Robbie was floored, in all the time he'd ever known the Sergeant Major, the only time he was smiling was when someone was about to get hurt. Holly and Chris smiled back at him, and darned if they didn't all three act like they'd known each other forever. The Sergeant Major was actually polite, solicitous, and it scared the hell out of Robbie. Then when Chris spoke, he was even more floored. "Robbie, you've met my Godfather before, haven't you?"

"Uh, yeah, sure, Sergeant Major Clagmore is our Division Sergeant Major."

"OH, really? Awesome! I love this man! He was with Dad at Fort Benning back in the day, all those thousands of years ago when I was born. You know, back before Dad decided to hang out with you schmucks in his 'second family'." With that she gave him a huge hug, and as the Sergeant Major picked up her bags, a detail of airborne troopers materialized to carry in the rest of his dad's baggage. Still shaking his head, he could only marvel at all the secrets his family had about dad and his past. Maybe he could pump Chris to find out why everyone was so intimidated by someone who, to him, was never anything but a dad.

Outside the Operations building, the wind was still howling when the entourage mounted into their vehicles for the short ride to the

Command facilities. Robbie noticed that the 'Gomer' had a hood over his 'hazmat' suit, and was being guided by hand everywhere they went. He was also mesmerized at the fact that his older sister was sitting next to the Sergeant Major, and they were laughing and poking at each other like school kids. To make it even more bizarre, his baby sister, Holly, actually seemed to be in charge of both the prisoner and the mounds of equipment that were accompanying this circus. Meanwhile, his General was locked into some pretty deep discussions with General Greene and his father when their convoy entered the long underground tunnel leading to the Allied Headquarters complex. When the convoy pulled up to the off-loading point, they were greeted by his dad's newest junior aide, a very scruffy Canadian Lieutenant that, to Robbie, looked like he was about 180 years old. He was introduced by Holly as Lieutenant Shiwak, and Robbie discovered that the Lieutenant was not only an Inuit, but he was a scout and an ASOC operator from the Canadian Armed Forces. The ideas now swirling around in his head simply made no sense, so for the first time in his life, he decided that silence was the better part of valor.

Staying fairly close to his boss, Robbie was still lost in his thoughts when he felt a hand on his shoulder. Turning around, it was his dad, who was smiling at him. "Son, how are you doing up here?"

"Fine. Uh, Sir."

"It's okay, when it is just us around, a hug and a 'hi Dad' will work just fine."

"Yessir. I guess I'm just trying to absorb everything. I'm surprised you didn't bring Mom along."

"Me, too. She wanted to be here, but we can't all be in one spot. In fact, you're going to be leaving here soon, too."

"Me? Where the hell am I going? Uh, ...Sir."

"You will be escorting Chris and Holly back out of here, once they are done setting up all their equipment and material I need for later."

"Dad, what is going on here?"

"Son, you don't really have a need to know, so I won't be telling you just yet. I can say that when all of this comes into play, assuming it ever comes into play, you'll be back here to assist in it. I just want to make sure that both Chris and Holly are NOT here for it, and I will be counting on you to get them the hell out of here."

"So, you think it might get dicey here?"

"It could happen, and I don't want to run any risk of having the whole damn family wiped out at once. Unfortunately, both Chris and Holly are vital to the set up, so they had to be here to get us going. Once they're done, I will have them out of here, and you're going to make damn sure they go."

"What makes you think that they won't leave, and that I will need to escort them?"

"Geez, son! You're not that thick, are you? Weren't you part of the conspiracy to keep me from this headquarters?"

"Yeah, I guess I'm guilty. So, you think they'll be hard-headed about leaving, just like you were being kind of hard-headed about wanting to be out here?"

"Bingo! Hard-headed runs in the family. Some of the most stubborn people on the earth are Patricks. Hell, you should have known MY dad in his heyday. The only thing on earth harder than his head was a diamond."

"Yessir. I get it. I'll make sure they go when it is time, even if I have to hog tie them to get them out."

"Excellent! Get with my senior Aide, Lieutenant Colonel Cho, and my other junior Aide, Captain Dubronin, and they will give you instructions on the plan for the evacuation."

"Dubronin? A Russian? You hate Russians!"

"Son, it is a new world, and Captain Dubronin is one of the finest officers I've ever seen come out of that part of the world. Besides, his Dad is an old .... shall we say, acquaintance of mine."

"Dad, is this another one of those family secrets?"

"Son, don't ask questions like that, you know better."

"You mean like not knowing that Clagmore is Chris' Godfather?"

"Actually, that wasn't a secret. I guess it just never came up, because it was in another lifetime. It was back when I was still with Chris' mother, WAY before your time."

"Dad?"

"Yeah."

"This 'need to know' shit is getting old."

"Tell me about it. Maybe someday, I'll give you the rest of these stories, but until then, you'll just have to be content in making your own."

"Dad. You always sound like a frickin' fortune cookie when you say stuff like that last statement."

"Ah, Grasshopper. You're finally getting it. Now get your ass to work, and don't forget to check in with Colonel Cho and Captain Dubronin! Got it?"

"Yes, Sir. General, Sir."

"Smart ass!" The last comment came with a big hug, and General Patrick strode off to his new quarters to get settled in. There would be briefings, and then there was the little matter of getting the evacuation information from Dubronin and Cho. Robbie had a feeling that things were about to get very interesting around this rock.

The Harbor of Pevek, Russia:

The USS Los Angeles surfaced right outside the harbor entrance. Taking advantage of the retreating ice pack, she was moving into the harbor to dispatch her passengers and equipment. Her mission was simple, she was to meet with an ASOC observation team already in Pevek, hand off her unique and very top secret payload, and then return to her station to maintain her harassment and monitoring of any Gomers that might transit her patrol area. Surfacing in the early dawn light, she followed the standard protocol of verifying that the skies were clear and that there were no Gomers anywhere near her position. Once in position, the Captain of the USS Los Angeles spotted the small cabin cruiser that they were told to expect. It pulled alongside, and a bow and stern line secured the small boat to the side of the submarine. Then, as he watched from the bridge on top of the 'sail,' several escorts were passing someone in a hazmat suit over the side and into the cabin cruiser.

The crew of the smaller boat immediately directed the delivered personnel, with all their equipment, inside the cabin and out of sight. Without the exchange of any other messages or words, the smaller boat cast off and returned to the shore on the far side of the harbor. Watching the smaller craft move away, the Captain turned to his Executive Officer. "Well, XO, that was an interesting trip. Dutch Harbor to Pevek, and with the oddest cargo I've ever seen."

"Captain. Did you get a good look at the freak in the suit?"

"Not really. They kept the hood covered, and nobody would tell me squat. In fact, I was specifically ordered not to ask."

"Well, sir. The hood slipped back there as they were transferring it to the little boat, and I swear to God, it looked like some of the Gomers we've seen floating after a good kill."

"XO, when they say don't ask, it also means you don't look, you don't tell, you haven't seen squat. Got it?"

"Aye, Aye, Sir. I got it."

"Good, now get us back to our original station and set the watch. Let's see if we can find some Gomers to kill."

"Aye, Aye, Sir."

Supreme Allied Headquarters, (SAHQ - Forward/Pacific):

The War Room of this particular headquarters complex was definitely state of the art. The design and construction began during the last Gomer war, and the previous experiences with Gomers and their weapons were fully integrated into the entire complex. Despite being this high tech, it was also the kind of complex bunker system that made me very uncomfortable. As General Patton was often quoted as saying, "Fixed fortifications are monuments to the folly of man. If it was built by man, it can be destroyed by man." I happened to agree, except instead of being destroyed by man, I was pretty convinced that a Gomer wouldn't have much trouble, either. I'd seen Diamond Head, and I already knew from personal experience that the Gomers had the ability to level the entire island, regardless of how deep we dug the hole.

It was this very concern that made it imperative that all non-essential personnel be evacuated from the complex the second they became non-essential. Chris and Holly were both about to be non-essential. The equipment had been set up, checked, antenna arrays were hard wired or cabled, with the radio output to specifically emanate from several islands away along the same Aleutian Island chain. We even incorporated various relay stations to make it appear as though the signals were being sent from Komandorskie Island, Attu Island, and Kiska Island simultaneously. We hoped that it would throw off the Gomers, much the same as the system had worked on Prince Charles Island near Baffin Island in the Greenland Campaign. When we got word from the USS Los Angeles that their cargo and charges were delivered, we knew it was time. I handed the mission over to Captain Dubronin and Lieutenant Patrick. Neither Chris nor Holly knew what hit them. They thought they were being taken to lunch to celebrate the completion of their tasks in getting things set up. Without fanfare, their brother and my junior Aide had them on an outbound aircraft. I'm not sure I'll ever know the full story, but ostensibly it involved 'let's get some food in Seattle, and we can pick up some additional equipment there for later.'

Chris was hot, and to say otherwise would be a gross understatement. Still, there was no way my daughter, the mother to my only grandson, was going to be at a place that could be ground zero in a heartbeat. I did not want Holly or Doctor Cobb at our location either, since they could be our last shot later on the communications side of things. Captain Dubronin was another story, and for the cause of diplomacy, I just opted to err on the side of caution. As for Robbie, I knew it was going to upset him if he missed things, but somebody had to be the 'Judas goat', and after a little secret discussion, I agreed to get him back by the first available transport, while Dubronin would escort Dr. Cobb and Chris back to the Rear Headquarters. Holly, on the other hand, was now going to be in the Rockies with General Greene's rear staff. Granted, anywhere on the planet was a potential target, but we were about to turn up the heat sufficiently to make Dutch Harbor one of the last places anyone in their right mind would want to be sitting when it started.

Once the signal came back that the flight was safely in Seattle, we locked down the airspace, and Robbie headed to his alternate transport for return. As a result, Operation Phone Call and Operation Siberian Express began with him onboard the USS Helena, en route to Dutch Harbor. As it turned out, he had a ring side seat for the opening of our Siberian campaign.

CHAPTER XIV

Supreme Allied Headquarters, (SAHG - Forward/Pacific):

When our weather reports showed significant improvement and the retreat of the key portions of the ice pack, we initiated both of our new main operations. The first, Operation Siberian Express, was a massive bombardment all along the front of all key Gomer enclaves. Taking care not to destroy what we believed were the weapons arrays that were aimed overhead, we focused instead on any above ground structures that were built by the Gomers during the last several months. Our ASOC personnel were again playing a key role in making sure that our firing wasn't wasted. Their intelligence work was highly satisfactory and their "eyes" on target were invaluable. The bombardment would be followed by the initial transmissions that were to comprise Operation Phone Call.

While not a great name for an operation, it sure fit the circumstances. The initial message that was sent by Sergeant Major Clagmore and General Greene was again transmitted, but this time it was followed by several hours of very precise missile and artillery fire onto various targets around the various main Gomer Enclaves. After several hours, the bombardment would be halted, and then followed by the second message from me, which would be transmitted with an adequate period of total silence to allow for a reply. Once the time to reply had passed, the bombardment would resume. The cycle of message, bombardment, message, bombardment, would continue for the first three days of the operation. On the morning of the fourth day, our two main Army Groups began their 'movement to contact' with the various Gomer perimeters.

As these operations were ongoing, our major Naval units were in place, along with scattered batteries of Gomer Guns, whose sole mission was to deny anyone the use of the airspace above the various Gomer enclaves in Siberia. With each passing night, the losses to the several Gomer Fleets being sent to relieve their comrades were considerable. While we had negligible losses, we did have some among the various naval units. Usually, these casualties involved personnel in the wrong place at the wrong time on deck. The side effects of a Gomer Gun were considerable to anyone exposed, and the deck of a major fleet unit was no exception.

Our Air Forces were playing a key role in the bombardment of the enclaves, as were our strategic submarine forces. As the ASOC personnel would call in requesting fire missions, they would be met with immediate assistance either from the Naval or the Air Force assets that were on call and nearby. When our main ground artillery and mobile Gomer Guns got closer to the Gomer enclaves on the second day, the shelling and/or Gomer gunfire was devastating to anything that was down range. Moving ever forward, our 21st Army Group from the Ural Mountains had completely encircled one of the main Gomer enclaves, while the 42nd Army Group was encircling a second Gomer enclave. The Russian Army Group was in the process of encircling the third main Gomer enclave when we ordered a 24 hour stand down from firing. During this period, our Army Groups were to consolidate their positions, prepare their fields of fire, and put the finishing touches to an all-out assault that would take place on my orders no earlier than 48 hours after the initial cease fire.

During this same time frame, General Greene was running another critical operation. This one was code named Visitor. His mission was to take full advantage of the first 24 hour stand down to release his envoy at or near the main entrance to a Gomer enclave. The initial period of cease fire was to allow the envoy the chance to make it to his leadership, and to convey a message personally from me. Commander Algatok had been selected, briefed, and prepared for his release. His trip from Dutch Harbor to Pevek on board the USS Los Angeles was nothing compared to his trek from Pevek to what we believed to be the main Gomer enclave. Traveling by day with a low light filter on the visor to his climate suit, it was no doubt harrowing to him. Still, we did all we could to keep him as comfortable as possible and to provide his sustenance. Through his interpreter, Lieutenant Shiwak, General Greene personally saw to many of Commander Algatok's needs.

The entire mission wasn't an easy process, but after almost a week of travel via submarine, small boat, truck, small aircraft, and then other more makeshift conveyances, he was smuggled into an area very near to ASOC's forward headquarters. The subterfuge was necessary, mainly to prevent Commander Algatok from acquiring much useful information about us that might help the Gomers. Our hope was to convince him of the vastness of our organization, and the need for the Gomers to cooperate with us. On the final day of the bombardment cycle, Commander Algatok was moved forward to a point almost within sight of what was believed to be the main Gomer base. The following evening, right before sunset and at the conclusion of the transmission of the last message, Gomer Commander Algatok was released and pointed towards his comrades. They now had roughly 46 hours left before the gates of hell would open to swallow them all, and Commander Algatok knew that this was coming. He would either convince them of our sincerity, or he would perish alongside his peers.

Popigaj, Russia, Gomer Enclave #2:

Watching through high powered night vision binoculars, Lieutenant Shiwak watched as Commander Algatok moved into the entrance of the enclave. Lieutenant Shiwak was instructed that upon seeing Algatok back into the Gomer fold, he was to immediately proceed by the fastest transportation back to Dutch Harbor. Turning away from the scene, he crawled slowly back to the ASOC team that had acted as their escorts. Scanning the sky above them, they saw the movement of several Gomer Fighter class ships off to their north and east. Moving as quickly as they dared, the team finished burying the Gomer's climate suit and began heading back into the scrub that made up their hideaway. Despite his orders, the fastest transportation this night was going to be no transportation.

Given his language skills with the Gomers, Lieutenant Shiwak was now too important to risk any more than necessary. This trip had been necessary, but now with Algatok back amongst his own kind, the ASOC team mission was to protect and deliver Lieutenant Shiwak back home safe and sound. Riding out the night was harrowing, but not something that Shiwak hadn't done before. In fact, his movements near the Gomers in Greenland were part of what landed him this job in the first place. Looking at the faces of those around him,

Lieutenant Shiwak had an epiphany. He was damn glad to be headed back somewhere else. What Lieutenant Shiwak didn't know was that General Patrick and the key members of his staff were really giving everyone the 24 hour cease fire order to insure that Lieutenant Shiwak would be able to escape and return.

With the return of the sun, Lieutenant Shiwak was hustled westward to the extraction point. Within 4 hours, he was on a fast transport aircraft that was hurtling ahead of the twilight line. It was a much faster trip out than it had been getting into Russia. This time, within 24 hours of dropping Algatok off at his "main gate," Lieutenant Shiwak was back inside the confines of the Supreme Allied Headquarters Forward at Dutch Harbor. In the last week, Lieutenant Shiwak had circumnavigated the globe. No mean feat for a simple Inuit kid from Northern Canada, and while it wasn't a record for speed, it sure was a record for him in distance. He just hoped like hell he didn't ever have to do it again. His nerves were more than a little frayed. Then again, it might have been because of that creepy Commander Algatok. Exhausted, the Lieutenant drifted off into his first real sleep in almost a week.

11th Airborne Division Headquarters, Dutch Harbor, Alaska:

Sergeant Major Clagmore was pacing the Division Command Post more than a little agitated. The Division was going to be moving forward to Kamchatka, but he wasn't making the move. Instead, he was being attached to General Patrick's staff, while the most senior Regimental Sergeant Major would be filling in for him. The Sergeant Major had never missed a move with his unit before, and his anger was only exceeded by his knowledge that something mighty big must be going on, otherwise there was no way he would be denied this chance to get back into a good fight.

"Hey, L-T, do you have a clue why I'm being left here?"

"No, Sergeant Major, not really ... unless it has something to do with that thing you made the tape about."

"Dammit. I knew that crap would bite me in the ass. Hell, I don't speak that Gomer crap, so why do I have to stay here? Shit!"

"Sergeant Major, I don't know the details, but believe me when I tell you that my Dad wouldn't be dragging you away if it wasn't for something he feels is a pretty good reason."

"What did you just say?"

"I said that my Dad wouldn't be dragging you away if it wasn't for a good reason."

"You know somethin', Loo'tenant? That might be the first really smart thing you've ever said out loud."

"Damn, Sergeant Major, cut me some slack. You sound like my sister when you say shit like that."

"YOUR SISTER? See, just when I think you're not a complete waste of space and that there is hope for your ass, you say some crap like that and change my mind again completely. 'Your sister?' Shit, slick, you should be half as smart as either one of them!" With that the Sergeant Major wheeled around and left to go grab his gear and head for the Allied Headquarters complex. Muttering all the way out the door, he didn't see the huge grin spreading over Lieutenant Patrick's face, or hear the small mutter under his breath, "Gotcha, you old bastard. I gotcha!" Once the Sergeant Major was gone, the Lieutenant took a look around and realized that he felt something he'd never thought he would ever feel. "Damn, I'm going to miss that guy a LOT. I just hope he's back before we get into the really deep Kimchee."

Popigaj, Russia, Gomer Enclave #2:

The ASOC team that evacuated Lieutenant Shiwak moved back into place after hustling him to the extraction point. Their observations were invaluable, and they were just a part of the network of operators placed in key observation posts around the enclave. In fact, one team was within stone throwing distance of the Gomers' main airstrip. It was this team that would offer some very interesting observations. The first was the flight patterns that were now in place, and the second was that within a few hours of Algatok's arrival, a Fighter Class ship was seen rocketing straight up and into space. This information was duly passed on, but what threw the team more than anything was the change in flight patterns.

"Hey, skipper, why do you reckon that Fighter took that route? I've never seen one do that before, have you?"

"Dude, that was impressive, wasn't it. Straight up! Normally they act like airplanes, I guess to save power, but this thing went like a rocket. Okay, code it, and send it."

"Yessir."

"OH, and Schmoltz, make sure you send that other traffic pattern stuff. Maybe somebody back in the rear can make sense of it."

"Yessir. That is so weird, too, they come in, and just kind of dive on the place."

"Right, get our estimates of altitude for that maneuver, and let them know that we've only seen the Fighter Class doing it. Hell, I haven't seen a Carrier Class ship in days, and they sure aren't trying that rocket thing, either."

"I've got it, and we'll code it out on the ELF ASAP."

"Excellent! Now with the sun up, we'll start back to normal shifts. From what I understand, things are going to get kind of hot around here over the next couple of days. Send the message, and get some rest."

Supreme Allied Headquarters, (SAHG - Forward/Pacific):

When I entered the War Room, several of my staff members couldn't wait to snatch me with their versions of critical information. After being inundated with information, three things jumped out at me. The first was that my oldest daughter was now officially back at our Rear Headquarters, and that Holly was back to work in General Greene's lab facilities with Dr. Abramson and his personnel. The second and third big chunks of information were requiring a lot more thought on my part. The report from the ASOC team left us all with something to ponder, and as the staff was trying to make sense of it, something in the back of my mind was triggered, and it hit me. Asking to see the message again, I called General Roberts over, and then had General Samuel Kaminski, USAF, join us. General Kaminski was a temporary fill to my staff to take the place of General Stephenson when he moved up to my Chief of Staff. The unfortunate events of the air crash had put much of this in turmoil, but as the Commander of the 12th Air Force, General Kaminski was a good choice to fill in as my Allied Air Operations Officer. I passed the message around, and while General Roberts didn't get it at first, I saw the clear flash in Kaminski's eyes. I think we both hit on the tactic, and it made perfect sense.

"Well, General Roberts, what do you think?"

"Sir, I got nothing. It just seems odd, but I guess it makes sense if that is the only way in or out. We do have coverage of the airspace pretty much all the way around that one enclave."

"Bingo! We are hurting them, or they wouldn't be doing it this way."

General Kaminski chimed in and related, "Yessir, it isn't all that different than when we do a tactical take-off in, say, an F-16 or F-15. The idea is to get clear of the ground, gain as much altitude as possible, and to stay out of range of anyone that might be shooting at you."

"I know, during Vietnam, helicopter pilots, more specifically the Dustoff or Air Medical Evacuation pilots, would employ a technique for getting into a landing zone that involved some rather violent maneuvers. They would fly above the area at an altitude above the effective range of ground fire, then once directly over the LZ or landing zone, they would begin a rather violent and rapid spiraling descent from altitude to flare and land on the ground. When I was younger, I performed this maneuver myself in training, and it would push the aircraft pretty close to its outer structural limits, especially when the temperature was working against you."

General Roberts, looking a little puzzled, asked, "The temperature is working against you?"

"J-T, when you're flying the old Huey or UH-1, the hotter temperature, coupled with an increase in density altitude, tends to sap the aircraft of all its usable power. In short, you could run out of power, altitude, and ideas at pretty much the same time. The proverbial busting of ass was never out of the question, and it was not a maneuver for the weak of heart. I've seen more than one crew chief in the back lose his lunch in the process."

"So, General, what exactly does that mean?"

"Well, now we are seeing evidence that the Gomers are doing the same kind of thing, and probably for the same reasons. Their Fighter Class ships are coming over their enclaves and beginning a similar violent descent from directly overhead of the enclave. This means that our ground fire must be having a significant impact, and it is forcing them to modify their tactics for getting into or out of the enclave."

General Kaminski then chimed in, "The idea that no Carrier Class ships are moving, either in or out, also tells us that their flight characteristics in our atmosphere are such that they very likely can't perform the maneuver. So, right now, they were not risking their movement, because we are denying them the airspace they need for take-off and landing."

"That sums it up, Sam. I think we're on the same page. Now with that information, we should be able to nail their Carrier Class ships on the ground, since it is a good bet that they aren't going to be able to escape."

General Kaminski looked at me and back to General Roberts, and simply said, "I'm going to pass that word to OUR fighters. We might finally have some fun ground targets to nail on our way in and out of their enclaves on tomorrow's sorties."

When we got to the third piece of information, it was not as puzzling, but it too offered additional insight about the Gomers and their ships. We knew that their Fighter Class ships were maneuverable, but the 'rocket' takeoff suggested that perhaps we had underestimated some of their capabilities. We would need to watch closely for any change of attack tactics based on this ability, and we would also need to be more watchful of anything overhead that might 'fall' on us, as opposed to following the normal curvature approaches we'd previously seen from space. We knew their Fighters could hover, since we'd seen that throughout this war and the last one, but their usage in being able to get in and out of the enclaves, virtually unmolested, was a new twist. As for the purpose of the lone Fighter, those of us who know about Algatok's trip back to his friends all had a pretty good guess about why the Fighter left the way it did, and was going where we thought it would go. Seems that someone was taking his message seriously, or at least that was our sincere hope.

We broke up our little meeting, and both General Roberts and General Kaminski headed off to issue their respective orders and guidance. I was extremely tickled to see that General Kaminski was also passing on this latest air intelligence to Admiral Lynch, so that the information could be provided to the various Battlegroups and the Naval Aviators who might be defending the Battlegroups. The nugget about the spiral approach from overhead onto a target was also passed on, so that defensive formations could be modified as necessary to counter the potential threat. If the Gomers were using mostly Fighters, then this could be a problem for some of our Big Gun Battlegroups, since their defense would be far more reliant on their anti-Fighter capabilities, than on knocking out the big guys with their big guns. The Gomer Bubble was always an option, but most weren't thrilled with it. Ask anyone on the USS New Jersey, which only now was finally rejoining the fleet.

I was walking out of the War Room to get some fresh air when someone yelled, "Hey General, we have movement!"

Turning back around, I couldn't pinpoint who yelled, and then I heard General Kaminski's voice repeating the same thing. As I headed over to him, he looked up and said, "Sir, we have a large move. Looks to be a formation of at least two Mountain Class Ships, four Battleship Class ships, and about a dozen Carrier Class ships. They are all hauling ass towards Mars, with an ETA of about thirteen to fourteen hours. They appear to be escorting the two Moon Class ships back to their prior locations, and the Moon Ship behind the Moon is also moving, but only slightly."

"Where is that one headed?"

General Kaminski thought for a second and said, "Not sure, Sir. It has shifted position, but it only appears to be changing orbits, to a lower one."

"Not good! Reckon he got our message from that Gomer, Algatok?"

"Can't tell sir, but he is definitely hugging the Moon closer than before."

"Okay, keep me advised. Any other movement towards us?"

"Not that we can detect. They are apparently taking their assets further back, and maybe into a more defensive posture."

"I hope that is because of us, as opposed to something else coming."

"Shoot, I hadn't thought of that one before, uh......"

"Okay, General Kaminski, get all our eyes pointed outwards, let's make sure the skies are clear back towards the original Gomerville, or Tornit, or whatever the hell we're calling it these days. We might need to worry about more of these Gomers, or maybe even the other nastier ones."

"Yessir. Standby, and I'll get a quick check with our other sky observers. Shouldn't take more than five minutes."

I will assure you that it was a very long five minutes, but General Kaminski came back with good news. He and his observers found nothing else, and no other movement that would indicate that the Gomers were moving for any other reason than our message to them from Algatok. Algatok must have suspected that we were going to target their large stuff, since they were doing what they could to get it out of our reach. We'd take that, even if it wasn't the optimal response, since now we could hopefully eliminate the Gomers in Siberia, much the same way as we had in Greenland.

Supreme Allied Headquarters, (SAHQ - Rear):

When Chris returned to the rear headquarters, she was more than a little upset with her dad. Basically, he had run her and Holly out, in some dinosaur belief that they needed to be protected. Chris was extremely torqued about that latter notion, since she felt that she was far more useful in her job when she could interact directly with her dad. This telephone, third party setup through Aides and staff members was making her life a lot more difficult. Holly, on the other hand, realized that she might be more useful back in the lab, so despite the fact she had been 'run out' she at least was focused on her new project. Leah did all she could to assuage the hard feelings, and while it was to some affect, it still made Chris a little angry. It wasn't until she thought about her son and husband, that she realized that her dad was probably right. She didn't like it, but he was probably right. A few days later, she realized that he had been dead right.

Holly was also less than pleased, but now working with Dr. Abramson, she had shifted to the topic of Mars, and all of the data information from the Gomers' ships gave her several new problems to work out. This time she was pouring through all the research available, to include the work of the various probes to Mars, such as the Curiosity, Sojourner, Spirit and Opportunity. Knowing what they knew about Gomers, one of her new goals was to see why the Gomers had such a fascination with Mars. It was a problem that took her mind off what was going on, and this time, it was a very good thing. Like her sister, at the end of the week, she was really very glad she wasn't anywhere near Dutch Harbor.

11th Airborne Division, Headquarters, Kamchatka, Russia:

The Division was settling into their new headquarters near the Petropavlovsk-Kamchatsky Airport, and both Lieutenant Patrick and his boss, the Division Commander, were really missing Command Sergeant Major Clagmore. This new guy just wasn't the same, and it was readily apparent that Sergeant Major Clagmore WAS the 11th Airborne Divisions' personality. The mood was different, and the edge just didn't feel quite right. Then again, Robbie recognized that it might be his own bias, but whenever Clagmore was around, things were more squared away and steady. Like his sisters, he wasn't wild about the latest arrangements, but at least he was still close to the thick of it, and shortly, he was thinking they might be directly on top of it. As he was walking back into the Division Command Post, the Division Commander waved him over to look at the latest message from their Higher Headquarters, the 42ⁿᵈ Army Group.

TO: ALL ARMY, CORPS, AND DIVISION COMMANDS
FROM: GENERAL RICHARD DAVIS
MESSAGE: 42-120
SUBJECT: ATTACK, DUTCH HARBOR

BE ADVISED, AS OF 0700Z THIS MORNING, SUPREME ALLIED HEADQUARTERS WAS ATTACKED BY GOMERS. FIGHTERS FROM AT LEAST TWO CARRIER CLASS SHIPS STRUCK WITH HORRIFIC FORCE AND WEAPONRY. CASUALTIES WERE HEAVY TO DEFENDING FORCES. ATTACK EMPLOYED SPIRAL TECHNIQUE AS DESCRIBED IN PREVIOUS MESSAGE, INTELLIGENCE 42-010I. BE ON ALERT ACCORDINGLY.

R. DAVIS
COMMANDING GENERAL
42ᴺᴰ ARMY GROUP

The Division Commander put his arm around his Aide and simply said, "We have no idea who was there."

Robbie could only stare at the message as he replied, "Geez, General, what DO we know, aside from this?"

"Well, we know we need to disperse our force, and keep a better watch above. The bastards came in from directly overhead, and it was not at the twilight line either. They waited until it was dark, and dropped in from above. Rumor has it they even brought in one of the Carrier Class ships, which either crashed, or played kamikaze, directly on the headquarters facilities."

"Son of a bitch...... Sorry, General. I think I might need a minute to maybe work some shit out."

"Fine, son, but don't take long. We're going to have to get our butts out in the trenches to make sure we've got all our eyes, ears, and weapons pointed upward."

"Yessir."

The rest of the day, Lieutenant Patrick focused on his duties, and probably would have made Sergeant Major Clagmore blush. He was a whirlwind, because now the Gomers had truly made it personal. This feeling was mirrored around the world, as each soldier, in each unit, from squad to Army Group, and each sailor, from the destroyers up to the Montana Class Battleships, were even more galvanized into killing Gomers. Granted, the Headquarters was a war time target, but that mattered little to anyone who already hated the Gomers.

SECTION 4

DESPERATION AND THE GLOBAL WAR

Chapter XV

Shortly after the strike on Dutch Harbor, the Gomers in all three of their main enclaves were struck by more weaponry than anyone thought possible. The offensive was now begun in earnest, as ground forces started their direct attack of the enclaves with everything they had available. Like Tierra del Fuego, this time it was hole to hole, with the fighting sometimes even taking the form of personal hand to hand combat. The next message from the Supreme Allied Headquarters had little effect on the average fighting man, but it did make everyone else, from the President down to at least a couple of Lieutenants, feel a whole lot better.

SUPREME ALLIED HEADQUARTERS

FROM: *GENERAL PATRICK*
TO: *ALL ARMY GROUPS*
SUBJECT: *LOCATION OF HEADQUARTERS*

BE ADVISED, ALL COMMUNICATIONS TO CONTINUE TO BE ROUTED TO THIS HEADQUARTERS VIA FLAGSHIP USS ALASKA. OPERATION SIBERIAN EXPRESS TO CONTINUE AS SCHEDULED. YOUR GUIDANCE IS TO KILL GOMERS, KILL GOMERS, AND THEN KILL MORE GOMERS! PATRICK

USS HELENA/USS ALASKA, SEA OF OKHOTSK, RUSSIA:

The fortunes of war are often taken for granted by many of the participants. This case was no exception. I, along with several members of my key staff, was in transit towards the USS Alaska when the strike at Dutch Harbor took place. Sure, we'd noticed that the Gomers had changed tactics, and we knew we were always vulnerable at Dutch Harbor, but it wasn't some sixth sense that led me to pull key staff, and my personal staff out of our forward headquarters. Instead, it was operational need. If we needed to pull a negotiation team together, this would require a more forward location. Moreover, the Psyops campaign we knew could lead them back to us sooner or later, and finally, that bastard Gomer, Commander Algatok, had seen Dutch Harbor. We knew it was probably compromised, so we left it in the hands of a skeleton staff, and were in the process of moving it all forward. The USS Alaska had been coordinated as my flag ship for quite some time, and along with the USS Montana and the *new* USS Iowa on the Atlantic side, each of these ships was equipped with the perfect command post for our operations. Like the last war, this was another one I intended to spend at sea. Unfortunately, not everyone I knew has his sea legs yet.

"General, can I speak to you just a minute?"

"Sure, Sergeant Major, what's on your mind?"

"Sir. Please don't tell anyone . . . but this boat is killing me."

"Sergeant Major, are you just a little sea sick?"

"Fuck, yeah. I didn't join the Navy for a reason. Now you can fly me anywhere you want, and you can even make me jump out of the damn plane, but this is bull shit."

"Why is that?"

"I keep knocking the shit out of myself just going from one room to another. The damn walls are always moving up and down, and I swear to GOD, even the coffee tastes like someone with a serious case of dehydration drank it first."

"Sergeant Major. Not to worry. I've got you scheduled for a flight out later this afternoon. You're going home to the 11th Airborne. After that bullshit at Dutch Harbor, if they want to talk, I'll find you. Right now, I want you to kill as many of the bastards as you can find!"

"Amen, hallelujah! Thank you, sir. I'll go get my gear together."

"Good, but remember one thing. If I need you, then you need to get your ass back to me, double quick. Got it?"

"Sir! Yes, Sir!" With that exchange, I sent him on his way. I knew we couldn't keep a tiger like him in this small of a cage, and regardless of what happened, CSM Clagmore was too good at what he does to sit on the sidelines like this. Nope, there was only one answer, put him back to work.

11th Airborne Division, Headquarters, Kamchatka, Russia:

The Division Commander read the latest message from the Supreme Allied Headquarters and felt a real sense of relief. It wasn't that he lacked faith in the system, but General Patrick was the guy who saw them through the first war with the Gomers, and it would be General Patrick that would get them through this one. With Patrick you had hope, and with anyone else, you had a lot more uncertainty. Now he looked around for his Aide, who wasn't anywhere to be seen. He was about to step out when he was handed the next message, which brought a HUGE smile to his face. Ah, more good news. Looking around, he grabbed a Corporal, and said, "Find me my Aide. NOW!" The Corporal bolted from the tent, and hauled it out to the flight line where he found the Lieutenant giving some poor Sergeant absolute hell about how he was rigging the chutes. Skidding to a halt in front of the Lieutenant and snapping a salute, he advised Robbie that the General needed him ASAP. Not wasting time, Robbie and the Corporal ran back to the Division Command Post.

"Sir. You wanted to see me?"

"Yes, but first, you have got to stop screwing with the help! That isn't what you're here for, and if you're that hell bent, I can always find you a rifle platoon somewhere to play with! Do you understand me, Lieutenant?"

"Yes, Sir! Sorry, Sir."

"Good, now read this." With that the Division Commander handed Robbie the message which immediately brought a smile to his face. The waves of relief that fell over him were overwhelming. When he looked back at the Division Commander, it was funny, but he almost thought he saw a tear in his eye. Then his General said something else that put tears in both their eyes. "Lieutenant, grab a HUMVEE, and get out to meet the Navy Chopper that should be arriving any minute. It seems that someone decided to send Clagmore back to the family. And on your way out, tell that other guy to come see me. I honestly can't wait to send him back to his Regiment. Good guy, but NOT the brightest bulb I've ever seen in stripes." Robbie nodded, snapped off the best salute of his life, and literally ran out to the Motor Pool. With his dad okay and the Sergeant Major returning, all was right in his world.

Supreme Allied Headquarters, (SAHQ - Rear):

When her father's message crossed through the message center, someone had the foresight to get her a copy right away. Chris immediately contacted Leah, and told her that Dad was okay, and apparently had some fight left in him. After talking to Leah, she got hold of Holly and told her the same thing. Their collective sense of relief was palpable. Holly then told Chris that they might have solved the Martian question, but that it would take a little more work to determine if it was correct. Once they had something, then they would need to contact the staff with their findings. Chris appreciated the importance, but her feelings for the Gomers were no longer sympathetic on any level. As far as she was concerned, she didn't care if they liked Mars or not, since she hoped that they wouldn't live long enough to ever see it again. Her mood was also reflected in New Washington.

New Washington:

Gathering his Cabinet, key advisors, and the military liaison officers from General Patrick's staff, President Martin Blanchard asked the simple question. "Have any of our efforts to contact the Gomers received a response?" As the President peered around the table, there was no response, except from Richard Todd, the Secretary of Defense. "Not unless Dutch Harbor was their response, in which case, yes, Mr. President."

"Todd, I agree. That was a response, and honestly, it wasn't the one we'd hoped to receive. I have here a message from General Patrick, which was sent via personal courier. I want to share it with you, and then get your opinions." Unfolding the paper, the President began reading:

Dear Mr. President,

It is my belief, and the belief of my staff intelligence officers, that the Gomers are, on some level, now reading our mail. This is why you are in receipt of this message via personal courier, and why we advertised the casualties as far higher than the actual numbers for the destruction of Dutch Harbor. As you know, and with your permission, our headquarters was virtually deserted at the time of the Gomer strike. This is also why we were careful to only transmit my post strike message via ELF to all headquarters.

I interpret the Gomer attack on Dutch Harbor as an attempt to respond negatively, or at the very least, to force a negotiation between us, where we will be negotiating from a position of weakness. As a result, I have given orders to escalate our activities to a full offensive on all three of the Gomer Enclaves in Siberia.

Additionally, I would like to humbly and officially request authorization for the employment of "Red Dragon", with such weapon to specifically target the Moon Class Ship, which is currently behind the Moon at low altitude. I recognize that we are very limited in the actual number of these weapons which are even now being built, but it would seem that the Gomers require a more drastic gesture to make our point. It would be my intent to not only keep the pressure up, but to make it so severe that they will have no choice but to negotiate or perish, and it is my belief that the release of one "Red Dragon" is necessary to accomplish this end.

My Courier will standby. I await your guidance, your humble servant,
Michael Patrick

The President set the letter down on the desk, and the room remained quite silent. The first to speak was the Secretary of State, Timothy Case, "Mr. President, I am not comfortable with such a weapon being released, but at the same time, I agree with General

Patrick's assessment. I think they are trying to back us into a corner, take out key leadership, and then force us either into negotiations or just out-right destruction. Either way, we lose little by turning General Patrick loose with Red Dragon."

Secretary Todd slowly nodded his head and then said, "Mr. President, I agree with Tim, but I do have a question."

"Go ahead."

"Sir. What do we tell the Russians and other allies in all this? Do we get their approval, or do we just do it?"

Before President Blanchard could reply, the National Security Advisor spoke up, "Sir. If I might interject?"

"Sure, Dr. Khelm."

"Sir. This entire project was classified Top Secret - NOFORN, meaning there was absolutely no foreign dissemination of the information to any of our allies. The list of people on this planet that even have a clue that such a thing even exists is extremely limited. As I look around, I can say that it is pretty much limited to those of us in this room, General Patrick, General McDaniel in the 14th Air Force at Vandenberg, and the scientists that helped build it and get it fielded."

"So, what is your point, Dr. Khelm?"

"Mr. President, I wouldn't tell a damn soul. I would just do it, and if anyone asks what happened, I think it would be that the Gomers flew too low to the Moon."

"Dr. Khelm, are you telling me to keep it hushed up?"

"Yes, Mr. President, that is exactly what I am saying. And for whatever it is worth, I saw a report this morning that Dr. Abramson's people have now cranked out two more of these monsters. That should bring our total for this weapons system up to six. If we fire the first prototype, we lose little in the way of strategic capability, just in case we need the newer types for other targets."

"I hadn't thought of that one. You're saying launch the first prototype of the weapon, and save the other five for later?"

"Mr. President, I realize that the first Red Dragon is not as powerful as the latter versions, but it does have the ability to get this job done. If the tests are any indication, the first one should be more than enough to eliminate the target General Patrick wants eliminated."

"Thank you, Dr. Khelm. Anyone else have any thoughts?" Waiting for more comments that didn't come, the President then continued. "Okay, Colonel, you've been waiting patiently on the sidelines. I want you to repeat for the benefit of these gentlemen the verbal message you were to convey to me from General Patrick."

"Mr. President. General Patrick was pretty specific that I only pass that on to you. He was rather adamant that it was personal in nature."

"Son. I'm the President, and I don't mind sharing this one. So, go ahead!"

"Yes, sir. Mr. President. I was instructed to tell you that General Patrick does not want a response in the classical sense. Instead, he 'only wants to know your answer if and/or when you decide to fire the thing.' He explained that 'I have to remain out of the actual loop, since I will still need credibility with our allies that I didn't know it was coming.' In other words, he wants to be able to plausibly deny any knowledge of what was going on here. He said, 'in case the Russians start asking questions, I want to be able to shrug it off as news to me.'"

"Thank you, Colonel. Okay, it sounds like General Patrick is in agreement with Dr. Khelm. What do you think, Tim?"

"Sir, as the Secretary of State, I would probably be better served to say that I understand that we need to send a message. I am very uncomfortable hitting someone with something like Red Dragon, when we're still hoping to talk to them."

"Okay, that sounds very officious. Now, please feel free to knock off the bullshit for posterity, and tell me what YOU think."

"Sir, I would knock them on their ass. After Dutch Harbor, regardless of whether we took serious casualties or not, it hardly sounds like good faith on their part. Nope, hit them, and hit them very hard. Maybe Patrick is right, and it will force them to finally understand that we mean serious business."

"Thank you, Tim. I appreciate your sentiment. Now then, what about you, Secretary Todd?"

"I have to agree with General Patrick and Dr. Khelm. Telling anybody would be a mistake, and as far as I am concerned, my opinion hasn't changed. I say release the weapon, and let's finally see if it works."

"Well, I know it will work, because it is the same principle as that employed by the USS New Jersey and the USS Morton, and we know it worked there. This is just a lot bigger, meaner, and far more devastating. Okay. Colonel, I want you to hand carry a message to Vandenberg to General McDaniel."

"Yes, Sir."

"And Colonel, you will NOT, repeat NOT, advise General Patrick of our decision, nor will you be allowed to return to his headquarters until AFTER Red Dragon is deployed."

"Actually, Sir. General Patrick was hoping you would say that, and he has authorized me leave en route to the USS Alaska. My family lives pretty close to Vandenberg, over the Pac Mountain facilities, so with your permission."

"By all means, Colonel. We'll have the message done in a few minutes, get you the code information, and then have you on your way."

"Thank you, sir."

Vandenberg Air Force Base, California:

True to his word, President Blanchard had the Colonel on his way, and within 8 hours, the Colonel was standing in front of General Randolph McDaniel, the Commander of the 14th Air Force, at Vandenberg Air Force Base, in California. Handing the General the sealed codes, the official message from the President, and both General Patrick and the President's personal greetings, he was about to walk out when he stopped and asked. "Sir, how long do I have for my leave?"

"Son, you can take as long as you want, but if you want to know when the light show will happen, I am pretty sure you won't have enough time to really unpack your bag."

"Thank you, General. I appreciate it. One other thing, and it didn't make a whole lot of sense, but....."

"Let me guess, Patrick has an unofficial message you're supposed to give me?"

"Actually, yes. He wanted me to tell you that when you had the ball rolling, he would appreciate hearing a short update about the ball game."

"I figured as much. Thanks, Colonel, and enjoy your leave." Saluting the General, the Colonel headed out of the office. Before the Colonel even reached the parking area, General McDaniel had the mission being sent out via land line teletype to the missile personnel responsible for the deployment of the "Red Dragon".

Near Bozeman, Montana. Mission Command Center:

An alarm sounded simultaneously with the teletype going berserk in the Command Center. The Air Force Major on duty immediately jumped, mainly from the surprise. Things had been quiet lately, and the Major had been reading a letter from his brother, who was a Marine on Kamchatka, Russia. When the klaxon went off and the teletype bells rang, he was re-reading the part of the letter that had described how miserable the winter had been and how busy the Marines were getting ready for the Gomers. Part of the Major was glad he wasn't freezing his ass off too, but he was also a little jealous at being shoved into a corner far away from the action. When those alarms went off, aside from almost giving him a heart attack, he was genuinely hoping that it wasn't just another drill. Reaching the teletype, he began reading the message that was scrolling over the ancient, antique machine. He laughed to himself that such a machine was even in existence, much less a key part of their missile technology, but after the First Gomer War, many decided that some of the old pre-transistor technology would be more resistant to the Gomers.

Taking a closer look at the message, he realized that this was no drill. Instead, his heart rate quickened, and he initiated the lock down procedures in and around the facility and got his partner over to confirm everything. This would be a HOT shot, and the boys hundreds of feet above were even now going through their pre-launch cycle of securing the facilities overhead. He had served down here countless hours and, aside from drills, had never been involved in anything close to this type of thing. His job was simple, he and his partner were responsible for the Red Dragon project, and it was their job to control the three Silos in Montana that were dedicated to that project. As they went through the pre-launch sequence, the targeting coordinates were being forwarded directly from Vandenberg to the one missile that they were authorized to launch. As the codes were verified, and then confirmed a second time, he and his partner began the countdown sequence. Finally, as he reached zero, both the Major and his partner turned their keys.

Several miles away, in Silo #236, the large ICBM began lifting from its underground home. Increasing speed until the requisite velocity to break Earth's gravitation was reached, it looked to the world like a lumbering children's toy. Painted in red lead paint, with a coating of gray lead base paint over the red, it crawled higher in the sky with only the flames and vapor trail marking its departure from the underground facility. Knowing what they had unleashed, but not knowing exactly where it was going, they did the after-launch checklist, and then began the process of securing the silo and the rest of the facility.

Turning to his partner, the Major simply muttered, "Probably just a test of that older model, since if they were going to shoot Gomers, you'd think they would use the new ones."

The young Captain said, "Yeah, it figures we'd get all this excitement for nothing. Hell, NOTHING ever happens here." As the Captain turned back to his check list items, and then his cheap novel, the Major picked his letter up and went back to reading about the cold and the 'real' action.

Vandenberg, Air Force Base, California:

General McDaniel was in his Operations section where they were tracking the missile. Turning to his Aide, he said, "Get this message off to General Patrick."

"Yessir."

"Write. McDaniel to Patrick. Vandy v. West Point is now underway. Care to wager?"

"Sir?"

"Just send it, and wait for the reply!"

"Yessir!" Scurrying to the Communications section, the message was sent. Within a few minutes the reply returned, and the Lieutenant ran back to his boss.

"Sir. I've got General Patrick's reply."

"Okay, what's he say, son?"

"Uh..... Patrick to McDaniel. No Wager yet, but advise as to score."

"Excellent." Turning back to the display, General McDaniel lit a cigar and sat back to watch things as they unfolded. This was a new animal they were sending out, and honestly, he was as curious as the rest of the crowd. Knowing that this was happening, Dr. Abramson entered the room, almost completely breathless from his sprint over to the Command Center from the helipad. The folks in the know were all waiting, and given the speeds involved, they were going to have a long wait. As the missile delivery system continued towards the Moon, there was no activity seen from the Gomers. It was sincerely hoped that they would not see anything, and that without a constant rocket flare following the Rocket, there was little they could see since it was shielded in lead. Unlike the other Moon shots taken to this point, this particular weapon was now being driven by momentum. Sure, there were minor adjustments being made, but they were only little bursts of the thruster to provide stability and directional control at key times along the flight path. Given this mode of delivery, there was nothing to do in the Command Center but watch and wait.

New Washington:

The longer the wait, the more impatient President Blanchard was becoming with the whole process. News from the Front was pretty good, and the President was taking comfort in the fact that the 21st Army Group had broken through the main defenses at the first Gomer enclave near the Ural Mountains. Looking at his own Military Aide, Lieutenant General Maria Hookman, he was smiling and commenting on the advances being made. It seemed that the only place that there was an issue was with the Russians and General Igor Sevitch, who was the Russian Airborne Forces Commander. They were the primary force responsible for a second Gomer Enclave, but apparently the best they could do was a stalemate. Neither gaining nor losing ground, General Patrick, General Whitney, and General Larkin were doing their best to kick them harder and hope that they could catch up to the other forces. Finally, the President was extremely pleased to note that the 42nd Army Group was also inside the Main Gomer enclave, and having sufficient success to keep almost the entire Gomer Fighter fleet housed there, on the ground.

Reading these latest reports, he was a little surprised when Dr. Henrich Khelm broke into the office unannounced and issued a rather loud, "MR. PRESIDENT! Check out the news!" The National Security Advisor immediately turned on the TV in the President's underground "Oval Office" without even saying an 'excuse me'. More than a little annoyed, the President was immediately mesmerized when he saw the pictures and heard the words from the announcer.

"Just a few minutes ago, a rather interesting explosion was seen on the back side of the moon. Our cameras have kept an almost constant watch on the Moon since the arrival of the Gomers some months ago. Just a few minutes ago, we got these pictures. As you can see, there is a faint light that grows in intensity to almost the brightness of the sun. Then it appears that there is a second explosion. As you can see, there is also a cloud of what appears to be dust coming from behind the Moon. Dick, have you spoken with anyone that knows what this could be?"

"Well, Alvin, we've tried to get someone to comment from the Allied Headquarters, but our sources indicate that they don't have a clue. It was speculated by one source that maybe the Gomers had something go wrong, which might have caused their Moon ship to explode. We're still working on it, but we just don't know at this point."

"Thanks, Dick. Folks, that was Dick Knox, from the New Pentagon, reporting. Again to recap, we have an explosion....."

Turning the TV off, the President turned to Dr. Khelm, and said, "Do you have a press release worked up for this yet?"

"Actually, we have the one we agreed on some days ago when this thing was launched."

"Okay, run it. Right now, we will plead our ignorance, just like the New Pentagon doesn't have a clue, then neither do we. Who knows, maybe it hit a mine."

"Yessir."

"Oh, and Dr. Khelm, as much as I appreciate your letting me know, next time, knock!"

"Sorry, Mr. President."

Vandenberg Air Force Base, California:

The cheers in the room were deafening. Dr. Abramson was beside himself with joy, as was General McDaniel. Lighting a cigar, General McDaniel hoisted a large bottle of scotch from his desk drawer and poured himself and Dr. Abramson a rather healthy shot. Then he turned to his Aide and said, "Lieutenant, I'd ask you to join us, but right now, you have to get to the message center. Send this message to General Patrick. 'First Period score. Vandy 1, West Point Zero.'"

"First period?"

"Damn, Lieutenant. Just send the message!"

"Yessir."

Turning to Dr. Abramson, he asked, "Well, Doc, how soon before the new and improved model is up and running?"

"In three days it will be loaded and ready to go. The range on it is much longer, and we can detonate on signal. It should work to keep them at a distance."

"Excellent. I'm sure General Patrick will be glad to hear it. I know damn well I'm glad. So what do you think of the prototype?"

"Actually, General, it worked, which is more than I really expected. The wave patterns were perfect, and it was our first real test of a 'Gomer' based THz bomb. When we came up with the 'Gomer Bubble' for the Navy, we had this notion that it might work in reverse."

"Okay, we've fired the first one, and we now are having a victory drink. Do you think it is about time somebody fully explained to me how this damn thing works?"

"Sure. The concept weapon, which is the one that just went off directly behind the Moon ship, was designed to create THz waves in such a strength as to allow it them to amplify and multiply immediately after being emitted into a series of highly focused energy waves."

"Excuse me?"

"General, in essence, it is an exponential T-wave weapon that will push against the side of a target with such a dynamic over-pressure, so as to crush that target under multiple minutely focused, but extremely high frequency, THz wave pressures."

"Still not real clear."

"Sound, General. THz waves are in a higher part of the electromagnetic spectrum, and we figured out how to focus them like the Gomers do with their weapons. You're familiar with the idea of Gomer Guns, and this is similar, only more powerful and deadly. In this case, we took that extremely high end of the spectrum, and were able to focus something akin to a microwave type beam into waves that would crush whatever it hits. It even has the joy with our newer version of burning what it hits, assuming there are other sources of combustion present. We don't know this for sure, but we believe it might even boil the fluids from the inside out of anything it hits."

"HOLY SHIT! So, we just fried a bunch of Gomers we can't even see, while they were hiding behind something as big as the Moon?"

"Yes, General, that is precisely what we did, and that is precisely why General Patrick really did NOT want to use it before. See, the down side is that we don't know for sure what it might do to the chemistry of the Moon. Right now, I'm even waiting to see if we've changed the orbit of the Moon."

"GOD, I hope not. Tides and all....."

"Still, General, it was all in a good day's work. Say, do you have any of those cigars left?"

"Sure! Here, and here's a light!"

CHAPTER XVI

USS Alaska, Supreme Allied Flagship, Sea of Okhotsk:

Frustration would be the primary word of the day. While we were getting excellent results from each of our main units in both the 21st and 42nd Army Groups, the Russian Forces were not quite as aggressive as we had hoped, especially since this was their soil we were defending. Finally, it was time to have a little meeting with General Igor Sevitch. Loading Captain Dubronin into the Seahawk, we began our journey by flying to the USS Nimitz, where we hopped a flight on a V-22 Osprey, headed to the Russian Command Group's headquarters near Jakutsk, Russia. This was already an issue for me, since Jakutsk was too damn far to the rear, and it certainly was not helpful for the field commander to be so far from the action. I hoped that a surprise appearance would perhaps light the necessary fire to get things moving.

On landing, General Sevitch, who was warned that we were coming when we refueled on the mainland, was out to meet us with full honors. It was quite the show and precisely what I did not need, want, or would tolerate from a Commander in a combat zone. General Sevitch was very hospitable and actually kind of likeable. Unfortunately, I saw precisely what General Larkin warned me I would see, and I was not impressed. Making polite discussion was one thing, but pissing away opportunities in combat was another entirely. Finally, after allowing him to play host for the requisite period, I got him and Captain Dubronin in a more private conference.

"General Sevitch. You have a lovely command, and your hospitality is wonderful."

"Da. Thank you, General."

"General Sevitch. Let me be clear, lovely commands and hospitality won't win this war. With your permission, please let me offer a few observations that might help us all achieve that victory."

"Certainly, General."

"Igor, you will have to do several things that I think might help. First, you need to move closer to the front, and let your soldiers see you lead. I'm not saying go into the enclaves, but I am saying you will need to visit your Army Commanders to make them push harder."

"Da, I can do this."

"Good. You will also need to get your subordinate commanders closer to the Gomers, too."

"Certainly."

"Finally, you need to spend less time on giving me a show, and more time on getting the job done. I hate to tell you this, but your government has given me the authority to bring in help if you bog down or I think you need it."

"Da. I know this."

"Good, because if you don't start moving this show, and attack the enemy with all you have, then I'm going to bring in that help."

"Sir. We take help!"

"General Sevitch, the help I'm talking about won't come from Americans dying for Russia. Instead, if you don't get this Group moving, the help is coming from China and Japan."

"Nyet! You cannot do this."

"General Sevitch. I'm as serious as I can be. Do you know Captain DUBRONIN here?"

"Nyet."

"Well, Captain Dubronin is the son of Yuri Dubronin. Does that help any?"

"Da."

"Then you know I'm telling you exactly what his Father already knows. If you don't light a fire under your group, one of two things is going to happen. You will be replaced, OR I am going to fill you up with Chinese and Japanese reinforcements. Do either of those options sound good to you?"

"Nyet. No. I will do my best to light fire."

"Excellent, General!" On those words, I threw my arm around him and we walked out of his private quarters. All that his soldiers saw was our friendship and my respect for their boss. On the flight out, Captain Dubronin looked at me and asked, "Sir, would you really bring in the Chinese to our sacred lands?"

"Captain, if it means getting the Gomers off the planet, yes I would."

Thinking for a minute, Captain Dubronin then said, "Sir. That was good motivator, but I hope you don't bring in Chinese."

Smiling, I said, "Me too, Alex, me too. Let's hope that Igor gets the message and starts moving those armies forward. Then it won't even have to be an option."

On short final back to the USS Nimitz, I was greeted with the message from General McDaniel, "Vandy 1, West Point Zero." The messenger from the cockpit looked at me quizzically, and I laughed. When we landed, I went immediately to the MH-60, Seahawk, that returned me to my Flagship, USS Alaska. Once on board, I began reviewing the videos taken from various angles and the multiple BDA assessments that were prepared by the scientists and the USAF personnel responsible for such things. There was no question, the weapon worked like a champ, and that surprised me. I was expecting a large fizzle, but it was a roll of the dice that worked. Scratch one Moon Class ship and the primary support base for the Gomers in Siberia. Now we would really turn up the heat.

As the twilight line approached, every weapon system we could bring to bear was focused on each of the disputed portions of the enclaves, and the approaches both to and from each of those enclaves, bombarding them without mercy. The expression of the day was, "If the Gomer is flying, then he be dying." The same was true for almost all of the outer rings of the defenses surrounding each of the Gomer enclaves, and into the main defenses of the same enclaves. My talk with General Sevitch also must have paid off, since even the Russian Forces were making unprecedented strides as they pushed deeper inside the enclave itself.

All in all, we were pushing harder and faster and the results were stunning. While this was taking place, more drama was forming in space near the Moon. The fleet that had escorted the two Moon Class ships to Mars was now headed towards the Moon. Presumably to assess the damage, but we saw it as potential movement back in our direction, and we were on alert accordingly. What we did not want to see was another attempt at a Dutch Harbor-like attack on any of our naval or ground forces. I also sent a message back to New Washington and all of our mountain facilities to warn them to be on alert for an overhead attack. I think at this point, everyone from the scientific community down to the amateur astronomer with a back yard telescope was watching the skies in all directions.

Supreme Allied Headquarters, (SAHQ-Rear):

General Clark was the Rear Commander, which was something he did not care to deal with at all. He was up to his eyeballs in logistical problems, so when the Doctors all descended on him with their vital information for the "boss" he couldn't wait to hand it off.

I had been hopping back and forth between the Army Groups and visiting forward units when I got a message that indicated that I was needed in the rear. Already exhausted from flying back and forth all around Russia when I got the message, I informed the flight crew to get us an aerial- tanker, we were headed to the rear barn. The crew was most accommodating, since they had just bounced out of an airfield near Pevek, Russia, and were ready for any excuse to land at an airport that wasn't quite such a challenge. Turning the aircraft around, they assessed the amount of daylight left before we would land near Seattle, Washington. It would be close, but we made it with a little light to spare. Taking advantage of the layover, I got perhaps the first full night of sleep I had seen in months. The following morning, we were up with the dawn, and headed east to the Allied Headquarters facilities.

When I reached the War Room, General Clark, who looked like he had seen the inside of a ringer washer, was actually glad to see me.

"General Patrick! Thank GOD you're here!"

"Glad to see you, too. So, what is so important that I had to leave the comforts of a combat zone to head back here to hang out with my family?"

"Well, sir. The Eggheads were chomping at the bit, and they swear they have something you have to know."

"Any idea what it is so important?"

"Not really. They started the chatter, but it wasn't registering with me."

"Okay, where are they? I need to get my butt back to the front. We're getting close, Dave, we really are getting close."

"I know, General. I've been reading the reports, but they swear that this might be something we need to know moving forward. I can get them here in about an hour."

"Okay, well, I'm going to grab a bite to eat, and get updated on the latest. Have them get here and get me briefed. I'll plan on my departure back to the USS Alaska for 3 hours from now. Tell them I'm on a short leash, and I don't have time to screw around."

"You got it, Sir. I'll even warn the flight crew."

"Thanks." True to my word, I had finished a bacon sandwich and was just pouring another coffee as I read the latest message traffic, when Dr. Clarkson, Dr. Marvin, and Dr. Cobb wandered into the War Room.

"Okay, gentlemen. What was so important that you had to get me back here?"

Dr. Clarkson began, "Sir, we have confirmed why the Gomers are so focused on keeping their last two ships near Mars."

"Are you serious? You drug my ass back here for that? Might I ask the relevance, or more to the point, why should we care?"

"Sir. It is what is motivating them. What we believe is their entire reason for attacking us here, and why they have acted the way they have to this point."

"Okay, I'm listening."

"Doctor Marvin will do our presentation, and he will be followed by Dr. Cobb. Dr. Marvin figured it out, and Dr. Cobb confirmed it, with the help of Dr. Patrick, I might add."

"Let's do it then. I've got a war to fight."

Dr. Marvin took up the presentation, despite my being a little miffed at the whole affair. This was definitely one of those times where I didn't give a damn about the science anymore. We were on the verge of kicking the Gomers off the planet, and this was a distraction. I did my best to listen to Dr. Marvin as he continued with his briefing, but it was starting to hit me that these motivations could be very useful, but only on another plain of existence.

"...... so the toxicity of Mars is precisely why the Gomers like the place. For them it is a perfect location to colonize. It is far enough from our Sun to not get the same energy levels, it is a polar planet, on an axis, which contains perchlorates, or chlorinated hydrocarbons, that they use as part of their photosynthesis like feeding process. It exists in our soil, but at more nominal and safer amounts. On Mars, this component would be toxic to us, but the Gomers don't mind it at all. We even had a school of thought several years ago that considered the question of how to get the perchlorates out of the soil and process it into oxygen. Of course, the Gomers don't need to do that, since oxygen isn't necessarily a key component for their respiration."

"Alright, Doctor. Where does this become relevant?"

Dr. Cobb took on the presentation by answering. "Sir, they are attempting to colonize Mars. It is why they are here in our solar system."

"Does that mean that the two remaining Moon Ships are full of colonists?"

"Exactly! While they still have some military capability in both of those ships, it would appear that they are mainly for defense."

"Okay, gentlemen, how can you know this?"

"Sir. The chemical process led us to go back to the prisoners to ask questions about their purpose for being here on Earth. The Prisoners almost to a ma.... okay to a Gomer, all said it was to keep us from attacking them on Mars. It was preemptive, since they knew we had sent probes to Mars, and they knew we had the capability of reaching that planet."

"How would they know that we could reach Mars, when even we don't have a viable mission profile for reaching the damn place yet?"

"Sir. They have been here before, and we were nowhere as advanced as we are today. They just assumed....."

"Dammit! Look, I've played along, but if this is any way reliant on a Gomer's opinion or statement, then I'm done playing. Algatok damn near cost me my life, and the lives of most of my staff. I will trust a Gomer as far as I can toss him, and his damn climate suit, into a 500 knot headwind!"

"Well, we've got some empirical data to support the composition of Mars, and we know that those two ships have tried to stay there for most of the conflict. They only ventured back this way when we took out a lot of their fleet with the first attack near the Moon. We have some communications with them, and we've intercepted some more communications that we have been able to decipher in a limited fashion."

"What about Algatok? He leaves, and within a couple of days, Dutch Harbor is pounded back to the Stone Age. What the hell was that about?"

"Well sir. We think it was because they were hoping to twist our arms into a better deal for them."

"Geez, you think!?! I hate to be hostile to this, and deep down I'm probably not as hostile as I appear, but seriously? They have done nothing but kill and lie since we started dealing with them. A lot of good men have died, and a lot more will die, all because we want to chat with these bastards? About something that may or may not be coming our way, what are they called? Oh, yeah. Tornit. You know, I really don't know that I care anymore. Right now, the only good one is a dead one."

"General! We believe that with this information, we can put together a better message to send them that just might bring them to the table. We destroyed their main command ship, the one near the Moon. When we showed the enhanced video to the prisoners, they reacted significantly. Some even demonstrated a true sense of loss."

"Enhanced video? What is that?"

"If you recall, they don't see in the same spectrum as we do, so we had to enhance it by broadcasting it at a different frequency level."

"Okay, I remember. So, they showed a sense of loss? What does that mean really? That some Gomer had buddies on the ship we blew up, or that they were now feeling alone, or maybe it is because they realize that we will personally kick their asses off the planet? Again, I'm not getting the message, since negotiations just don't seem possible at this point. Sure these guys surrendered, but wasn't it when their trans...... Wait a minute. Get rid of their ride, and they get compliant?"

"That is one way of putting it. We destroyed their main command ship, the one with the bulk of their military command structure. So, now maybe the 'civilian' or colonist Gomers will be more compliant."

"All right. Let's say for the sake of argument that you have hit on something. What do you want us to do?"

"Send another message only this time from you and the President. Something a little more benign or friendly."

"You're kidding right? Friendly, as in 'come on down for tea, we love you'? How about we just sing Kumbaya to their asses, and thank them for killing millions of people? No, Doctor. I think blasting their Moon ship was a message. Just like their hitting Dutch Harbor was a message. How about this for a plan? We retransmit our messages from before, take the approach we took before they hit Dutch Harbor, and let's see what they do this time. If that was a military command ship we destroyed, as you suggest, then maybe this time the civilians will take the smart road. That might substantiate your theory. I know that one huge difference this time is that we have shown them we can take out their Moon Ships, AND we are sitting inside their enclaves kicking their teeth down their throats on a more personal level."

"I think being nice works well with the prisoners, so I was hoping we could take that approach to their government....."

"Doctor, the only message I'll send the bastards, and I'm pretty sure it is the only message the President will want to send, is give up or we will shove it a little further up your ass. Of course, we'll say it far more politely. Now then, I've only got one more question."

Looking a little crestfallen, Dr. Clarkson responded, "Yessir?"

"You said you were deciphering some of their traffic, and I assume you're translating some of their wording. Are you getting anything from it, anything that we know isn't a plant or deception transmission?"

"Actually, we can read some of it, we understand less of it, and to be perfectly honest, we have no idea from the lack of inflection that we can interpret, whether it means something one way or another."

"Inflection, as in certain languages, say Yiddish for example, the inflection will dictate the meaning, and the Gomers have inflection?"

"Exactly, and to be brutally honest, part of what you were told was supposition based on our best analysis as to certain inflections we are not able to fully interpret."

"Well, this trip hasn't been a total waste, I got a bacon sandwich out of the deal. Okay, Dr. Clarkson, how about this. Why don't we send them a copy of an Oxford Dictionary, keep pounding the shit out of them, and maybe one of them will learn enough of our language to finally speak to us for a change. I know in Greenland, when we were kicking their asses around the ice, they were motivated to communicate, so they just laid down and called it a day. I would notice that the Gomers in Siberia aren't taking that approach at all. Instead, they are fighting to the bitter end. Hell, last night, one of our units was all but wiped out by a damn Banzai kind of charge out of one of their holes."

"Sir..."

"Doctor Clarkson. Let me say this for the benefit of all three of you. You guys, along with Dr. Abramson, have been the life blood for our fight. You're the brains of the operation, and you have no idea how valuable each and every one of you are to me. I mean that, even on a personal level. In fact, if you guys were in uniform, each of you would have earned more medals than any 10 soldiers for your contributions. Now I'm sure this one is as important, but PLEASE don't forget what has to be done. NOBODY wants this to end anymore than I do, and trust me, I realize that with the alleged Tornit out there, I don't want to take these guys out if we don't have to do it. I just need you to start thinking outside the box again. You've got this information you think is relevant, but it needs to be developed more. I've been hard on you today, but I will assure you that it isn't you, it is my frustration over not ending this sooner than later. Every day that goes by, we're losing men, and nothing pisses me off more than losing people."

"We understand, sir, but we do think we're onto something."

"No question, you're onto something, but it needs to be something besides their motivation. It needs to be concrete enough that we can act on it. Right now, their motivations are not that big a secret. Whether they want to defend themselves preemptively or whether they are here to steal energy, doesn't mean a thing to the guy who is about to die because a Gomer has him by the throat."

"Yessir."

"Oh, and good work intercepting signals. Now from that we might learn more about motivations, and more specifically, what will get them to leave. Now that is the motivation I want."

"We're working it, and we'll get you something soon."

"While we are on this subject, I've got another burning question."

"Yessir?"

"You remember all the data information? Those cyber 'computer' files we've obtained from their downed ships? Oh, and the data from that Mountain Ship General Greene captured in the last war? Has anyone come close to cracking into that yet?"

"No, sir. We've got people working on it, but we haven't been able to find the key to get into it yet."

"Assuming the bastards keep records, wouldn't that tell us whether this was all real or some BS they are tossing at us?"

"Yessir."

"Then keep after it. Otherwise, what we have is what THEY want us to know."

"Yessir."

"Thanks, gentlemen, I know a lot of people who would appreciate it. And seriously, please don't take today too much to heart. I wasn't kidding, we wouldn't be even close to this far ahead if it wasn't for all you have done. On behalf of a very grateful world, I do thank you."

There was no question that this was the hardest butt chewing I could have given them, but out of the ashes did come the idea of renewing "Operation Phone Call". Only this time, it was going to be a new message that incorporated the destruction of their Moon Ship, and the state of their forces in Siberia. This time it would be something to really get them thinking about what they had to lose. Maybe this time, we could get some of that right 'inflection' going in what we were sending them. Then again, maybe it would be Algatok all over again. All I knew was that if I ever got my hands on that dirty SOB, it was going to be VERY personal.

I was about to leave my office to catch my flight when Holly, who apparently was back in town with her scientist friends, caught me on the way out. She looked mortified, and I knew already that word of the ass chewing had filtered back to her world. When she walked up, she gave me the obligatory hug, but then launched into her assault on me. Taking her by the arm, we walked back into my office, where Chris was waiting. Chris I knew was in agreement with me on the question of Gomer diplomacy, but she also didn't want to see the family erupt into a classic case of "Patrick-cide warfare." When we sat down, Holly started her tearful "how could you pick on the scientists" speech. When I related my side of it, she seemed to calm down a little, and then I threw her a bone, which she promptly used to beat me in the head. I told her that I wanted her to help me get a new speech recorded to be transmitted to the Gomers. She refused, saying instead that she couldn't since Dr. Cobb wasn't talking to her at the moment. It was then, for the first time since she was little, that I let the baby of the family hold it.

"Holly, dammit. I've got people getting blown to hell around the globe, and you're sitting here whining because some snot-nosed prima donna won't talk to you? What the hell, is he your damn boyfriend or something?"

"God! No, dad. I am actually dating a guy that works with John, you know, your son-in- law John. He is a chemist."

"Holly, I'm not here to discuss your love life, I just wondered what was so important about this joker, Dr. Cobb."

"Dr. Cobb is no joker, and we've made great strides. He was the one to finally figure out that the inflections of the speaker could change the message."

"What are you trying to say here?"

"I'm saying I can't help you, only he can, and right now his tail feathers are a little singed."

"Good, then maybe he will get his head out of his ass and help. Seriously, we need him to do his job, so if you want to help, get him talking again, and get me what is in those damn data files. Right now, I don't give a rip how, but just get him to stop being so far into the clouds. If he really wants there to be peace, then he's going to have to cooperate, or I guess we can find a new egghead and start over. Right now, we have a little thing called a war going on, and honestly, I don't have time for this crap."

"Dad! You are insufferable."

"Then by all means pass on your sympathy to your Mother, but in the meantime, get Cobb moving on helping you get the message done, otherwise, I will find someone who will."

"It doesn't work that way, but okay. I'll talk to him."

"Good. Now what the hell is up with this chemist guy? Does he have a name?"

"Actually he does, it is James."

"James? James what?"

"James Evans."

"When all this is over, I'll have to meet him. Now, give me a hug, and go make Dr. Cobb see the light."

Heading back out of the office, I gave Chris a hug, and then changed course to head to my quarters to see Leah for a few minutes. We didn't have long, so she didn't give me a hard time about the "Holly is upset at dad" incident. I knew she probably knew all about it, but far be it from me to poke anything with a stick at this point. We had a few minutes, and we didn't waste it discussing business. Within the hour, I was back to the flight line, and then headed back to the west trying to stay ahead of the twilight line. I had another forced layover in Seattle, and then we were off to find the USS Alaska.

USS Alaska, Supreme Allied Flagship. Sea of Okhotsk:

The trip around the various commands that had turned into the science junket had been a huge diversion from where I needed to be located. Back on board the USS Alaska, I was finally able to get a handle back on Operation Siberian Express. The three Gomer enclaves were now reduced to two. The balance of the 21st Army Group was shifting to assist the Russian Army Group, which was still having trouble with their particular enclave. They were far beyond where they were on my first visit, but still behind the curve when it came to results. As our reinforcements were arriving, the Russians were finally able to move deeper into the enclave. The real problem was to verify that the positions were actually being eliminated, before moving onward. With the arrival of the American forces, the reduction of Gomer positions was becoming far more systematic and precise.

The 42nd Army Group had the largest of the three enclaves to clear, and it was going as well as could be expected. This was the home of what we believed to be the Gomers' main base on Earth, and it was certainly the best defended. We were keeping the Gomers' Fighter Class ships on the ground, and it was working so well that there had not been a Gomer ship spotted in the air for several days. The Gomer fleet that had moved from Mars to the Moon was still holding position near the moon. We maintained the alert posture for their movement, but so far, they were still acting the same as when they had to do the clean up after our first Moon Strike. Their patterns appeared to be that of a search and rescue operation. General Thayer and the Air Forces were monitoring this movement, and advising us so that ground defense postures could be set accordingly.

It was two nights later that the Gomers' fleet began to move, and this time Vandenberg was on full alert and waiting. Coming above the twilight line, well above Earth, it was determined by their angle of descent that they were about to try one more Dutch Harbor type attack, only this time, it was quite apparent that the target was going to be at or near New Washington, the new Pentagon, and our Rear Headquarters.

Chapter XVII

USS Alaska, Supreme Allied Flagship. Sea of Okhotsk:

When the information flashed over the command net, I immediately snapped my chief concerns to the staff. "I need to know how many, what type ship, and what is their ETA to New Washington?" The defenses for each of those locations, New Washington, the new Pentagon, and our Rear Headquarters, were excellent, but they had their limits. As the reports came back, it was clear to me that we were going to have a hard night ahead of us. Admiral Lynch was quick to point out that the initial projections indicated the Gomer fleet moving towards the US East Coast had an estimated time of arrival of about 45 minutes. "General, the attack force now headed to the target consists of two Mountain Class ships, four Battleship Class ships, and eight Carrier Class ships."

"What is the status of our strategic air defenses, you know, the damn mines!"

"Vandenberg reports all Green and hot, Sir."

"Excellent, now then, let's liven things up a little. Admiral?"

"Aye, Sir."

"Admiral Lynch, I want all Pacific Big Gun Battlegroups, to include this one, to maximize their UHF and VHF traffic immediately! All Carrier Battlegroups are to become holes in the water."

"Sir? You want us to transmit?"

"You heard me, tell all the battleships to transmit on VHF and UHF Guard Frequencies. I don't care if they send their damn laundry lists, I want as much emission in those frequencies ranges as possible. And tell them I want the transmissions to continue for the next 45 minutes or until I tell them to quit, whichever is sooner."

"Aye, aye, sir. Isn't that running the risk that their big stuff will come after....."

"Exactly my point! While you're at it, double check the positions of all submarine assets working with the Big Gun Battlegroups. If we have anyone at least 100 miles away to our west, then they need to be doing the standard bait transmissions, but ONLY after we have stopped."

"Okay?"

"Dammit, Admiral. None of our assets can hold off a Mountain or Battleship Class ship if they decide to hit New Washington or any of our other Mountain facilities. Look, the Gomers have a stand-off range of anywhere from 50 miles for their Battleship classes, up to roughly 100 miles from their Mountain Class ships. We can shoot them out of the sky at about 20 miles, which is great for Carrier Class and Fighter Class ships, but isn't worth a damn for the big ones. If they decide to put one of the big bastards over the target and unleash, then the folks back home will have one very ugly night."

"So, you're thinking of making us better targets, to draw the heat off."

"That is exactly right. I still remember Diamond Head and Dutch Harbor. We have to be a real hot target, so instruct your commo guys to send my 'screw you Gomer' messages on all frequencies. We have to draw them our way, or the folks back home could be well and for truly fucked. Got it?"

"Yessir. I've got it!"

"Good, now start sending, and General Roberts, keep all Gomer course and distance information headed to me. The timing for this will be tough, and I'll need to know the instant the Gomer Fleet makes any changes or modifies the flight path. Oh, and Admiral Lynch."

"Yessir?"

"Make sure to tell the Carrier Battlegroups to get all of their aircraft up to immediate standby status for a maximum effort. They need to be prepared to launch everything they have that can hit the Gomers from a distance. Now is the time to break some more of those modified X-51A2 Waverider missiles out of the crates."

As the staff scrambled to issue the orders, our own Battlegroup turned out to the east heading for plenty of open water. We were no longer a hole in the water, but instead were sending as much radio traffic as we could find. Intermixed with my message to the Gomers were the messages of General Greene and Sergeant Major Clagmore. The other Big Gun Battlegroups were doing the same thing, only they were sending other things that ranged from the Old Testament to the Tokyo phone book. We were also sending these forces on convergent courses towards one another, all aimed to a common point as far out to sea as we could make it. My hope was that the Gomers would think we were about to have a major meeting, and that I was the guest of honor.

Supreme Allied Headquarters, (SAHQ-Rear):

General Clark was digging through the latest message traffic from General Patrick and the staff on board the USS Alaska. Confounded beyond belief, none of what was happening or what he was reading made any real sense to him. "Now why in the hell would he be yelling at the world, with the whole damned Gomer fleet bearing down on our mountains?" As he pondered all this, he was even more frustrated that radio traffic from the USS Alaska appeared to be all out-bound, and that there was nothing in the way of response from their ELF/VLF inquiries to the senior staff. He was still pondering all of this when his Aide yelled for him to pick up the phone line.

"General Clark here."

"General, what is the status of your evacuation?"

"Who the hell is this?"

"President Blanchard! Dammit, now answer my question?"

"Sorry, Mr. President. Sir, we've got all the civilian personnel in the shelters, and our Air Defense weapons are all aimed and waiting on them to get into range. What is your status there?"

"I'm clear, along with most of the cabinet. We're still working the problem, but 2.4 million people are hard to move in a hurry. What is Patrick's status?"

"Sir, he is transmitting all over the VHF/UHF spectrum, and raising more hell than you can imagine with the Gomers. What I don't understand is the why, or what he might have in mind."

"Damn, Clark, I guess you might be the best logistician on the planet, but you don't know dick about tactics."

"Sorry? Mr. President.... uh, I guess I don't know this one."

"General, our esteemed General Patrick is trying to buy us all some time, and he is trying to make himself a better target for their big stuff. In other words, he is doing all he can to draw off the enemy."

"Mr. President, wouldn't that be suicide?"

"Probably."

"Then ....."

"Geez. Look, General Clark, start clearing out your people. From what I'm hearing you've got about 25 minutes to get as many people as possible to their alternate or shelter locations."

"Yessir. I would......" Before he could finish the sentence the line was dead. General Clark thought about General Patrick, and his family that he just saw earlier hauling it to the deep shelter, 'For your sake, General, suicide or not, I sincerely hope your plan works.'

Vandenberg Air Force Base, California:

General McDaniel was in his command post monitoring the oncoming fleet. As the Gomers neared the mine field, he was timing the launch of several strategic missile assets to try to slow the bastards down. Trying to watch it real time was somewhat of a challenge, and the lag time between position and firing point was yet one more of these challenges. He thought of it as duck hunting, where he had to lead the bird, before blasting it. He and his staff had done it before, but this time it was different. Their courses were different, since they were headed to a point as opposed to flying in an approach arc, and they were not coming into the same orbit angles as they were lining up to dive on their targets. The one thing that might help was that now they were bunching up to make their dives. As they watched, the smaller portions of the Gomer fleet, the Carrier Class and Fighters, were already moving through the minefield. The larger units were lined up with one of the Battleship Classes taking the lead. When the lead Battleship Class entered the mine field, General McDaniel realized that the first ship was being used to detonate the mines, and so long as the other capital ships followed the exact same path, they probably wouldn't be impacted. It was a good strategy, simply because McDaniel didn't have a damn thing to counter it, except the somewhat inaccurate missile fire.

Within seconds of entry, the lead Battleship Class ship struck the first mine. Turning to almost a broadside angle, it drifted on through the mine field, detonating a number of the other mines before it was ultimately incinerated. As it exploded into infinitesimal particles of space junk, the second Battleship Class ship stepped up to take the lead position. Moving past the wrecked and disintegrating first ship, this new Battleship Class ship was struck by the first of several missiles launched for the purpose of either destroying the targets, or at least forcing the larger ships into a different course away from New Washington. When the final Mountain Class ship left the target area, General McDaniel's 14th Air Force was responsible for one Mountain Class Ship, and two of the four original Battleship Class ships. Unfortunately, this still left enough Gomer combat power to completely destroy New Washington and the other mountain shelters.

Secure standby bunker near New Washington:

President Blanchard was less than impressed with the evacuation from New Washington. There were at least one million people still exposed in the underground levels that were already identified as areas that could expect total destruction. Granted these estimates were based on the Mountain and Battleship Class ship weapons, but even the Carrier Class could be expected to inflict upwards of 10,000 casualties, should they find and hit the exact right spot. Watching the course, speed, and other targeting information that was being forwarded to the bunker from Vandenberg, Air Force Base, the situation was anything but comforting. Turning to Dr. Khelm, he said, "Well, Doctor, it would appear that we only got half of their big stuff, and a handful of their smaller stuff. Any sign that General Patrick's plan might be working?"

"Nothing yet. It looks to me as if they are still headed to our three key locations here on the East Coast. It also appears that they will still have one big ship per location. I guess that would give them one good solid shot from a standoff range to hit us without doing a suicide run to the target."

"You're very comforting, Doctor. Okay, have you spoken to anyone about whether any of them are taking Patrick's bait?"

"I'm listening, like you, Mr. President."

"Dr. Khelm, must you always be an insufferable ...." Before he could finish the sentence, the President's Military Aide, broke in saying, "Mr. President! The Mountain Ship is making a turn. Looks like he is about to follow the twilight line towards the Pacific!"

"Thank GOD! Now what about the other two big ones?"

"Mr. President, they are NOT, say again, NOT turning."

"Great, does Vandenberg have anything else in their quiver?"

"Yes and no. They have some anti-satellite ordinance and aircraft available, but they are kind of a long shot against this large of a target."

"What is General McDaniel planning to do with them?"

"Mr. President. He is trying to use them, we'll know in a little while if it is effective. Apparently, the aircraft and their targets aren't at their optimal positions yet."

"Keep me advised."

"Mr. President?"

"Yes? Doctor Khelm."

"Sir, we do have our defenses around their main targets, surely with it now being just two Battleship Class ships, we've got some ability to drive them off?"

"Doctor Khelm. Don't you read the damn information sent to you by General Patrick and his staff? Have you read the damage assessments from Dutch Harbor? How about from Diamond Head from the last war?"

"Sir, I was only..."

"Dammit! How high up is 50 miles, Doctor?"

"I know, sir, but it is only two of them."

"Doctor, it would only take one of them to hit us in the right spot, and then we would have upwards of a million casualties."

"I see your point, Mr. President."

"Doctor, please see if you can light a fire under somebody to get more people to shelter in New Washington. Right now, we're looking at one hellacious loss."

USS Alaska, Supreme Allied Flagship. Sea of Okhotsk:

With the turn of the Mountain Class Ship towards the Pacific, the staff was electrified that the plan might actually work. Almost to a person, they were hoping that it was the ship that was going to originally target their rear headquarters, where most of them had family. Still keeping count on all of the ships, based on the observations from Vandenberg, the staff was praying that the other Capital ships would turn towards them before firing their main weapons. Trying to pull a plan out of my ass, I literally was thinking a mile a minute. Then it hit me. "General Roberts. Send a Flash Immediate message to both the 21st and 42nd Army Groups. Tell them to commence firing all artillery on the center points of each of the remaining enclaves. They are not to endanger engaged forces, but they are still to step up the firing tempo to maximum. I don't care if they fire every artillery shell they have, they have to keep firing. Hell, maybe that will turn the last two big ones."

"Yessir!" General Roberts turned to send out the message via ELF/VLF, and I turned back to Admiral Lynch. "Admiral, once the Gomer gets within 250 miles of our location, you are to stop all transmissions, but only for a moment. How close is our closest submarine to the west?"

"Sir. Uh.... the USS Helena is about 15 miles to our west."

"Good. The second we stop transmissions, they are to begin sending the same messages we've been sending, and in the same Order. They are also to head at flank speed precisely due west from our position. In the meantime, tell the USS Alaska Battlegroup Commander to turn towards the Gomer and move to flank speed for the whole group."

"Sir? You mean turn directly towards him?"

"Exactly, it is an old 'air to air' technique for helicopters versus fast movers. We turn towards him, go to maximum speed, then force him to change his dive angle. If we can get him steep enough, the bastard might exceed his flight characteristics."

"Wow. I like it. Okay, so we turn towards him, run under him as he heads towards the USS Helena?"

"Yep. Then when he gets to his weapons range of 100 miles up, the Helena will stop transmitting, and then we'll start transmitting from behind his ass. As he steepens out, maybe it will force him to either pull up and change to the classic arc approach, or he will just bust his ass. Either way, it gives us a long shot chance to get rid of the bastard."

"Got it, sir." Turning, Admiral Lynch bolted from our command bridge to meet with the Captain of the USS Alaska and to send a message to the other Battlegroup Commanders, whose flags were flying from the USS Missouri, USS Alabama, and the USS New

Jersey. Making sure that the USS Helena had our exact transmission schedule, she took up our messaging on my order, and the Battlegroup turned and began the "haul ass" maneuver directly into the path of the Mountain ship.

Then we finally caught a break. Observers noted that the Battleship Class ships were now turning to intercept a follow-on course to follow the Mountain Class ship. They were faster, and were closing on their large companion, most likely in response to our stepped up artillery attacks on the enclaves. They were traveling above and slightly behind the Mountain Class ship, and we were waiting to see it unfold. Thanks to their turn and approach course, we then got lucky enough to catch our second break. The USS Missouri and USS New Jersey, both positioned about 100 to 200 miles to our east, would be close to being on a perfect course line for the approach of the Battleship Class ships. The USS Alabama was to our west, but she was not too far out of position to at least get some shots in, should we be blown out of the water.

Meanwhile, we were starting to get reports from our rear headquarters and New Washington. The Carrier Class Ships, having released their Fighters, were now attacking all three of our main facilities on the East Coast. The good news was that there were no major weapons being expended from distant ranges, but the flip side to this was that our air defenses in and around New Washington were catching it. In fact, they were catching it with both barrels. The anti-satellite missiles had little impact, even though they may have damaged some of the smaller ships. It wasn't until the Gomers entered the atmosphere that our anti-aircraft missiles could do much damage. Firing from the light side of the line, the fighters were heavily engaged and still losing aircraft from high-angle Gomer weapon hits. As the fleet of smaller Gomers got closer, the Gomer Gun Batteries took over, and it was here that we finally were able to significantly reduce the attacking force. Still, it was obvious to me that they were going to get hit, maybe not nearly as hard as Dutch Harbor, but that was little consolation to those of us with loved ones in the vicinity.

I was absorbing all this when Admiral Lynch turned to me, and said "Sir, the Mountain Class ship is 250 miles up and descending. I make her position roughly 100 miles east and forward of our position."

"So, she is 100 miles away, but 250 miles up?"

"Aye, sir."

"Okay, watch her altitude, and let me know when she is 100 miles away from the USS Helena."

"Yessir......... She is now descending, and about 120 miles from the Helena."

"Descending how much?"

"Working on it, sir. . . . . . Okay, she is now 80 miles up, and 100 miles from the Helena. She is past the vertical for our position."

"Good! Switch off the Helena, and turn on our noise!"

"Aye, Aye!"

"Tell the bridge to standby for MY orders."

"Sir?"

"I'm taking command of the Group."

"Yessir."

"Bridge?"

"Bridge, Aye! Yes, General."

"Bridge, I want you to be prepared for a hard turn to Port on my order, bring all guns to broadside to Port, and have them track the target! They will fire in the turn! ALSO, tell communications to be prepared to switch it back to the Helena on my Order."

"Aye, Aye, Sir."

"Admiral, keep giving me the numbers."

"Sir. Okay, we're up running hot. The Target is now almost vertical trying to turn into us. Sir, he is at 50 miles, and descending rapidly...... His turn is trying to tighten, but his nose is still about 40, no, make that 45 degrees out."

"Good, keep the numbers running. Bridge, Standby!"

"Bridge, Aye."

"Admiral? Keep giving me the numbers!"

"Sir, he is still unable to completely get his nose turned, he is trying to level out sir, his range is 30 miles....... 25 miles, ... his turn is almost complete now. His speed is down to around 300 knots, and his range is 20 miles. ..... Nose is at....."

"BRIDGE, HARD LEFT RUDDER, FIRE ALL MAIN BATTERIES! GIVE'M HELL!"

On that command, the USS Alaska heeled over into a very tight turn, bringing all the main guns on target of the now turned Gomer. Our first shots were deadly accurate, and our tight turn made us harder for them to acquire. As the first salvos left the gun barrels, I ordered, "Communications. Switch all comm to the Helena. Bridge! Straighten her out on a parallel course to the Gomer, and continue firing main guns. Once the power levels are up, fire all Gomer Batteries, and maintain constant fire."

The noise was deafening, and the smell was incredible. In fact, as I looked around at my staff, it was clear that they were all overwhelmed with the sheer violence of the noise from the firing. The sounds of twelve 18" gun tubes firing on rapid fire, with the power and sound of the four main Gomer Guns doing the same, not only took away most of your senses, but the concussions alone would even steal your breath. Our escorts were now having their plates filled too, as waves of Fighter Class ships whirled into the attack. In the midst of this noise, Admiral Lynch was waving at me with his "OH CRAP" look. Leaning into me he yelled, "SIR, THE BATTLESHIP CLASS GOMERS ARE NOW ABOUT 250 MILES

OUT, AT AN ALTITUDE OF 100 MILES AND DESCENDING IN OUR DIRECTION."

"WELL, ADMIRAL, IT HAS BEEN DAMN NICE KNOWING YOU! ASK THE USS MISSOURI AND THE USS NEW JERSEY IF THEY CAN HELP US HIT THOSE BASTARDS!"

"SIR. THE MISSOURI IS IN POSITION, BUT THE NEW JERSEY WILL BE OFF TOO FAR TO THE EAST."

"WELL, NO SENSE IN WASTING THE MIGHTY MO. JUST TELL THEM I WOULD APPRECIATE ANYTHING THEY COULD DO TO HELP."

"GENERAL, BRIDGE!"

"GO AHEAD, BRIDGE!"

"GENERAL, THE DAMN MOUNTAIN SHIP JUST TRIED TO TURN, AND WELL, SHE IS GOING NOSE FIRST INTO THE SEA!"

"BRIDGE, CEASE FIRE MAIN BATTERIES! ADVISE THE DESTROYERS TO BEGIN ANTI-SUBMARINE OPERATIONS. LET'S KILL THIS BASTARD ONCE AND FOR ALL!"

"AYE, aye, sir." With the sound of the main batteries no longer firing, it was now our first chance to take a full breath in what seemed hours. My ears were still ringing, my hearing was shot, but when the overwhelming noise stopped, we could still hear the Gomer Batteries charging and firing from all over the ship, along with the smaller 37mm, 5" and 6" anti-aircraft batteries that were fitted with sulphur rounds.

"Admiral. Get me a status on the Gomers headed our way, and tell the Battlegroup Commander that with my compliments, he now has the Con!"

"Sir, the two Battleship Class ships are now roughly over the USS Missouri's position, and she and her escorts are engaging!"

"General, Bridge!"

"Go, Bridge!"

"General, the USS Howard reports multiple hits on the underwater Gomer. We are still tracking."

"Excellent, keep me posted. What about the Fighters?"

"Sir, the Battlegroup Commander advises that he just gave the USS McCampbell and USS Antietam permission to fire their bubbles."

"Understand. We will hang on. " Turning to my staff, I advised them to hold on, we were firing bubbles. Everyone grabbed their nearest rail, seat, or table, and held on. Looking around, I realized that it was right out of an old submarine movie where the crew was hanging on during a depth charge attack.

"Standby, General. We have Bubbles firing.......... NOW!" The feeling that comes from being under a Gomer Bubble can probably only be described as standing under a shower of sparks. The tingling of the skin, the raising of hair, and the static charge that seems to surround you are all very uncomfortable. Once the feeling passed, it was just in time to hear the Admiral's voice yelling that the USS Missouri had very minor damage, and that one of the Battleship Class ships was now headed our way, doing what appeared to be the "slash and burn" as it fired at the water along its flight path. If that were true, then this would be the first time the Gomers employed that as a sustained tactic over water. New twists called for new solutions. Unfortunately, I was just about out of ideas.

CHAPTER XVIII

Secure standby bunker near New Washington:

President Blanchard was rapidly losing his patience with his own staff, since they were not exactly forthcoming with the information he wanted. Never a man to sit on his hands, he was at this point wishing that he was still in the Army, or at the very least, somewhere closer to the fighting. The damage and action reports were finally starting to trickle in to the President's War Room, but it still it wasn't fast enough. The picture they were painting was making the President feel almost physically ill. A Gomer Carrier Class ship had executed the spiral maneuver over New Washington, in almost the same form as over Dutch Harbor. This time though, it wasn't against a nearly empty headquarters complex, but instead, an underground urban area. Now there were civilians sheltered in the deeper regions of the overall cave system, and the President was terrified at the potential losses from such an attack. As the initial unconfirmed reports of civilian casualties were mounting, another report indicated that a second Gomer Carrier Class ship had deliberately crashed into the side of the mountain housing the new Pentagon. This information was confirmed, and it was clear that they too had suffered casualties, but nobody could say how many. What was driving the President almost to the edge was that the numbers were not coming in to him fast enough to either confirm or refute the numbers and types of wounded or killed that were being estimated by his staff.

With each passing minute, the President was more agitated than he'd been in years. "Dammit. Doctor Khelm, can't anyone give me at least their best guess as to what is going on around New Washington?"

"Sir, we're going through the reports as they come in, but they just aren't arriving fast enough."

"Doctor, tell my Military Aide to get in here and advise the Secret Service detail, we're headed out."

"Mr. President. You can't go right now, the Gomers are still out there in the attack mode. The Action Reports indicate that we've made some serious progress, but it is too fluid for you to leave this facility."

With an almost quiet fury, the President fixed his National Security Advisor with a glare that could have frozen water at 200 yards. Speaking slowly and deliberately, "Doctor. I am the President. I will go where I am needed, and I will go when I damn well please. IS THAT UNDERSTOOD?"

"Yes. Mr. President. I understand exactly what you're saying, and I agree that you should go, but just not yet. Those people will need you a whole lot more when this is done. Besides, right now the people it would take off the line to keep track of you would be too distracting. Like it or not, you will not be doing anyone any favors wandering around out there right now. Please just wait, and I'll even go with you."

"OKAY! You are right, but at least get me better information, then maybe I won't feel the need to go see for myself."

Seeing this exchange, the Military Aide entered the room and stepped up to the President. "Doctor. Mr. President, I've got some news for you. Most of it you're going to like, some you won't."

"Okay, General. SPIT IT OUT."

"Yessir. Okay, New Washington was hit, and the Gomer Carrier Class ship crashed outside the facilities and over the eastern entrance leading towards Washington, D.C. Civilian casualties were minimal, since most were still trying to evacuate to the west when we locked it all down. The deep shelters were untouched, and only a few hundred people, out of the almost 1.25 million still inside, were injured or killed at the time and point of impact."

"Geez, that IS good news. What about other ships or damages?"

"There were none of any major size. The Anti-Gomer Gun Batteries took casualties, but around New Washington, they are still reporting up to 85% effective. As for the new Pentagon complex, the losses there were mostly military, but it was a much more significant hit. The mountain complex is still operational, but portions of the facility collapsed. They had two Gomer Carrier Class ships hit their facilities. There were also Fighter Class ships that literally tried to fly into three of the 15 entrances. Damndest thing anyone had ever seen. The civilian casualties at the new Pentagon are unknown, since three of the four tunnels leading to the main civilian shelter and family quarters collapsed. Once they dig their way in, we'll have better numbers. Right now, it could be a few, or a lot, we just don't know yet."

"SHIT, I know some of those people. I've even got a few relatives in that facility. Please keep me posted. Now what about the Supreme Allied Headquarters complex?"

"Mr. President. We can't get in touch with General Clark or any of his staff right now, via land line or radio. We have no clue, but it would appear from reports coming from nearby that another Gomer Carrier Class ship may have been shot down in that area, and that it may have crashed into their mountain. Casualties from their Gomer Gun Batteries appear negligible though, and they are at about 98%."

"Son of a bitch. Okay, has any of this information filtered out to General Patrick and his boys on the USS Alaska?"

"No, Mr. President, it hasn't."

"Why the hell not?"

"Mr. President. The last we heard the USS Alaska was under attack from the Gomers' Mountain Class ship, and they had two Gomer Battleship Class ships headed directly towards them. We've been unable to keep up with the signals, but the intercept information and the signals coming from that area haven't quite made sense to us."

"What are you saying?"

"Mr. President, I'm saying that things are VERY confused out there, and we don't really have a clue. We intercepted a message from the USS Alaska to the USS Missouri just a little while ago, and it simply said, 'Do what you can'."

"That doesn't sound good, does it?"

"No, Mr. President, it doesn't sound good at all, although, the signals are continuing from somebody out there, so it can't be a total wash. At least not yet. OH, and General Patrick, right before the Mountain Class should have intercepted them, sent out a call for all artillery to expend maximum effort on the enclaves. We think that it is probably the reason we only got hit by the Carrier Class ships."

"Thank God, it was only their Carrier Class ships. Hell, they've done enough damage, can you imagine what one of their really big ones would have done, and from a distance we couldn't have stopped." Looking around at both Dr. Khelm and his Aide, there was a mere nodding of heads. "Okay, keep me updated, and Doctor, see what you can find out about General Clark and Allied Headquarters." The President then did something he hadn't done in years. He put his head in his hands, and asked for someone to bring him "a pack of damn smokes, and I don't give a crap what brand!"

Supreme Allied Headquarters, (SAHQ - Rear):

The explosion overhead was loud, but not particularly damaging to the room or his hearing. Sure, some dust fell, and the equipment was jarred around some, but otherwise, there was nothing outwardly significant about the damage. Getting to his feet, General Clark surveyed the headquarters war room and asked if everyone was okay. Not hearing anything to the contrary, he picked up the phone to contact his observers around the facility. "Dammit. Deader than a doornail. Shit! Okay, Colonel, send runners around, and get me a damage report. While you're at it, see what the hell is wrong with the land line." The facilities Colonel bolted from the room and began his survey of the entire facility. Unfortunately, since the facility was almost 25 miles of underground tunnels and shelters, it would take a while, especially since the phone system was inoperative. Assembling his personnel, he dispatched them in all directions using little hand held radios.

While the facilities officer was starting the damage assessment, General Clark was asking his staff for information. Going around the room, he realized quickly that nobody had anything. All real time information, ELF/VLF, and even the seldom used UHF/VHF systems were all off line. They had power, but their communications were completely cut off from the rest of the world. As the enormity of this hit both General Clark and his staff, a very uncomfortable feeling circled the room at about the speed of light. Sensing that things could get out of control in a serious hurry, General Clark took the reins, and gave everyone something to do. "Okay, people. Calm down, and start using all of your back up systems. Whether it is phone, telegraph, or fucking smoke signals, we will contact someone out there. In the meantime, use runners, and let's get a handle on how badly we are hit, and with what. ALSO, someone get me some information about the shelters. Our civilians that took refuge from the government quarters all need to be eyeballed and checked for casualties. Let's make sure that they are okay, and that they DO NOT panic. It isn't time for that yet." General Clark sat back down, and half turned away from the room when he muttered to himself, 'now who tells the General not to fucking panic?'

Snapping out of his thoughts, General Clark summoned the Sergeant Major to him. "Sergeant Major. How far to the nearest Gomer Gun Battery fire control center?'

"Uh, General, it would be about three to four miles from here, on the next ridge."

"Good, within PRC range. Okay, Sergeant Major, take your ass and at least two or three PRC 77s, you know the old FM radios that never seem to work when you need them, and get your ass to that Fire Control point with the ELF hook up."

"Sir? The Gomers will just home in on the FM transmission."

"Yeah, I know. So take a repeater, and drop it somewhere remote on the way."

"Uh, that won't work sir. That would take me at least an hour to get it set up and get to the fire control point."

"Sergeant Major. Nothing else is working, we've already got our people using the little hand held radios just to find out what is going on inside the complex, and let's face it. Don't you think they already know where the hell we are?"

"Uh..... yessir. I reckon they do."

"GOOD, I'm glad it finally meets with your approval. Now get your ass moving. You've got thirty minutes!"

"Yes, Sir. General." The Sergeant Major headed out, and as he left, he passed the facilities engineer who was coming in to the room. "General?"

"Go ahead, Colonel. How bad is it?"

"They hit the Communications tunnel, the transmissions facilities, and the main phone junction point."

"Damn, those things are at least a half mile apart."

"Yessir, but between their weapons and the crashed ship, it has collapsed some of the tunnels and all three rooms where all our communications were routed."

"What about the lowest level stuff, like the Comm room and the civilian shelters?"

"Sir. We don't know yet. We've had to send people out of the complex and around to the lower entrances. Right now, we're completely cut off from that part of the mountain, because there is a Gomer ship basically sitting inside a large part of our headquarters."

"GEEZ, where at exactly?"

"Below the former 'Whitehouse', you know, General Patrick's quarters, and along that lower main tunnel running down to the science labs."

"Crap, anyone in that area?"

"We're checking now sir, but I've got no word on casualties at this point. I know we have them, I just have nothing as to numbers."

"Do what you can and keep me posted."

USS Alaska, Supreme Allied Flagship. Sea of Okhotsk:

The Gomer Battleship was now about 50 miles out, and we were doing our best to resemble that 'hole in the water' while moving away from the last position where we'd sent any signals. The USS Helena was now sending her messages again, but this was little comfort given what the Gomers were now doing. Fortunately, the Gomer Bubble had taken care of the fighters, and our escorts had only suffered minimal damage as a result of that Bubble. The hits they'd taken earlier from the Gomer Fighters was another story, but nobody was in danger of sinking, at least for the moment. Thankfully, the USS Missouri Battlegroup had take down one of the two Gomer Battleship Class ships, which left us with a very sick Mountain Class ship that was still lurking beneath us in the sea. We were now facing the lone remaining Battleship Class ship which was busy scorching the water as it headed directly towards us. Noting the relative positions between our ship and the Gomer, Admiral Lynch approached me and asked, "General? What are you orders?"

"Admiral, I got nothing. Let's take a walk down to the bridge, I want to talk to the Battlegroup Commander."

"Okay, but you're probably not very popular down there right now."

"I know, which is why I think I need to go down there. You're going since you might be able to at least pick me up off the deck after he punches me." I stood up then, and we walked down the two levels to the main Bridge where the Battlegroup Commander was sitting on the Captain's chair. Entering the Bridge, a sharp looking Marine Corporal snapped to a parade ground position of attention and announced very loudly, "GENERAL ON THE BRIDGE!"

Apparently, this was another gaff on my part, but at this point, I figured what the hell. "Admiral Pellman?"

"Yes, General."

"Admiral, I wanted to come down here personally to convey a couple key things to you."

"Go ahead, General."

"Admiral Pellman, I want to compliment you on the excellent job you have done with this Battlegroup, and I want to formally apologize for taking personal command a little while ago."

"Uh...... General, I uh......"

"Admiral. What I did would normally be unforgivable, and I would fully understand it if you wanted to knock my ass to the deck. It was NOT my lack of faith in you, your skills, or the skills of any officer or man onboard this ship, or even in your group. It was instead my own history that made me do it. We executed a classic move that is taught to Army Aviators when faced with a fast mover that is trying to kill us. Unfortunately, the only way I could make it work was to be holding the controls. In this case, that meant having to simply do it. I want to formally apologize, and I would ask that the log of this ship and of your command reflect that apology."

"Sir. General. I am honored that you would come down here and say something. I understand, and for whatever it is worth, I'd like the log to reflect that your apology is accepted, and that the General was actually responsible for some good shooting. In all honesty, I'm not sure I'd have the balls to pull it off...."

"Admiral, I'm sure you would have, if you could have read my mind, and I have complete faith in you. Besides, Generals, even of the Army, should never get too grabby with another officer's woman, and face it, the USS Alaska is your woman. It won't happen again."

"General, I would be happy to let it happen again, but only if you got the same result. Now, any ideas about this big guy headed towards us?"

"Nothing beyond what you're doing, Admiral. Although......."

"What, General?"

"Admiral, where is the Mountain Class right now?"

"Sir? Uh, standby. CIC?"

"CIC, Aye."

"Where does the McCampbell have that big ass Gomer cornered?"

"Sir. USS McCampbell reports that the Gomer is about 4,000 feet below them, and apparently holding stationary."

"General, that means that the Gomer is about 3,000 yards, over there." Pointing to the west of us, it hit me.

"Admiral, let's get over to the west of it. In fact, you might want to get the whole Battlegroup to the west of it."

"Why?"

"I am hoping that the Battleship Class won't slash and burn over his buddy. I'm also thinking that maybe they are going to slash and burn all around, to maybe rescue some of their buddies who are still down there."

"Maybe so. General, I think I know how to confirm that idea, too. . . . CIC."

"CIC Aye."

"CIC, can you monitor for any Terahertz transmissions from either the Gomer below or the one coming?"

"Aye, sir. I can confirm that there have been some burst transmissions, but we have no idea what they were, other than being very brief."

"Could it be like a homing signal?"

"Maybe sir." Turning back to me, Admiral Pellman asked, "What do you think, sir?"

"Admiral. We used to do a long and short count on the FM radios, and we would use those signals to directionally find someone who was downed or needed extraction. I think you've hit the nail on the head."

"Sir, with your permission."

"By all means. I'll leave you to it."

"Thank you, sir." Turning to his operations officer, Admiral Pellman started issuing the orders that would put his Battlegroup in position to take advantage of any potential rescue attempts by the Gomers. I motioned to Admiral Lynch, and as we departed, I heard "GENERAL OFF THE BRIDGE".

Supreme Allied Headquarters, (SAHQ - Rear):

It was a huge struggle, but General Clark was finally getting the information he needed. The tunnels were damaged, some collapsed, but the loss of life was minimal. The count was 14 security personnel, and about 25 members of the Communications staff. There were no known civilian casualties; however, there were a handful of the science civilians that were either missing or unaccounted for at the moment. This was in part because the laboratory facilities were cut off thanks to a collapsed tunnel. Facilities personnel and the combat engineers were working feverishly to reach that part of the complex, which housed a number of Gomer prisoners, along with the scientists that were working with them. Out of concern, General Clark also verified that all of General Patrick's family appeared to be fine. The youngest, Holly, was actually not in the laboratory for once, since she was helping get General Patrick's mother to a shelter. He even double checked that Chris' husband John wasn't working, and that she, her husband, and their son were all safely away from that part of the mountain. General Clark was married, but they weren't fortunate to have children. In a lot of ways, he thought of General Patrick's kids as the children and grandchildren he knew he would never have with his wife.

Now came the hard part. How to tell everyone the good news, and their status. The Sergeant Major he sent to the Gomer Gun Battery fire control center was taking his damn sweet time. It would be almost an hour and a half before the Sergeant Major reported back.

"General?"

"Sergeant Major, it is about damn time."

"Sorry, Sir. When we got out there, the attack was still going on with the Fighters. We're up now."

"Good, I need you to get the word to all stations via the fire control centers ELF."

"Yessir. What word?"

"Okay, here is our report. Send it in the clear, and repeat each word verbatim. Got it?"

"Yessir." Once the Sergeant Major responded, General Clark read out the damage assessment, and even passed on the good news about the civilians. He didn't go into detail about the scientists, since among the missing were Dr. Marvin and Dr. Cobb, and he didn't want to concern anyone unless or until he knew for sure their status.

Secure standby bunker near New Washington:

The President was no longer pacing the floor, and he wasn't nearly as agitated as before. In fact, between the cigarettes, the scotch, and the continuing flood of information, he was doing much better. It was pretty clear that the Gomers had failed in the goals of their attack. The civilian casualties were minimized in all three locations. The military casualties were higher, especially around the new Pentagon, but even they were well below the initial estimates. All three mountain complex facilities, New Washington, Supreme Allied Headquarters, and the new Pentagon, had a combined loss of life that would be less than 450 to 600 people. While still a higher sounding number, these numbers were actually well below anything even the optimists were predicting. Considering that almost 3.6 million people lived at or near these three locations, the low numbers were pretty damned impressive. It was in no small measure to the credit of the military forces to the west drawing off the Gomers' largest ships that these numbers were so low.

The President was also delighted that the Gomers' attacking forces were decimated in the process. Only a handful of the Fighter Class ships were able to escape, and even they would eventually succumb to air attacks by the Air Forces as they attempted to leave the target areas. There were a number of Carrier Class ships that were now crashed and scattered around the landscape, and the Fourth Army personnel responsible for security were already scouring through the wreckage. Their mission was to find and take all the prisoners that they might encounter in the wrecks, and to make sure that there weren't any other Gomers that might still be wandering around the countryside. The one thing still bothering the President was the burning question for which there was no answer. What was going on in the Pacific? It had been hours since they'd heard from anyone on the USS Alaska. According to his staff, not even the USS Helena was sending signals anymore. Right now, that part of the Pacific area was being deadly quiet, without anything coming from the key players. It was almost like they weren't there.

USS Alaska, Supreme Allied Flagship. Sea of Okhotsk:

Admiral Pellman did an excellent job of placing his Battlegroup near the Mountain Class Gomer, but away from the approaching

Battleship Class ship. Turning the entire area into a quiet zone, there were no emissions of any kind. Instead, the Battlegroup was communicating entirely by signal light. The Battleship Class ship was continuing the "slash and burn" firing over the water, but it was being done in a pattern. It was obvious that they could not see or hear our fleet, and that the impact of their weapons were nothing more than a waste of their power. They were just hoping to clear the area around their wounded Mountain Class ship, but they were not coming too near the monster that was lying below us. We waited for what seemed to be a pretty long time, when Admiral Lynch turned and reported, "General. CIC just advised the bridge that the Battleship Class is no longer firing."

"Excellent, my guess is that now things are about to get very damn interesting. Tell Admiral Pellman to expect the Mountain Class to start surfacing at any time now."

"Aye, Sir. The group is at battle stations, and all weapons are trained on the Battleship Class."

"Great. I guess you and I get to sit this one out and be spectators." As I looked around, General Roberts walked over to us, and joined the conversation. "General? Why hasn't Admiral Pellman just gone ahead and engaged the Battleship Class ship?"

"General Roberts, that is an excellent question. The Battleship Class is in range of our big guns and our Gomer Guns, so Admiral Lynch, care to educate General Roberts?"

"Sure. T-J, if we wait, we can catch the Mountain Class on the surface, AND get the Battleship Class ship along with her fighters. We already know that killing the Mountain Class underwater is a VERY difficult proposition. On top of that, if we time it right, we can catch the Battleship Class at a more advantageous angle. Hopefully, we can nail it before it can launch any of its Fighters, too."

"Won't they launch Fighters to pick up people from the Mountain Class?"

"Maybe, T-J, but we're hoping that the Battleship Class is going to try to be an escort for the wounded Mountain Class, as opposed to just picking up survivors. If that is the case, then they won't be launching Fighters since it would slow them down on the recovery. I think Admiral Pellman is counting on them trying to be in a hurry to get their biggest asset out of here."

"Kind of a long shot, isn't it?" Looking at both Admiral Lynch and me, you could see the lingering doubt over his face.

"T-J, Admiral Lynch has laid it out, now let me just tell you that this entire war has been long shots. Some have worked, and some haven't. Look at the debacle at Dutch Harbor. Hell, that was pure luck that got us out of there before they hit."

"General Patrick. I would take your luck of the Irish any day."

"T-J, I've got a lot of dead staff, and enough metal in my ass, to disprove that theory!"

The time spent in idle discussion was nothing more than a cover for our nervousness. We had rolled the dice in the first place, trying to lure the Gomers' big stuff away from our mountain facilities. We were now about to either cash in our chips, or pull off a major victory. The line between the two outcomes was so thin as to be virtually non-existent. The minutes were dragging by, and we were now working on hours. Finally, we heard what we wanted to hear. The big Mountain Class ship beneath us was starting to rise to the surface.

"General!"

"I know, I heard. He is coming up. How fast is he rising?"

"Sir, it looks like about 1500 feet a minute."

"SO, we've got what, about two more minutes?"

"Yessir. Admiral Pellman has the fleet ready to fire."

"Tell Admiral Pellman that this is his show, my orders are simple. Inflict maximum damage to all enemy targets. Good luck and good shooting!" General Roberts raised his eyebrows, and asked, "General. Do you think we should have a plan for breaking the engagement and getting the hell out of here? Just in case?"

"Nope, T-J, this is it. For all the marbles. Let my order ride. We either kick their ass here, or we've got bigger problems as the twilight line heads back around to New Washington again. There can be no draw, or escape. This time we're in it for the finish."

"Yessir." General Roberts and Admiral Lynch exchanged glances, and we then became mere witnesses to one of the more epic sea battles in the history of mankind. It would be short, violent, and more brutal than anything I'd ever seen.

Chapter XIX

USS Alaska, Supreme Allied Flagship. Sea of Okhotsk:

Given our far more sweeping responsibilities, the personnel in the Allied Headquarters' Combat Information Center, (CIC), monitored a lot more information than the personnel in the Battlegroup's CIC. If the Allied Staff wasn't onboard the USS Alaska, then this function would be taking place in a War Room which meant this was a game of semantics, as opposed to function. The Battlegroup, which included the USS Alaska and her escorts, was more concerned with those things taking place in her tactical area of operations. The result was simple, if I wanted information about what was taking place around the ship, I had to monitor the Battlegroup's CIC, as opposed to my own. At this moment, I was being forced by the circumstances to monitor both the local news and the more global situation.

Globally, we were pouring everything we had into the two remaining Gomer enclaves in Siberia, with very little respite in our advances or in our high volume of artillery fire. Based on my overall assessment of the situation, and given the fact that the Gomers' remaining Battleship Class ship was now parked about 15 miles to my east, I directed that a message via ELF be sent to reduce the rate of artillery fire, but that our ground forces were to continue their advance. With that decision, mainly to save on our special sulphur based ammunition, I left the ground campaign in the hands of my staff. I had a very strong feeling that the key to the whole war was probably taking place right outside the hull of the USS Alaska, and I thought it imperative that the local situation be closely monitored. Quoting my old friend, Command Sergeant Major Clagmore, "Life is all about pissing on fires. If you don't want to get burnt, you HAVE to start with the one closest to your feet, and THEN work your way out!"

Leaving the Allied Staff behind in our CIC, I grabbed Admiral Lynch, and we made our way out onto the "Admiral/General's Bridge." From here, I could monitor the Battlegroup's CIC and I could visually follow at least part of what was going on. In other words, I had made a conscious decision to follow the local news, and as a result, I had the best seat in the house for what was probably the last sea battle of the war. Stepping out on my bridge, it took a few minutes for my eyes to adjust to the darkness, but fortunately, the latest in night vision binoculars were handy and I could get a very clear view of the surface of the water as it began to boil. There, about 2500 yards away, a portion of the Mountain Class Ship was breaking the surface. I could also hear the voice over the intercom indicating that the Battleship Class ship was moving towards our location at minimal speed. As the course, speed, elevation, and other key information were being passed to Admiral Pellman, we finally obtained visual contact with the Battleship Class as she approached. She was truly a monster, and to see one this close was enough to make anyone extremely concerned.

The Battleship Class ship was now about 5,000 yards away, and it appeared as though she was going to be launching her fighters. I saw movement along the side of the Battleship Class as she began opening up four outer doors. Then I saw two streaks of light pass our position at very high speed in the direction of the Gomer. I was completely mesmerized, as these two flickers split up, with one striking the starboard and port side of the Gomer at the exact same instant. The explosions were impressive, but not enough to bring it down. Almost simultaneously, a bell rang to warn us that all main batteries were about to commence firing. Within about 2 seconds, the main guns opened fire in all their 18" glory. The salvo left the ship, and it felt as though we were being pushed sideways as the guns fired. As before, the sound was completely deafening, and the concussion of the blasts almost sucked the air from your lungs. There was no question that each round counted, and as the Gomer Gun Batteries from both the USS Alaska and her Cruiser escort, the USS Antietam, added to the din, it was clear that the Gomer was going to be doomed, but she sure wasn't going down without a fight.

In the time between the first Cruise Missile hits from the USS Helena and the USS Alaska opening fire with her main guns, the Gomer Battleship Class managed to launch a dozen or so of her Fighter Class ships. The resulting exchange of gunfire was incredible and accurate from both sides. The Battleship Class ship took aim at the first of the destroyers firing at the Fighter Class ships approaching the USS Alaska. The blue/green burst of light emanating from the front of the Gomer struck the USS McCampbell forward of her bridge. The entire bow was simply gone, and as the ship plowed forward at full speed, she sank almost immediately. Honing in on the section of the Gomer Battleship where the weapon was located, the USS Alaska had several 18" hits in and around that section of the Gomer's hull. Our own Gomers Gun Batteries were also seriously damaging sections all along the hull of the Gomer. As we watched, huge chunks of the Gomer were falling away and crashing into the sea.

While the Gomer Battleship was being struck by our main batteries and missiles, several of their Fighter Class ships were diving and firing at the USS Alaska and the USS Antietam. The USS Stethem was doing her best to keep them off us, just as our secondary batteries were doing all they could, but both the USS Alaska and the USS Antietam suffered hits. Some were significant. The USS Antietam was struck in the bridge area and was unable to maintain her rate of fire for several minutes. The USS Alaska lost one of the aft Gomer Gun Batteries and a portion of the after superstructure nearest the aft fire direction control. Transferring the fire control function from the aft to the forward fire direction control for all guns was almost immediate, but it did interrupt firing for a few seconds. The casualties were growing with each such hit, and they would continue to happen over the next several minutes.

The USS Alaska's secondary batteries were finally catching up to the volume of attackers. With the help of the USS Stethem, the dozen or so attackers were virtually eliminated. The Battlegroup did not have a single ship that hadn't suffered at least some damage, and with the loss of the USS McCampbell, it was definitely not a one-sided fight. The Gomer Battleship Class was now settling into the water in a nose down position. Her splash into the surface of the sea produced a small wave, but it did little to stop the constant firing against the Gomer's hull. When the behemoth was almost level in the water, several secondary explosions could be heard, and she simply broke apart.

The entire time of this engagement, the Mountain Class ship still had not completely surfaced. There was only a portion of her hull visible, and it wasn't until after the Battleship Class was destroyed that she began to fire with what must have been her secondary batteries. They were just as dangerous to us, but at least they weren't as devastating as their main batteries. Our angle was to the left rear, and most of the firing was being attempted from forward. As she cut loose with a shot at the USS Antietam, the Cruiser heeled over and turned away from the direction of the Gomer. The hit was aft near the stern, but it was still completely devastating. The USS Antietam started taking on water, and her speed dropped until she eventually was rendered dead in the water. Now that she was a sitting duck, I got a request directly from Admiral Pellman over the old fashioned bridge pipe. Admiral Lynch looked over at me, and said, "Sir. Admiral Pellman for you."

When I got over to the bridge pipe, which was nothing more than a voice tube leading down to the deck below, Admiral Pellman didn't waste any time, "General. Request permission for the USS Alaska to engage at close range."

"Granted. By close range I assume you mean....."

"Yessir, I do! I just figured I should ask you, this being the flagship and all......"

"Do it, Admiral! We'll worry about that crap later. I'll advise my staff to brace."

"Thanks, General!" Closing the lid on the tube, I motioned Admiral Lynch to hold on, and I stuck my head back into the Allied CIC. "Ladies and Gentlemen. Grab something and hold on to your asses. It is about to get very bumpy here. Marine Guard, be on standby for possible enemy contact that could be up close and personal." Not really waiting on a reply, General Roberts turned and looked at me. His eyes were the size of saucers, and he said, "General? Should we be....."

"General Roberts. Grab a side arm, and the deck. Seriously, it is going to be a load of fun here in about 3 minutes."

Stepping forward to my bridge position, Admiral Lynch passed me a pistol belt with a .45 pistol contained in a standard issue USN holster. Then he handed me a Kevlar helmet, which I promptly put on. I couldn't help but chuckle, since I already had my .45 tucked in my waist band. Looking around at some of the faces around me, I realized that this was really my element. "Now this is some damn combat I understand!" At the same time that I was advising everyone to hold on, Admiral Pellman had issued his orders to the ship. We had turned directly towards the Mountain Class Gomer and were now traveling at flank speed, which best guess was around 32 knots. Only the forward batteries were firing, but it was still an impressive sight. I can only imagine what might be passing through the Gomer's mind as he saw all that firing coming his way.

I didn't have time to imagine much else, since when we rammed the Mountain Class ship, it was with all we had to offer. Throwing everyone to the deck, the force of our forward momentum, and the rather sudden stopping, was tremendous. The sound of the USS Alaska tearing through the Gomers' hull was horrific, and honestly, our steel versus the composite crap they used turned out to not be that fair of a fight. It reminded me a little of those old "Ginsu knife" commercials, where the knife cut through the old beer can. We didn't know that their hull was going to be that fragile when Admiral Pellman decided to ram, and the effect sure was not what any of us had expected. Instead, we had been prepared to actually do the old "boarders away" to keep the Gomers off our hull, or to directly attack the Gomers in what was left of their ship. Fortunately, that simply became completely unnecessary.

There is no question that our ramming damaged the hull of the USS Alaska, but she had definitely delivered far more punishment than she received. The Mountain Class ship fell away rapidly, and began going down. This wasn't a controlled crash or an attempt to get away, and it sure wasn't the plan of the Gomers to submerge. Instead, she was going down the hard way, and this time there was no way she was coming back. The Sonar operators from around what was left of the Battlegroup all reported hearing the ship break up and eventually explode in the deep waters around our position. The wreckage surrounding our little fleet was equally impressive. Within seconds of the end of this engagement, any ships that were still able to maneuver engaged in the search and rescue operations for our men from the USS McCampbell. Unfortunately, there were only three survivors, who had been blown off the deck when she first was hit. Of the three that were pulled out of the water, one would later succumb to his wounds. Casualties around the rest of the Battlegroup were also high.

USS Missouri Battlegroup, nearing the USS Alaska, Sea of Okhotsk:

It was a few hours after the dawn line had passed, and the Commander of the USS Missouri Battlegroup couldn't believe his eyes. Nearing the waters around the last known position of the USS Alaska, it was obvious to even an idle observer that something significant had taken place here. Remaining off the radio, they could only survey the scene through the eyes of the helicopter scouts using signal lights. The reports were incredible. There were no Gomers, which was good news, but apparently the USS Alaska's original Battlegroup was greatly reduced. The first helicopter crew was landing, and the pilot in command was rushed to the bridge to give a more detailed report of what he was seeing.

"Admiral."

"Commander, what the hell is going on over there?"

"Sir. The USS Alaska looks pretty banged up. Her communications equipment appears to be shot out. The USS Antietam is, well, sinking, sir. Going down by the stern, it doesn't look good. The USS Stethem is providing escort, and even she has a small list."

"Is that it?"

"Yessir. The USS McCampbell is nowhere to be seen. Neither is the USS Helena."

"Damn! Okay, get your ass back in the air, and get a status on the Alaska. Does she need assistance, does she need communications equipment, and does she need to transfer General Patrick's flag?"

Leaving the bridge at a dead run, the Captain of the USS Missouri called up to the Admiral's Bridge. "Admiral. We have the USS Helena surfacing and coming abeam of us."

"Great, Captain. That is at least one we didn't lose."

"Sir. They are signaling that they have Allied Supreme Commander and his staff on board, and they are requesting that we take them, and assume position as Allied Supreme Headquarters Flagship."

"Excellent! Okay, make it happen, Captain. I'll be aft when they arrive on the helipad."

"Aye, Aye, Sir."

It would take several minutes for the transfers to begin, and almost a 45 minute period before the helicopter crews were able to get all of the Allied Staff personnel on board. Greeting General Patrick and Admiral Lynch was not what Admiral Becker had expected. He was thinking that these guys would be pretty down, but instead, they were bounding off the aircraft the happiest he'd ever seen either Admiral Lynch or the old man. As General Patrick stepped on deck, the red flag with the five white stars was broken out and now flying above the USS Missouri. Admiral Becker laughed to himself, and thought that it was almost like the old man had come home. General MacArthur's flag at the end of World War II, and General Patrick's flag at the end of the First Gomer War, had both flown from the USS Missouri. Now, hopefully, this is where she would fly for the end of this one.

"Admiral Becker! Good to see you again. Good job with the earlier Gomer Battleship. So, what is your status and the status of your ship?" General Patrick got right down to business.

"Sir, we have some minor damage, mostly cosmetic. We took a hit on the starboard side just aft of the secondary guns, but nothing is leaking. Casualties were mostly minor wounds, but we lost one KIA, after one of their Fighters bounced off that part of the ship."

"Sorry to hear about your man, but that at least sounds like you managed a better night than we did."

"So, I see, sir. Looks a little rough. How is Admiral Pellman?"

"Full of fight! Good man, nothing personal, but I'm going to miss him!"

"Yessir!"

"Now then, Admiral, can we get back up on the radio net? The information I just got on the USS Helena tells me that things are beyond fluid at the moment."

"Yessir. Welcome home, and we'll have you up and running as soon as you can get to my old bridge. I'll move my stuff in with the Captain."

"Thanks, Admiral, but you don't need to move. You are more than welcome to hang out with me on our bridge. In the meantime, can you send Admiral Pellman plenty of help? Those boys earned their pay last night, and we need to get them any assistance we can." Turning to Admiral Lynch, "Get the carrier battlegroups in gear, and have them send what assistance they can, too. The Alaska will make it, but I'm damn worried about the Antietam."

The pomp and circumstance now completed, the Allied Headquarters was back up and running at full bore, and we had a lot on our plate. The ground campaign in Siberia was taking a major turn for the weird.

New Washington:

President Blanchard was taking the chance to head back to his quarters within the New Washington mountain complex. The defenses had been beefed up by pulling in a number of reserve Gomer Gun Batteries. There were also a great deal more security personnel surrounding the facilities, just in case of a Gomer ground incursion. The President was making his return mainly to calm the remaining populace and to assess the situation within the complex. He was also being careful not to lift the evacuation orders, keeping most of the population out of the facility, while still trying to get the rest of the people out just in case of another attack. There was no saying that the assaults were over, especially since there were still two of their Moon Class ships remaining just out of range near Mars. The plus was that it would take time for them to launch another attack, and the President was counting on that warning period to make sure that this time, the evacuation of the population would be completed.

The thing that bothered him the most was that General Patrick was still out of the loop, and for all he knew, could well be dead.

Other than one short transmission that had come in garbled from the USS Helena, there was nothing coming out of that part of the Pacific area. The only real comforting news was that there was no sighting of either of the Gomer Battleship Class ships or the monstrous Mountain Class ship passing into the Siberian areas. It had taken hours, but he was getting contact restored with both the new Pentagon and Allied Headquarters facilities in the rear. At least now he was able to monitor the war again, but most of the news he was receiving was just very confusing. The Gomers in both of the remaining enclaves were now undertaking what could be best described as a ground offensive. It was coordinated, but poorly executed. It would have made sense if it had an air component, but now that their Fighter Classes and Carrier Classes had been neutralized, this was just madness.

Taking stock of the evacuation situation and the damages in and around the "underground city," the President was marveling at the amount of damage that had been avoided by the diversion of the larger Gomer ships from the attack. He was talking to a repair crew when his military aide approached and said, "Mr. President. We just heard from General Patrick. He is alive and well, and I've got the battle damage assessment and report from their headquarters."

"Excellent! Give it to me."

"Sir, it might be better if we do this back in the war room, where we can show you more details."

Looking at the workmen, President Blanchard, said, "Can you at least tell me if it was a victory?"

"Sure, and yes, it was a victory. In fact, considering the stakes, it was a HUGE victory."

As the aide finished the statement, the workmen began cheering, and the President was able to conclude his visit on a high note. Smiling at the small crowd, he got back into his Presidential golf cart and, along with his military aide, rushed back to the War Room. Walking in, the President turned to Dr. Khelm and said, "Okay, Doctor, give it to me straight."

"Sir, the Gomer fleet did not survive the night. General Patrick's plan worked and the big ones all took the bait going after his flag ship. We got the two remaining Battleship Class ships, and the Mountain Class ship." The President was doing his best to be stoic about it, but the sense of joy was ever increasing, at least until Dr. Khelm continued with the actual report of the battle. Reading through the attacks, the loss of ships and personnel, and then the ramming, the President could only shake his head. "Damn. Sounds like a really long night for those boys." Dr. Khelm continued to explain that General Patrick and staff were all alive and well, having shifted their flagship from the wounded USS Alaska to the USS Missouri Battlegroup. Breathing a sigh of relief, the President asked, "So, what is going on with the ground campaign?"

"Sir. General Patrick kicked the airborne into play just an hour or so ago. They will be dropping the entire IXth Airborne Corps on the 42nd Army Group's Pacific Enclave, while the XVIIIth Airborne Corps will be dropped on the 21st Army Group's Ural area Enclave. Their drop is scheduled for first light over each target."

"Sounds like General Patrick thinks we're down to the end game."

"Yessir, he does. Most of our staff and scientists agree. The two remaining Moon Ships are still near Mars, and while they might carry their offensive or defensive fleets with them, the intelligence we've gathered from the prisoners indicates that they are committed to Mars, and not Earth."

"What do YOU think, Doctor Khelm?"

"Sir. I've seen nothing to counter that, especially since the Gomers have made no effort to reposition either of their Moon Ships closer for launching offensive operations."

"I hope you're right about this, since I would hate to commit the whole team without knowing that it is really the end game."

11th Airborne Division, Staging Area, Syagannah, Russia:

The Division Commander and his aide, Lieutenant Patrick, had just returned from the airfield and were going to be meeting with his Commanders. As the crowd of both Regimental and Battalion Commanders entered the Division Command Post, the word of the naval engagement was already drifting around the room. Taking the podium, the Division Commander began reading the After Action Report submitted by the USS Alaska. The details were stark, but it was quite apparent that a major event had taken place, and that it was a pretty darn big victory for the good guys. The room was electrified, when the Division Commander then called the room to attention. Turning, both General Davis, the 42nd Army Group Commander, and the IXth Airborne Corps Commander walked in and had a seat. Within a minute, they were followed by General Patrick.

"Gentlemen. Tomorrow morning, when it is first light over the Urals, we will be launching both of the Airborne Corps into the largest airborne combat assault in history. You, as the lead airborne forces, will be dropped on the target drop zones, and open the door to the very heart of each of their two remaining enclaves. Your commanders, from General Davis, through General Powers, to your own Commander, will brief you on your exact targets and time lines. I'm only here to wish you God speed and good luck. Yesterday, I had the privilege of seeing the USS Alaska and her group in action against those same Gomers. You men are every bit as dedicated and tough, and just like those men, I feel pretty confident that you will get the job done. Gentlemen, it is my honest belief that this could be the blow that ends this damn war! So, make it count!"

Turning, General Patrick left the room, and then each commander took his turn in providing their guidance and information. When Lieutenant Patrick was able to excuse himself from his boss, the Division Commander, he barely had a minute to catch up to his father, who was about to step into his aircraft. The only thing that helped him catch up was that Command Sergeant Major Clagmore was actually stalling his dad on the flight line. As Lieutenant Patrick ran up, he stopped, saluted, and then had his dad greet him with a hug. "Son, be careful. I've been where you're about to go. Listen to the Sergeant Major, and keep your damn head down. No heroes in this family. Understand?"

"Dad, I'll do my best, but don't give me that crap about no heroes. I just heard about the Alaska, and there is no way you didn't have your prints all over that one."

"Sergeant Major?"

"Yes, General."

"Sergeant Major, take this boy behind the wood shed and explain to him the importance of keeping one's head down. While you're at it, you might give him the speech about two eyes, two ears, and one mouth."

"Yessir!" Smiling, General Patrick gave his son a brief hug and got back on the aircraft. Soon, they were winging out to the next division staging area, and before the day was done, General Patrick would visit each of the airborne units prior to their dropping on the Gomers. Watching the aircraft lifting off, Lieutenant Patrick asked the Sergeant Major about the two eyes and ears thing. Looking the Lieutenant up and down Sergeant Major Clagmore explained, "L-T, God himself gave you two eyes, two ears, and one damned mouth. Do you know what that means?"

"No, Sergeant Major, what does it mean?"

"It means look and listen twice as much as you run that damned mouth!"

"Thanks, Sergeant Major. Sounds like good advice, especially given our job for tomorrow."

"No shit, L-T. Now get back to the old man, and lock and load. We've got a very early morning ahead of us."

"Yes, Sergeant Major!"

USS Missouri, Supreme Allied Flagship. Sea of Okhotsk:

The evening and night before were a blur. I had tried to visit all of our Airborne Division Commanders prior to this morning's operation, and was barely back to the ship before the two Airborne Corps started their loading process. I was tempted to sit it out at the 42nd Army Group Headquarters with General Davis, but thought better of it. I knew if I were present, I would either make people nervous or would be too tempted to stick my nose where it didn't belong. Besides, the travel and the exhaustion that goes with it helped keep my mind off the fact that I had just ordered my own son into combat. It was going to be a very bloody affair, and my staff was telling me that our losses could well be extensive. Knowing this didn't make my decision any easier, and knowing that my son would be among those forces sure as hell didn't make it any easier. Still, it had to be done. I had catnapped or 'power napped' where I could on the flights, but it was just a few minutes here and there. Stepping back into the USS Missouri's Allied CIC, Admiral Lynch and General Roberts were standing there to greet me with big smiles.

"General. We are damn glad you're back. Something big is going on, and it just might be the break we've been waiting to get."

"Huh?"

"Sir. Gomers in both enclaves are starting to give up! They started their big counterattack, but it folded up about an hour ago. They are lying down."

"What?"

"Sir. What do you want to do about the Airborne Operations?"

"Okay, give them the status, but send them in anyway. We can use them as security, and unless or until somebody in charge actually surrenders, we can't count on this being the real thing."

"Yessir. What do we tell them, though?"

"Tell them to meet force with force, peace with peace. If they are truly surrendering, then the drop should be unopposed, and we can use our forces as prisoner guards. If they mean business still, then we'll drop the hammer on them and kill anything that moves."

"Yessir. Makes sense."

"General Roberts, when is the last time we sent out the surrender messages?"

"Uh, I guess yesterday from the USS Helena, right before the big one."

"Okay, give that a shot, and do it while our airborne guys are in the air. How long before the first drop, and which drop zone?"

"Sir. First drop will be in about an hour and fifteen minutes, and it will on the Ural side Gomer enclave. The Drop Zone is right on their remaining strong point."

"Okay, send it again, only add that for them their time has run out. Surrender or die! Go ahead and send the addition, and keep me posted on the drops, especially if there is any resistance."

"General. We'll get the message coded into their 'language' and give you a countdown when they are 15 minutes out from the drop."

"Excellent. Now as for the message, send it in English, in the clear, on UHF/VHF, and then get Lieutenant Shiwak to repeat the same message and send it in his language. That will start it, and then if you get Doctor Clarkson's software version, then fine, send it, too, as a third variation on the message."

"Why bother in English?"

"Because I made a crack at the eggheads a few weeks ago about sending the bastards an Oxford Dictionary so they could learn our language, and sure enough, Doctor Clarkson and Doctor Marvin did just exactly that. I was kidding, but maybe we'll see if the Gomers have decided to learn our language."

"Okay, General. We will give it a shot. You want a general signal sent into space, or just to the enclaves?"

"Go for broke. Send it out to the world, and beyond, let the Gomers hear it wherever they might be ......"

The next several hours would tell us what our next step would require, but for the first time in over a year, I was guardedly hopeful. Not optimistic, just hopeful.

CHAPTER XX

USS Missouri, Supreme Allied Flagship. Sea of Okhotsk:

At less than thirty minutes from the first drop by the 82nd Airborne Division, the reports from both the 21st Army Group and the 42nd Army Group indicated that our message must have reached someone in the Gomer High Command. The two remaining Gomer enclaves were laying down their weapons and were not providing any return fire. This clearly was not their normal routine, since they had been actively defending their positions well past the passage of the Dawn line. Specifically, on the Pacific side in the 42nd Army Group's area, the Gomer enclave ceased all operations and defense almost two hours before the Dawn line passed through their area.

The original scheme, or plan of battle, had been similar to the one we had used with great success in the First Gomer War during the Tierra del Fuego battles. It was simple. The 82nd Airborne Division and the 11th Airborne Division were to drop directly on top of the Gomers' strong points, with these initial assaults to commence within a few minutes of one another. The two airmobile divisions, the 101st Airborne Division and 108th Airborne Division, were to follow 30 minutes later, with an air assault into the outer ring of the drop zones where the parachute infantry were to land. Finally, once the aircraft assigned the initial airdrop mission had completed their turnaround, they were to deploy the remaining two Airborne Divisions, the 17th Airborne Division and the 13th Airborne Division, either into the

Drop Zones secured by the 82nd and the 11th Divisions, or on any additional stronghold targets that might appear to us once the mission began.

Our concept was to hit them will little warning from above, and then for the air assault forces to establish a more secure landing area that would facilitate the air movement of heavier units into the very heart of the two enclaves. When the Gomers finally made it clear that they were giving up, both the 11th Airborne Division and the 82nd Airborne Division were already in the air and approaching their release point for the final run into the Drop Zones. What the 82nd Airborne troopers found on landing was nothing short of a miracle. The Gomers were all face down and their weapons were clearly not within their possession or control. They had simply given up. Within a very short period of time, we were getting an almost identical report from the Commander of the 11th Airborne Division. Still, exercising caution, the airmobile Divisions also began their deployments with a tactical air move. Everyone was guarded, but there was absolutely no resistance. The Gomers were all docile, compliant, and after a short logistical issue related to a shortage of hazmat or prisoner protection suits, the remaining "Gomer Army" was now under our complete control.

On board the USS Missouri, my staff and I were reveling in the emotions of watching the complete capitulation of a deadly enemy. This is a difficult thing for most soldiers, and for us, it would be particularly difficult. The mission concept of "kill or be killed" was now forced by circumstances into the mission of trying to keep your enemy alive and under peaceful control. The concept of making peace or even entering into the simplest of negotiations can be equally problematic. Minds do not snap from one mode to the other very easily, and nobody reflected this more than Command Sergeant Major Clagmore. When it became quite apparent that things were falling apart for the Gomers, I sent word forward to both ASOC and the 11th Airborne Division, for them to get both General Daniel Greene and Sergeant Major Clagmore to my location by the fastest available transportation. General Greene was headed in my direction within 10 minutes. Sergeant Major Clagmore, on the other hand, almost had to be arrested and drug to an aircraft for transport. On the plane ride to the USS Missouri, he let anyone and everyone know that he was truly upset that he wasn't allowed to kill any more Gomers, and that he had to leave his beloved 11th Airborne Division behind.

I hated to pull either General Greene or Sergeant Major Clagmore back to the USS Missouri, but across the globe, we were getting a rather strange transmission in the Terahertz bands. This message repeated in a cycle, and it was in surprisingly good, even if somewhat stilted, English. "We will meet your leader at location of your choice to discuss terms for peace."

After monitoring this transmission for almost an hour, the President contacted me to discuss this latest message.

"Mike? Are you guys monitoring the Terahertz signals?"

"Yes, Mr. President, we are. What do you think?"

"Mike, according to Doctor Clarkson, Doctor Abramson, and Doctor Marvin, this is a genuine message."

"What does Doctor Cobb think?

"Mike, we lost Doctor Cobb. Since the attack on your headquarters facilities, he was the one guy we couldn't find in the rubble of the collapsed tunnels around the labs. Doctor Marvin was with him when they got hit, but he came out without a scratch, and there is just no sign of Dr. Cobb."

"Wow. This is the first I heard that Doctor Cobb was even missing."

"Sorry about that, too, since I think him and Holly were kind of close friends."

"Thanks, but I got word that she is okay, which honestly is all that matters to me personally. Now the loss of Doctor Cobb is kind of problematic with this message coming in."

"True, but Doctor Clarkson and Doctor Marvin are convinced."

"Well, who do you propose is our 'leader'? I mean talk about your alien cliché! 'Take me to your leader' is about the biggest one I can think of at the moment."

"I know, but since you're the Supreme Allied Commander, my guess is that it would need to be you. I'll get Secretary Case on it right now, but if anything breaks, you'll need to be ready."

"Marty, just how in the hell am I supposed to be ready? What terms? What conditions? How do I consult, and with whom do I consult?"

"Mike, I don't have the answer yet, but you need to gather up the folks from your original plan. Who was it again?"

"Mr. President. I was going to use General Greene, Sergeant Major Clagmore, and Lieutenant Shiwak, our Inuit Scout from the Canadian Armed Forces."

"What about Dubronin's kid?"

"I can add him if you want, and I guess while I'm thinking about it, should we include any other Allied Representatives from my staff?"

"Maybe, but for now, keep it to the people we've already talked about. I'm going to see if someone from Doctor Marvin's team can come and join your team, too."

"Mr. President. You can send anyone you want, so long as it is not Holly."

"Mike, there is no way in hell I'd do that to you. Nope, I'll get Doctor Marvin to find another linguist type."

"Thank you, Mr. President." Hanging up the phone, I realized that we would all have to prepare rather quickly for what would be coming next. Now that I was ordered to assemble "my" negotiation team and to be prepared to engage in the "end game" dance, the pressure was probably as intense as awaiting combat. Within 7 hours, we were given the official word to standby and be prepared to move on very short notice. Apparently, we were waiting for the eggheads to confirm the location and source of the message before we issued our official reply. In the meantime, General Greene and I were working hard on two things. Our first issue was to decide on a location for this potential meeting, which was actually the easy part of the equation. The harder part was deciding on how to deal with the Gomers.

Our dilemmas included an awful lot of questions. For example, we had to decide whether it was a trap, what security we would need, and more to the point, just exactly what terms were we going to try and negotiate. How could we go from an all out "kill or be killed" genocidal war, to a position where we would have some give and take and actually negotiate for peace? What kind of peace? Were the older intelligence reports correct? Were we making peace, only to forge an alliance to fight a future enemy? If so, what would the world say about any such alliance, especially after the human death toll of the two wars around the globe easily exceeded 2.8 billion people? The time was ticking away, and we were no closer to the answers to any of these questions. Each of these questions was sent to the President and to the Secretary of State, but there was very little guidance or consensus as to what the answers should be, or how we were even supposed to negotiate our position.

These questions were bouncing around among my staff and me, when it hit me. For the very first time in a number of years, I was being asked to be a lawyer again. This time, instead of litigating an issue in a courtroom, I was being asked to represent the largest client you could ever find, the Earth and all of her inhabitants. It was 24 hours after our receipt of the Gomers' first message, when Secretary of State Timothy Case finally contacted me with some answers.

"General? Secretary Case here. Do you have a minute?"

"Absolutely, Mr. Secretary. I've been hoping you would contact me."

"Well, General. First of all, after consulting with most of the world's leaders, it has been decided by consensus that you will lead the negotiations on behalf of all the United Nations. I was told to inform you that your appointment as the Supreme Allied Commander is expanded to include command of all United Nations Forces, which I guess technically, was already the situation. So, it is official. You are to negotiate with the Gomers on behalf of everyone."

"So, when the alien says 'take me to your leader', I'm the guy holding the head?"

"I guess that covers it."

"Then tell me, Mr. Secretary. Just exactly what am I supposed to ask them to do or not do, aside from getting the hell off of our planet?"

"I can say that there is no real consensus on any terms, beyond them leaving."

"Mr. Secretary, not wishing to sound rude, but can you at least tell me what our position will be if they ask us to forge some potential alliance for any future threat?"

"No, General. I can't tell you at this point. I doubt legally you can forge any alliance beyond peace terms without some mandate from the various nations or possibly the United Nations."

"Wonderful. Okay, so I go to a negotiation, without a real position, except to tell them to get the hell out? I mean seriously, what about future problems with this other kind of Gomer that their prisoners have told us will be coming here?"

"On that point, General, I'm authorized to tell you, on behalf of the President, that you may commit the United States, and only the United States, to such a potential agreement. Beyond our support, it will fall on the United Nations to either buy into it, or not."

"Mr. Secretary, what about the UK, China, and Russia? Has anyone asked them yet?"

"Yes, but so far, no answer from any of those parties. I can tell you that the UK will likely buy into it, as will our more traditional European allies. I think Israel will go for it, but right now, there are more open questions than answers. Have you tried using your aide to ask his father?"

"Actually, he does have a call in now, but we still haven't heard anything. I will also use my Allied Staff to consult with their respective Governments. Any idea about how long I have before this comes about?"

"No, General, I don't. Once Doctors Abramson, Marvin, and Clarkson get their answers, we'll let you know."

"Thank you, Mr. Secretary." Breaking the connection, I immediately assembled the foreign officers on my staff and briefed them on the overall scheme and questions we were all facing. They all consulted with their governments, but I was really waiting on Russia and China to either opt in or out, when it came to any potential alliance that might come up. There was a lot of soul searching, and more than a little resistance to even dealing with the enemy, but we decided that our involvement with the Gomers would be dependant in large part on a number of questions we would ask at any meeting. Assuming one was ever held, and assuming we were dealing with someone or something with whom we could enter into negotiations.

In the interim, Admiral Lynch informed the USS Missouri Battlegroup Commander to set a course for St. Lawrence Island in the Bering Straits. Similarly, the USS Nimitz Battlegroup and two additional attack Submarines were also to converge in that area within the next two days. General Greene suggested the location, based on his ability to saturate it with ASOC personnel. We also selected the location to facilitate the cold and limited light levels that the Gomers valued so highly. Another, and pretty significant reason, was that we wanted a place that would allow for the naval forces to maneuver quickly if necessary. Despite the notion that the Gomers supposedly wanted to talk peace, history told us that we still needed to be prepared to hit them hard if it were necessary.

When Dr. Marvin and Dr. Clarkson finally confirmed the source and veracity of the Gomers' initial message, our Terahertz reply message was sent to the Gomers. "The appointed Representative of Earth will meet with you at Savoonga, on the northern coast of St. Lawrence Island, Alaska. It is the largest island in what we refer to as the Bering Sea. There is an airport located on the island, with the coordinates of 63° 41' 11" N, 170° 29' 33" W. You shall travel in an unarmed transport ship, without escort, to Earth, where you will land at the coordinates for the airport. Your representatives will be provided safety clothing, if necessary, and you will be provided further transportation to our final location for negotiations. We expect your reply to these conditions within the next three Earth hours, before we set the time for any such negotiations." The message was repeated every few minutes over the next three hours, utilizing the exact same procedure and frequency that the Gomers used in their initial message to us. Their answer came at precisely 2 hours and 59 minutes after our first transmission. "We agree, set time please." Located a full day out of St. Lawrence Island, we sent a reply to meet us in 36 hours. This was timed to coincide with the passage of twilight over Savoonga, and it gave us 12 hours to get our final pieces in place.

Savoonga Airport, St. Lawrence Island, Alaska:

Only minutes before the appointed hour, we were advised that the Gomer Transport class ship was passing into the atmosphere. General McDaniel's personnel at Vandenberg, Air Force Base, had tracked the craft from the instant it was launched from one of the Mars-based Moon Class ships. It was unaccompanied, and all the telemetry and imagery we obtained confirmed that the Transport was of the class and type we had already encountered in Greenland. Despite it being alone, General McDaniel maintained a hand on the trigger, just in case. The Transport crossed into Alaskan airspace, just north of the Arctic Circle, and picked up an escort of several lead painted and fully armed Naval variants of the F-35 aircraft. Each of them had been launched by the USS Nimitz, which was holding station near St. Lawrence Island. When the transport touched down, the craft was met by representatives from the 511th Parachute Infantry Regiment, from the 11th Airborne Division, who provided the initial security and the honor guard. I had Sergeant Major Clagmore cull the division to cobble together the tallest, meanest- looking troopers we could find. When the Gomer Transport opened the main doors, the Honor Guard marched forward to either side of the designated pathway. They presented a very intimidating picture, and as the Gomers' party disembarked their craft, it was clear that they were extremely hesitant. Finally, the four Gomers, led by a rather stately Gomer, began walking forward from their transport between the rows of Airborne Troopers.

General Roberts, as my representative, approached the Gomers and offered them a hand salute. After introducing himself, he asked if they required any protective clothing to feel comfortable in the environment. This offer was refused by the senior Gomer, and General Roberts told them to accompany him to the waiting transport which, after some more hesitation, they approached with great trepidation. It was deliberately our intent to keep them uncomfortable, and their being transported to the harbor via dog sled was just one more such expression of that intent. Once they were to the coast, they were loaded onboard the 'Admiral's Barge' for their final journey to the deck of the USS Missouri. We could have transported them by helicopter, but we wanted to gauge their reaction to the things that would be more out of the ordinary or basic for them.

The entire process from their landing, to their being led into the Senior Officers' Wardroom, took a little better than an hour. I was informed when they were seated, and General Roberts gave me the brief description of their demeanor and actions on the way to the ship. They had said little, but then I already knew that, since they'd been photographed, video recorded, and 'bugged' for their entire journey. I again took my time, opting to have a brief smoke, while I let them stew for almost another half hour. Then with all the pomp and circumstance we could muster, I was ushered into the room, where I sat down across the table from the Gomer who was identified as the leader or chief negotiator for the Gomers. Taking my seat, I simply stared at the Gomer for almost a full minute, before picking up a microphone and asking him if he could function in our language, or would he require a translator. His reply came through a speaker set up on the table for just this conversation. "No. We can translate your words based on language sample provided."

"Fine. Let me introduce myself. I am General of the Army, Michael Patrick. I am the Supreme Allied Commander of all the United Nations' Forces defending Earth. With whom am I speaking?"

"I am Councilor Ormak, and I represent the Glavanna High Council. We are prepared to discuss with you peace." Watching Ormak closely, I was able to finally detect the device around his neck which allowed him to transmit and apparently receive our discussion. I could only surmise that this was also a translator of some type. Continuing his remarks, Ormak referred to me as "General of the

Army, Michael Patrick, Supreme Allied Commander of the United Nations' Forces defending Earth, we Glavanna wish to end all hostile actions with you and your people."

"Councilor Ormak. We too would like to find peace, but we need to ask you some questions first."

"Yes. General of the Army, Michael Patrick, Supreme Allied Commander of the United Nations' Forces defending Earth."

"Councilor Ormak. If it is appropriate within your protocol, I would ask that you call me General Patrick."

"Yes. General Patrick. That would be acceptable."

"May I refer to you as Councilor Ormak?"

"Yes. General Patrick. That would be acceptable."

"Councilor Ormak. Why have you attacked Earth?"

"General Patrick. We did not attack Earth. We were attempting to remove what we saw as a dangerous infestation on Earth."

"Councilor Ormak, you will have to explain what you mean by infestation."

"General Patrick. We come to Earth, many of your years before. The inhabitants were largely animals and primitive life forms. When our scouts return about 1500 of your years ago, we saw life forms that were only a little more advanced, who were using simple tools, and living simply."

"Councilor Ormak, how is that a dangerous infestation?"

"General Patrick. We return about 30 of your years ago and found a warrior culture. A culture that had advanced into space, and we believed with warrior-like intent. You are no longer simple. You were dangerous infestation that could threaten our new home."

"Councilor Ormak. I'm a good listener, can you explain to me the new home and why you need such a new home?" It was now time to find out if the Tornit story from the prisoners was actually going to be the Gomers' official line.

"General Patrick. We leave home planet after millions of years. It was necessary for two reasons. The first is that our Sun is sick and failing. The second is Tornit have driven all life from our Sun. They have enslaved and killed all they encounter. In search for new home, we considered your world, but it has too many problems and infestations. We finally arrived at what you call Mars, or the 4th planet from your Sun. We find the climate best, and while there are poisons to us on that planet, we hope to find a way to deal with them. We are living in our main ships, while we consider problem. We worried that you were servants of the Tornit. The transmissions and the transmitter on your Moon gave us belief that you were dangerous to our survival. As subservient to the Tornit, it was important that you must be eliminated."

"Councilor Ormak. I think we have met the Tornit, only a few short years ago. It was their attack that left the transmitter on the Moon. Just as we defeated you, we defeated them."

"General Patrick. You defeated their small expedition. They are many more, with far greater numbers. They outnumber us and you, and they will absorb and destroy all that is encountered. We intercepted their ship after it left your planet, and we destroyed it. It was General Algatok's belief that they were from here and returning to their home planet on a routine mission."

"Councilor Ormak. Did you just refer to General Algatok?"

"General Patrick. Algatok was our Supreme Warrior Chief, until killed several nights ago in his Military Command ship."

"Councilor Ormak. We had a prisoner who represented that he was Commander Algatok, and we returned him to you in good faith to seek an accord between us. Is this the same Algatok?"

"General Patrick. Yes, he is the same Algatok who escaped from you. It was he that ordered additional attacks, even though the High Council wished to discuss your messages with you."

"Councilor Ormak. Algatok did not escape. We returned him in a good faith effort to seek peace to perhaps join forces to meet the Tornit."

"General Patrick. It no longer matters. Algatok is dead."

"Actually, Councilor Ormak, it matters. You could have achieved an alliance then, but now, things are different. You have killed almost a third of our population, and we have already shown that we can defeat the Tornit. You see, Councilor, we learn pretty fast here, and we haven't stopped learning either. Why should we help you? Why should we care what happens to you?"

"General Patrick. I have no answer. We can but only ask for your mercy."

"Councilor Ormak. We will consider your words. I will now consult with the various world leaders. Can your staff discuss the issues related to the return of your prisoners?"

"Yes, General Patrick. We too have prisoners of your people, so an exchange can be made." With his last remark, I did my best to keep a straight face. He has prisoners from our world? I wondered how many prisoners, where were they now, and from what operation were they taken? We had billions of dead around the globe, but from our combat operations, we just didn't have many missing. Most of what we had seen were people just blowing up before our very eyes. Finally, trying to appear bored, I asked the question. "Councilor? How many prisoners do you have? We need a close count, so we can determine where and how to make an exchange."

"General Patrick. We are holding about 2,000 people, who we took as prisoners in what you call Siberia and Greenland."

"Councilor, I am informed that we are holding somewhere around one million of your . . . . . . soldiers."

"General Patrick. We sent almost five times the number. Where are the rest?"

"Councilor, to my knowledge, they are now dead."

"Thank you, General Patrick, for your honesty."

"Councilor Ormak, I am now going to consult with my Government and the other governments around the world. Can my staff get you anything?"

"No, thank you, General Patrick. We wait."

Stepping out of the Wardroom, I had General Greene stay in the room to babysit Ormak, while the rest of the staff began their discussions with the Gomers about prisoners. True to my word, I went straight to my stateroom, and began my rather lengthy encrypted conversation with the President and Secretary Case. Once I had my instructions, I made my way back into the Wardroom and sat back down in front of Ormak. This time I would be the one with at least a few surprises.

"Councilor Ormak, I consulted with my Government and the other governments around the world. Some of our Governments will entertain discussions with you regarding a form of joint defense against the Tornit. The terms for these Governments will be that you share ALL of your information about the Tornit. You must not withhold any information, and you will give our scientists access to all of the technology that you possess to assist them in finding ways to counter the Tornit threat. This information will also include access to your data files and information about both the Tornit and your interactions with the Tornit."

"General Patrick? I will need to discuss with Council, but these terms seem acceptable."

"Councilor Ormak, I'm not done. In addition, you and your forces are to leave our planet and our Moon, only to return at pre-selected points, and only then with permission from myself or my headquarters. You will come only in unarmed craft, and you will fly to our world and then off again, using only preset course information. Do you understand those terms?"

"Yes. General Patrick. What of our possible settlement on Mars?"

"Councilor Ormak. I have been instructed to advise you that we will honor your request to settle on Mars, without harassment or attacks from Earth. In that regard, we wish to leave you in peace. We will have no involvement in your internal affairs, unless or until they infringe on our world. At which point, we reserve the right to defend ourselves, or to engage in such activities as may be necessary to protect our planet. I was also instructed to tell you that we will entertain the possibility of your people submitting an ambassador to our world to continue negotiations and to maintain some form of diplomatic relationship."

"General Patrick. May I be candid?"

"Councilor Ormak, I believe that is our purpose for talking today. Yes, please do be candid."

"General Patrick. The issue of Mars settlement is difficult for us. We have issue with decay of materials and may be unable to survive."

"Councilor Ormak. That is my surprise for you. We think we know why, and we can offer you some assistance, but such assistance can only come with the acceptance of all our terms, and especially the provision of all information in your possession that is related to the Tornit."

"General Patrick. I will consult with the High Council."

"Councilor Ormak, we can provide you with the use of our communications facilities, or we can return you to your transport. We will leave the decision up to you."

"General Patrick. I will return to my transport. I am sure you understand."

"Councilor Ormak, I certainly understand, but please also understand that the entire time you are in transit and onboard your ship, you will be under observation by people who have been ordered to terminate your very existence, if you so much as twitch in a threatening manner."

"General Patrick. You are most direct, but you must know that my people must be assured that I have not been coerced into making these terms of peace."

"I do understand, Councilor, but remember, our peace is dependent on our being assured that you are no longer a threat to

OUR world. Please do not violate our trust, otherwise, we will not discuss any terms. Next time, your surrender will be unconditional, or we will all be dead."

"General Patrick. Our answer will be transmitted on the same frequencies, and you will have our answer in one of your Earth days, 24 of your hours, after my return."

"Excellent. Councilor Ormak, we will await your answer, and you will be provided more detailed information about where to meet for the execution of any documents required to solidify the peace."

"Documents?"

"Yes. On our planet, we make all of our agreements in writing, and that writing is signed by all of the parties to that agreement. If this is too foreign of a concept, then we can video the event, and you can be given a copy for posterity."

"I think I understand, General Patrick. You need official recording of our agreement to your terms."

"That's right, Councilor Ormak. This will be for your benefit and ours. If a dispute arises in the future about the terms, or the agreement among the parties, then it serves as a record of what took place."

"Ah, I understand, General Patrick."

"Councilor Ormak. Have a safe journey."

"General Patrick. Thank you." Councilor Ormak and I rose from our seats together, and he was escorted from the Wardroom to the helicopter pad and then flown back to his transport ship. Now it would be a simple matter of waiting for their response, and to begin the coordination for what we hoped would be an exchange of prisoners and information.

General Greene and I watched the helicopter with the Gomers on board lift off from the deck of the USS Missouri. Turning to me, General Greene said, "General, that was about the creepiest thing I have ever seen or done."

"Daniel. I have a feeling we're going to have to get used to creepy as the new normal."

"I know, General, but there is still something about all this that just doesn't feel right."

"I agree. How are we coming on cracking their data files?"

"General, we've made zip in the way of progress. The access keys are tough, and may be based on equations that are not within our ability to crack right now."

"Daniel. If they buy into the agreement, and if they provide us access to what they know about these alleged Tornit, then maybe the answer will be in all of that information."

"General, it is sure worth a shot. We'll see how this develops, but it could be that we could just get their access key by asking for it."

"I'm not so sure about that one, but if you have some way to get the access code or formula, or whatever the hell it would be, to get into those files, then give it a try. I want a second data set to examine, if nothing else to verify their story. So, the stuff we need to crack is from both the First War, and now this Second War with these jokers. Maybe by comparing the data from then to what they are telling us now will give us some real answers."

"General, I agree. I wouldn't trust these Gomers any further than I could toss one of them."

"OH, and Daniel?"

"Sir?"

"This has priority for your guys. The President is aware of my concerns, and he agrees that we need those answers. We have to keep focused, and we will have to hedge our bets, since we have no idea what we're doing if we don't know the real truth."

"Yessir. We'll keep working on it. We'll also keep an eye on all exchanges with the Gomers if it comes down to it."

"Excellent! Keep me posted as you go along." We stepped back into the warmth of the ship, just as the Captain gave the orders to move the USS Missouri out of the harbor and back towards Alaska.

Chapter XXI

Supreme Allied Headquarters, (SAHQ - Main):

Councilor Ormak was true to his word. One day after his return to his home ship, we were sent a message that they accepted all terms for peace. The result was the beginning of more negotiations, discussions, and exchange of both information and prisoners. Of the roughly 2,200 prisoners that were returned to Earth, it was readily apparent that the Gomers had been searching for our weaknesses, just as we had searched for their weaknesses. Each of the former POW's was grossly under nourished, suffering from exposure, and apparently ill from the various environmental effects of the Gomers' ships. We were seeing some rather extreme psychological issues to go along with the symptoms of radiation sickness. Fortunately, there were no invasive viral diseases, but the overexposure to the radiation of space, and/or the lack of shielding from their radioactive emissions, was sufficient to kill off many of the prisoners shortly after their return.

The treatment of the Earth's people in captivity was one more of the hundreds of sticking points for many of the World's leaders as they attempted to negotiate the finer points of a peaceful alliance with the Gomers. We had treated their prisoners with care and respect. Still, many of them died in captivity, at least before we had identified that our environment was causing the prisoners harm. I knew that they had the same issue, but that was little comfort to those who died in the process. There were other problems, not the least of which was our overwhelming distrust of the Gomers. Perhaps it was because we could not read their emotions, or perhaps it was because we were inherently incapable of trusting anyone, especially those who had worked so hard to kill us in their genocidal attacks. Either way, trust was the real issue and it would be the constant stalker of all our negotiations.

As weeks turned into months, the negotiations were as scientific as they were diplomatic. President Blanchard, Secretary of State Case, and the United Nations representatives became quite embroiled in meetings, discussions, and arguments amongst themselves. The scientific community, to include Dr. Clarkson, Dr. Abramson, Dr. Marvin, and others from around the globe, was as excited as small children at Christmas. The information about the Gomers and their Tornit enemies was leading to almost daily technological advances and breakthroughs. It was as if the Gomers had part of the puzzle while we held the rest of it. The Gomers metallurgical technology was in some ways extremely advanced, while in others it was completely deficient. It would be the combination of what they knew, with what we could achieve, that would lead to more breakthroughs that benefitted both the Gomers and the population of Earth. We were able to boost weapons power, along with our own propulsion systems, to retrofit and modify several of our key weapons systems. In short, the science was overwhelming when combined and was giving our entire World a boost forward.

It would take the better part of a year for the powers at the United Nations to dust off their *Protocol for Alien Contact* and for the various countries around the world to hammer out an agreement with the

Gomers. Some things required my input, and there were a number of meetings that required my presence regarding future defense issues. As the Agreement was reached, signed, video recorded, and audio recorded in no less than 350 languages, to include Gomer, our World was faced with the next pressing question: "Now what?"

I know for my part, I was tired to the level of almost pure exhaustion. The almost three years of constant work, countless cigarettes, and billions of cups of coffee were taking their toll. The one meal days, four hours sleep a night, and the inability to enjoy even the simple things with my family, had put me in a horrid frame of mind. I wasn't the least bit excited about scientific breakthroughs anymore. I was tired of beating my head against the wall of trying to mediate or assist in forming accords. It was getting so bad that even the sound of a phone ringing would almost make me physically ill. Thanks to the exhaustion, I reached a personal decision that led to a rather dramatic phone conversation with my old friend, President Martin Blanchard.

"Mr. President. I am a Reservist; the war has been over for a year. At what point do you let me off active duty and send my ass home?"

"General Patrick. You remember that Fifth Star?"

"Yessir."

"That means there is no leaving active duty. You, sir, are Regular Army and have been ever since we gave you those last two Stars in the first war."

"Mr. President. With all due respect, if I had known that, I'm not sure I would have taken the Fourth Star, much less the Fifth one."

"Such is War, General."

"Mr. President. Again, with all due respect, would it be too much trouble if you shoved those last two stars up your ass and sent me home?"

"Hah! Mike, cut the crap! You don't want to go home, you really don't. You've got too much to do here, and besides, the alliances we have would fall on their ass without you. You're too key to this whole mission. Besides, what about the Tornit?"

"Mr. President. What damn good will I be with the Tornit when I'm too tired to give a damn anymore? Besides, there are other guys who can deal with this garbage. Generals Larkin, Davis, Whitney, Greene, and Admiral Lynch, all have a handle on this."

"Nobody has a handle on this, not even me. We need you!"

"Marty, dammit. Let me retire or something. I've GOT to get the hell away from this stuff. It is killing me, and you should know that better than anyone."

"Mouse! Sorry. I'll give you a couple months leave if you want, but other than that, you're on the hook."

"Geez. Remember when your predecessor as the Chairman of the Joint Chiefs had me drug back from being retired and into the Army

Reserves? Remember how it was supposedly to deal with the fallout from some dip-doodle 'Arab Spring'?"

"Yes, I do."

"Well, I told him then, just like I'm telling you now. I might as well have joined the damn Mob, since it is probably easier to quit them than it is to get away from Special Operations or the military."

"I know all that, and maybe I agree a little with you, but Mike?"

"Yes. Mr. President."

"Mike, your country, oh hell, the Earth needs you. What about your grandson? What kind of life do you want him to have? Enslaved to some ET?"

"Dammit, boss, that is hitting below the belt!"

"It might be, but there it is. Now you still want to retire?"

"Okay. I won't retire, but I at least need a sabbatical."

"Sure. What do you want, a month?"

"How about six months?"

"No wonder you negotiate well with the Gomers. Okay, you've got two months."

"No sir. I get six, or I just say piss on it and walk away as a nothing. You do know that is an option, and right now, my 'give a damn' is completely broken!"

"Okay! Deal, you get your damn six months. BUT for those six months, you have to stay in contact, and you have to remain reachable."

"Okay. Mr. President. I will be handing off command to a temporary Acting Commander, say, in a week?"

"Done. Who you going to stick with it while you're on leave?"

"Sir. I'm actually thinking General Whitney can handle it. General Larkin and General Davis are still tied up with their Army Groups and the transfer of material to and from the Gomers. General Whitney is my Senior Deputy, at least since General Richardson was taken in for treatment for his heart. I'm also thinking that General Clark can fill in for Whitney until I get back."

"General Patrick, that sounds like a deal, but my terms are not negotiable. You WILL keep in touch, you WILL keep your headquarters posted on your location, and you WILL keep them advised as to your general location at all times. Do I make myself clear?"

"Yes. Marty, I've only got one more question."

"What?"

"Do you need me to submit a daily report on toilet paper usage, or can I at least have the freedom to ....."

"Smart ass!" The silence of the phone line was immediate and left me with a smile on my face. For the first time in several years, I was going to get my break. Now how long, or where, were questions that were still in the air, but at least the light at the end of the tunnel was no longer an oncoming train. Stepping away from it all, and allowing my family to step away too, was something we all needed. My only hope was that we could enjoy it before the other shoe dropped, since it might be our last chance forever.

We were all packed and about to head out for our long-awaited family vacation, when General Greene sent me a message to contact him ASAP. To this day, I have no reason why it triggered something in me, but it did, and with the little red flags dancing in my head, I picked up the phone and got General Greene on the line.

"Daniel.. . . Patrick here. You needed to talk to me?"

"Yessir. Boss, we might have a problem."

"Nothing but problems, Daniel, so what is yours?"

"Sir, we've been getting some interesting information from some Terahertz intercepts, and there is something not right here."

"What do you mean, not right?"

"Sir. I can't put my finger on it exactly, but my gut says that somebody isn't being on the level here. These intercepts might be nothing, but we're not able to piece it together yet."

"Okay, so what do you want from me?"

"Well. I need your authority to do some more 'snooping' and digging into our new friends. I also wanted to ask if you still wanted us to 'check the dogs for fleas'?"

"Absolutely. I have been having the same misgivings, and I know that you're probably right that things are not as they seem. Might be why we have held onto a few things, and will continue to hold them close."

"Yessir, and I've also taken the liberty to make sure we have plenty of flea dip handy."

"Excellent. Keep me posted. Do you know how to reach me?"

"Yessir. You're going to be at your old favorite haunt, and my folks will never be far away."

"Great. In that case, I'll see you when I get back!"

"Yessir." Hanging up the phone, I turned back to my bride, and said those immortal famous words used for all trips, "Are we there yet?" She smiled and we headed off to get that much needed break. After my discussion with General Greene, I knew absolutely that we were going to need every second of it, and that the odds of my getting the full six months were probably very long indeed.

APPENDICES

APPENDIX I

ORDER OF BATTLE

US NAVAL FORCES

PACIFIC FLEET

3rd Fleet, Battle Groups

TF-31.1

BB   USS Alabama
CG   USS Mobile Bay
DDG USS Howard
        USS Spruance

TF-31.2

BB   USS New Jersey
CG   USS Port Royal
DDG USS Fitzgerald
        USS Higgins

7th Fleet, Battle Groups

TF-71.1

BB   USS Missouri
CG   USS Vincennes
DDG USS O'Brien
        USS O'Kane

TF-71.2

BB   USS Alaska
CG   USS Antietam
DDG USS McCampbell
        USS Stethem

TF-74

CVN USS Ronald Reagan
USS George Washington
LHD USS Boxer
USS Makin Island
CG USS Princeton
USS Chosin
USS Valley Forge
DDG USS Russell
USS Benfold
USS Cushing

TF-38

CVN USS Nimitz
USS Carl Vinson
CG USS Shiloh
DDG USS Shoup
USS Hopper

TF-78

CVN USS John C. Stennis
USS Kitty Hawk
CG USS Lake Erie
DDG USS John Paul Jones
USS Decatur
USS Briscoe

ATTACK SUBMARINES ASSIGNED TO THE PACIFIC FLEET:

SSN 688 Los Angeles

SSN 698 Bremerton

SSN 701 La Jolla

SSN 705 City of Corpus Christi

SSN 707 Portsmouth

SSN 711 San Francisco

SSN 713 Houston

SSN 715 Buffalo

SSN 716 Salt Lake City

SSN 717 Olympia

SSN 718 Honolulu

SSN 721 Chicago

SSN 722 Key West

SSN 724 Louisville

SSN 725 Helena

SSN 752 Pasadena

SSN 754 Topeka

SSN 758 Asheville

SSN 759 Jefferson City

SSN 762 Columbus

SSN 763 Santa Fe

SSN 770 Tucson

SSN 771 Columbia

SSN 772 Greeneville

SSN 773 Cheyenne

ATLANTIC FLEET

2nd Fleet Battle Groups,

TF - 20.1
BB   USS Montana
CG   USS San Jacinto
DDG USS Morton
      USS Gregg
      USS Inoye

TF - 20.2
BB   USS Wisconsin
CG   USS Vicksburg
DDG USS Oscar Austin
      USS Ignatius

TF-25
BB   USS North Carolina
CVN USS Abraham Lincoln
LHD USS Wasp
      USS Bataan
      USS Iwo Jima
CG   USS Gettysburg
      USS Vella Gulf
      USS Thomas S. Gates
DDG USS Bulkeley
      USS Laboon
      USS The Sullivans
      USS Porter

4th Fleet Battle Groups

TF-40.1
BB   USS Massachusetts
CG   USS Monterey
DDG USS Stout
      USS O'Bannon

TF-40.2
BB   USS Iowa
CG   USS Cape St. George
DDG USS Winston Churchill
      USS Mitscher

TF-27

CVN USS Harry Truman
     USS Dwight D. Eisenhower
CG   USS Hue City
     USS Ticonderoga
DDG USS Arleigh Burke
     USS Ramage
     USS Ross

TF-47

CVN USS Theodore Roosevelt
     USS G. H. W. Bush
CG   USS Anzio
     USS Yorktown
DDG USS Barry
     USS Carney
     USS Mahan
     USS Thorn

ATTACK SUBMARINES ASSIGNED TO THE ATLANTIC
FLEET:

SSN 690 Philadelphia
SSN 699 Jacksonville
SSN 700 Dallas
SSN 706 Albuquerque
SSN 708 Minneapolis-Saint Paul
SSN 709 Hyman G. Rickover
SSN 710 Augusta
SSN 714 Norfolk
SSN 719 Providence
SSN 720 Pittsburgh
SSN 723 Oklahoma City
SSN 750 Newport News
SSN 751 San Juan
SSN 753 Albany
SSN 755 Miami
SSN 756 Scranton
SSN 757 Alexandria
SSN 760 Annapolis
SSN 761 Springfield
SSN 764 Boise
SSN 765 Montpelier
SSN 766 Charlotte
SSN 767 Hampton
SSN 768 Hartford
SSN 769 Toledo

APPENDIX II

KEY PERSONNEL

ALLIED GROUND FORCES

General Edward Whitney,
USA (Atlantic Command)

21ST ALLIED ARMY GROUP - Field Marshal Sir William Fuller, UK (Atlantic) (KIA) General Jerry Larkin, US

<u>FIRST ARMY - Lieutenant General Daniel Mickelson</u>

II Corps. - Major General Clyde Stubben

5th Infantry Division
36th Infantry Division
4th Armored Division

V Corps. - Major General Marvin Russell

6th Infantry Division
42nd Infantry Division
7th Armored Division

XXI Corps. - Major General Michael Decatur

    10th Mountain Division
    102nd Infantry Division
    9th Armored Division

THIRD ARMY - Lieutenant General S. L. Simpson

VII Corps. - Major General William H. Prosser

    99th Infantry Division
    106th Infantry Division
    1st Armored Division

VIII Corps. - Major General Alvin Simpkins

    8th Infantry Division
    18th Infantry Division
    8th Armored Division

XVIII Airborne Corps. - Major General James Sturdivant

    17th Airborne Division
    82nd Airborne Division
    101st Airborne (Airmobile) Division

SEVENTH ARMY (Allied composite Army)- Lieutenant General Karl Kessler, Germany

I French Corps. - Lieutenant General Henri Reneau

I German Corps. - Major General Hermann Smetzler

II German Corps. - Major General Rudolph Heinz

I Spanish Corps. - Major General Francisco Carlos

EIGHTH BRITISH ARMY (UK) - General Sir. Edward Fitzhugh Mallory

X Corps. - Lieutenant General David Thatcher, Royal Army

XX Corps. - Lieutenant General William Houser, Royal Army

XXX Corps. - Lieutenant General Stephen Wintergable, Royal Canadian Forces

PACIFIC THEATER

General Stephen Richardson, USA, (Pacific Command)

42nd ALLIED ARMY GROUP - General Richard Davis, USA

<u>SIXTH ARMY - Lieutenant General Manuel "Manny" Ortiz, USA</u>

III Amphibious Corps. - Major General D. E. James, USMC

1st Marine Division
2nd Marine Division
3rd Marine Division
15th Marine Expeditionary Unit (MEU)

XIVth Corps. - Major General David Chandler

2nd Cavalry Division
2nd Armored Division
25th Infantry Division

IX Airborne Corps. - Major General John J. Powers

11th Airborne Division
13th Airborne Division
108th Airborne (Airmobile) Division

EIGHTH ARMY (US) - General Winfield David Smith

I Corps. - Major General John Montgomery

4th Infantry Division
7th Infantry Division
3rd Armored Division

X Corps. - Major General Thomas Westerman

28th Infantry Division
29th Infantry Division
5th Armored Division

XXIV Corps. - Major General George Foster

1st Cavalry Division
24th Infantry Division
77th Infantry Division

<u>TENTH ARMY - General Roberto Guzeman, USA</u>

XX Corps. - Major General Mark Scutarski, USA

21st Infantry Division
12th Infantry Division
14th Infantry Division
10th Armored Division

I Australian/New Zealand Corps. - Lieutenant General Edmond Hurt, Australian Army

I Japanese Corps. - Lieutenant General Hideki Tochihara

CHINESE ARMY GROUP- General Xi Jintao, PLAGF

Composed of 18 Group Armies, One through Eighteenth Army Groups. Each Group is approximately the same composition and strength as a US Corps. These Sixteen Corps sized elements are the equivalent of Six Armies, and are all under the command of the Chinese Forces. Relations with the PLAGF and the PLAN, are excellent under the current conditions, and both forces have had no difficulty in working with the Allied Command as a semi autonomous grouping of forces.

RUSSIAN ARMY GROUP - General Vladimir Petrofsky, Russian Federation

Composed of 10 Field Armies, the Field Armies were each were organized into Four Corps, with Four Divisions assigned to each

Corps. The strengths of each element was about 75% the strength of a comparable United States Army Force. Once the diplomatic relations eased prior to the Siberian Campaigns, the working relationship improved slowly. Per the arrangements between the United States and Russia, Russian Forces operated separately, and answered directly to the Allied Command to General of the Army Michael Patrick. Their operations were coordinated and eventually, prior to the execution of the Campaign, this Army Group Command was shifted to the Command of General Gerald "Jerry" Larkin, USA, where it operated as an autonomous grouping of forces, under the 21st Army Group (after the death of Field Marshal Fuller, UK).

ALLIED NAVAL FORCES

CHINESE NAVAL GROUP - Admiral Zao Tse Hue, PLAN, is providing a number of diesel submarines, and frigate/corvette size surface escorts. All operating in conjunction with the US 7th Fleet, during the Anti-Gomer operations.

RUSSIAN NAVAL GROUPS - Admiral Viktor Suchkov, Russian Federation, Consisted of the Black Sea, Baltic Sea, and Pacific fleets. While there were a few surviving surface combatants, most were of the destroyer or frigate types. The largest surviving surface ship was a single Missile Cruiser, the Varyag, in the Russian Pacific Fleet. The majority of naval assets were 15 nuclear powered submarines, and 20 diesel/electric submarines. These assets were relied on heavily in their respective areas to assist in the escort of transports in conjunction with the applicable US Fleet for that theater of operations.

JAPANESE NAVY - Admiral Tanaka Sato, JPNDF. Japan contributed 15 additional Destroyer class escorts, mostly US Arleigh Burke Class, which operated in conjunction with both the US Navy's 7th and 3rd Fleets.

ROYAL AUSTRALIAN NAVY - Admiral David Hugh McDermott, RAN. Australian naval forces, were comprised of a number of submarine and surface vessels, to include sealift and escort type ships. These forces also were operating as part of the US Navy's 3rd and 7th Fleets, providing both escorts and active participation in all seaborne operations.

US AIR FORCES

First Air Force	Lieutenant General L. L. West
Second Air Force	Lieutenant General G. Foster
Eighth Air Force	Lieutenant General T. J. Lilly
Tenth Air Force	Lieutenant General A. Brooks
Eleventh Air Force	Lieutenant General C. C. Nowak
Twelfth Air Force	Lieutenant General S. Kaminski (trsfr'd)
	Lieutenant General D. F. Stout
Eighteenth Air Force	Lieutenant General R. S. Young
United States Air Forces Southern Command	Lieutenant General F. R. Casner

ALLIED AIR FORCES

RAF -	General Sir. Harold Manning
RCAF -	General David Horn
RAAF -	General Donald Taviner
Danish AF -	General Bjorg Christian
Norwegian AF -	General Lars Hanson
Finland AF -	General Svork Sevotstock
France AF -	General Robert Marcel Delamey
German AF-	General Heinrich Hoefer
PLAAF-	General Tsi Xi Woo
Russian Fed. AF-	General Pyotr Nemerov

| Russian Strategic Missile Forces - | General Mikail Tuporovski |
| Russian Airborne Forces - | General Igor Sevitch |

STRATEGIC RESERVE US FORCES

Naval Forces: (Adm. Charles Steadman)

Atlantic: SSBN   USS West Virginia
   USS Louisiana
   USS Florida
   USS Georgia

Pacific: SSBN   USS Pennsylvania
   USS Kentucky
   USS Ohio
   USS Michigan

10th Fleet (Attack)
   SSN   USS Virginia
   USS Texas
   USS Hawaii
   USS North Carolina

Air Forces: (General Quentin J. Thayer, Jr.)

14th Air Force, Vandenberg, CA, General Randolph McDaniel

Allied Special Operations Command

USSOCOM
JSOC
1st SFOD-D
2nd SFOD-D
75th Ranger Regiment (3 Battalions)
95th Ranger Regiment (3 Battalions)
160th SOAR
USAF Special Operations Wing
Seal Teams, USN
Seal Team 2
Seal Team 6
Seal Team 8
SAS
RC SAS/Armed Forces
Australian SAS
Danish/Finland/Sweden/Norway Special Operators
to operate in the Arctic Regions, in conjunction with
indigenous recruited personnel.

US Special Forces

1st SF Group
3rd SF Group
5th SF Group
7th SF Group
10th SF Group
19th SF Group
20th SF Group

US Artillery/Gomer Batteries (ASOC) +

101st Gmr Arty Brigade *
202nd Gmr Arty Brigade
303rd Gmr Arty Brigade
110th Gmr Arty Brigade
120th Gmr Arty Brigade
121st Gmr Arty Brigade
145th Gmr Arty Brigade
173rd Gmr Arty Brigade
181st Gmr Arty Brigade
210th Gmr Arty Brigade
804th Gmr Arty Brigade
903rd Gmr Arty Brigade
1101st Gmr Arty Brigade

(Each Gmr Arty Brigade is comprised of three battalion of three Batteries apiece. Each Battery is comprised of 1 Main Gmr Gun and 3 ADA Gmr Guns; a Battalion is 4 Main Guns with 12 ADA pieces; while the Brigade is 12 Main Guns with 36 ADA pieces.)

* The 101st Gmr Arty Brigade was virtually destroyed in the battle of Prince Charles Island, Canada, but was eventually reconstituted prior to the Russian Campaigns.

+ Additional Gmr Arty Brigades were assigned to various key locations, and are NOT listed here, but were instead base forces for New Washington, SAHQ, various key ports around CONUS, and the New Pentagon. There were, at the conclusion of the war, an additional 40 such additional Brigade sized units, which were apportioned to deploying units as follows: One Brigade assigned to each US Army Group HQ, one Brigade assigned to each US Army HQ, and an additional Brigade assigned to each Corps HQ. (Ultimately this was roughly one Battalion for each Operational Combat Division.)

FOURTH ARMY (US) (CONUS)(Deployable) General Walter G. Crouse, USA

IV Corps. Lieutenant General Howard Masters (CONUS Reserve)

45th Infantry Division (Conus Security) (Security Reserve)
50th Infantry Division (Conus Security) (East Coast Port Security)
98th Infantry Division (Conus Security) (New Washington Area)

XXII Corps. Lieutenant General Phillip Travis (Strategic Reserve) (Infantry)

63rd Infantry Division (Conus Security) (Allied Hq area)
68th Infantry Division (Conus Security) (New Pentagon area)
51st Infantry Division (West Coast Port Security)

XV Corps. Lieutenant General Larry Waxman (Strategic Reserve) (Armor)

20th Armored Division
21st Armored Division
23rd Armored Division

<u>SECOND ARMY (US) (CONUS)(Training) - General Willard Washington</u>

XXXI Corps. Lieutenant General James E. Fien (Advanced Unit Training/USAR/NG Training)

107th Infantry Division (Tng)
59th Infantry Division (Tng)
14th Armored Division (Tng)

73rd Aviation Brigade (Tng)
121st Artillery Brigade (Tng)
339th Engineer Brigade (Tng)

1st OPFOR/GOMER Group

XXXII Corps. Lieutenant General Harmon Clarkson (Special/ Advance Training)

145th Airborne Brigade (Tng)
15th Air Defense Brigade (Gmr)
18th ADA Brigade (Conventional)
293rd Artillery Brigade/School (Gmr)

803rd Artillery Brigade/School (Conventional/S&P)

170th Special Tactics/Research Detachment/School

JFK Warfare Center and School

XXXIII Corps. Lieutenant General April S. Freeman (f/k/a
TRADOC)

Armored Center and School

Infantry Center and School

Engineer Center and School

Artillery Center and School

Aviation Center and School

Logistics Center and School

Medical Center and School

ADA Center and School

C&GSC

War College,

Center for Strategic Studies

US NAVAL CONSTRUCTION COMPLETED DURING THE SECOND GOMER WAR:

USS Montana, BB+
USS Iowa, BB+
USS Alaska, BB+
USS South Carolina, BB
USS Morton, DDG+
USS Gregg, DDG+
USS Halsey, DDG
USS Fuller, DDG

+   Engaged in combat operations either in Greenland, or in support of later operations in both the Ural and Siberian Campaigns.

BB   Battleship
DDG   Destroyer

NATIONAL COMMAND AUTHORITY

President Martin "Marty" Blanchard

National Science Advisors: Dr. Anthony Abramson, Dr. Walter J.
                              Clarkson, and Dr. George Marvin; Dr.
                              Dana Cobb, (MIA).
Secretary of State   The Honorable Timothy Case
Secretary of Defense   The Honorable Richard Todd
National Security Advisor: Dr. Henrich Khelm

SUPREME ALLIED COMMAND

Commander: General of the Army, Michael "Mighty
                    Mouse" Patrick, USA

Deputy Commander   Field Marshal Sir William Fuller, UK, Army
                    (KIA)
                    General Edward "Whit" Whitney, USA

Aides: Captain Randy Bowen, USN (KIA); Lieutenant
                    Colonel David Cho, USA; Major T. G. Fellers,
                    USAF; Captain Alexander Dubronin, Russian

Federation; Lieutenant/Captain Nathan Shiwak,
Canadian Armed Forces

Chief of the Allied Staff:	General Edward "Whit" Whitney, USA (Transferred)
	General Anthony Stephenson, USAF (KIA)
	Major General T. James "T-J" Roberts, USA
Chief of Allied Air Ops:	General Anthony Stephenson, USAF (KIA)
	General Samuel Kaminski, USAF
Chief of Allied Ground Ops:	General Gerald "Jerry" Larkin, USA (21ST Army Group)
Chief of Allied Logistics:	General David Marvin Clark, USA (also Rear Detachment Commander, SAHQ).
Chief of Allied Naval Ops:	Admiral Carl Lynch, USN
Chief of Allied Intelligence:	General David Campbell, AUS Army
Chief of Pacific Planning:	Rear Admiral Li Dejiang, PLAN, China
Chief of Atlantic Planning:	Vice Admiral Klaus Blucher, German Navy.

Chief of Allied Spec. Ops: Lieutenant General Daniel Greene, Jr., USA

Deputy: Major General James Anawak, Canadian Forces
Deputy: Major General Sir. Martin Talbot, SAS, UK
Deputy: Brigadier General Bjorg Christenson, Norway
Deputy: Brigadier General Deacon Jones, USA, (Liaison, SAHQ).

Russian Liaison Officer: Brigadier General Vladimir Karnaukhov, Russian Army
(MIA on return to Government of Russian Federation)

JOINT CHIEFS OF STAFF

CHAIRMAN: General of the Army, Michael Patrick, USA

Vice Chairman: General William C. Mahan, USAF

ARMY: General Gerald "Jerry" "Green Giant" Larkin, USA

NAVY: Admiral Charles "Chuck" Steadman, USN

AIR FORCE: General Quentin Thayer, USAF

MARINE Corps: General Albert C. Durham, USMC

Director of the Joint Staff: Lieutenant General Stephen C. Carpenter, USMC

J-1   Major General Drew Sullivan, USMC

J-2   Rear Admiral Albert H. King, USN

J-3   Major General Timothy Roberts, USA (Trsf'd to Allied Staff)
      Major General Alan E. Townsend, USA

J-4   Major General David Marvin Clark, USA (Trsf'd to Allied Staff)
      Major General Thomas Jackson, USA

J-5   Major General Stephen Hickman, USAF

J-6   Major General R. E. Caughman, USAF

J-7   Major General Thomas Moss, USMC

J-8   Rear Admiral Anthony Brinkman, USN

J-9   Major General Hank Carter, USAR

ABOUT THE AUTHOR

Michael S. Pauley is a Navy brat and an old soldier who, throughout his military career, served in all three components of the United States Army. He is also a licensed attorney in South Carolina, who is admitted in the United States District Court for the District of South Carolina, the United States Court of Appeals for the Fourth Circuit, and before the United States Supreme Court. Mr. Pauley is a former Judicial Law Clerk for the Honorable Chief Justice Jean H. Toal, Supreme Court of South Carolina, as well as a former Prosecuting Attorney for the Office of Disciplinary Counsel. Currently in the private practice of law as a partner in LIDE AND PAULEY, LLC, Mr. Pauley concentrates on both State and Federal Constitutional law; law enforcement defense; civil rights law; and appellate litigation. Born in Beckley, West Virginia "back when dinosaurs roamed the earth," Mr. Pauley resides in Lexington, South Carolina, along with his bride. Mr. Pauley is a member of the United States Naval Institute and the American Legion, Post 154, Tybee Island, Georgia. You can find out more by either following Mr. Pauley on Twitter @michaelspauley; Tumblr at http://thegomerwars.tumblr.com; or on his web page at www.michaelspauley.com.